THE MAN I

CW00377094

THE MAN IN BLACK

Macabre Stories from
Fear on Four

BBC BOOKS

Published by BBC Books,
a division of BBC Enterprises Limited,
Woodlands, 80 Wood Lane, London W12 0TT
First published 1990
This compilation © BBC Books, 1990.
For information on individual copyright holders
see page 7.
ISBN 0 563 20904 6
Designed by Trevor Vincent
Set in 10/12 pt Meridien by Ace Filmsetting Ltd, Frome
Printed and bound in Great Britain by Clays Ltd, St Ives plc
Cover printed by Clays Ltd, St Ives plc

Contents

Acknowledgements

The Publishers would like to thank the following for their kind permission to reproduce copyright material:
The Beast with Five Fingers by William Fryer Harvey, © 1947 by E. P. Dutton & Co., Inc. and reproduced by kind permission of Weidenfeld & Nicolson; *Snipe 3909* by Graeme Fife, © Graeme Fife 1990 and reproduced by his kind permission; *The Dead Drummer* based on an original radio script by David Buck, © the Estate of David Buck 1990, adaptation for this compilation by Haydn Middleton, © Haydn Middleton 1990 and reproduced by kind permission of Haydn Middleton and the Estate of David Buck; *Fat Andy* by Stephen Dunstone, © Stephen Dunstone 1990 and reproduced by his kind permission; *The Dispossessed Daughter* by Katharine Nicholas, © Katharine Nicholas 1990 and reproduced by her kind permission; *The Specialty of the House* by Stanley Ellin, © the Estate of Stanley Ellin 1990 and reproduced by kind permission of the author's Estate; *The Face* by E. F. Benson, © the Estate of K. S. P. McDowall 1990 and reproduced by kind permission of the Estate of K. S. P. McDowall; *A Child Crying* by James Saunders, © James Saunders 1990 and reproduced by his kind permission; *The Horn* by Stephen Gallagher, © Stephen Gallagher 1989 and reproduced by his kind permission; *The Monkey's Paw* by W. W. Jacobs, © the Estate of W. W. Jacobs 1990 and reproduced by kind permission of The Society of Authors as the literary representatives of the Estate of W. W. Jacobs; *William and Mary* by Roald Dahl, © Roald Dahl 1990 and reproduced by his kind permission; *Every Detail but One* by Bert Coules, © Bert Coules 1990 and reproduced by his kind permission; *The Snowman Killing* by J. C. W. Brook, © J. C. W. Brook 1990

Foreword

From your Storyteller, The Man in Black, welcome to this anthology of the macabre. I am a past master at tingling the nerve ends of the imagination since I first invited you to an *Appointment with Fear* on the BBC Home Service in September 1943. Later, in 1949, the country would close its curtains, switch off the lights, huddle round the wireless set and wait nervously for its weekly half hour of horror in my own series *The Man in Black*.

I'm still around, ageless as fear itself; still emerging from the basement of Broadcasting House to bring you tales from those parts of the mind other tales don't reach. *Fear on Four* they call it now, different name but same mixture of fear and horror.

In George Orwell's *1984*, Winston Smith is taken to Room 101 to be confronted by his own deepest fear – in his case, rats. I know that each one of you has some secret fear – some secret horror – perhaps like Winston Smith it is rats, or perhaps the fear of the telephone, of the dentist's drill, of being buried alive, of the walking dead, of a revengeful spirit. Who can tell? – only you. Radio has allowed me to recount all manner of stories based on the dark side of human nature. Now these stories have been brought together in this anthology. Some are accepted classics – 'The Beast with Five Fingers' and 'The Monkey's Paw'. Some are from modern masters of the genre – Stanley Ellin, Stephen Gallagher, Roald Dahl and John Wyndham. Others began life as radio plays and have since been re-written as short stories. Included are works by dramatists such as J. C. W. Brook, Gwen Cherrell, Bert Coules, Stephen Dunstone, Graeme

Fife, William Ingram, Katharine Nicholas, James Saunders, Martyn Wade and Nick Warburton. It has proved a rich field – cannibalism, the supernatural, the unborn, and the undead.

Stephen King, the American grand-master of horror, pays tribute to the power of radio in stimulating his imagination when, as a boy, he listened spellbound to his country's masters of the macabre such as Arch Oboler. Today, radio drama in the United States is struggling towards a revival and one day Oboler's work may be heard again. He wrote scores of plays for the series *Lights Out* including *A Day at the Dentist's*. It was a particular pleasure for me to acknowledge Oboler's work in asking James Saunders to write a modern reconstruction of Oboler's original radio concept (his play had long since disappeared). The idea remains pure radio, asking the listener to fill in the gaps and decide in his imagination what is happening. James Saunders' story does exactly the same. I still shiver when I ponder the implications – but please read on – experience the same thrill of horror.

Meanwhile I shall be locked away deep in Broadcastng House seeking out the unusual and disturbing for my next series of *Fear on Four* on Radio 4. Remember fear is always there – somewhere – searching for victims.

Good reading. Good listening.

The Man in Black

THE BEAST WITH FIVE FINGERS

William Fryer Harvey

*William Fryer Harvey was born in Yorkshire in 1885. Ill-health,
which interrupted his medical training, was exacerbated during
the First World War when, serving as a doctor, he saved a stoker
petty officer from a flooded engine room. His lungs never recovered
from the fumes and he died in 1937 at the age of 52. A master of
psychological horror, his first book was a volume of ghost stories,
MIDNIGHT HOUSE (1910). THE BEAST WITH FIVE
FINGERS followed in 1928 and MOODS AND TENSES was
published in 1933.*

---

*THEY SAID IT WAS – YOU'LL EXCUSE ME, SIR –
A HAND THAT THEY SAW. EMMA TROD ON IT ONCE
AT THE BOTTOM OF THE STAIRS.*

The story, I suppose, begins with Adrian Borlsover,
whom I met when I was a little boy and he an old man.
My father had called to appeal for a subscription, and before
he left, Mr Borlsover laid his right hand in blessing on my
head. I shall never forget the awe in which I gazed up at his
face and realised for the first time that eyes might be dark
and beautiful and shining, and yet not able to see.

For Adrian Borlsover was blind.

He was an extraordinary man, who came of an eccentric
stock. Borlsover sons for some reason always seemed to
marry very ordinary women; which perhaps accounted for
the fact that no Borlsover had been a genius, and only one
Borlsover had been mad. But they were great champions of
little causes, generous patrons of odd sciences, founders of

querulous sects, trustworthy guides to the bypath meadows of erudition.

Adrian was an authority on the fertilisation of orchids. He had held at one time the family living at Borlsover Conyers, until a congenital weakness of the lungs obliged him to seek a less rigorous climate in the sunny south-coast watering-place where I had seen him. Occasionally he would relieve one or other of the local clergy. My father described him as a fine preacher, who gave long and inspiring sermons from what many men would have considered unprofitable texts. 'An excellent proof,' he would add, 'of the truth of the doctrine of direct verbal inspiration.'

Adrian Borlsover was exceedingly clever with his hands. His penmanship was exquisite. He illustrated all his scientific papers, made his own wood-cuts, and carved the reredos that is at present the chief feature of interest in the church at Borlsover Conyers. He had an exceedingly clever knack in cutting silhouettes for young ladies and paper pigs and cows for little children, and made more than one complicated wind-instrument of his own devising.

When he was fifty years old Adrian Borlsover lost his sight. In a wonderfully short time he adapted himself to the new conditions of life. He quickly learnt to read Braille. So marvellous indeed was his sense of touch, that he was still able to maintain his interest in botany. The mere passing of his long supple fingers over a flower was sufficient means for its identification, though occasionally he would use his lips. I have found several letters of his among my father's correspondence; in no case was there anything to show that he was afflicted with blindness, and this in spite of the fact that he exercised undue economy in the spacing of lines. Towards the close of his life Adrian Borlsover was credited with powers of touch that seemed almost uncanny. It has been said that he could tell at once the colour of a ribbon placed between his fingers. My father would neither confirm nor deny the story.

Adrian Borlsover was a bachelor. His elder brother, Charles, had married late in life, leaving one son, Eustace, who lived in the gloomy Georgian mansion at Borlsover Conyers, where he could work undisturbed in collecting material for his great book on heredity.

Like his uncle, he was a remarkable man. The Borlsovers had always been born naturalists, but Eustace possessed in a special degree the power of systematising his knowledge. He had received his university education in Germany; and then, after post- graduate work in Vienna and Naples, had travelled for four years in South America and the East, getting together a huge store of material for a new study into the processes of variation.

He lived alone at Borlsover Conyers with Saunders, his secretary, a man who bore a somewhat dubious reputation in the district, but whose powers as a mathematician, combined with his business abilities, were invaluable to Eustace.

Uncle and nephew saw little of each other. The visits of Eustace were confined to a week in the summer or autumn – tedious weeks, that dragged almost as slowly as the bath-chair in which the old man was drawn along the sunny sea-front. In their way the two men were fond of each other, though their intimacy would, doubtless, have been greater, had they shared the same religious views. Adrian held to the old-fashioned evangelical dogmas of his early manhood; his nephew for many years had been thinking of embracing Buddhism. Both men possessed, too, the reticence the Borlsovers had always shown, and which their enemies sometimes called hypocrisy. With Adrian it was a reticence as to the things he had left undone; but with Eustace it seemed that the curtain which he was so careful to leave undrawn hid something more than a half-empty chamber.

Two years before his death, Adrian Borlsover developed, unknown to himself, the not uncommon power of

13

automatic writing. Eustace made the discovery by accident. Adrian was sitting reading in bed, the forefinger of his left hand tracing the Braille characters, when his nephew noticed that a pencil the old man held in his right hand was moving slowly along the opposite page. He had left his seat in the window and sat down beside the bed. The right hand continued to move, and now he could see plainly that they were letters and words which it was forming.

'Adrian Borlsover,' wrote the hand, 'Eustace Borlsover, Charles Borlsover, Francis Borlsover, Sigismund Borlsover, Adrian Borlsover, Eustace Borlsover, Saville Borlsover. B for Borlsover. Honesty Is the Best Policy. Beautiful Belinda Borlsover.'

'What curious nonsense!' said Eustace to himself.

'King George ascended the throne in 1760,' wrote the hand. 'Crowd, a noun of multitude; a collection of individuals. Adrian Borlsover, Eustace Borlsover.'

'It seems to me,' said his uncle, closing the book, 'that you had much better make the most of the afternoon sunshine and take your walk now.'

'I think perhaps I will,' Eustace answered as he picked up the volume. 'I won't go far, and when I come back, I can read to you those articles in *Nature* about which we were speaking.'

He went along the promenade, but stopped at the first shelter, and, seating himself in the corner best protected from the wind, he examined the book at leisure. Nearly every page was scored with a meaningless jumble of pencil-marks; rows of capital letters, short words, long words, complete sentences, copy-book tags. The whole thing, in fact, had the appearance of a copy-book, and, on a more careful scrutiny, Eustace thought that there was ample evidence to show that the handwriting at the beginning of the book, good though it was, was not nearly so good as the handwriting at the end.

He left his uncle at the end of October with a promise to return early in December. It seemed to him quite clear that the old man's power of automatic writing was developing rapidly, and for the first time he looked forward to a visit that would combine duty with interest.

But on his return he was at first disappointed. His uncle, he thought, looked older. He was listless, too, preferring others to read to him and dictating nearly all his letters. Not until the day before he left had Eustace an opportunity of observing Adrian Borlsover's new-found faculty.

The old man, propped up in bed with pillows, had sunk into a light sleep. His two hands lay on the coverlet, his left hand tightly clasping his right. Eustace took an empty manuscript book and placed a pencil within reach of the fingers of the right hand. They snatched at it eagerly, then dropped the pencil to loose the left hand from its restraining grasp.

'Perhaps to prevent interference I had better hold that hand,' said Eustace to himself, as he watched the pencil. Almost immediately it began to write.

'Blundering Borlsovers, unnecessarily unnatural, extraordinarily eccentric, culpably curious.'

'Who are you?' asked Eustace in a low voice.

'Never you mind,' wrote the hand of Adrian.

'Is it my uncle who is writing?'

'O my prophetic soul, mine uncle!'

'Is it anyone I know?'

'Silly Eustace, you'll see me very soon.'

'When shall I see you?'

'When poor old Adrian's dead.'

'Where shall I see you?'

'Where shall you not?'

Instead of speaking his next question, Eustace wrote it. 'What is the time?'

The fingers dropped the pencil and moved three or four times across the paper. Then, picking up the pencil, they wrote: 'Ten minutes before four. Put your book away Eustace. Adrian mustn't find us working at this sort of thing. He doesn't know what to make of it, and I won't have poor old Adrian disturbed. Au revoir!'

Adrian Borlsover awoke with a start.

'I've been dreaming again,' he said; 'such queer dreams of leaguered cities and forgotten towns. You were mixed up in this one, Eustace, though I can't remember how. Eustace, I want to warn you. Don't walk in doubtful paths. Choose your friends well. Your poor grandfather . . .'

A fit of coughing put an end to what he was saying, but Eustace saw that the hand was still writing. He managed unnoticed to draw the book away. 'I'll light the gas,' he said, 'and ring for tea.' On the other side of the bed-curtain he saw the last sentence that had been written.

'It's too late, Adrian,' it said. 'We're friends already, aren't we, Eustace Borlsover?'

On the following day Eustace left. He thought his uncle looked ill when he said good-bye, and the old man spoke despondently of the failure his life had been.

'Nonsense, uncle,' said his nephew. 'You have got over your difficulties in a way not one in a hundred thousand would have done. Every one marvels at your splendid perseverance in teaching your hand to take the place of your lost sight. To me it's been a revelation of the possibilities of education.'

'Education,' said his uncle dreamily, as if the word had started a new train of thought. 'Education is good so long as you know to whom and for what purpose you give it. But with the lower orders of men, the base and more sordid spirits, I have grave doubts as to its results. Well, good-bye Eustace; I may not see you again. You are a true Borlsover, with all the Borlsover faults. Marry, Eustace. Marry some good, sensible girl. And if by any chance I don't see you again, my will is at my solicitor's. I've not left you any legacy, because I know you're well provided for; but I thought you might like to have my books. Oh, and there's just another thing. You know, before the end, people often lose control over themselves and make absurd requests. Don't pay any attention to them, Eustace. Good-bye!' and he held out his hand. Eustace took it. It remained in his a fraction of a second longer than he had expected and gripped him with a virility that was surprising. There was, too, in its touch a subtle sense of intimacy.

'Why, uncle,' he said, 'I shall see you alive and well for many long years to come.'

Two months later Adrian Borlsover died.

Eustace Borlsover was in Naples at the time. He read the obituary notice in the *Morning Post* on the day announced for the funeral.

'Poor old fellow!' he said. 'I wonder whether I shall find room for all his books.'

The question occurred to him again with greater force when, three days later, he found himself standing in the library at Borlsover Conyers, a huge room built for use and not for beauty in the year of Waterloo by a Borlsover who was an ardent admirer of the great Napoleon. It was arranged on the plan of many college libraries, with tall projecting bookcases forming deep recesses of dusty silence, fit graves for the old hates of forgotten controversy, the dead passions of forgotten lives. At the end of the room, behind the bust of some unknown eighteenth-century divine, an ugly iron corkscrew stair led to a shelf-lined gallery. Nearly every shelf was full.

'I must talk to Saunders about it,' said Eustace. 'I suppose that we shall have to have the billiard-room fitted up with bookcases.'

The two men met for the first time after many weeks in the dining-room that evening.

'Hallo!' said Eustace, standing before the fire with his hands in his pockets. 'How goes the world, Saunders? Why these dress togs?' He himself was wearing an old shooting-jacket. He did not believe in mourning, as he had told his uncle on his last visit; and, though he usually went in for quiet-coloured ties, he wore this evening one of an ugly red, in order to shock Morton the butler, and to make them thrash out the whole question of mourning for themselves in the servants' hall. Eustace was a true Borlsover. 'The world,' said Saunders, 'goes the same as usual, confoundedly slow. The dress togs are accounted for by an invitation from Captain Lockwood to bridge.'

'How are you getting there?'

'There's something the matter with the car, so I've told Jackson to drive me round in the dogcart. Any objection?'

'Oh dear me, no! We've had all things in common for far too many years for me to raise objections at this hour of the day.'

'You'll find your correspondence in the library,' went on Saunders. 'Most of it I've seen to. There are a few private letters I haven't opened. There's also a box with a rat or something in it that came by the evening post. Very likely it's the six-toed beast Terry was sending us to cross with the four-toed albino. I didn't look because I didn't want to mess up my things; but I should gather from the way it's jumping about that it's pretty hungry.'

'Oh, I'll see to it,' said Eustace, 'while you and the captain earn an honest penny.'

Dinner over and Saunders gone, Eustace went into the library. Though the fire had been lit, the room was by no means cheerful.

'We'll have all the lights on, at any rate,' he said, as he turned the switches. 'And, Morton,' he added, when the butler brought the coffee, 'get me a screwdriver or something to undo this box. Whatever the animal is, he's kicking up the deuce of a row. What is it? Why are you dawdling?'

'If you please, sir, when the postman brought it, he told me that they'd bored the holes in the lid at the post office. There were no breathing holes in the lid, sir, and they didn't want the animal to die. That is all, sir.'

'It's culpably careless of the man, whoever he was,' said Eustace, as he removed the screws, 'packing an animal like this in a wooden box with no means of getting air. Confound it all! I meant to ask Morton to bring me a cage to put it in. Now I suppose I shall have to get one myself.'

He placed a heavy book on the lid from which the screws had been removed, and went into the billiard-room. As he came back into the library with an empty cage in his hand, he heard the sound of something falling, and then of something scuttling along the floor.

'Bother it! The beast's got out. How in the world am I to find it again in this library?'

To search for it did indeed seem hopeless. He tried to follow the sound of the scuffling in one of the recesses, where the animal seemed to be running behind the books in the shelves; but it was impossible to locate it. Eustace resolved to go on quietly reading. Very likely the animal might gain confidence and show itself. Saunders seemed to have dealt in his usual methodical manner with most of the correspondence. There were still the private letters.

What was that? Two sharp clicks and the lights in the hideous candelabras that hung from the ceiling suddenly went out.

'I wonder if something has gone wrong with the fuse,' said Eustace, as he went to the switches by the door. Then he stopped. There was a noise at the other end of the room, as if something was crawling up the iron corkscrew stair. 'If it's gone into the gallery,' he said, 'well and good.' He hastily turned on the lights, crossed the room, and climbed up the stair. But he could see nothing. His grandfather had placed a little gate at the top of the stair, so that children could run and romp in the gallery without fear of accident. This Eustace closed, and, having considerably narrowed the circle of his search, returned to his desk by the fire.

How gloomy the library was! There was no sense of intimacy about the room. The few busts that an eighteenth-century Borlsover had brought back from the grand tour might have been in keeping in the old library. Here they seemed out of place. They made the room feel cold in spite of the heavy red damask curtains and great gilt cornices.

With a crash two heavy books fell from the gallery to the floor; then, as Borlsover looked, another, and yet another.

'Very well. You'll starve for this, my beauty!' he said, 'We'll do some little experiments on the metabolism of rats deprived of water. Go on! Chuck them down! I think I've got the upper hand.' He turned once more to his correspondence. The letter was from the family solicitor. It spoke of his uncle's death, and of the valuable collection of books that had been left to him in the will.

> *There was one request* [he read] *which certainly came as a surprise to me. As you know, Mr Adrian Borlsover had left instructions that his body was to be buried in as simple a manner as possible at Eastbourne. He expressed a desire that there should be neither wreaths nor flowers of any kind, and hoped that his friends and relatives would not consider it necessary to wear mourning. The day before his death we received a letter cancelling these instructions. He wished the body to be embalmed (he gave us the address of the man we were to employ – Pennifer, Ludgate Hill), with orders that his right hand should be sent to you, stating that it was at your special request. The other arrangements about the funeral remained unaltered.*

'Good Lord,' said Eustace, 'what in the world was the old boy driving at? And what in the name of all that's holy is that?'

Someone was in the gallery. Someone had pulled the cord

attached to one of the blinds, and it had rolled up with a snap. Someone must be in the gallery, for a second blind did the same. Someone must be walking round the gallery, for one after the other the blinds sprang up, letting in the moonlight.

'I haven't got to the bottom of this yet,' said Eustace, 'but I will do, before the night is very much older;' and he hurried up the corkscrew stair. He had just got to the top, when the lights went out a second time, and he heard again the scuttling along the floor. Quickly he stole on tiptoe in the dim moonshine in the direction of the noise, feeling, as he went, for one of the switches. His fingers touched the metal knob at last. He turned on the electric light.

About ten yards in front of him, crawling along the floor, was a man's hand. Eustace stared at it in utter amazement. It was moving quickly in the manner of a geometer caterpillar, the fingers humped up one moment, flattened out the next; the thumb appeared to give a crablike motion to the whole. While he was looking, too surprised to stir, the hand disappeared round the corner. Eustace ran forward. He no longer saw it, but he could hear it, as it squeezed its way behind the books on one of the shelves. A heavy volume had been displaced. There was a gap in the row of books, where it had got in. In his fear lest it should escape him again, he seized the first book that came to his hand and plugged it into the hole. Then, emptying two shelves of their contents, he took the wooden boards and propped them up in front to make his barrier doubly sure.

'I wish Saunders was back,' he said; 'one can't tackle this sort of thing alone.' It was after eleven, and there seemed little likelihood of Saunders returning before twelve. He did not dare to leave the shelf unwatched, even to run downstairs to ring the bell. Morton, the butler, often used to come round about eleven to see that the windows were fastened, but he might not come. Eustace was thoroughly unstrung.

At last he heard steps down below.

'Morton!' he shouted. 'Morton!'

'Sir?'

'Has Mr Saunders got back yet?'

'Not yet, sir.'

'Well, bring me some brandy, and hurry up about it. I'm up in the gallery, you duffer.'

'Thanks,' said Eustace, as he emptied the glass. 'Don't go to bed yet, Morton. There are a lot of books that have fallen down by accident. Bring them up and put them back in their shelves.'

Morton had never seen Borlsover in so talkative a mood as on that night. 'Here,' said Eustace, when the books had been put back and dusted, 'you might hold up these boards for me, Morton. That beast in the box got out, and I've been chasing it all over the place.'

'I think I can hear it clawing at the books, sir. They're not valuable, I hope? I think that's the carriage, sir; I'll go and call Mr Saunders.'

It seemed to Eustace that he was away for five minutes, but it could hardly have been more than one, when he returned with Saunders.

'All right, Morton, you can go now. I'm up here, Saunders.'

'What's all the row?' asked Saunders, as he lounged forward with his hands in his pockets. The luck had been with him all the evening. He was completely satisfied, both with himself and with Captain Lockwood's taste in wines. 'What's the matter? You look to me to be in an absolutely blue funk.'

'That old devil of an uncle of mine,' began Eustace – 'Oh, I can't explain it all. It's his hand that's been playing Old Harry all the evening. But I've got it cornered behind these books. You've got to help me to catch it.'

'What's up with you, Eustace? What's the game?'

'It's no game, you silly idiot! If you don't believe me, take out one of those books and put your hand in and feel.'

'All right,' said Saunders; 'but wait till I've rolled up my sleeve. The accumulated dust of centuries, eh?' He took off his coat, knelt down, and thrust his arm along the shelf.

'There's something there right enough,' he said. 'It's got a funny, stumpy end to it, whatever it is, and nips like a crab. Ah! no, you don't!' He pulled his hand out in a flash. 'Shove in a book quickly. Now it can't get out.'

'What was it?' asked Eustace.

'Something that wanted very much to get hold of me. I felt what seemed like a thumb and forefinger. Give me some brandy.'

'How are we to get it out of there?'

'What about a landing-net?'

'No good. It would be too smart for us. I tell you, Saunders, it can cover the ground far faster than I can walk. But I think I see how we can manage it. The two books at the end of the shelf are big ones, that go right back against the wall. The others are very thin. I'll take out one at a time, and you slide the rest along, until we have it squashed between the end two.'

It certainly seemed to be the best plan. One by one as they took out the books, the space behind grew smaller and smaller. There was something in it that was certainly very much alive. Once they caught sight of fingers feeling for a way of escape. At last they had it pressed between the two big books.

'There's muscle there, if there isn't warm flesh and blood,' said Saunders, as he held them together. 'It seems to be a hand right enough, too. I suppose this is a sort of infectious hallucination. I've read about such cases before.'

'Infectious fiddlesticks!' said Eustace, his face white with anger; 'bring the thing downstairs. We'll get it back into the box.'

23

It was not altogether easy, but they were successful at last. 'Drive in the screws,' said Eustace; 'we won't run any risks. Put the box in this old desk of mine. There's nothing in it that I want. Here's the key. Thank goodness there's nothing wrong with the lock.'

'Quite a lively evening,' said Saunders. 'Now let's hear more about your uncle.'

They sat up together until early morning. Saunders had no desire for sleep. Eustace was trying to explain and forget; to conceal from himself a fear that he had never felt before – the fear of walking alone down the long corridor to his bedroom.

'Whatever it was,' said Eustace to Saunders on the following morning, 'I propose that we drop the subject. There's nothing to keep us here for the next ten days. We'll motor up to the Lakes and get some climbing.'

'And see nobody all day, and sit bored to death with each other every night. Not for me, thanks. Why not run up to town? Run's the exact word in this case, isn't it? We're both in such a blessed funk. Pull yourself together, Eustace, and let's have another look at the hand.'

'As you like,' said Eustace; 'there's the key.'

They went into the library and opened the desk. The box was as they had left it on the previous night.

'What are you waiting for?' asked Eustace.

'I am waiting for you to volunteer to open the lid. However, since you seem to funk it, allow me. There doesn't seem to be the likelihood of any rumpus this morning at all events.' He opened the lid and picked out the hand.

'Cold?' asked Eustace.

'Tepid. A bit below blood heat by the feel. Soft and supple too. If it's the embalming, it's a sort of embalming I've never seen before. Is it your uncle's hand?'

'Oh, yes, it's his all right,' said Eustace. 'I should know

24

those long thin fingers anywhere. Put it back in the box, Saunders. Never mind about the screws. I'll lock the desk, so that there'll be no chance of its getting out. We'll compromise by motoring up to town for a week. If we can get off soon after lunch, we ought to be at Grantham or Stamford by night.'

'Right,' said Saunders, 'and tomorrow – oh, well, by tomorrow we shall have forgotten all about this beastly thing.'

If, when the morrow came, they had not forgotten, it was certainly true that at the end of the week they were able to tell a very vivid ghost-story at the little supper Eustace gave on Hallowe'en.

'You don't want us to believe that it's true, Mr Borlsover? How perfectly awful!'

'I'll take my oath on it, and so would Saunders here; wouldn't you, old chap?'

'Any number of oaths,' said Saunders. 'It was a long, thin hand, you know, and it gripped me just like that.'

'Don't, Mr Saunders! Don't! How perfectly horrid! Now tell us another one, do! Only a really creepy one, please.'

'Here's a pretty mess!' said Eustace on the following day, as he threw a letter across the table to Saunders. 'It's your affair, though. Mrs Merritt, if I understand it, gives a month's notice.'

'Oh, that's quite absurd on Mrs Merritt's part,' replied Saunders. 'She doesn't know what she's talking about. Let's see what she says.'

Dear Sir [he read]: *This is to let you know that I must give you a month's notice as from Tuesday, the 13th. For a long time I've felt the place too big for me; but when Jane Parfit and Emma Laidlaw go off with scarcely as much as an 'If you please,' after frightening the wits out of the other girls, so that they can't turn out a room by themselves or walk alone down the stairs for fear of treading on half-frozen toads or hearing it run along the passages at night, all*

I can say is that it's no place for me. So I must ask you, Mr Borlsover, sir, to find a new housekeeper, that has no objection to large and lonely houses, which some people do say, not that I believe them for a minute, my poor mother always having been a Wesleyan, are haunted.

> *Yours faithfully,*
> *Elizabeth Merritt*

P.S. – I should be obliged if you would give my respects to Mr Saunders. I hope that he won't run any risks with his cold.

'Saunders,' said Eustace, 'you've always had a wonderful way with you in dealing with servants. You mustn't let poor old Merritt go.'

'Of course she shan't go,' said Saunders. 'She's probably only angling for a rise in salary. I'll write to her this morning.'

'No. There's nothing like a personal interview. We've had enough of town. We'll go back tomorrow, and you must work your cold for all it's worth. Don't forget that it's got on to the chest, and will require weeks of feeding up and nursing.'

'All right; I think I can manage Mrs Merritt.'

But Mrs Merritt was more obstinate than he had thought. She was very sorry to hear of Mr Saunders's cold, and how he lay awake all night in London coughing; very sorry indeed. She'd change his room for him gladly and get the south room aired, and wouldn't he have a hot basin of bread and milk last thing at night? But she was afraid that she would have to leave at the end of the month.

'Try her with an increase of salary,' was the advice of Eustace.

It was no use. Mrs Merritt was obdurate, though she knew of a Mrs Goddard, who had been housekeeper to Lord Gargrave, who might be glad to come at the salary mentioned.

'What's the matter with the servants, Morton?' asked

Eustace that evening, when he brought the coffee into the library. 'What's all this about Mrs Merritt wanting to leave?'

'If you please, sir, I was going to mention it myself. I have a confession to make, sir. When I found your note, asking me to open that desk and take out the box with the rat, I broke the lock, as you told me, and was glad to do it, because I could hear the animal in the box making a great noise, and I thought it wanted food. So I took out the box, sir, and got a cage, and was going to transfer it, when the animal got away.'

'What in the world are you talking about? I never wrote any such note.'

'Excuse me, sir; it was the note I picked up here on the floor the day you and Mr Saunders left. I have it in my pocket now.'

It cerainly seemed to be in Eustace's handwriting. It was written in pencil, and began somewhat abruptly.

'Get a hammer, Morton,' he read, 'or some tool and break open the lock in the old desk in the library. Take out the box that is inside. You need not do anything else. The lid is already open. Eustace Borlsover.'

'And you opened the desk?'

'Yes, sir; and, as I was getting the cage ready, the animal hopped out.'

'What animal?'

'The animal inside the box, sir.'

'What did it look like?'

'Well, sir, I couldn't tell you,' said Morton, nervously. 'My back was turned, and it was half way down the room when I looked up.'

'What was its colour?' asked Saunders. 'Black?'

'Oh, no, sir; a greyish white. It crept along in a very funny way, sir. I don't think it had a tail.'

'What did you do then?'

'I tried to catch it; but it was no use. So I set the rat-traps

27

and kept the library shut. Then that girl, Emma Laidlaw, left the door open when she was cleaning, and I think it must have escaped.'

'And you think it is the animal that's been frightening the maids?'

'Well, no, sir, not quite. They said it was – you'll excuse me, sir – a hand that they saw. Emma trod on it once at the bottom of the stairs. She thought then it was a half-frozen toad, only white. And then Parfit was washing up the dishes in the scullery. She wasn't thinking about anything in particular. It was close on dusk. She took her hands out of the water and was drying them absent-minded like on the roller towel, when she found she was drying someone else's hand as well, only colder than hers.'

'What nonsense!' exclaimed Saunders.

'Exactly, sir; that's what I told her; but we couldn't get her to stop.'

'You don't believe all this?' said Eustace, turning suddenly towards the butler.

'Me, sir? Oh, no, sir! I've not seen anything.'

'Nor heard anything?'

'Well, sir, if you must know, the bells do ring at odd times, and there's nobody there when we go; and when we go round to draw the blinds of a night, as often as not somebody's been there before us. But, as I says to Mrs Merritt, a young monkey might do wonderful things, and we all know that Mr Borlsover has had some strange animals about the place.'

'Very well, Morton, that will do.'

'What do you make of it?' asked Saunders, when they were alone. 'I mean of the letter he said you wrote.'

'Oh, that's simple enough,' said Eustace. 'See the paper it's written on? I stopped using that paper years ago, but there were a few odd sheets and envelopes left in the old desk. We never fastened up the lid of the box before locking it in. The hand got out, found a pencil, wrote this note, and shoved it through the crack on to the floor, where Morton found it. That's plain as daylight.'

'But the hand couldn't write!'

'Couldn't it? You've not seen it do the things I've seen.' And he told Saunders more of what had happened at Eastbourne.

'Well,' said Saunders, 'in that case we have at least an explanation of the legacy. It was the hand which wrote, unknown to your uncle, that letter to your solicitor bequeathing itself to you. Your uncle had no more to do with that request than I. In fact, it would seem that he had some idea of this automatic writing and feared it.'

'Then if it's not my uncle, what is it?'

'I suppose some people might say that a disembodied spirit had got your uncle to educate and prepare a little body for it. Now it's got into that little body and is off on its own.'

'Well, what are we to do?'

'We'll keep our eyes open,' said Saunders, 'and try to catch it. If we can't do that, we shall have to wait till the bally clockwork runs down. After all, if it's flesh and blood, it can't live for ever.'

For two days nothing happened. Then Saunders saw it sliding down the banister in the hall. He was taken unawares and lost a full second before he started in pursuit, only to find that the thing had escaped him. Three days later, Eustace, writing alone in the library at night, saw it sitting on an open book at the other end of the room. The fingers crept over the page, as if it were reading; but before he had time to get up from his seat, it had taken the alarm, and was pulling itself up the curtains. Eustace watched it grimly, as it hung on to the cornice with three fingers and flicked thumb and forefinger at him in an expression of scornful derision.

'I know what I'll do,' he said. 'If I only get it into the open, I'll set the dogs on to it.'

He spoke to Saunders of the suggestion.

'It's a jolly good idea,' he said; 'only we won't wait till we find it out of doors. We'll get the dogs. There are the two terriers and the under-keeper's Irish mongrel, that's on to rats like a flash. Your spaniel has not got spirit enough for this sort of game.'

They brought the dogs into the house, and the keeper's Irish mongrel chewed up the slippers, and the terriers tripped up Morton, as he waited at table; but all three were welcome. Even false security is better than no security at all.

For a fortnight nothing happened. Then the hand was caught, not by the dogs, but by Mrs Merritt's grey parrot. The bird was in the habit of periodically removing the pins that kept its seed- and water-tins in place, and of escaping through the holes in the side of his cage. When once at liberty, Peter would show no inclination to return, and would often be about the house for days. Now, after six consecutive weeks of captivity, Peter had again discovered a new way of unloosing his bolts and was at large, exploring the tapestried forests of the curtains and singing songs in praise of liberty from cornice and picture-rail.

'It's no use your trying to catch him,' said Eustace to Mrs Merritt, as she came into the study one afternoon towards dusk with a step-ladder. 'You'd much better leave Peter alone. Starve him into surrender, Mrs Merritt; and don't leave bananas and seed about for him to peck at when he fancies he's hungry. You're far too soft-hearted.'

'Well, sir, I see he's right out of reach now on that picture-rail; so, if you wouldn't mind closing the door, sir, when you leave the room, I'll bring his cage in tonight and put some meat inside it. He's that fond of meat, though it does make him pull out his feathers to suck the quills. They say that if you cook – '

'Never mind, Mrs Merritt,' said Eustace, who was busy writing; 'that will do; I'll keep an eye on the bird.'

For a short time there was silence in the room.

'Scratch poor Peter,' said the bird. 'Scratch poor old Peter!'

'Be quiet, you beastly bird!'

'Poor old Peter! Scratch poor Peter; do!'

'I'm more likely to wring your neck, if I get hold of you.' He looked up at the picture-rail, and there was the hand, holding on to a hook with three fingers, and slowly scratching the head of the parrot with the fourth. Eustace ran to the bell and pressed it hard; then across to the window, which he closed with a bang. Frightened by the noise, the parrot shook its wings preparatory to flight, and, as it did so, the fingers of the hand got hold of it by the throat. There was a shrill scream from Peter, as he fluttered across the room, wheeling round in circles that ever descended, borne down under the weight that clung to him. The bird dropped at last quite suddenly, and Eustace saw fingers and feathers rolled into an inextricable mass on the floor. The struggle abruptly ceased, as finger and thumb squeezed the neck; the bird's eyes rolled up to show the whites, and there was a faint, half-choked gurgle. But, before the fingers had time to lose their hold, Eustace had them in his own.

'Send Mr Saunders here at once,' he said to the maid who came in answer to the bell. 'Tell him I want him immediately.'

Then he went with the hand to the fire. There was a ragged gash across the back, where the bird's beak had torn it, but no blood oozed from the wound. He noted with disgust that the nails had grown long and discoloured.

'I'll burn the beastly thing,' he said. But he could not burn it. He tried to throw it into the flames, but his own hands, as if impelled by some old primitive feeling, would not let him. And so Saunders found him, pale and irresolute, with the hand still clasped tightly in his fingers.

'I've got it at last,' he said, in a tone of triumph.

'Good, let's have a look at it.'

'Not when it's loose. Get me some nails and a hammer and a board of some sort.'

'Can you hold it all right?'

'Yes, the thing's quite limp; tired out with throttling poor old Peter, I should say.'

'And now,' said Saunders, when he returned with the things, 'what are we going to do?'

'Drive a nail through it first, so that it can't get away. Then we can take our time over examining it.'

'Do it yourself,' said Saunders. 'I don't mind helping you with guinea-pigs occasionally, when there's something to be learned, partly because I don't fear a guinea-pig's revenge. This thing's different.'

'Oh, my aunt!' he giggled hysterically. 'Look at it now.' For the hand was writhing in agonised contortions, squirming and wriggling upon the nail like a worm upon the hook.

'Well,' said Saunders, 'you've done it now. I'll leave you to examine it.'

'Don't go, in heaven's name! Cover it up, man; cover it up! Shove a cloth over it! Here!' and he pulled off the antimacassar from the back of a chair and wrapped the board in it. 'Now get the keys from my pocket and open the safe. Chuck the other things out. Oh, Lord, it's getting itself into frightful knots! Open it quick!' He threw the thing in and banged the door.

'We'll keep it there till it dies,' he said. 'May I burn in hell, if I ever open the door of that safe again.'

Mrs Merritt departed at the end of the month. Her successor, Mrs Handyside, certainly was more successful in the management of the servants. Early in her rule she declared that she would stand no nonsense, and gossip soon withered and died.

'I shouldn't be surprised if Eustace married one of these days,' said Saunders. 'Well, I'm in no hurry for such an event. I know him far too well for the future Mrs Borlsover to like me. It will be the same old story again; a long friendship slowly made – marriage – and a long friendship quickly forgotten.'

But Eustace did not follow the advice of his uncle and marry. Old habits crept over and covered his new experience. He was, if anything, less morose, and showed a greater inclination to take his natural part in country society.

Then came the burglary. The men, it was said, broke into the house by way of the conservatory. It was really little more than an attempt, for they only succeeded in carrying away a few pieces of plate from the pantry. The safe in the study was certainly found open and empty, but, as Mr Borlsover informed the police inspector, he had kept nothing of value in it during the last six months.

'Then you're lucky in getting off so easily, sir,' the man replied. 'By the way they have gone about their business, I should say they were experienced cracksmen. They must have caught the alarm when they were just beginning their evening's work.'

'Yes,' said Eustace, 'I suppose I am lucky.'

'I've no doubt,' said the inspector, 'that we shall be able to trace the men. I've said that they must have been old hands at the game. The way they got in and opened the safe shows that. But there's one little thing that puzzles me. One of them was careless enough not to wear gloves, and I'm bothered if I know what he was trying to do. I've traced his finger-marks on the new varnish on the window-sashes in every one of the downstairs rooms. They are very distinctive ones too.'

'Right or left hand, or both?' asked Eustace.

'Oh, right every time. That's the funny thing. He must have been a foolhardy fellow, and I rather think it was him that wrote that.' He took out a slip of paper from his pocket. 'That's what he wrote, sir: "I've got out, Eustace Borlsover, but I'll be back before long." Some jailbird just escaped, I suppose. It will make it all the easier for us to trace him. Do you know the writing, sir?'

'No,' said Eustace. 'It's not the writing of anyone I know.'

'I'm not going to stay here any longer,' said Eustace to Saunders at luncheon. 'I've got on far better during the last six months than I expected, but I'm not going to run the risk of seeing that thing again. I shall go up to town this afternoon. Get Morton to put my things together, and join me with the car at Brighton on the day after tomorrow. And bring the proofs of those two papers with you. We'll run over them together.'

'How long are you going to be away?'

'I can't say for certain, but be prepared to stay for some time. We've stuck to work pretty closely through the summer, and I for one need a holiday. I'll engage the rooms at Brighton. You'll find it best to break the journey at Hitchin. I'll wire to you there at the "Crown" to tell you the Brighton address.'

The house he chose at Brighton was in a terrace. He had been there before. It was kept by his old college gyp, a man of discreet silence, who was admirably partnered by an excellent cook. The rooms were on the first floor. The two bedrooms were at the back, and opened out of each other. 'Mr Saunders can have the smaller one, though it is the only one with a fireplace,' he said. 'I'll stick to the larger of the two, since it's got a bathroom adjoining. I wonder what time he'll arrive with the car.'

Saunders came about seven, cold and cross and dirty. 'We'll light the fire in the dining-room,' said Eustace, 'and get Prince to unpack some of the things while we are at dinner. What were the roads like?'

'Rotten. Swimming with mud, and a beastly cold wind against us all day. And this is July. Dear old England!'

'Yes,' said Eustace, 'I think we might do worse than leave old England for a few months.'

They turned in soon after twelve.

'You oughtn't to feel cold, Saunders,' said Eustace, 'when you can afford to sport a great fur-lined coat like this. You do yourself very well, all things considered. Look at those gloves, for instance. Who could possibly feel cold when wearing them?'

'They are far too clumsy, though, for driving. Try them on and see;' and he tossed them through the door on to Eustace's bed and went on with his unpacking. A minute later he heard a shrill cry of terror. 'Oh, Lord,' he heard, 'it's in the glove! Quick, Saunders, quick!' Then came a smacking thud. Eustace had thrown it from him. 'I've chucked it into the bathroom,' he gasped; 'it's hit the wall and fallen into the bath. Come now, if you want to help.' Saunders, with a lighted candle in his hand, looked over the edge of the bath. There it was, old and maimed, dumb and blind, with a ragged hole in the middle, crawling, staggering, trying to creep up the slippery sides, only to fall back helpless.

'Stay there,' said Saunders. 'I'll empty a collar-box or something, and we'll jam it in. It can't get out while I'm away.'

'Yes, it can,' shouted Eustace. 'It's getting out now; it's climbing up the plug chain. No, you brute, you filthy brute, you don't! Come back, Saunders; it's getting away from me. I can't hold it; it's all slippery. Curse its claws! Shut the window, you idiot! It's got out.' There was the sound of something dropping on to the hard flagstones below, and Eustace fell back fainting.

For a fortnight he was ill.

'I don't know what to make of it,' the doctor said to Saunders. 'I can only suppose that Mr Borlsover has suffered some great emotional shock. You had better let me send someone to help you nurse him. And by all means indulge that whim of his never to be left alone in the dark. I would keep a light burning all night, if I were you. But he *must* have more fresh air. It's perfectly absurd, this hatred of open windows.'

Eustace would have no one with him but Saunders.

'I don't want the other man,' he said. 'They'd smuggle it in somehow. I know they would.'

'Don't worry about it, old chap. This sort of thing can't go on indefinitely. You know I saw it this time as well as you. It wasn't half so active. It won't go on living much longer, especially after that fall. I heard it hit the flags myself. As soon as you're a bit stronger, we'll leave this place, not bag and baggage, but with only the clothes on our backs, so that it won't be able to hide anywhere. We'll escape it that way. We won't give any address, and we won't have any parcels sent after us. Cheer up, Eustace! You'll be well enough to leave in a day or two. The doctor says I can take you out in a chair tomorrow.'

'What have I done?' asked Eustace. 'Why does it come after me? I'm no worse than other men. I'm no worse than you, Saunders; you know I'm not. It was you who was at the bottom of that dirty business in San Diego, and that was fifteen years ago.'

'It's not that, of course,' said Saunders. 'We are in the twentieth century, and even the parsons have dropped the idea of your old sins finding you out. Before you caught the hand in the library, it was filled with pure malevolence – to you and all mankind. After you spiked it through with that nail, it naturally forgot about other people and concentrated its attention on you. It was shut up in that safe, you know, for nearly six months. That gives plenty of time for thinking of revenge.'

Eustace Borlsover would not leave his room, but he thought there might be something in Saunders's suggestion of a sudden departure from Brighton. He began rapidly to regain his strength.

'We'll go on the first of September,' he said.

The evening of the thirty-first of August was oppressively warm. Though at midday the windows had been wide open, they had been shut an hour or so before dusk. Mrs Prince had long since ceased to wonder at the strange habits of the gentlemen on the first floor. Soon after their arrival she had been told to take down the heavy window curtains in the two bedrooms, and day by day the rooms had seemed to grow more bare. Nothing was left lying about.

'Is the fire laid? Good, but it may not burn. I know – the oil from that old reading-lamp and this cotton-wool. Now the match, quick. Pull the sheet away, you fool! We don't want it now.'

There was a great roar from the grate, as the flames shot up. Saunders had been a fraction of a second too late with the sheet. The oil had fallen on to it. It, too, was burning.

'The whole place will be on fire!' cried Eustace, as he tried to beat out the flames with a blanket. 'It's no good! I can't manage it. You must open the door, Saunders, and get help.'

Saunders ran to the door and fumbled with the bolts. The key was stiff in the lock. 'Hurry,' shouted Eustace, 'or the heat will be too much for me.' The key turned in the lock at last. For half a second Saunders stopped to look back. Afterwards he could never be quite sure as to what he had seen, but at the time he thought that something black and charred was creeping slowly, very slowly, from the mass of flames towards Eustace Borlsover. For a moment he thought of returning to his friend; but the noise and the smell of the burning sent him running down the passage, crying, 'Fire! Fire!' He rushed to the telephone to summon help, and then back to the bathroom – he should have thought of that before – for water. As he burst into the bedroom there came a scream of terror which ended suddenly, and then the sound of a heavy fall.

This is the story which I heard on successive Saturday evenings from the senior mathematical master at a second-rate suburban school. For Saunders has had to earn a living in a way which other men might reckon less congenial than his old manner of life. I had mentioned by chance the name of Adrian Borlsover, and wondered at the time why he changed the conversation with such unusual abruptness. A week later Saunders began to tell me something of his own history; sordid enough, though shielded with a reserve I could well understand, for it had to cover not only his failings, but those of a dead friend. Of the final tragedy he was at first especially loath to speak; and it was only gradually that I was able to piece together the narrative of the preceding pages. Saunders was reluctant to draw any conclusions. At one time he thought that the fingered beast had been animated by the spirit of Sigismund Borlsover, a sinister eighteenth-century ancestor, who, according to legend, built and worshipped in the ugly pagan temple that overlooked the lake. At another time Saunders believed the spirit to belong to a man whom Eustace had once employed as a laboratory assistant. 'A black-haired, spiteful little brute,' he said, 'who died cursing his doctor because the fellow couldn't help him live to settle some paltry score with Borlsover.'

From the point of view of direct contemporary evidence, Saunders's story is practically uncorroborated. All the letters mentioned in the narrative were destroyed, with the exception of the last note which Eustace received, or rather, which he would have received, had not Saunders intercepted it. That I have seen myself. The handwriting was thin and shaky, the handwriting of an old man. I remember the Greek 'e' was used in 'appointment'. A little thing that amused me at the time was that Saunders seemed to keep the note pressed between the pages of his Bible.

I had seen Adrian Borlsover once. Saunders I learnt to

38

know well. It was by chance, however, and not by design, that I met a third person of the story, Morton, the butler. Saunders and I were walking in the Zoological Gardens one Sunday afternoon, when he called my attention to an old man who was standing before the door of the Reptile House.

'Why, Morton,' he said, clapping him on the back, 'how is the world treating you?'

'Poorly, Mr Saunders,' said the old fellow, though his face lighted up at the greeting. 'The winters drag terribly nowadays. There don't seem no summers or springs.'

'You haven't found what you were looking for, I suppose?'

'No, sir, not yet; but I shall someday. I always told them that Mr Bolsover kept some queer animals.'

'And what is he looking for?' I asked, when we had parted from him.

'A beast with five fingers,' said Saunders. 'This afternoon, since he has been in the Reptile House, I suppose it will be a reptile with a hand. Next week it will be a monkey with practically no body. The poor old chap is a born materialist.'

SNIPE 3909

Graeme Fife

Graeme Fife has written two children's books, plays, features and a large number of stories about composers, also a dramatised biography of Vivaldi for radio. His ARTHUR THE KING was broadcast on BBC Radio in 1990 and he has written an accompanying BBC book, ARTHUR THE KING: THE THEMES BEHIND THE LEGENDS.

The phone rang. Mary lifted the receiver and spoke: 'Snipe 3909.' There was no reply. Mary repeated the number. There was no reply. She put the receiver down, and resumed painting.

The estate agent was one of the old school, courteous as a family doctor. He arrived, smiling sunnily, at ten o'clock precisely. Optimism and encouragement radiated from him like the bloom of a ripe apple.

'Charming, Mrs Luckham, charming,' he muttered as she showed him round the cottage. He made notes on a clipboard.

The decision to sell the cottage had been harder for Mary to reach than to take. She had decided on a fresh start, a clean break with the past, as the past still clung so tenaciously to her. Divorce never seemed to deal out its hurts even-handedly. Simon had merely replaced her with someone else in their house, their bed; while she was dogged by the nightmare of those final, crucifying months with him. What a cruel sham it had been, knowing that even as he pretended to make an effort at renewal, she was sharing him with the someone else now comfortably installed in what had been theirs. Hers. That agony had all been so futile in the end.

Even the cottage they had bought – as a refuge from the pressures of work in town – had become part of the wounding pattern of her life. The Retreat they had called it; but the cottage with country views, their weekend solace, had now so cruelly lived up to a different side of its name.

Mary had hoped to escape the memories, to give herself a chance to think and reconstruct. Instead, she merely retreated into the entire shambles of the past. Was it vengeance? Was it part of the slow tearing to pieces of her life? And why her, only? Didn't Simon deserve his share, Simon now blithely doling out the fruits of their partnership to someone else?

To buoyant Mr Hampton, though, blissfully or discreetly unaware of Mary's reasons for selling, The Retreat offered only reasons to be cheerful.

'A lick of paint, well done,' he said. 'Amazing how persuasive a lick of paint can be. Small trick of the trade,' he confided. 'Not that I think we'll have any trouble selling for you, Mrs Luckham. Secluded rural position; excellent views of woodland; mature garden; rustic charm . . .'

'You mean overgrown and dilapidated?' said Mary.

'Think positive, Mrs Luckham, think positive,' he said. The phone rang.

'Excuse me.' Mary went into the other room. She picked up the receiver and spoke: 'Snipe 3909.' She listened and heard a slow melancholy whistling, two notes high, two notes low, two notes just above, two notes lower, each note the same length. Quietly, as if not to arouse some fear that slumbered in her, she put the receiver down. Involuntarily she caught her breath; her stomach clenched.

'Wrong number?' said Mr Hampton artlessly, when she came back.

'Wrong . . .? Oh, yes, wrong number,' said Mary. Mr Hampton stared up at a small damp patch on the ceiling and made another note on his clipboard.

'What about the price?' she asked, with an effort.

He pondered a moment then answered with avuncular charm, as if it were a matter of his generosity. 'I've been mulling that over. Let's go for it, shall we? Why not?'

'You don't think it will put people off?'

'I think we should cross that bridge when we come to it. One thing, though, it might well be an idea to clean out the gutters. We don't want to overdo the rustic charm, do we?'

'You mean having the lawn overflowing onto the roof?' she said.

He laughed, as if that were an essential part of his etiquette too, and consulted his clipboard. 'Well, I think that's everything. I could get someone to do the gutters for you if you like?' She nodded.

She walked with him to the car.

'We'll be in touch,' he said, 'but don't hesitate to call, of course. Cheerie-bye, dear lady.' With that he drove off. The phone rang.

'Snipe 3909.'

A woman's voice answered: 'Mary, darling? Rachel. Listen, I'm in a fearful dash but Craig said he'd do the valuation of the porcelain for you as soon as you like. He's just working out his own catalogue so it's no problem.'

'Oh, that's very sweet of him,' said Mary. 'Why don't you both come for an early drink?'

'Love to,' said Rachel.

'How about today? I could do with a break from gloss and turps.'

'Not possible, darling, sorry. Tomorrow?'

'Fine. Say six-thirty.'

'We'll be there. Any more of those phone calls?'

'Yes. Just now, actually.'

'Tell the police.'

'Oh, I don't know,' said Mary.

'Tell the police,' said Rachel. 'That's what they're there for.

Can't do any harm.'

'Yes,' said Mary, 'yes, all right. When I go shopping.'

'Good girl. See you tomorrow.'

The police sergeant was as helpful as he could be in the circumstances. Threats or lewd suggestions constituted grounds for direct action – the telephone exchange might give her a new number as a matter of priority. However, silence did not constitute grounds for action. Whistling did not warrant official priority, not even persistent whistling and silence.

'Whistling?' he'd said. 'It's probably kids.' Then he added: 'One thing I *can* do, madam, seeing as how you are a bit remote out there, is get the patrol car to call in on its way past. Show a presence.'

'Oh, thank you,' said Mary.

'Try not to fret. You strike me as being the sensible type, anyway.'

They're all so optimistic about me, thought Mary.

At home again, she had barely climbed to the top of the stepladder, paintbrush and pot in her hand, when the phone rang. She listened as a man's voice spoke her name.

'Mary.'

She didn't reply.

'Mary.'

She stuttered. 'Who is this?'

'Don't move, Mary,' he said. 'Don't sell the house. Don't go away.' His voice lilted, half-crooning.

'Who are you?' she said, distantly, as if she were uncertain of any human presence.

'You know, Mary,' he said. 'That's the trouble. You know but won't admit it.'

A nausea of fear and rage boiled into her throat. She barked into the phone, 'Leave me alone' and slammed the receiver down. Trembling, she went back into the sitting-room. Sunlight streamed in through the curtainless windows. Suddenly the fresh paint of the picture rails smelled sour.

An hour later the phone rang again. She clambered down the ladder and gingerly lifted the receiver. 'Snipe 3909,' she said. Mr Hampton of Stockwell and Rowley answered, informing her, with audible satisfaction, that a gentleman on the lookout for an immediate purchase was very keen to view.

'A cash buyer, Mrs Luckham. We'll be in touch, naturally,' he said. 'Fingers crossed.'

Mary put the receiver down and went back to her painting. Like a pulse beating in her head came the notes of that crude tune the man had whistled – la-la la-la . . . la-la la-la – hypnotically over and over again until the shrill of the doorbell abruptly jarred the rhythm. Mary went out into the hallway and saw a shadow looming across the frosted panels of the door. 'Who is it?' she said.

'Police, madam,' came the reply.

Mary opened the door. A tall, young constable stood on the gravel of the drive. He saluted with a casual wave of his hand. 'Just calling to say we're here if you need us,' he said.

Mary felt a sudden warmth. 'Oh. That's kind.'

The policeman smiled. 'Any more phone calls recently?'

'Er, yes, not very long ago in fact.'

'Ah.' He paused, frowning, and asked, 'Did he threaten you, or . . .'

'No.' And then suddenly it came to her. The tune he had whistled. A nursery rhyme. 'Mary, Mary, quite contrary'.

'Are you all right, madam?' asked the policeman, observing her distraction.

'It's nothing,' she said.

Thunder rumbled a long way off. The constable sniffed the air. 'Looks as if we're in for some rain I'm afraid,' he said.

'Yes,' replied Mary mechanically.

The storm arrived as dusk fell and lasted several hours. The curtainless window panes in the sitting-room became watery mirrors. Pitch darkness pressed its face against the glass, the rainlike tears streaming down its cheeks. Mary felt the sightless eyes of the night on her. Taut with apprehension, she phoned Simon. The ringing tone went on and on, dulling her senses . . . dring-dring, dring-dring . . . Ma-ry Ma-ry. Simon's voice shocked her out of the reverie.

'Luckham.'

'It's me,' she said.

'Oh,' he sounded instantly annoyed. 'What do you want?'

'Simon . . .' she began, but he didn't wait for her to gather up any more words.

'Oh God,' he sighed. 'I recognise *that* tone.'

'Listen, I want to talk to you.'

'Well, I'm afraid it's not wildly convenient now,' he said, his chill, dismissive tone like a cold draught round the neck. 'We're just going out to dinner. It'll have to wait.'

'It can't wait,' she said, exasperated. Why should everything have to happen at *his* convenience? Bloody Simon.

'If you've phoned up for a row,' he said, 'you're out of luck. I'm not playing.'

'It's about selling the cottage.'

'What about it?'

'I want to sort out the money,' said Mary.

'We agreed all that.'

'No.' She tried to contain her anger. '*You* agreed all that. As it is, I've got all the expenses and the . . .' She paused. He said nothing. Her patience snapped '. . . while you just sit back and do as you please, like some king and queen.'

'If by that,' he said, 'you mean Fenella, which I take it you do, you can go to hell.'

Mary's anger slackened into weariness. 'Oh, who cares?'

she said. Forcing the words out as if they were in a foreign language, she pleaded, 'I just want to sort it out. Please.'

'Then sort it out,' he said. 'I've got to go.'

'Very convenient,' she said.

'Good-bye, Mary. And don't forget the porcelain, either.' He put the phone down.

'That's not yours, you bastard. Damn you . . .' She shouted into the dialling tone. Tears seeped into her eyes as she put the phone down. Almost at once, as if the caller had chosen his moment with exact cunning, the phone rang. She picked it up without thinking.

'Snipe 3909.'

The voice said, 'Ma-ry? Ma-ry?' She didn't reply. 'You won't move, will you, Mary? Finish the decorating and stay, won't you?'

'Go to hell,' she screamed and slammed the phone down. A gust of wind slapped the side of the house. Again the phone rang.

'I said go to hell,' she screamed into the mouthpiece. The man's voice at the other end of the line, startled, repeated, 'Is that Mrs Luckham?'

Mary stood in the brightly-lit room staring nonplussed at her reflection in the windows. 'Yes?' she said. 'Who is this?'

'Mr Elwin,' said the man. 'Through Stockwell and Rowley. About viewing the cottage.'

'At this time of night?'

'Oh, I do apologise,' he said.

'Isn't it rather late to call?'

'I do apologise,' said the man. 'Mr Hampton gave me the number and . . .'

She breathed in deeply and said, 'Yes, I understand. When were you thinking of?'

'I wondered if the day after tomorrow would suit you? In the morning?'

'Fine,' she said flatly. 'What time?'

'Say ten o'clock. Depending on a couple of appointments. Hopefully.'

Hopefully, she thought, hopefully. 'Yes,' she said.

'I'll phone if I get held up for any reason. The place sounds just right.'

'I hope so,' said Mary. 'Good-bye.'

Next morning Mary woke to the insistent ringing of the phone. Half asleep, she stumbled downstairs to answer it and heard a breathy whistling. 'Mary, Mary, quite contrary . . .' She put the phone down. A chill of horror fluttered through her. Upstairs the alarm clock shrilled and a dull clunk like a door slamming shook the side of the house. Mary gasped with fright. She heard footsteps on the gravel outside. Nerving herself, she looked out of the window and saw a man in overalls climbing up a ladder past the side window. Mary tightened the belt of her dressing gown and, ignoring the insistent blast of the alarm upstairs, went into the garden. The man in overalls was poking at the gutters.

'What do you think you're doing?' she asked.

'Oh,' he said, turning round, 'I thought the place was empty.'

'Does it *look* empty?'

'Not now it doesn't.'

'Didn't you think to knock? Do you know what time it is?'

He shifted position on the ladder. 'Well, from what Mr Hampton told me . . .'

'Oh, never mind,' she said.

'I had to come on my way somewhere else,' he said, 'to fit you in.'

'All right.' She turned to go.

'Because they haven't been done for some time, have they?' He dropped a clump of sodden grass onto the path to prove the point.

'I'm sure they haven't,' she said and went inside.

Craig and Rachel arrived at seven o'clock that evening. Mary opened a bottle of wine. They drank and talked awhile, then Craig went off into the study to price Mary's collection of porcelain cups, presents from Simon, many of them.

'We'll miss you, you know,' said Rachel.

'I shall miss you, too, but . . . I do so want a fresh start.'

'Yes,' Rachel smiled, 'and there are always visits. Did you go to the police?'

'Yes. They said they'd send the patrol car from time to time. They've been once.'

'Good. That's something.'

Mary sighed. 'You know, it's almost as if he can see me. That's what it feels like anyway. I get to the top of the stepladder and the phone rings. I don't know, other things too. It's like being watched.'

'I'm not surprised with the curtains down,' said Rachel. 'How awful. He hasn't caught you with your knickers down, has he?' And at once she regretted her stupid flippancy. 'Oh, darling, forgive me.'

Mary shook her head and smiled a faint, tired smile.

Eventually Craig rejoined them, full of warm good humour. What a lucky bird you are, Rachel, thought Mary.

'Good news, my love, good news,' said Craig. 'Two or three thousand there, I should say.'

'What?' said Mary, eyes widening.

'Conservative estimate. Do you want me to arrange a sale?'

'Would you?'

'Pleasure.'

'I'll pay you.'

'No you won't. Leave it to me.' He sipped the last of his wine and put his hand on Rachel's shoulder. 'Well, Mrs T., we'd better be going, I guess.'

Rachel stood up and kissed Mary. 'Take care darling.

Sooner you get the curtains back the better.'

'If I'd left them up they'd be thick with paint by now.'

Craig put both his arms round Mary and kissed her. Oh, you lucky bird, Rachel, Mary thought again.

Minutes after she had waved them good-bye the phone rang. She let it ring for a long time. It didn't stop. She took the receiver off and replaced it. It began to ring again. She lifted the receiver, pressed the cradle down, held it, let it up again. There was no dialling tone. Instead she heard a man whistling the opening notes of a familiar tune. She depressed the cradle a second time, then began to dial the number of the police station. Even as the dial clicked round she heard a man's voice saying: 'Mary, Mary, please listen.'

She stopped dialling, slammed down the receiver; picked it up and dialled the number again.

'It's no good, Mary,' his voice said, 'I've got your line and I intend to keep it as long as I like. A radio phone has its special uses, you see.'

Mary looked into the mirror of the curtainless windows. The man's voice went on. She listened as if in a trance. 'I want to talk, Mary. You never let me talk. Standing there in your blue track suit with your lovely hair tied all back with a purple ribbon.'

'How do you know?' she whispered.

'How do you think?' he said.

Oh my God, he can see me, she thought; watching me with a damned phone, watching me.

'I've only ever been allowed to look at you, Mary, not touch. Never . . . touch. Reach out and touch yourself for me, Mary. Go on, do as I say. You've always looked straight through me like I was glass. Like I was a shop window. But I am ever so near to you now, Mary.'

She trembled. 'Leave me alone. Oh God, please leave me alone.'

'Oh, I'm not going to leave you alone,' he said, his voice

moaning like a low wind. 'Not like you left me alone. I can comfort you, Mary. Don't you need comfort, Mary, Mary, quite contrary?'

Numb with fear she replaced the receiver, its weight leaden in her hand. In a sudden access of panic she ran through the house, locking every door, every window upstairs and down. Feverishly she hauled at the heap of curtains in the corner of the room; anything to make her invisible, to block out the windows, to blind him.

She heard a car drive up, its wheels crunching on the gravel. She saw its headlights beaming onto the hedge. Engine switched off. Door opened and shut. Footsteps. The doorbell shrilled like an alarm through the house. At that same instant, the phone began to ring like another peal of obscene laughter from the loathsome voyeur. She left the phone and went into the hallway. A shadow loomed across the glazed panels of the door.

'Who is it?' she whispered.

The doorbell rang again.

'Who is it?' Fear jerked the whisper uncontrollably into a yell.

'Police, madam. Just passing. To see if you're OK.'

She opened the door. A young police constable stood outside. She didn't recognise him. The telephone rang on.

'Thank you, thank you,' she said. 'It's ringing now.' She pointed hopelessly.

The constable stepped into the hallway. He closed the door behind him and followed the sound of the ringing. He picked up the receiver, listened and looked across at Mary and shook his head. She clasped her arms tight about her. He replaced the receiver and shrugged his shoulders.

'Well, madam, I think we had better sort out what we're going to do. You look white as a sheet.'

'Oh, I'm just a bit shaken. Would you, would you like a cup of tea?'

'That would be appreciated. I'll just go and get my things from the car: better make a statement.'

Mary went into the kitchen and filled the kettle. The policeman went out, took the radio phone from where he had left it by the door and put it back in the car, then returned to the house and locked the front door noiselessly behind him. No need to lock any other doors – he had seen Mary doing that. As he walked down the hallway Mary heard him whistling a familiar tune.

THE DEAD DRUMMER

David Buck
ADAPTED BY HAYDN MIDDLETON

Haydn Middleton was born in 1955 and educated in Reading and Oxford. His publications include three contemporary novels that deal with the magic history of the island of Britain: THE PEOPLE IN THE PICTURE, THE LIE OF THE LAND, and THE COLLAPSING CASTLE. He is married with two small children.

The two men lurched against each other as they crossed the stormswept plain. That night the unsheltered moorland seemed as endless as the ocean, and although both men knew the ocean, neither knew the moor. Matthew – the elder of the two at almost thirty – realised that they should never have wandered from the roads, so it cheered him to see a signpost looming ahead.

'That's rare difficult writing,' sighed Billy Boy when Matthew peered up through the rain in an attempt to decipher it. 'There's numbering figures mixed up in there too, I shouldn't wonder.'

Matthew, needing all his concentration, raised an arm to keep him silent. 'This way-post,' he announced at last, pointing, 'tells us we're to Lavington this way . . . and Devizes that.'

'And what do the third arm say?'

Matthew shook his head. He was a big man, broad-shouldered; a monstrous tattoo on his forearm showed Bonaparte swinging from a gibbet. 'The writing's quite worn away there, but the figure says one mile.'

'If it's signposted so,' Billy Boy said at once, his tarred sailor's pigtail bobbing as he stamped his feet, 'then it must be worth a man's labour to reach it. An inn, think you?'

'That or a pond or a swamp or some man's grave . . .'

Suddenly Billy Boy stiffened. 'What were that sound?'

'Eh?' said Matthew, looking in the direction of the sign's third arm. 'I heard naught.' There was a distant thunderous rumble. 'But aye, I heard that.' He looked away. 'And 'twere thunder, plain and simple.'

Billy Boy shook his head. 'It were *him*, Matthew.' His weasel eyes darted. 'And he's coming closer.'

'Then step out, man, for God's sake! Thunder or bogeyman, I want to be under cover when it do come.'

They came to the inn. Matthew knocked loudly on its door. At first there was no response. Matthew looked up to see a light at the window, and then that window being thrown open. 'Who's below?' called the landlord.

'Two travellers from the Wars. Soaking wet and Godforsaken lost.'

The window was pulled shut. Moments later, from the other side of the door came the sounds of a key turning and bolts being drawn. At the same time a clap of thunder broke, and a terrified cry escaped Billy Boy.

'Now keep your mouth shut about your fancies,' Matthew hissed. 'Don't say a word. Whatever it is out there, it's not what you think.'

'Come in, come in,' laughed the landlord as the door opened. 'You're not the first to stray off the paths, nor shan't be the last.'

'I trust we did not disturb your rest,' said Matthew when they were inside, and the door had been shut firmly on the lashing rain.

The landlord simply smiled. 'You're sailormen?' he asked Matthew. They nodded. 'Place yourselves by the fire, Gentlemen. You'll be requiring a jar directly, I'm sure. I'll mull up some ale, then go warm your beds.'

'Landlord . . .' Matthew began. 'What'll this cost in hard

cash? For though the King be dear to us, we don't carry his picture to any great extent.'

The landlord bent to load new logs onto the fire. 'I do what I can,' he said in a low voice, 'for those who has fought for their country. My inn doors'll never be closed to such as you – and your friend.'

'Well, Billy Boy, ain't that a Christian spirit on the kind gentleman?'

'Ay, that's for certain sure, Matt.' But as the landlord was leaving the room, a heavy crash of thunder swamped the room and Billy Boy gave another involuntary cry.

'Storm's getting closer,' said the landlord, eyeing him strangely.

As soon as he was gone, Billy Boy tugged on Matthew's coat. ''Tis he,' he murmured. 'He with the drum.'

'There's no drum, damn you! What you hear, 'tis thunder.'

'Ay. Ay, thunder. But beat upon a drum. His snare drum. Isn't that what ye call it? A right, tight little side drum that sits at a lad's hip? It's that sound I do hear. Not thunder . . .'

A loud thunderclap sliced his speech in half. His eyes bulged as its reverberations died away. 'Thunder,' said Matthew. 'Rattlin' the shutters and the windys in their sashes.'

'A drum, I say,' Billy walked over to the window. 'I hear that drummer-boy coming closer, ever closer out there over the plain. He's after me, sure.'

Matthew narrowed his eyes in perplexity as the landlord returned with two pots of ale. 'Will you keep us company here by the fire?' Matthew asked him. He nodded and took his place. 'A good brew, ain't it, Billy Boy?'

Billy came away from the window, sat a little apart from the other two, and sipped at the mull. 'Ay.'

'Put life into the dead, it would,' said the landlord slowly.

'Eh?' cried Billy Boy to Matthew, leaping up. 'What did he mean?'

Matthew smiled. 'Hush man. Sit down.'

'"Life in the dead"? What meant he by that?'

'He meant naught, on my soul. Now sit, do, and beg his pardon.'

Billy Boy did so; gladly the landlord granted it. 'He speaks before he thinks,' Matthew tried to explain.

The landlord nodded. 'And lashes out with those great hands of his, I shouldn't wonder. I'd not like to be at the rough end of his temper.'

Matthew shook his head. 'He's gentle as a lamb. Now he's nervous, but he'll be better directly.' He raised his eyes at a rumble of thunder. Billy Boy started violently. 'It's just his way,' Matthew explained, 'his fancy – of a drummer.' He lowered his voice. 'And there's a reason for that fancy . . .'

For a moment the three of them listened as the thunder rolled nearer still, sounding for all the world like an approaching drum. Billy Boy wrung his hands. 'Oh, tell him the tale, Matt Boy,' he murmured. *'Tell* him . . .'

Matthew frowned uncertainly, drank deep, then wiped his lips, staring into the crackling fire. 'Billy was once a soldier,' he began, 'and a good 'un. A sergeant, no less: well-trusted, stout, reliable, and sober. So one day there's a command for him to take the regimental pay to a detachment a dozen mile away or more, packed on a string of mules . . .'

'A grave responsibility,' nodded the landlord. Outside the thunder rolled slowly like a drum, louder and louder as Matthew spoke.

'A young drummer-boy were chosen to go with him, to while the time away.'

'Brand were his name,' added Billy Boy, staring. 'Abel Brand.'

The landlord looked from Billy to Matthew. 'Go on,' he said after a pause.

'Well, they stopped by the way – in a little wood – to keep

the sun off their heads while they shared a rough meal. Now this is what makes the tale. There were bandits in them parts, rovers. And as soon as Billy slipped the rifle off his shoulder and leaned it against a rock, they struck . . .'

'I can still hear his cries!' Billy Boy interrupted.

'So they killed him? The drummer?' said the landlord.

'Spit him on their swords,' nodded Matthew. 'And Billy Boy here fought like the deuce, but there were too many, so he ran.' He saw Billy shaking his head. 'Don't take it bad. You're no coward, Billy. No reason you shouldn't run, not if the lad was dead.'

'He was dead all right.' Billy looked up wildly. 'Only question is . . why don't he *stay* so?' The drum-beats continued outside, brisk, inexorable.

The landlord shifted on his bench. 'The thunder still troubles you, sir?'

'Thunder, you call it?'

The landlord widened his eyes. 'What else would you have me call it?'

'Ha!' was all Billy Boy could say, and then: 'Oh, make it stop, sir.'

The landlord laughed. 'Don't worry, man. Storm'll blow over soon.'

At that Billy Boy rushed to the window and flung open the shutters. 'But *he*'ll still be there! Brand. Abel Brand! Do you not see him? There, there! So proud and stiff in his marching . . .'

Matthew rose and guided Billy Boy back to his bench. 'Steady, Billy. Steady now, old lad.'

'Drummer-boy indeed,' grinned the landlord. 'But tell me – what harm should this sprite wish you? As your shipmate says, you did no harm to him. And ghosts is many things, but there's always a logic to what they do. They'll not carry you off for no reason, I promise you.'

Billy Boy seemed not to hear. 'He and his damnable drum.'

He's come with his rataplan to take me down to hell.' Then, seeming to recover himself, he glared at the landlord. 'Is it reasons you want? Oh, I'll give you reasons . . .'

'Billy?' said Matthew, puzzled now. 'What mean you?'

Billy laughed wretchedly. 'Oh, Matthew, Matthew, you take care of me like a brother. You think I'm something cracked, but I've a knowledge in my soul you never even dreamed of.'

Matthew looked over into the landlord's furrowed face. The rain beat against the walls. The inn-sign creaked. Suddenly Billy Boy started. 'You hear him now?' he demanded. 'The drum, for God's sake. The drum!'

Matthew, his eyes still on the landlord's, nodded slowly, humouring his friend. 'I hear it, sure.'

'Tap to his rhythm, then,' Billy Boy challenged.

'I . . .' Matthew began. 'I have not the skill . . .'

'Liar!' cried Billy Boy. 'You hear nothing. Neither of you.' His eyes dropped. 'But he's outside now. He's come as far as he will. Now he'll wait.'

'For what?' asked the landlord.

Billy Boy shook his head and moved from the wall. 'For me. 'Tis only my fear protects me now, for it keeps me awake, and he'll not take me open-eyed. He'll wait till my eye-lids droop, then sneak in by the chink of a casement, then *off* with my soul!'

The landlord stood. 'Tell me this true,' he said to Billy Boy. 'What wrong did ye do to young Brand? There's maybe a detail or so you left out.'

Billy Boy, to Matthew's alarm, was nodding. His eyes seemed wild in his head. 'I left him, it's true,' he whispered. 'And with a six-inch of steel in his ribs!'

The landlord swallowed. 'Who put it there?'

Billy Boy's wild eyes, all melancholy now, turned on him. 'I did.'

'Not the bandits?'

Billy Boy twisted his neck, as if he were hearing his drummer again. 'There never was no bandits.' Matthew closed his eyes.

The landlord frowned. 'You stabbed him in cold blood, then?'

'I had to. Don't you see? He had a secret. A knowledge – of what I intended.'

Matthew moaned. But the landlord cut in. 'You intended. . .'

'Ain't it obvious, man? To rob the mules of their packs. Take the money, and what else of value. Wave good-bye to the flag.'

The landlord nodded. 'He refused to act with you, young Brand, so you cut him down? In cold blood.'

Billy Boy narrowed his eyes at him. 'Your words, Mister, but 'taint so. The blood pumped hot in my veins. This here in my brow has not done throbbing since. But I couldn't let him go. Don't you see? He'd have told all.'

The landlord gave him a dry look: 'He told more dead than alive.' Outside the thunder pealed on through the rain. Beats on a drum. Thunder and rain.

Billy Boy rushed his hands to his ears. 'He still does, too! He still tells them all they want to know! Don't you hear, don't you *hear*? Circling this inn now . . .' Smartly he drew a jack-knife from his belt and snapped it open. 'Quiet, you demon. If I can kill you once, I can kill you twice.'

Billy Boy's words had come as the most awful revelation to Matthew. He had known that his young companion was subject to dreams and terrors, and that once he had been rich. But that was all. 'Steady, old friend,' he murmured.

Billy Boy appeared not to hear. He looked to left and right, the knife still poised. 'At sea, I was safe when the press come and took me. He was a soldier, you see, young Brand. A land-demon only. But now the Wars are done. Hard to find a ship, hard to find . . .' At that he pitched forward, falling heavily in a kind of stupor.

Matthew went to him and knelt. 'He's wore himself out,' he said. 'A bad conscience can do that to a man.'

'Best get him to bed,' answered the landlord. 'Can't turn him out of door.'

Matthew looked up at him. 'You believe in the demon?' he asked, hushed.

The landlord stooped to raise Billy Boy by his armpits while Matthew took his legs. 'I don't believe, nor disbelieve. Now pick up that knife of his. It gives me the creeps. This way, through the door and up the stairs ... .'

As they lowered the senseless form onto the bed, Matthew tilted his head. 'The thunder,' he said softly. 'It's stopped.'

Both men listened. 'Ay,' said the landlord, 'for the present. But nothing's to be read by that. All thunder stops some time. There, get his shoes off.'

Complying, Matthew sighed, 'His eyes is shut. He didn't want them shut.'

'You can close the eyes of the dead,' replied the landlord, 'but you can't open the eyes of the living. What are you doing with that knife of his?'

Matthew placed the jack-knife under Billy Boy's pillow. As he did so, new thunder growled low outside. 'There, Billy,' said Matthew. 'There's your knife, to keep you safe.' And he left the room ahead of the landlord.

Once downstairs, the landlord grew pensive. 'A charm,' he said, 'would work better than a knife, I'm thinking. And I have one, a dolly, somewheres.' He re-entered the tap-room, mounted a stool, and removed a corn dolly from above the bar. 'Farmers and folk do set great store by these, though I myself hold no belief in them.'

Matthew touched it. ''Tis quaintly woven. Could Billy have it?'

The thunder rumbled again, just like a muffled drum-roll. 'I suppose so,' said the landlord. 'Just for tonight, ay. Fill your pot, pray. I'll take this up and put it by his bed – against the sprite.'

Matthew obediently refilled his pot as the landlord went back up the wooden stairs. Again, he thought he heard the drum- beat outside. He was confused: the landlord said he didn't believe in charms yet he nailed one up on a beam; he himself didn't believe in spirit drummer-boys, yet sure enough he could hear one now. *Rataplan, rataplan . . .* Receding now. 'Abel Brand,' Matthew said under his breath, clutching at his pot of ale. Abel Brand. Deeper into the distance. And was he leaving because of the charm? Or was it *because his work was done*? 'Oh my God . . .' said Matthew more loudly.

At that moment his words were swamped by a piercing cry from above. Matthew rushed to the stairs, to find the landlord coming slowly down. 'I was too late,' the landlord told him ruefully. 'The wee drummer got there first.'

'What do ye mean?' gasped Matthew.

'His throat is cut from ear to ear. Wi' his own knife.'

'Billy!' Matthew breathed, moving to go up the stairs but finding the landlord barring his way. 'It's not an instructive sight,' was all he said.

'I've been in battle, man,' Matthew countered. 'I've seen the worst.'

The landlord would not move. ''Tis not the blood nor the cut. 'Tis the expression on his face. I'll not forget it as long as I live.'

'Oh Billy!' cried Matthew, surging past him up the stairs. 'Billy!'

At ten the next morning, when all outside was fresh and calm, Matthew stood on the upper level of the barn attached to the inn, watching the undertaker complete the business of laying out Billy Boy.

'Take a last look, then,' said the undertaker. 'I'll nail him up anon.'

Matthew shook his head. 'Do it straightaway, if you please. All my prayers is said.' Then, as the undertaker went about his work, Matthew continued: 'I have to tell you this, though: neither he nor I had sufficient funds to see you paid – leastways, not as you deserve. I mean, we have naught.'

The undertaker drove in his last nail, smiled, and straightened up. 'That's no worry to me. Here, give me a hand down these steps, eh?'

Puzzled, Matthew helped him ease the coffin off its trestles and over to the barn's steep wooden steps. 'You surely didn't come here out of charity?' he asked.

The undertaker shook his head, amused at the idea. They began to descend.

'Then who shall pay you?' demanded Matthew.

'I'm paid. The innkeeper saw me right.'

'The landlord? Here?'

'He's a soft-hearted one, is Jed; and powerful generous to such as have worn the King's uniform.' Matthew nodded, aware of the truth of that. 'He lost his young lad in the wars. Reckon Jed thinks he owes it his memory to care for the military, so to speak.'

Matthew stiffened. The coffin tilted. 'A . . . young lad?'

'Killed in action. Drummer-boy, he were. Here, careful now . . .'

Matthew staggered a little as he reached the level ground. 'Jed . . .?'

'The landlord here,' replied the undertaker. 'Jed Brand.'

'Ay,' said another voice, suddenly close to them both. 'Such is my name.' Matthew opened his mouth but could not speak. 'Ha,' the landlord went on. 'Scared you, did I?' Still Matthew could only gape and stare.

'Here,' said the undertaker to him, 'hoist your end up, lad,

61

onto the cart. Help, Jed, there, if you will.' The three of them lifted the coffin onto the waiting cart. Humming a merry tune, the undertaker then lashed it into place, mounted the cart, and backed up the horses.

'Farewell, then; and thankee,' called the landlord.

'Any time, Jed Brand,' called back the undertaker, as the cart rumbled away through a scatter of chickens.

Watching it go, the landlord came and stood by Matthew's side. 'Well, sir,' he sighed at length. 'I wish your stay had been a happier one.'

Matthew looked at him. 'He called you Brand.'

The landlord stared into the distance after the cart. 'And why not? That's my handle, as they say.'

'It's what the lad was called – Abel Brand.'

The landlord looked back at him. 'It's a common enough name in these parts. Why, what's troubling you, sir? You've gone powerful pale.'

'When,' faltered Matthew, 'when you went up to Billy's room with the charm . . .'

'I cut his throat. Is that what you're thinking?'

'Why not? You had cause enough.'

'Oh, sir,' the landlord remonstrated. 'I'm an innkeeper. I'm proud of my calling. We have standards, we landlord folk. And murder, as I think you'll agree, sir . . .'

'Well. Say on. Damn you, say on!'

The landlord turned on his heel. 'Murder, sir,' he continued over his shoulder, 'is a most fearful breach o' hospitality. Most fearful.'

FAT ANDY

Stephen Dunstone

*Stephen Dunstone gave up full-time German teaching ten years
ago in order to write. Since then, he has written regularly for
Radios 3 and 4, winning a RADIO TIMES Drama Award and a
Giles Cooper Award. His work has been translated into French,
German, Norwegian, Hebrew, Icelandic, Japanese, and Russian.*

———————————

Andrew and his mother were walking through St
Leonard's churchyard, on their way back from the
shops. It was a short cut they had been taking for the last
forty years or so, and it was pleasanter than going by the
road: there was the well-kept grass, the beautifully trimmed
hedge, the daffodils in spring, the swallows nesting over the
south transept window . . .

'That window's going to be filthy before long,' said Millie.

But Andrew's mind was not on swallows – he was grap-
pling with a difficult thought. For the church was to be
made redundant, and the important issue for Andrew – the
thing Andrew was trying to puzzle out – was this: when
would God's spirit actually leave? Would it be when the
Bible and prayer books were removed, or would He wait
until the roof fell in? Andrew had special reasons for wanting to know.

'I saw a damp patch in the vestry this morning,' Millie
was saying. 'It's a leak in the plumbing, I expect. Wasn't the
roof, we haven't had rain. Might be the mains, under the
floor.'

'Mains is off,' said Andrew.

'Doesn't mean you can't get water,' said Millie. 'You don't
get water when the mains is *on* sometimes, so you could
easily get it when it's off. You should look.'

'God's going,' said Andrew. 'Bad'll come.'

'Don't talk daft. God doesn't want dafties.'

He didn't answer.

'Oh, now would you look at that!' exclaimed Millie, as they passed a well-tended grave. 'Is that the cats been playing around? They've scattered all the flowers you put out. Would you believe it?'

But Andrew was panting away down the path, the shopping bag swinging against his legs.

He shut the church door behind him – rather loudly in his haste – and stood on the worn stone step, getting his breath back. He looked around the old walls, seeking reassurance. Yes: God was still here.

Safe now, he could let the pictures come into his head. They'd been coming a lot recently.

In the pictures a wave crashes on a rocky beach; two children are playing among the pools: a girl and a boy. No one else is in sight. The boy does not seem to be enjoying himself.

Their voices – her voice – is carried on the breeze: 'Can't catch me! Can't catch me!' Then, with a sudden burst of inspired rhyming: 'Cos you're much too FAT, got a face like a big cow PAT!'

But he has almost caught her. He lunges – a fat boy's lunge – she squeals and runs off across the rocks. 'FatAndyfatAndyfatAndy fatAndy . . . can't catch me . . . '

It seems he doesn't want to play any more; he turns to go back the way they came.

Instantly: 'Where are you going?' calls the girl. 'Come back! Spoil sport!'

But he plods resolutely along the shingle. The girl runs to catch him up.

'I didn't mean it,' she says. 'Please play.'

He ignores her.

'Honestly, you're really nice, I really think so.'

He falters.

She dangles bait. 'I want to show you something.' He stops, looks

at her. 'It's a secret, it's a really special secret. Do you want to know?'
His look tells her he does, very much.
'Then you've got to catch me. I won't run too fast.' And she's off
again; off down the beach and onto a rock, where – coquettishly, like
some shore-bird in a mating display – she calls: 'Andy . . . Andy . . .
Andy . . . Andy . . .'
He makes up his mind – he cannot live without the secret – and he
trots after her. Instantly, she's away into the distance, calling into the
wind:'FatAndyfatAndyfatAndyfatAndy . . .'

The pictures faded, and Andrew blinked in the sunlight that
shafted through the south transept window, undimmed by
swallows' droppings.

He whispered to God: 'It wasn't cats. I've kept her sleeping, till now, but she knows, see. She knows you're going.'

The next day, Andrew was in the church again, with his
mother, collecting hassocks and piling them up. Millie was
looking out for the ones she had embroidered; Andrew was
wondering if a bargain could be struck with God. If they left
a hassock, and Andrew came and knelt on it, and if they left
a prayer book and a hymn book somewhere, couldn't He be
persuaded to stay? It wouldn't be like before, but He could
pretend. Couldn't He?

'Aren't you going to go and look at that damp?' said
Millie. 'It might be doing something in the crypt.'

'Not my job any more,' said Andrew petulantly.

'Someone'll have to look: you don't want a flood.' They
carried on piling. 'I hope it's fine for the vicar's little speech
tomorrow,' said Millie, after a while.

'Is it after that, God goes?' said Andrew. 'Is it what the
vicar says?'

'It's nothing to do with the vicar, it's the bishop signing a
paper, I expect.'

'I hope he never signs it,' said Andrew.

'You're soft in the head,' said his mother.

Outside, somewhere, a dog barked. Andrew dropped the hassock he was holding and looked up, ready for flight. 'What was that?'

'A dog, silly.'

'Wild dog?'

'Quite soft in the head,' said Millie. But he didn't hear her.

The girl and boy are walking side by side, close to the water, talking.

'Why are you fat?' asks the girl.

'Don't know,' says the boy, simply.

'I expect they could operate,' says the girl. 'My father says they can do anything in hospital. I expect they could slice bits off.'

'Don't want to go to hospital.'

'They'll have machines they can bring and do it at home for you.'

'Don't want machines.'

'I'd hate to be fat,' she says. 'I'm glad I'm beautiful. I won our class beauty competition. It's my bone structure.'

'Where are we going?' asks the boy. 'What's the secret you're going to show me?'

'Do you want to hold my hand?'

He thinks about it. 'All right.'

'Well you can't!' And she runs off again. 'Cos you're too fat! FatAndyfatAndyfatAndyfatAndy . . .'

At the appointed time, a handful of ancient faithfuls gathered in the churchyard to hear the vicar's little speech and see Andrew get his present. All those years of keeping the churchyard looking so nice: it was only proper he should get his thanks. The sun shone benignly down.

'His whole life,' the vicar was saying, 'has been dedicated to the service of simple beauty: witness his devotion to the remembrance of young Joanne, who was taken so untimely from her family all those many, many years ago. It is Andrew in his unquestioning faith and selflessness who has acted as a model to us all, tending the memory of a blessed innocent with the flowers of God's garden. I would love to say "Long may it all continue thus", but alas . . .'

And on he went, talking about dwindling congregations, straitened times, and the recent problem of subsidence. But Andrew wasn't listening. He was staring with widening eyes at a certain headstone. It was at a tilt, surely it was at a tilt. It hadn't been yesterday. His breath began to come fast and shallow. He turned, blundered past his mother, past the vicar and ancient faithfuls.

'Andrew!' bellowed his mother. 'Come back here, this is for you!' But he was gone, into his refuge.

Once inside, he leant his head against the wall, waiting for his pounding heart to ease. He laid his cheek against the cool plaster, touched its solidity with his hands. He stood there without moving.

The girl must have waited for him to catch up, because they're walking together again.

'It must be very boring being called Andrew,' she says.

But he doesn't reply. So much of what she says confuses him. They walk on. Looking straight ahead of her, the girl says 'I think you're in love with me.' His heart beats faster, but again he says nothing, and she rounds on him, almost ferociously: 'Are you?'

'Where are we?' says the boy. ' I don't know where we are.'

'You're stupid. I don't think I'm going to show you my secret any more,' she says, carelessly.

'Please.'

'I'm going to push you in the sea and watch you float away to America.'

He looks anxiously at her. 'Don't push me in.'

'I will. After three. One –'

'Don't!' He starts to run off. 'I'm going back, I don't want to see your secret, you're horrid.'

'No, I'm not, please Andrew,' she calls. 'I won't be horrid again, cross my heart and hope to die, I promise I won't push you in.'

'I'll push you in.' But he has stopped running.
They stand on the rocks, facing each other.
'Shall we play kiss chase?' says Joanne.

Andrew sat at the foot of the stairs, staring unseeing at a spot on the hall carpet. The vicar'd said the church would have to be padlocked from tomorrow, and Andrew'd got upset, so his mother had had words with him: told him to pull himself together. But he *was* together, he didn't need pulling; she didn't understand; she didn't *know*. He didn't like it when his mother scolded him.

He sat up, aware suddenly that he could see her reflection in the hall mirror, standing on the stairs above him. He'd thought she was outside.

'Mother?' he said, to the reflection.

A voice that was not her voice spoke softly from behind him: 'Andrew . . .'

He leapt up in panic, turned to face the voice, but there was no one there. He rushed along the hall, through the kitchen and out of the back door.

'Mother, Mother, Mother,' he cried, in the garden.

'Yes, dear, I'm here, what's happened?'

'She . . . she . . . she . . . she . . . she . . . she . . .'

'Shh, there . . .'

'She . . . she . . .'

Millie put her arm around his quivering shape. 'Who, dear?'

'She was in there, she was you.'

'Who was, dear?'

'Joanne, she was pretending to be you. Is *this* you? You're not her still?'

'No, dear, I'm always me and no one else, especially when I'm picking beans.'

He buried his face in her shoulder. 'She's the Devil,' he murmured.

'Now, now, Andrew, she's your little friend.'

He looked at his mother earnestly. 'Never let her be you. She mustn't get in.'

The boy and girl have left the beach: she has led him into the most beautiful place in the world, where the sound of water dripping in solitary drops into a rock pool echoes off every facet of the vaulted chamber, and where the sunlight reflects in ripples across the rock ceiling.

She talks in a hushed voice. 'Isn't it lovely?'

'It's lovely,' he agrees. He likes her again, now.

'I discovered it, and no one else knows about it.'

He feels like her only friend. 'It's like heaven,' says the boy.

But she has to spoil everything. 'I don't believe in heaven,' she says.

The boy is upset. 'You have to!'

'I don't believe in hell either.'

'But you have to!'

'Why?'

'Cos . . . cos . . . when you die.'

'Huh.' She's contemptuous. 'When I die I shall rot away, like everyone else.'

It disturbs him, what she says. ''Tisn't like that!'

'And when I'm buried, wild dogs will come and dig up my grave and my ghost will come and haunt you!'

'No! No!' cries the boy.

But she climbs nimbly over the rocks towards the obscurity in the recesses of the cave. 'It's even better further in, it gets spooky.'

'Wait! Don't leave me alone,' he calls, fearfully. 'Joanne . . . ! Joanne . . . ?'

His voice echoes unanswered.

Andrew looked up from where he sat on the sanctuary step. The vicar was standing quietly at the back.

'Vicar?' said Andrew. The vicar walked slowly up the

aisle and stopped in front of him.

'Andrew, old chap,' he said.

'Don't let the bishop sign the paper,' said Andrew.

But it was not in the vicar's hands. He sat beside Andrew, and talked gently with him for about half an hour. Afterwards they both walked across to Andrew's house, where Millie had the kettle on.

The vicar and Millie chatted and drank their tea, while Andrew munched custard creams and pondered the vicar's earlier words. He didn't exactly understand what a psychological anxiety transference was, but the vicar, who knew about such things, had assured him that the Devil was not involved. Without wishing to get too technical (the vicar had said) it basically meant that Andrew had a fertile imagination, and though, goodness me, there was nothing wrong with imagination, no, it simply meant that these recent . . . worries had been caused by too much *thinking*. However, there were two things Andrew had to be completely clear about: firstly, there were no such things as ghosts (except the Holy Ghost, and that was something different), and secondly, even if there were, they couldn't possibly appear as another person. Categorically not.

Andrew took another custard cream. He felt curiously elated. It wasn't real, none of it was real. If he told it all to go away, it would. It was all in his head. All he had to do was say to himself, 'It's my imagination' (this was the vicar's suggestion), and it would disappear, pouff!

That evening Millie had a W.I. meeting. It was raining when she returned. She stamped her wet feet on the mat and shook her raincoat.

'Wet,' said Andrew, who had come to greet her in the hall.

'I don't know about locking the church,' she said, 'they should padlock the churchyard. Wretched animals.'

'What animals?' said Andrew.

'Scuffling, digging, scratching up the earth, never did like dogs. Shooed them off though. Mind the way, I'll have to change these shoes.'

Andrew froze. Wild dogs . . . When Millie had stomped upstairs, he tiptoed to the sitting-room window, lifted the corner of the curtain and looked churchwards. What a fool he'd been. Oh what a fool! He'd let himself be taken off guard, and now she was free, she was out. He could feel the numbness of terror taking hold inside his head.

He looked round the room. Here was obviously no longer safe: she would be coming for him any moment. The question was: could he make it to the church if he made a dash for it now, or would she be waiting for him to do just that, waiting in the darkness in the bushes beside the path? He took a deep breath and ran out of the house.

It was raining hard, but he scarcely noticed it. He opened the garden gate and lumbered out onto the church path. The bushes seemed full of menace, but he stared ahead of him as he ran, fixing his eyes on the south porch.

He reached the church, flung open the door, slammed it behind him and almost fell down the step. He knew the electricity was off, but he didn't need lights: not in here. He made his way forward to the front pew, and sat, relieved. He'd made it.

Now that the immediate panic was over, he made his plan. What he was going to do was this: he was going to spend all night here, and when they came with the padlock he'd take it away from them. Then he'd live here for ever. For ever.

The cave goes back a long way, narrowing, twisting and opening again into gloomy, chill places. The boy has followed the girl's voice into darkness, and now he has lost her.

'Joanne . . . ?' he asks. 'Joanne . . . ?

Her voice comes from where he did not expect it, some distance away. 'Here I am.'

'Where? I can't see you.'

'You should eat more carrots, and not so many sweets.' *The voice seems to move about in the darkness.*

'I'm going,' *says the boy,* 'I hate you.'

'I thought you wanted to kiss me,' *says the girl's voice, from some-where else. He doesn't answer.* 'Don't you?'

'You're ugly,' *he says.*

'Not as ugly as you. You ought to be put down. We had a puppy once that was really ugly, and I drowned it. It was easy. I could drown you too, easy-peasy. Just leave you in here and wait for the tide to come in.'

'No you couldn't, you're not going to touch me, I'm going.'

'You don't know the way out, fatty.'

'Do!' *he says. He hates her. He hates her.*

Instantly there is the sound of scrambling, and of falling stones, muddled with its own echo, then silence.

'Joanne . . . ?' *says the boy, afraid.*

There is no sound, then, suddenly, close to his ear: 'Booh!'

He lashes out, seizes what his hands find.

'Ow, stop it, get off, stop it, Andrew!' *She wrenches herself free and runs crunching across pebbles.* 'FatAndyFatAndyFatAndyFatAndy FatAndy . . .'

He grabs whatever is at his feet – small stones, shingle – and flings it in fistfuls at the sound of the voice.

'Don't! Stop it! Ow, Andrew! Don't!'

He picks up bigger pebbles, flings them, panting, a constant bar-rage, not stopping, throwing indiscriminately, heavy stones, crying because he only wanted to be her friend.

'Don't, Andrew, don't!' *She's almost screaming.* 'Andrew, don't, don't, don't, don't . . . ! Andrew! Andrew! Andr –'

Her cries stop abruptly, but he does not seem to notice. He continues flinging stones, panting heavily. Then he turns and stumbles across the pebbles. He yells back to her: 'And I do know the way out. I do. I do!' *And he is gone: returned to the sunlight and the sound of the sea breaking on the shore.*

72

Andrew heard the church door open far behind him. He turned round. Torchlight bobbed.

'Andrew?' said his mother's voice.

'Mother,' said Andrew.

'What are you doing here?'

He could tell she was approaching, from the footsteps and the way the light moved. The footsteps came right up to him.

He thought. 'I came to look at the leak,' he said.

'At this time of night?' She turned and walked away towards the crypt stairway door.

Reluctantly, he got up and walked after the bobbing light. She opened a door; listened. 'It's doing well.'

Andrew caught up. 'Sounds bad. Shine the torch.' But the stone stairs twisted out of sight.

'Down you go,' said Millie.

'We should get the vicar. We can't do anything.'

'Nonsense. On you go. You'll need your hands – I'll hold the torch.' She lit the first few steps for him.

'I don't like it, it's steep,' said Andrew. He reached the bend. 'Are you coming? You've got to come, Mother.' The light went out. 'Mother! What have you done? Turn it on!' There was no answer. 'I can't see!'

From the blackness at the top of the stone stairs came the soft voice that was not his mother's. 'You should eat more carrots and not so many sweets. I told you before.'

The chill went through him. 'Mother? Where are you?'

'She's not here,' said the soft voice. 'She's never been here.'

'She came in just now.'

'No,' said the voice. 'That was me.'

'You can't do that,' said Andrew. ''Tisn't possible. Vicar said.'

'The vicar!'

He tried the magic words. 'It was 'magination.'

'Shows how much he knows.'

'And it wasn't you last time, in the house. It was

73

'magination.'

'Oh yes, *that* was your imagination. But it was such a good idea I couldn't resist it. Do you mind?' The voice seemed to be coming closer, down the stairs, coming closer through the darkness, floating invisibly towards him. He backed down a step.

'You're not real,' he cried. 'You're not real! God, she's not here, tell her to go away! God?'

'He's not here either. He went this afternoon.' The voice was close now. 'Did you think He was staying till tomorrow?'

'You're not here, you're not here!'

The voice stopped an inch from his face. 'Don't you want to kiss me?'

Andrew leaned back from the touch of the long dead lips, slipped down a step. 'Don't come near me, leave me alone!'

But the voice was so close he could almost feel its breath. 'Kiss me . . .'

'No!' he cried. He lurched away from the terrible embrace, tripped, stumbled, lost balance, flung his hands out to save himself but grasped only air, and fell . . .

There were three inches of water in the crypt, but Andrew's head made a sharp crack as it hit the stone. He lay awkwardly, twisted, his legs half on the bottom steps, his face down.

The water lapped his cheek. He didn't move.

Her feet nice and dry, Millie came downstairs. The front door was open again. 'Andrew?' she called, peering out into the rain from the doormat. 'Are you out there? What are you playing at?' No answer. She looked in the sitting-room, in the kitchen. Back at the front door, she called again: 'Andrew? I'm making some cocoa, I'm putting it on now. You know you don't like it with skin on.' That'll bring him if he's coming, she thought.

She pushed the door to and went to get the milk out of the fridge.

Somewhere else, the tide is coming in. A wave races foaming up the beach, across the rocks, and into a cave at the base of the cliff. A few moments later the water surges back through the pebbles to rejoin the sea and gather itself for the next wave. An hour later there is no cave to be seen.

When morning comes, the sea has retreated and the sun shines down once more. The rocks dry in the warmth of the new day.

THE DISPOSSESSED DAUGHTER

Katharine Nicholas

THE DISPOSSESSED DAUGHTER was Katharine Nicholas's first play for radio. Hitherto she'd written three Morning Stories for Radio 4 and a history book about the social effects of unemployment between the wars. Katharine currently lives in Wales where she works as a solicitor. She is married to a TV drama producer and has one daughter.

When his new daughter was born David Pritchard gave up work and stayed at home to look after her. It was a big change to be in the house all day but he found it quite satisfying. He learned to cook, grew vegetables in the garden and enjoyed the freedom of being able to organise his own daily schedule. He loved little Jane and she was calm and pink and contented in his care. A perfect baby.

David's only sorrow was that he saw so little of his wife, Ellen. She was so busy, newly promoted at the school. She was planning and organising, teaching and helping out at school clubs, outings, even trips abroad in the holidays.

'I am the breadwinner now,' she said. 'You chose to stay at home and I take my work seriously. Teaching is not a nine till four job and not even a nine to five one.'

David wanted to say that *last* time he had made real efforts to spend time at home to be with his wife and the baby. He could not say it though, so much went unsaid in the Pritchard household. Their first daughter, Imogen, had died suddenly and inexplicably at three months old. Ellen had got up in the night, checked on the sleeping baby and found her in eternal sleep. Jane had been quite unplanned. She had been born almost nine months later on Ginny's birthday. It was perhaps this quirk of fate which her mother found hardest to bear.

David displaced his sorrow with love for the new daughter. Ellie could not. In fact, what happened was that while David put aside all thought of the daughter he had lost, Ellie could not think of the one she had. Of late, though, David had seen his wife standing by the cot of the beautiful little Jane and gazing down with loving kindness. Were things getting better at last? Everyone said they would. Then one night he heard her.

'Goodnight, Ginny.'

'You mustn't,' he said. 'We loved Ginny but Ginny is dead. We have another lovely daughter. She's a new, different person.'

'I can't deny her,' was all his wife would say to him.

January came, that cold, quiet time after Christmas, with festivities all gone and no hope of spring. Ginny had died in January. Ellie worked harder than ever. She took pills to make her sleep and saw little of Jane. David felt low, strained by caring; caring for wife and child, and strained by his own suffering in spite of himself. He began to feel lonely at home. The house was isolated in the depths of the country. They'd moved there with the prospect of parenthood but now the days were dark and no lights were visible from their house. The only sound which travelled to them was that of the church bells from over the hill.

One night as they settled into bed there was a scream from Jane's room. Normally she never woke but this sound came over loud and clear on their baby-listening device. David went immediately into Jane's room. She was awake and peaceful, just lying there looking at the wall. David watched her for a moment and it was only when he returned to Ellie's side that he realised the sound they'd heard was not really like a baby's cry at all.

So what was it? Ellen grew irritated as he mulled over this mystery. David had heard of receivers picking up sounds from other people's houses but they had no neighbours. So where had that awful scream come from?

The anniversary of their first born's death dawned bright and clear. Ellen would be away all day. The weather provided such a positive invitation to go out of doors that after Ellen had set off, David took Jane in her pram to the churchyard. He had his flowers ready. As he placed them on the little grave he felt something of the pain of loss he normally denied himself. But there was Jane, so pretty and angelic, gazing around her.

'Hallo.' It was the vicar. A new vicar. David went to church only occasionally.

'Hallo.' David was not best pleased at being interrupted.

'I'm sorry, am I disturbing you?'

'No. That's my first born. My daughter and I were just saying hallo.' David surprised himself at his frankness. Perhaps the man would leave him alone now.

'Of course. Imogen Mair Pritchard. A beautiful name. Died just a year ago.'

The clergyman was grave and deep in thought. David didn't know whether he wanted to speak to the man or not. There was something about his direct approach. And he had a sad look about him. He was thin, dark and wore untidy clothes. He looked unloved thought David.

'You seem to be new.' David realised it was some months since he'd been to matins. 'Though I don't come to church as often as I might.'

'I'm sorry, I should have introduced myself. Russell Williams. I start my ministry today. On Candlemas.'

'David Pritchard.' The two men shook hands.

'And this is Jane Elisa?' The vicar asked.

'How do you know that?'

'I've been making it my business to know who my new parishioners will be. I look forward to seeing more of you. And Mrs Pritchard.'

'Oh, Ellie's not a church-goer,' said David. 'Never was much, but since . . .'

Williams looked serious. 'Even the clergy find it difficult to reconcile everything to a loving God. Indeed some of us believe that Good and Evil are still fighting for possession of the world. I should come and see her.'

David wondered how Ellie would react to Mr Williams.

'I don't think now would be the best time – give her a little longer perhaps.'

'I shall be thinking of you,' said Williams solemnly. 'Tell me, have you had Jane Elisa christened?'

'Perhaps soon.'

David and Ellie had never got round to having Ginny baptised and, although neither was very devout, it upset both of them.

'It worries you.' Williams was a perceptive man.

'Well, it's Ginny,' David looked at the small grave. 'I have thoughts of her being in limbo.' Again he was surprised at how honest he could be with this stranger.

'A state which is neither heaven nor hell. These old myths are very powerful,' Williams acknowledged. 'The Church likes to think itself more enlightened these days. Still you should have Jane Elisa baptised. She's a beautiful girl. And so good!'

David felt justly proud. 'I hardly know I've got her most of the time.'

'You are very blessed.'

David got home to a phone call from his wife. She would be late. It was only to be expected. He filled the kettle idly. Suddenly all hell broke loose with the pipes banging in Janey's room where she was having her afternoon sleep. The clatter registered loud and clear on the listening device yet when David got upstairs there was not a sound to be heard and Jane was facing the wall once again in perfect repose. Assuming that the receiver had exaggerated a temporary air-lock in the pipes, David went back to the kitchen. The caco-phony started again. He wrenched the plug of the receiver from the electric socket and the noise died. The house was silent. What the hell was going on?

'Welsh bloody water.'

When Ellie did come home her baby daughter was back in bed for the night. David had cooked a meal for the two of them but Ellen had eaten already. She said little through what was left of the evening. That night the wind rose. Out-side their bedroom window David could see the trees shift like troops mustering on a hill-top. He'd hoped to find some way of diverting Ellen from the anniversary of Ginny's death but she was determined to remember. When he tried to comfort her in bed she reminded him that a year ago Imogen had died as Jane was conceived. Her words were so grim he gave way to anger.

'For heaven's sake Ellie, stop torturing us with the past.' Ellen cut him off.

'She's not past. Not for me.'

The bedside phone began to ring. Irritated by the interrup-tion David lifted the receiver. No one spoke and the phone continued to ring. Then the listening device picked up the noise. He tried repeatedly to disengage the phone until it finally stopped. He looked next door. Jane was fine, fast asleep. She had just rolled over and was facing the wall.

'Are you sure she's fine?' Ellen was concerned.

'Of course, sweetheart. It's just that stupid machine. We don't really need it anymore. She never wakes.'

'No, we must.' Ellen was insistent. It was unusual for her to be so definite about Jane's upbringing. 'She might change her habits. Children do. I want to keep it.'

They were woken in the night by the telephone ringing again. David picked up the receiver. Again the ringing would not stop. By now Ellen was awake.

'Stop it for God's sake,' she said.

'It won't stop. I'm trying . . .'

'Disconnect it then!' Ellen screamed. David pulled the phone out of its socket and all was quiet. Then in the silence there was a sudden roar over the listening device, an unmistakably bestial roar.

'Janey!' Ellen was in tears. David went to see his daughter. He came back and disconnected the baby alarm as well.

'Bloody machine. Janey's fine.'

'What d'you mean fine?'

'Looking at the wall.'

'And you call that fine? She should be crying. Why doesn't she cry? The stupid child!' Tears began to course down Ellen's cheeks. David put his arms around her.

'Come, come and see her for yourself.'

She was half-awake but did not stir. The room was very warm. Had the heating come on? David went to open the window. It was fused, frame and window were like one solid piece of wood. He was filled with horror.

'The door!' David shouted and Ellen seemed to understand. She ran to the door and held it open.

'Don't let it go!'

He left the room. Ellen heard him plug in the phone and dial a number. 'Who are you ringing?'

'The vicar.'

'Why not the doctor – I trust him – we know him.'

'Listen, this isn't something you can treat with pills and sedatives. If this house is haunted we need a priest.'

'Just don't expect me to believe that.'

It was the Reverend Williams himself who answered. He was quite calm and swept away David's apologies for being called out so late.

'All part of the job,' he said. 'I'll be along straight away.'

Within minutes the doorbell rang. As David went downstairs, he could hear Ellen talking to their child.

'Imogen?' she said.

Mr Williams seemed almost jovial. He looked neater and tidier than before, even at this late hour. Tonight, he reminded David, was Candlemas, a christian festival imposed on the pagan ritual of Imbolc. Ellen looked at him suspiciously.

'I'm here to help you Mrs Pritchard,' he said.

Could he explain what was happening? Well, electrical discharges, odd happenings with machinery could affect people finely attuned to atmospheres.

'And the window?' said David.

'Sealed by the flames of hell,' Williams replied matter-of-factly.

'So you really do believe there is something going on?'

'Don't you?' Williams replied. 'And don't you Mrs Pritchard?'

He looked directly at Ellen before continuing:

'Spirits not assigned to God are more likely to be abroad on pagan nights like this.'

Ellen looked at the minister, bravely hostile.

'David, make him go.'

'He's here to help us, darling.' But David himself did not know how to react to what was happening. 'Look, how serious is all this?' he asked.

'Serious enough for me to come when I was invited in. We need to protect – what's the Name, Mrs Pritchard?'

'Go away.' Ellen glared at the vicar.

'Mrs Pritchard, what is your daughter's name?'

David was about to answer for his hysterical wife but he realised a curious battle of wills seemed to be going on between her and the minister.

'*Jane.*' Ellen was defiant.

Williams looked satisfied. 'That's better,' he said. 'Well now, why does little Jane Elisa face away from the Church?'

He looked at the parents.

'I think we should pray, all of us.' David knelt down by the cot but was suddenly stunned by Ellen shouting at Williams.

'Make that man go away! I've told you I don't believe in it. Go away!'

David's patience was gone too. How could she be so selfish? So uncaring?

'Think of the child for once. You care more for the one that's dead and gone than the one alive with us now. The one that's going to grow up with us.'

'I am thinking of her. Don't you see?' Ellen began to cry again. Williams watched them both dispassionately. David turned to him.

'Reverend – can you talk sense into her?'

'I think this is sense to Mrs Pritchard,' Williams' tones were cool in the hot room. 'She has renounced God. She has named Jane Elisa, and she has invited me in. She knows who I am. It is she who has put her child in danger.'

Ellen was quiet now. 'I wanted her back.'

'Of course.' Williams was soothing but David shouted.

'What are you both saying for Christ's sake? Ellen have you done something? What have you done?'

Williams held up his hand.

'Quiet, it's nearly midnight. Mrs Pritchard please leave the room. I shall pray for Jane.'

Ellen said nothing. She did not move but stared defiantly. David was beside himself with anger, frustration, disappointment, all the stress of the last year. Why was Ellen behaving in this ridiculous way? Williams looked genuinely worried as the church clock began to sound.

'Please Mr Pritchard!'

David pulled his wife and dragged her from the room. Did

she care nothing for their daughter? The door slammed shut. He turned to go back in but the door, like the window before it, would not move. At last David began to understand.

'Oh God, no!' He hammered on the door, shouting for Williams to open it, then turned to Ellen.

'What have you done?'

Without emotion she told him. When Jane was born she had prayed that God would take her away and give her back Ginny. At last she seemed quite calm.

'I made a bargain. Only not with God, with – whoever. And tonight he has come. I recognised him as soon as he came.'

David was stunned. 'Why didn't you tell me? Why didn't you say?'

'I wanted Ginny back. I didn't want to lose Jane. I did love her, you must understand, but Ginny!' She cried. And this time David could not comfort her. He did not wish to. The final chime of twelve sounded as David Pritchard realised what he'd done. He flung himself at the door but it was fused solid like the window frame and Janey was inside. David hammered on the door, flung his whole weight against the frame. The explosion of a mighty fire burst from inside the sealed room.

They fell back in terror as the white paint began to blister and peel. David hammered again, yelling frantically, but the heat beat him back. He turned on his wife, dragging her by the throat, forcing her head against the wall.

'What have you done? You've killed her.' He breathed. 'You've sold your own daughter to the Devil.'

He would have broken her neck but their struggle was cut short by a bestial roar. The entire house shook. In the silence that followed, the door to Janey's room swung open. No smoke, no flames, no sound.

They rushed in. The room was untouched. It was as if nothing had happened – except that the window was now open and Williams was nowhere to be seen. Before either of them could speak a cry filled the room. Jane lay in her cot, convulsed in misery, she stared with anger into their eyes. It took all night to comfort the child. Neither spoke of the fear each felt.

The two children were so alike. How could they tell which one now slept in the cot?

Every night as the parents put their daughter to bed they say 'God Bless'. And they hope that the wording is appropriate. But only time will tell. It was a long time before David went to church again. The new vicar is called Reverend Thomas, and he is short, round and cheerful with fair curly hair. Neither David nor Ellen have mentioned their worst fears to him.

THE SPECIALTY OF
THE HOUSE

Stanley Ellin

Stanley Ellin was born in Brooklyn, New York in 1916. His career as a writer began with the instant success of 'The Specialty of the House' (1948) which has been described as one of the finest crime stories of modern times. As well as two short story collections, MYSTERY STORIES (1956) and THE BLESSINGTON METHOD (1964), Ellin produced several novels, the most successful of which were DREADFUL SUMMIT (1948), THE KEY TO NICHOLAS STREET (1964), THE EIGHTH CIRCLE (1958) and MIRROR MIRROR ON THE WALL (1972). Stanley Ellin died in 1986.

'And this,' said Laffler, 'is Sbirro's.' Costain saw a square brownstone façade identical with the others that extended from either side into the clammy darkness of the deserted street. From the barred windows of the basement at his feet, a glimmer of light showed behind heavy curtains.

'Lord,' he observed, 'it's a dismal hole, isn't it?'

'I beg you to understand,' said Laffler stiffly, 'that Sbirro's is the restaurant without pretensions. Besieged by these ghastly neurotic times, it has refused to compromise. It is perhaps the last important establishment in this city lit by gas jets. Here you will find the same honest furnishings, the same magnificent Sheffield service, and possibly in a far corner, the very same spider webs that were remarked by the patrons of a half century ago!'

'A doubtful recommendation,' said Costain, 'and hardly sanitary.'

'When you enter,' Laffler continued, 'you leave the insanity of this year, this day, and this hour, and you find yourself for a brief span restored in spirit, not by opulence, but by dignity, which is the lost quality of our time.'

Costain laughed uncomfortably. 'You make it sound more like a cathedral than a restaurant,' he said.

In the pale reflection of the street lamp overhead, Laffler peered at his companion's face. 'I wonder,' he said abruptly, 'whether I have not made a mistake in extending this invitation to you.'

Costain was hurt. Despite an impressive title and large salary, he was no more than clerk to this pompous little man, but he was impelled to make some display of his feelings. 'If you wish,' he said coldly, 'I can make other plans for my evening with no trouble.'

With his large, cowlike eyes turned up to Costain, the mist drifting into the ruddy, full moon of his face, Laffler seemed strangely ill at ease. Then 'No, no,' he said at last, 'absolutely not. It's important that you dine at Sbirro's with me.' He grasped Costain's arm firmly and led the way to the wrought-iron gate of the basement. 'You see, you're the sole person in my office who seems to know anything at all about good food. And on my part, knowing about Sbirro's but not having some appreciative friend to share it is like having a unique piece of art locked in a room where no one else can enjoy it.'

Costain was considerably mollified by this. 'I understand there are a great many people who relish that situation.'

'I'm not one of that kind!' Laffler said sharply. 'And having the secret of Sbirro's locked in myself for years has finally become unendurable.' He fumbled at the side of the gate and from within could be heard the small, discordant jangle of an ancient pull-bell. An interior door opened with a groan, and Costain found himself peering into a dark face whose only discernible feature was a row of gleaming teeth.

'Sair?' said the face.

'Mr Laffler and a guest.'

'Sair,' the face said again, this time in what was clearly an invitation. It moved aside and Costain stumbled down a single step behind his host. The door and gate creaked behind him, and he stood blinking in a small foyer. It took him a moment to realise that the figure he now stared at was his own reflection in a gigantic pier glass that extended from floor to ceiling. 'Atmosphere', he said under his breath and chuckled as he followed his guide to a seat.

He faced Laffler across a small table for two and peered curiously around the dining-room. It was no size at all, but the half-dozen guttering gas jets which provided the only illumination threw such a deceptive light that the walls flickered and faded into uncertain distance.

There were no more than eight or ten tables about, arranged to ensure the maximum privacy. All were occupied, and the few waiters serving them moved with quiet efficiency. In the air were a soft clash and scrape of cutlery and a soothing murmur of talk. Costain nodded appreciatively.

Laffler breathed an audible sigh of gratification. 'I knew you would share my enthusiasm,' he said. 'Have you noticed, by the way, that there are no women present?'

Costain raised inquiring eyebrows.

'Sbirro,' said Laffler, 'does not encourage members of the fair sex to enter the premises. And, I can tell you, his method is decidedly effective. I had the experience of seeing a woman get a taste of it not long ago. She sat at a table for not less than an hour waiting for service which was never forthcoming.'

'Didn't she make a scene?'

'She did.' Laffler smiled at the recollection. 'She succeeded in annoying the customers, embarrassing her partner, and nothing more.'

'And what about Mr Sbirro?'

'He did not make an appearance. Whether he directed

affairs from behind the scenes, or was not even present during the episode, I don't know. Whichever it was, he won a complete victory. The woman never reappeared nor, for that matter, did the witless gentleman who by bringing her was really the cause of the entire contretemps.'

'A fair warning to all present,' laughed Costain.

A waiter now appeared at the table. The chocolate-dark skin, the thin, beautifully moulded nose and lips, the large liquid eyes, heavily lashed, and the silver white hair so heavy and silken that it lay on the skull like a cap, all marked him definitely as an East Indian of some sort, Costain decided. The man arranged the stiff table linen, filled two tumblers from a huge, cut-glass pitcher, and set them in their proper places.

'Tell me,' Laffler said eagerly, 'is the special being served this evening?'

The waiter smiled regretfully and showed teeth as spectacular as those of the major domo. 'I am so sorry, sair. There is no special this evening.'

Laffler's face fell into lines of heavy disappointment. 'After waiting so long. It's been a month already, and I hoped to show my friend here . . .'

'You understand the difficulties, sair.'

'Of course, of course.' Laffler looked at Costain sadly and shrugged. 'You see, I had in mind to introduce you to the greatest treat that Sbirro's offers, but unfortunately it isn't on the menu this evening.'

The waiter said, 'Do you wish to be served now, sair?' and Laffler nodded. To Costain's surprise the waiter made his way off without waiting for any instructions.

'Have you ordered in advance?' he asked.

'Ah,' said Laffler, 'I really should have explained. Sbirro's offers no choice whatsoever. You will eat the same meal as everyone else in this room. Tomorrow evening you would eat an entirely different meal, but again without designating a single preference.'

'Very unusual,' said Costain, 'and certainly unsatisfactory at times. What if one doesn't have a taste for the particular dish set before him?'

'On that score,' said Laffler solemnly, 'you need have no fears. I give you my word that no matter how exciting your tastes, you will relish every mouthful you eat in Sbirro's.'

Costain looked doubtful, and Laffler smiled. 'And consider the subtle advantages of the system,' he said. 'When you pick up the menu of a popular restaurant, you find yourself confronted with innumerable choices. You are forced to weigh, to evaluate, to make uneasy decisions which you may instantly regret. The effect of all this is a tension which, however slight, must make for discomfort.

'And consider the mechanics of the process. Instead of a hurly-burly of sweating cooks rushing about a kitchen in a frenzy to prepare a hundred varying items, we have a chef who stands serenely alone, bringing all his talents to bear on one task, with all assurance of a complete triumph!'

'Then you have seen the kitchen?'

'Unfortunately, no,' said Laffler sadly. 'The picture I offer is hypothetical, made of conversational fragments I have pieced together over the years. I must admit, though, that my desire to see the functioning of the kitchen here comes very close to being my sole obsession nowadays.'

'But have you mentioned this to Sbirro?'

'A dozen times. He shrugs the suggestion away.'

'Isn't that a rather curious foible on his part?'

'No, no,' Laffler said hastily, 'a master artist is never under the compulsion of petty courtesies. Still,' he sighed, 'I have never given up hope.'

The waiter now reappeared bearing two soup bowls which he set in place with mathematical exactitude, and a small tureen from which he slowly ladled a measure of clear, thin broth. Costain dipped his spoon into the broth and tasted it with some curiosity. It was delicately flavoured, bland to the verge of tastelessness. Costain frowned, tentatively reached for the salt and pepper cellars, and discovered there were none on the table. He looked up, saw Laffler's eyes on him, and although unwilling to compromise with his own tastes, he hesitated to act as a damper on Laffler's enthusiasm. Therefore he smiled and indicated the broth.

'Excellent,' he said.

Laffler returned his smile. 'You do not find it excellent at all,' he said coolly. 'You find it flat and badly in need of condiments. I know this,' he continued as Costain's eyebrows shot upward, 'because it was my own reaction many years ago, and because like yourself I found myself reaching for salt and pepper after the first mouthful. I also learned with surprise that condiments are not available in Sbirro's.'

Costain was shocked. 'Not even salt!' he exclaimed.

'Not even salt. The very fact that you require it for your soup stands as evidence that your taste is unduly jaded. I am confident that you will now make the same discovery that I did; by the time you have nearly finished your soup, your desire for salt will be non-existent.'

Laffler was right; before Costain had reached the bottom of his plate, he was relishing the nuances of the broth with steadily increasing delight. Laffler thrust aside his own empty bowl and rested his elbows on the table, 'Do you agree with me now?'

'To my surprise,' said Costain, 'I do.'

As the waiter busied himself clearing the table, Laffler lowered his voice significantly. 'You will find,' he said, 'that the absence of condiments is but one of several noteworthy characteristics which mark Sbirro's. I may as well prepare you for these. For example, no alcoholic beverages of any sort are served here, nor for that matter any beverage except clear, cold water, the first and only drink necessary for a human being.'

'Outside of mother's milk,' suggested Costain dryly.

'I can answer that in like vein by pointing out that the average patron of Sbirro's has passed that primal stage of his development.'

Costain laughed. 'Granted,' he said.

'Very well. There is also a ban on the use of tobacco in any form.'

'But good heavens,' said Costain, 'doesn't that make Sbirro's more a teetotaller's retreat than a gourmet's sanctuary?'

'I fear,' said Laffler solemnly, 'that you confuse the words, *gourmet* and *gourmand*. The gourmand, through glutting himself, requires a wider and wider latitude of experience to stir his surfeited senses, but the very nature of the gourmet is simplicity. The ancient Greek in his coarse chiton savouring the ripe olive; the Japanese in his bare room contemplating the curve of a single flower stem – these are the true gourmets.'

'But an occasional drop of brandy or pipeful of tobacco,' said Costain dubiously, 'are hardly over-indulgences.'

'By alternating stimulant and narcotic,' said Laffler, 'you seesaw the delicate balance of your taste so violently that it loses its most precious quality: the appreciation of fine food. During my years as a patron of Sbirro's, I have proved this to my satisfaction.'

'May I ask,' said Costain, 'why you regard the ban on these things as having such deep aesthetic motives? What about such mundane reasons as the high cost of a liquor licence, or the possibility that patrons would object to the smell of tobacco in such confined quarters?'

Laffler shook his head violently. 'If and when you meet Sbirro,' he said, 'you will understand at once that he is not the man to make decisions on a mundane basis. As a matter of fact, it was Sbirro himself who first made me cognisant of what you call "aesthetic" motives.'

'An amazing man,' said Costain as the waiter prepared to serve the entrée.

Laffler's next words were not spoken until he had savoured and swallowed a large portion of meat. 'I hesitate to use superlatives,' he said, 'but to my way of thinking, Sbirro represents man at the apex of his civilisation!'

Costain cocked an eyebrow and applied himself to his roast which rested in a pool of stiff gravy ungarnished by green or vegetable. The thin steam rising from it carried to his nostrils a subtle, tantalising odour which made his mouth water. He chewed a piece as slowly and thoughtfully as if he were analysing the intricacies of a Mozart symphony. The range of taste he discovered was really extraordinary, from the pungent nip of the crisp outer edge to the peculiarly flat yet soul-satisfying ooze of blood which the pressure of his jaws forced from the half-raw interior.

Upon swallowing he found himself ferociously hungry for another piece, and then another, and it was only with an effort that he prevented himself from wolfing down all his share of the meat and gravy without waiting to get the full voluptuous satisfaction from each mouthful. When he had scraped his platter clean, he realised that both he and Laffler had completed the entire course without exchanging a single word. He commented on this, and Laffler said: 'Can you see any need for words in the presence of such food?'

Costain looked around at the shabby, dimly lit room, the quiet diners, with a new perception. 'No,' he said humbly, 'I cannot. For any doubts I had I apologise unreservedly. In all your praise of Sbirro's there was not a single word of exaggeration.'

'Ah,' said Laffler delightedly. 'And that is only part of the story. You heard me mention the special which unfortunately was not on the menu tonight. What you have just eaten is as nothing when compared to the absolute delights of that special!'

'Good Lord!' cried Costain. 'What is it? Nightingales' tongues? Filet of unicorn?'

'Neither,' said Laffler. 'It is lamb.'

'Lamb?'

Laffler remained lost in thought for a minute. 'If,' he said at last, 'I were to give you in my own unstinted words my opinion of this dish, you would judge me completely insane. That is how deeply the mere thought of it affects me. It is neither the fatty chop, nor the too solid leg; it is, instead, a select portion of the rarest sheep in existence and is named after the species – lamb Amirstan.'

Costain knit his brows. 'Amirstan?'

'A fragment of desolation almost lost on the border which separates Afghanistan and Russia. From chance remarks dropped by Sbirro, I gather it is no more than a plateau which grazes the pitiful remnants of a flock of superb sheep. Sbirro, through some means or other, obtained rights to the traffic in this flock, and is, therefore, the sole restaurateur ever to have lamb Amirstan on his bill of fare. I can tell you that the appearance of this dish is a rare occurrence indeed, and luck is the only guide in determining for the clientele the exact date when it will be served.'

'But surely,' said Costain, 'Sbirro could provide some advance knowledge of this event.'

'The objection to that is simply stated,' said Laffler. 'There exists in this city a huge number of professional gluttons. Should advance information slip out it is quite likely that they will, out of curiosity, become familiar with the dish and thenceforth supplant the regular patrons at these tables.'

'But you don't mean to say,' objected Costain, 'that these few people present are the only ones in the entire city, or for that matter, in the whole wide world, who know of the existence of Sbirro's!'

'Very nearly. There may be one or two regular patrons who, for some reason, are not present at the moment.'

94

'That's incredible.'

'It is done,' said Laffler, the slightest shade of menace in his voice, 'by every patron making it his solemn obligation to keep the secret. By accepting my invitation this evening, you automatically assume that obligation. I hope you can be trusted with it.'

Costain flushed. 'My position in your employ should vouch for me. I only question the wisdom of a policy which keeps such magnificent food away from so many who would enjoy it.'

'Do you know the inevitable result of the policy *you* favour?' asked Laffler bitterly. 'An influx of idiots who would nightly complain that they are never served roast duck with chocolate sauce. Is that picture tolerable to you?'

'No,' admitted Costain, 'I am forced to agree with you.'

Laffler leaned back in his chair wearily and passed his hand over his eyes in an uncertain gesture. 'I am a solitary man,' he said quietly, 'and not by choice alone. It may sound strange to you, it may border on eccentricity, but I feel to my depths that this restaurant, this warm haven in a coldly insane world, is both family and friend to me.'

And Costain, who to this moment had never viewed his companion as other than tyrannical employer or officious host, now felt an overwhelming pity twist inside his comfortably expanded stomach.

By the end of two weeks the invitations to join Laffler at Sbirro's had become something of a ritual. Every day, at a few minutes after five, Costain would step out into the office corridor and lock his cubicle behind him; he would drape his overcoat neatly over his left arm, and peer into the glass of the door to make sure his Homburg was set at the proper angle. At one time he would have followed this by lighting a cigarette, but under Laffler's prodding he had decided to give abstinence a fair trial. Then he would start down the corridor, and Laffler would fall in step at his elbow, clearing his throat. 'Ah, Costain. No plans for this evening, I hope.'

'No,' Costain would say, 'I'm footloose and fancy free,' or 'At your service,' or something equally inane. He wondered at times whether it would not be more tactful to vary the ritual with an occasional refusal, but the glow with which Laffler received his answer, and the rough friendliness of Laffler's grip on his arm, forestalled him.

Among the treacherous crags of the business world, reflected Costain, what better way to secure your footing than friendship with one's employer. Already, a secretary close to the workings of the inner office had commented publicly on Laffler's highly favourable opinion of Costain. That was all to the good.

And the food! The incomparable food at Sbirro's! For the first time in his life, Costain, ordinarily a lean and bony man, noted with gratification that he was certainly gaining weight; within two weeks his bones had disappeared under a layer of sleek, firm flesh, and here and there were even signs of incipient plumpness. It struck Costain one night, while surveying himself in his bath, that the rotund Laffler, himself, might have been a spare and bony man before discovering Sbirro's.

So there was obviously everything to be gained and nothing to be lost by accepting Laffler's invitations. Perhaps after testing the heralded wonders of lamb Amirstan and meeting Sbirro, who thus far had not made an appearance, a refusal or two might be in order. But certainly not until then.

That evening, two weeks to a day after his first visit to Sbirro's, Costain had both desires fulfilled: he dined on lamb Amirstan, and he met Sbirro. Both exceeded all his expectations.

When the waiter leaned over their table immediately after seating them and gravely announced: 'Tonight is special, sair,' Costain was shocked to find his heart pounding with expectation. On the table before him he saw Laffler's hands trembling violently. But it isn't natural, he thought suddenly. Two full grown men, presumably intelligent and in the full possession of their senses, as jumpy as a pair of cats waiting to have their meat flung to them!

'This is it!' Laffler's voice startled him so that he almost leaped from his seat. 'The culinary triumph of all times! And faced by it you are embarrassed by the very emotions it distils.'

'How did you know that?' Costain asked faintly.

'How? Because a decade ago I underwent your embarrassment. Add to that your air of revulsion and it's easy to see how affronted you are by the knowledge that man has not yet forgotten how to slaver over his meat.'

'And these others,' whispered Costain, 'do they all feel the same thing?'

'Judge for yourself.'

Costain looked furtively around at the nearby tables. 'You are right,' he finally said. 'At any rate, there's comfort in numbers.'

Laffler inclined his head slightly to the side. 'One of the numbers,' he remarked, 'appears to be in for a disappointment.'

Costain followed the gesture. At the table indicated a grey-haired man sat conspicuously alone, and Costain frowned at the empty chair opposite him.

'Why, yes,' he recalled, 'that very stout, bald man, isn't it? I believe it's the first dinner he's missed here in two weeks.'

'The entire decade more likely,' said Laffler sympathetically. 'Rain or shine, crisis or calamity. I don't think he's missed an evening at Sbirro's since the first time I dined here. Imagine his expression when he's told that, on his very first defection, lamb Amirstan was the *plat du jour*.'

Costain looked at the empty chair again with a dim discomfort. 'His very first?' he murmured.

'Mr Laffler! And friend! I am so pleased. So very, very pleased. No, do not stand; I will have a place made.' Miraculously a seat appeared under the figure standing there at the table. 'The lamb Amirstan will be an unqualified success, hurr? I myself have been stewing in the miserable kitchen all the day, prodding the foolish chef to do everything just so. The just so is the important part, hurr? But I see your friend does not know me. An introduction, perhaps?'

The words ran in a smooth, fluid eddy. They rippled, they purred, they hypnotised Costain so that he could do no more than stare. The mouth that uncoiled this sinuous monologue was alarmingly wide, with thin mobile lips that curled and twisted with every syllable. There was a flat nose with a straggling line of hair under it; wide-set eyes, almost oriental in appearance, that glittered in the unsteady flare of gaslight: and long, sleek hair that swept back from high on the unwrinkled forehead – hair so pale that it might have been bleached of all colour. An amazing face surely, and the sight of it tortured Costain with the conviction that it was somehow familiar. His brain twitched and prodded but could not stir up any solid recollection.

Laffler's voice jerked Costain out of his study. 'Mr Sbirro. Mr Costain, a good friend and associate.' Costain rose and shook the proffered hand. It was warm and dry, flint-hard against his palm.

'I am so very pleased, Mr Costain. So very, very pleased,' purred the voice. 'You like my little establishment, hurr? You have a great treat in store, I assure you.'

Laffler chuckled. 'Oh, Costain's been dining here regularly for two weeks,' he said. 'He's by way of becoming a great admirer of yours, Sbirro.'

The eyes were turned on Costain. 'A very great compliment. You compliment me with your presence and I return same with my food, hurr? But the lamb Amirstan is far superior to anything of your past experience, I assure you.

All the trouble of obtaining it, all the difficulty of preparation, is truly merited.'

Costain strove to put aside the exasperating problem of
that face. 'I have wondered,' he said, 'why with all these
difficulties you mention, you even bother to present lamb
Amirstan to the public. Surely your other dishes are excellent enough to uphold your reputation.'

Sbirro smiled so broadly that his face became perfectly
round. 'Perhaps it is a matter of the psychology, hurr? Someone discovers a wonder and must share it with others. He
must fill his cup to the brim, perhaps, by observing the so
evident pleasure of those who explore it with him. Or,' he
shrugged, 'perhaps it is just a matter of good business.'

'Then in the light of all this,' Costain persisted, 'and considering all the conventions you have imposed on your customers, why do you open the restaurant to the public instead
of operating it as a private club?'

The eyes abruptly glinted into Costain's, then turned
away. 'So perspicacious, hurr? Then I will tell you. Because
there is more privacy in a public eating place than in the
most exclusive club in existence! Here no one inquires of
your affairs; no one desires to know the intimacies of your
life. Here the business is eating. We are not curious about
names and addresses or the reasons for the coming and
going of our guests. We welcome you when you are here; we
have no regrets when you are here no longer. That is the
answer, hurr?'

Costain was startled by this vehemence. 'I had no intention of prying,' he stammered.

Sbirro ran the tip of his tongue over his thin lips. 'No, no,'
he reassured, 'you are not prying. Do not let me give you that
impression. On the contrary, I invite your questions.'

'Oh, come, Costain,' said Laffler. 'Don't let Sbirro intimi-
date you. I've known him for years and I guarantee that his
bark is worse than his bite. Before you know it, he'll be

showing you all the privileges of the house – outside of invit-
ing you to visit his precious kitchen, of course.'

'Ah,' smiled Sbirro, 'for that, Mr Costain may have to wait
a little while. For everything else I am at his beck and call.'

Laffler slapped his hand jovially on the table. 'What did I
tell you!' he said. 'Now let's have the truth Sbirro. Has anyone, outside of your staff, ever stepped into the sanctum
sanctorum?'

Sbirro looked up. 'You see on the wall above you,' he said
earnestly, 'the portrait of one to whom I did the honour. A
very dear friend and a patron of most long standing, he is
evidence that my kitchen is not inviolate.'

Costain studied the picture and started with recognition.
'Why,' he said excitedly, 'that's the famous writer – you
know the one, Laffler – he used to do such wonderful short
stories and cynical bits and then suddenly took himself off
and disappeared in Mexico!'

'Of course!' cried Laffler. 'And to think I've been sitting
under his portrait for years without even realising it?' He
turned to Sbirro. 'A dear friend, you say? His disappearance
must have been a blow to you.'

Sbirro's face lengthened. 'It was, it was, I assure you. But
think of it this way, gentlemen: he was probably greater in
his death than in his life, hurr? A most tragic man, he often
told me that his only happy hours were spent here at this
very table. Pathetic, is it not? And to think the only favour I
could ever show him was to let him witness the mysteries of
my kitchen, which is, when all is said and done, no more
than a plain, ordinary kitchen.'

'You seem very certain of his death,' commented Costain.
'After all, no evidence has ever turned up to substantiate it.'

Sbirro contemplated the picture. 'None at all,' he said
softly. 'Remarkable, hurr?'

With the arrival of the entrée Sbirro leaped to his feet and
set about serving them himself. With his eyes alight, he

lifted the casserole from the tray and sniffed at the fragrance from within with sensual relish. Then, taking great care not to lose a single drop of gravy, he filled two platters with chunks of dripping meat. As if exhausted by this task, he sat back in his chair, breathing heavily. 'Gentlemen,' he said, 'to your good appetite.'

Costain chewed his first mouthful with great deliberation and swallowed it. Then he looked at the empty tines of his fork with glazed eyes.

'Good God!' he breathed.

'It is good, hurr? Better than you imagined?'

Costain shook his head dazedly. 'It is as impossible,' he said slowly, 'for the uninitiated to conceive the delights of lamb Amirstan as for mortal man to look into his own soul.'

'Perhaps –' Sbirro thrust his head so close that Costain could feel the warm, fetid breath tickle his nostrils '– perhaps you have just had a glimpse into your soul, hurr?'

Costain tried to draw back slightly without giving offence. 'Perhaps.' He laughed. 'And a gratifying picture it made: all fang and claw. But without intending any disrespect, I should hardly like to build my church on *lamb en casserole*.'

Sbirro rose and laid a hand gently on his shoulder. 'So perspicacious,' he said. 'Sometimes when you have nothing to do, nothing, perhaps, but sit for a very little while in a dark room and think of this world – what it is and what it is going to be – then you must turn your thoughts a little to the significance of the Lamb in religion. It will be so interesting. And now –' he bowed deeply to both men '– I have held you long enough from your dinner. I was most happy,' he said, nodding to Costain, 'and I am sure we will meet again.' The teeth gleamed, the eyes glittered, and Sbirro was gone down the aisle of tables.

Costain twisted around to stare after the retreating figure. 'Have I offended him in some way?' he asked.

Laffler looked up from his plate. 'Offended him? He loves

that kind of talk. Lamb Amirstan is a ritual with him; get him started and he'll be back at you a dozen times worse than a priest making a conversion.'

Costain turned to his meal with the face still hovering before him. 'Interesting man,' he reflected. 'Very.'

It took him a month to discover the tantalising familiarity of that face, and when he did, he laughed aloud in his bed. Why, of course! Sbirro might have sat as the model for the Cheshire cat in *Alice*!

He passed this thought on to Laffler the very next evening as they pushed their way down the street to the restaurant against a chill, blustering wind. Laffler only looked blank.

'You may be right,' he said, 'but I'm not a fit judge. It's a far cry back to the days when I read the book. A far cry, indeed.'

As if taking up his words, a piercing howl came ringing down the street and stopped both men short in their tracks. 'Someone's in trouble there,' said Laffler. 'Look!'

Not far from the entrance to Sbirro's two figures could be seen struggling in the near darkness. They swayed back and forth and suddenly tumbled into a writhing heap on the sidewalk. The piteous howl went up again, and Laffler, despite his girth, ran toward it at a fair speed with Costain tagging cautiously behind.

Stretched out full-length on the pavement was a slender figure with the dusky complexion and white hair of one of Sbirro's servitors. His fingers were futilely plucking at the huge hands which encircled his throat, and his knees pushed weakly up at the gigantic bulk of a man who brutally bore down with his full weight.

Laffler came up panting. 'Stop this!' he shouted. 'What's going on here?'

The pleading eyes almost bulging from their sockets turned toward Laffler. 'Help, sair. This man – drunk –'

'Drunk am I, ya dirty – ' Costain saw now that the man

was a sailor in a badly soiled uniform. The air around him reeked with the stench of liquor. 'Pick me pocket and then call me drunk, will ya!' He dug his fingers in harder, and his victim groaned.

Laffler seized the sailor's shoulder. 'Let go of him, do you hear! Let go of him at once!' he cried, and the next instant was sent careening into Costain, who staggered back under the force of the blow.

The attack on his own person sent Laffler into immediate and berserk action. Without a sound he leaped at the sailor, striking and kicking furiously at the unprotected face and flanks. Stunned at first, the man came to his feet with a rush and turned on Laffler. For a moment they stood locked together, and then as Costain joined the attack, all three went sprawling to the ground. Slowly Laffler and Costain got to their feet and looked down at the body before them.

'He's either out cold from liquor,' said Costain, 'or he struck his head going down. In any case, it's a job for the police.'

'No, no sair!' The waiter crawled weakly to his feet, and stood swaying. 'No police, sair. Mr Sbirro do not want such. You understand, sair.' He caught hold of Costain with a pleading hand, and Costain looked at Laffler.

'Of course not,' said Laffler. 'We won't have to bother with the police. They'll pick him up soon enough, the murderous sot. But what in the world started all this?'

'That man, sair. He make most erratic way while walking, and with no meaning I push against him. Then he attack me, accusing me to rob him.'

'As I thought,' Laffler pushed the waiter gently along. 'Now go on in and get yourself attended to.'

The man seemed ready to burst into tears. 'To you, sair, I owe my life. If there is anything I can do –'

Laffler turned into the areaway that led to Sbirro's door. 'No, no, it was nothing. You go along, and if Sbirro has any questions send him to me. I'll straighten it out.'

'My life, sair,' were the last words they heard as the inner door closed behind them.

'There you are, Costain,' said Laffler, as a few minutes later he drew his chair under the table, 'civilised man in all his glory. Reeking with alcohol, strangling to death some miserable innocent who came too close.'

Costain made an effort to gloss over the nerve-shattering memory of the episode. 'It's the neurotic cat that takes to alcohol,' he said. 'Surely there's a reason for that sailor's condition.'

'Reason? Of course there is. Plain atavistic savagery!' Laffler swept his arm in an all-embracing gesture. 'Why do we all sit here at our meat? Not only to appease physical demands, but because our atavistic selves cry for release. Think back, Costain. Do you remember that I once described Sbirro as the epitome of civilisation? Can you now see why? A brilliant man, he fully understands the nature of human beings. But unlike lesser men he bends all his efforts to the satisfaction of our innate natures without resultant harm to some innocent bystander.'

'When I think back on the wonders of lamb Amirstan,' said Costain, 'I quite understand what you're driving at. And, by the way, isn't it nearly due to appear on the bill of fare? It must have been over a month ago that it was last served.'

The waiter, filling the tumblers, hesitated. 'I am so sorry, sair. No special this evening.'

'There's your answer,' Laffler grunted, 'and probably just my luck to miss out on it altogether the next time.'

Costain stared at him. 'Oh, come, that's impossible.'

'No, blast it.' Laffler drank off half his water at a gulp and the waiter immediately refilled the glass. 'I'm off to South America for a surprise tour of inspection. One month, two months, Lord knows how long.'

'Are things that bad down there?'

'They could be better.' Laffler suddenly grinned. 'Mustn't forget it takes very mundane dollars and cents to pay the tariff at Sbirro's.'

'I haven't heard a word of this around the office.'

'Wouldn't be a surprise tour if you had. Nobody knows about this except myself – and now you. I want to walk in on them completely unsuspected. Find out what flimflammery they're up to down there. As far as the office is concerned, I'm off on a jaunt somewhere. Maybe recuperating in some sanatorium from my hard work. Anyhow, the business will be in good hands. Yours, among them.'

'Mine?' said Costain, surprised.

'When you go in tomorrow you'll find yourself in receipt of a promotion, even if I'm not there to hand it to you personally. Mind you, it has nothing to do with our friendship either; you've done fine work, and I'm immensely grateful for it.'

Costain reddened under the praise. 'You don't expect to be in tomorrow. Then you're leaving tonight?'

Laffler nodded. 'I've been trying to wangle some reservations. If they come through, well, this will be in the nature of a farewell celebration.'

'You know,' said Costain slowly, 'I devoutly hope that your reservations don't come through. I believe our dinners here have come to mean more to me than I ever dared imagine.'

The waiter's voice broke in, 'Do you wish to be served now, sair?' and they both started.

'Of course, of course,' said Laffler sharply, 'I didn't realise you were waiting.'

'What bothers me,' he told Costain as the waiter turned away, 'is the thought of the lamb Amirstan I'm bound to miss. To tell you the truth, I've already put off my departure a week, hoping to hit a lucky night, and now I simply can't delay any more. I do hope that when you're sitting over your share of lamb Amirstan, you'll think of me with suitable regrets.'

Costain laughed. 'I will indeed,' he said as he turned to his dinner.

Hardly had he cleared the plate when a waiter silently reached for it. It was not their usual waiter, he observed; it was none other than the victim of the assault.

'Well,' Costain said, 'how do you feel now? Still under the weather?'

The waiter paid no attention to him. Instead, with the air of a man under great strain, he turned to Laffler. 'Sair,' he whispered. 'My life. I owe it to you. I can repay you!'

Laffler looked up in amazement, then shook his head firmly. 'No,' he said, 'I want nothing from you, understand? You have repaid me sufficiently with your thanks. Now get on with your work and let's hear no more about it.'

The waiter did not stir an inch, but his voice rose slightly. 'By the body and blood of your God, sair, I will help you even if you do not want! *Do not go into the kitchen, sair.* I trade you my life for yours, sair, when I speak this. Tonight or any night of your life, do not go into the kitchen at Sbirro's!'

Laffler sat back completely dumbfounded, 'Not go into the kitchen? Why shouldn't I go into the kitchen if Mr Sbirro ever took it into his head to invite me there? What's all this about?'

A hard hand was laid on Costain's back, and another gripped the waiter's arm. The waiter remained frozen to the spot, his lips compressed, his eyes downcast.

'What is all *what* about, gentlemen?' purred the voice. 'So opportune an arrival. In time as ever, I see, to answer all the questions, hurr?'

Laffler breathed a sigh of relief. 'Ah, Sbirro, thank heaven you're here. This man is saying something about my not going into your kitchen. Do you know what he means?'

The teeth showed in a broad grin. 'But of course. This good man was giving you advice in all amiability. It so happens that my too emotional chef heard some rumour that I might have a guest into his precious kitchen and he flew into a fearful rage. Such a rage, gentlemen! He even threatened to give notice on the spot, and you can understand what that would mean to Sbirro's, hurr? Fortunately, I succeeded in showing him what a signal honour it is to have an esteemed patron and true connoisseur observe him at his work first-hand, and now he is quite amenable. Quite, hurr?'

He released the waiter's arm. 'You are at the wrong table,' he said softly. 'See that it does not happen again.'

The waiter slipped off without daring to raise his eyes and Sbirro drew a chair to the table. He seated himself and brushed his hand lightly over his hair. 'Now I am afraid that the cat is out of the bag, hurr? This invitation to you, Mr Laffler, was to be a surprise; but the surprise is gone, and all that is left is the invitation.'

Laffler mopped beads of perspiration from his forehead. 'Are you serious?' he said huskily. 'Do you mean that we are really to witness the preparation of your food tonight?'

Sbirro drew a sharp fingernail along the tablecloth, leaving a thin, straight line printed in the linen. 'Ah,' he said, 'I am faced with a dilemma of great proportions.' He studied the line soberly. 'You, Mr Laffler, have been my guest for ten long years. But our friend here –'

Costain raised his hand in protest. 'I understand perfectly. This invitation is solely to Mr Laffler, and naturally my presence is embarrassing. As it happens, I have an early engagement for this evening and must be on my way anyhow. So you see there's no dilemma at all, really.'

'No,' said Laffler, 'absolutely not. That wouldn't be fair at all. We've been sharing this until now, Costain, and I won't enjoy this experience half as much if you're not along. Surely Sbirro can make his conditions flexible, this one occasion.'

They both looked at Sbirro who shrugged his shoulders regretfully.

Costain rose abruptly. 'I'm not going to sit here, Laffler, and spoil your great adventure. And then too,' he bantered, 'think of that ferocious chef waiting to get his cleaver on you. I prefer not to be at the scene. I'll just say good-bye,' he went on, to cover Laffler's guilty silence, 'and leave you to Sbirro. I'm sure he'll take pains to give you a good show.' He held out his hand and Laffler squeezed it painfully hard.

'You're being very decent, Costain,' he said. 'I hope you'll continue to dine here until we meet again. It shouldn't be too long.'

Sbirro made way for Costain to pass. 'I will expect you,' he said. '*Au'voir.*'

Costain stopped briefly in the dim foyer to adjust his scarf and fix his Homburg at the proper angle. When he turned away from the mirror, satisfied at last, he saw with a final glance that Laffler and Sbirro were already at the kitchen door, Sbirro holding the door invitingly wide with one hand, while the other rested, almost tenderly, on Laffler's meaty shoulders.

THE FACE

E. F. Benson

As the son of an Archbishop of Canterbury, Edward Frederic Benson caused something of a stir when his candidly anti-episcopal first novel, DODO, was published in 1893. With record-breaking sales, it caused a 'boom' in the publishing world. Benson also wrote light fiction – the popular LUCIA novels – and biographies and contemporary histories of which AS WE WERE (1930) is probably the best known.

Hester Ward, sitting by the open window on this hot afternoon in June, began seriously to argue with herself about the cloud of foreboding and depression which had encompassed her all day, and, very sensibly, she enumerated to herself the manifold causes for happiness in the fortunate circumstances of her life. She was young, she was extremely good-looking, she was well-off, she enjoyed excellent health, and above all, she had an adorable husband and two small, adorable children. There was no break, indeed, anywhere in the circle of prosperity which surrounded her, and had the wishing-cap been handed to her that moment by some beneficent fairy, she would have hesitated to put it on her head, for there was positively nothing that she could think of which would have been worthy of such solemnity. Moreover, she could not accuse herself of a want of appreciation of her blessings; she appreciated enormously, she enjoyed enormously, and she thoroughly wanted all those who so munificently contributed to her happiness to share in it.

She made a very deliberate review of these things, for she was really anxious, more anxious, indeed, than she admitted to herself, to find anything tangible which could possibly warrant this ominous feeling of approaching disaster. Then there was the weather to consider; for the last week London had been stiflingly hot, but, if that was the cause, why had she not felt it before? Perhaps the effect of these broiling, airless days had been cumulative. That was an idea, but frankly, it did not seem a very good one, for, as a matter of fact, she loved the heat; Dick, who hated it, said that it was odd he should have fallen in love with a salamander.

She shifted her position, sitting up straight in this low window-seat, for she was intending to make a call on her courage. She had known from the moment she awoke this morning what it was that lay so heavy on her, and now, having done her best to shift the reason of her depression on to anything else, and having completely failed, she meant to look the thing in the face. She was ashamed of doing so for the cause of this leaden mood of fear which held her in its grip was so trivial, so fantastic, so excessively silly.

'Yes, there never was anything so silly,' she said to herself. 'I must look at it straight, and convince myself how silly it is.' She paused a moment, clenching her hands.

'Now for it,' she said.

She had had a dream the previous night, which, years ago, used to be familiar to her, for again and again when she was a child she had dreamed it. In itself the dream was nothing, but in those childish days whenever she had this dream which had visited her last night, it was followed, on the next night, by another, which contained the source and the core of the horror, and she would awake screaming and struggling in the grip of overwhelming nightmare. For some ten years now she had not experienced it, and would have said that, though she remembered it, it had become dim and distant to her. But last night she had had that warning dream, which used to herald the visitation of the nightmare, and now that whole storehouse of memory, crammed as it was with bright things and beautiful, contained nothing so vivid.

The warning dream, the curtain that was drawn up on the succeeding night, and disclosed the vision she dreaded, was simple and harmless enough in itself. She seemed to be walking on a high sandy cliff covered with short downgrass; twenty yards to the left came the edge of this cliff, which sloped steeply down to the sea that lay at its foot. The path she followed led through fields bounded by low hedges and mounted gradually upwards. She went through some half-dozen of these, climbing over the wooden stiles that gave communication; sheep grazed there, but she never saw another human being, and always it was dusk, as if evening was falling, and she had to hurry on, because someone (she knew not whom) was waiting for her, and had been waiting not a few minutes only, but for many years. Presently, as she mounted this slope, she saw in front of her a copse of stunted trees, growing crookedly under the continual pressure of the wind that blew from the sea, and when she saw those she knew her journey was nearly done, and that the nameless one, who had been waiting for her so long, was somewhere close at hand. The path she followed was cut through this wood, and the slanting boughs of the trees on the seaward side almost roofed it in; it was like walking through a tunnel. Soon the trees in front began to grow thin, and she saw through them the grey tower of a lonely church. It stood in a graveyard, apparently long disused, and the body of the church, which lay between the tower and the edge of the cliff, was in ruins, roofless and with gaping windows round which ivy grew thickly.

At that point this prefatory dream always stopped. It was a troubled, uneasy dream, for there was over it the sense of dusk and of the man who had been waiting for her so long, but it was not of the order of nightmare. Many times in childhood had she experienced it, and perhaps it was the subconscious knowledge of the night that so surely followed it which gave it its disquiet. And now last night it had come again, identical in every particular but one. For last night it seemed to her that in the course of these ten years which had intervened since last it had visited her the glimpse of the church and churchyard was changed. The edge of the cliff had come nearer to the tower, so that it now was within a yard or two of it, and the ruined body of the church, but for one broken arch that remained, had vanished. The sea had encroached, and for ten years had been busily eating at the cliff.

Hester knew well that it was this dream and this alone which had darkened the day for her, by reason of the night-mares that used to follow it, and, like a sensible woman, having looked it once in the face, she refused to admit into her mind any conscious calling-up of the sequel. If she let herself contemplate that, as likely as not the very thinking about it would be sufficient to ensure its return, and of one thing she was very certain, namely, that she didn't at all want it to do so. It was not like the confused jumble and jangle of ordinary nightmare, it was very simple, and she felt it concerned the nameless one who waited for her . . . But she must not think of it; her whole will and intention was set on not thinking of it, and to aid her resolution there was the rattle of Dick's latchkey in the front door, and his voice calling her.

She went out into the little square front hall; there he was, strong and large, and wonderfully undreamlike.

'This heat's a scandal, it's an outrage, it is an abomination of desolation,' he cried, vigorously mopping. 'What have we done that Providence should place us in this frying-pan? Let us thwart Him, Hester! Let us drive out of this inferno and have our dinner at – I'll whisper it so that he shan't overhear – at Hampton Court!'

She laughed: this plan suited her excellently. They would return late, after the distraction of a fresh scene; and dining out at night was both delicious and stupefying.

'The very thing,' she said, 'and I'm sure Providence didn't hear. Let's start now!'

'Rather. Any letters for me?'

He walked to the table where there were a few rather uninteresting-looking envelopes with halfpenny stamps.

'Ah, receipted bill,' he said. 'Just a reminder of one's folly in paying it. Circular . . . unasked advice to invest in German marks . . . Circular begging letter, beginning, "Dear Sir or Madam". Such impertinence to ask one to subscribe to something without ascertaining one's sex . . . Private view, portraits at the Walton Gallery . . . Can't go; business meetings all day. You might like to have a look in, Hester. Someone told me there were some fine Vandycks. That's all: let's be off.'

Hester spent a thoroughly reassuring evening, and though she thought of telling Dick about the dream that had so deeply imprinted itself on her consciousness all day, in order to hear the great laugh he would have given her for being such a goose, she refrained from doing so, since nothing that he could say would be so tonic to these fantastic fears as his general robustness. Besides, she would have to account for its disturbing effect, tell him that it was once familiar to her, and recount the sequel of the nightmares that followed. She would neither think of them nor mention them: it was wiser by far just to soak herself in his extraordinary sanity, and wrap herself in his affection . . . They dined out-of-doors at a riverside restaurant and strolled about afterwards, and it was very nearly midnight when, soothed with coolness and fresh air, and the vigour of his strong companionship, she let herself into the house, while he took the car back to the garage. And now she marvelled at the mood which had beset her all day, so distant and unreal had it become. She felt as if she had dreamed of shipwreck, and had awoke to find herself in some secure and sheltered garden where no tempest raged nor waves beat. But was there, ever so remotely, ever so dimly, the noise of far-off breakers somewhere?

He slept in the dressing-room which communicated with her bedroom, the door of which was left open for the sake of air and coolness, and she fell asleep almost as soon as her light was out, and while his was still burning. And immediately she began to dream.

She was standing on the seashore; the tide was out, for level sands strewn with stranded jetsam glimmered in a dusk that was deepening into night. Though she had never seen the place it was awfully familiar to her. At the head of the beach there was a steep cliff of sand, and perched on the edge of it was a grey church tower. The sea must have encroached and undermined the body of the church, for tumbled blocks of masonry lay close to her at the bottom of the cliff, and there were gravestones there, while others, still in place, were silhouetted whitely against the sky. To the right of the church tower there was a wood of stunted trees, combed sideways by the prevalent sea wind, and she knew that along the top of the cliff, a few yards inland, there lay a path through fields, with wooden stiles to climb, which led through a tunnel of trees and so out into the churchyard. All this she saw in a glance, and waited, looking at the sand-cliff crowned by the church tower, for the terror that was going to reveal itself. Already she knew what it was, and as so many times before, she tried to run away. But the catalepsy of nightmare was already on her; frantically she strove to move, but her utmost endeavour could not raise a foot from the sand. Frantically she tried to look away from the sand-cliffs close in front of her, where in a moment now the horror would be manifested . . .

It came. There formed a pale, oval light, the size of a man's face, dimly luminous in front of her and a few inches above the level of her eyes. It outlined itself: short reddish hair grew low on the forehead; below were two grey eyes, set very close together, which steadily and fixedly regarded her. On each side the ears stood noticeably away from the head, and the lines of the jaw met in a short, pointed chin. The nose was straight and rather long, below it came a hairless lip, and last of all the mouth took shape and colour, and there lay the crowning terror. One side of it, soft-curved and beautiful, trembled into a smile, the other side, thick and gathered together as by some physical deformity, sneered and lusted.

The whole face, dim at first, gradually focused itself into clear outline: it was pale and rather lean, the face of a young man. And then the lower lip dropped a little, showing the glint of teeth, and there was the sound of speech. 'I shall soon come for you now,' it said, and on the words it drew a little nearer to her, and the smile broadened. At that the full, hot blast of nightmare poured in upon her. Again she tried to run, again she tried to scream, and now she could feel the breath of that terrible mouth upon her. Then with a crash and a rending like the tearing asunder of soul and body she broke the spell, and heard her own voice yelling and felt with her fingers for the switch of her light. And then she saw that the room was not dark, for Dick's door was open, and the next moment, not yet undressed, he was with her.

'My darling, what is it?' he said. 'What's the matter?'

She clung desperately to him, still distraught with terror.

'Ah, he has been here again,' she cried. 'He says he will soon come to me. Keep him away, Dick.'

For one moment her fear infected him, and he found himself glancing round the room.

'But what do you mean?' he said. 'No one has been here.'

She raised her head from his shoulder.

'No, it was just a dream,' she said. 'But it was the old dream, and I was terrified. Why, you've not undressed yet. What time is it?'

'You haven't been in bed ten minutes, dear,' he said. 'You had hardly put out your light when I heard you screaming.'

She shuddered.

'Ah, it's awful,' she said. 'And he will come again . . .'

He sat down by her.

'Now tell me all about it,' he said.

She shook her head.

'No, it will never do to talk about it,' she said, 'it will only make it more real. I suppose the children are all right, are they?'

'Of course they are. I looked in on my way upstairs.'

'That's good. But I'm better now, Dick. A dream hasn't anything real about it, has it? It doesn't mean anything?'

He was quite reassuring on this point, and soon she quieted down. Before he went to bed he looked in again on her, and she was asleep.

Hester had a stern interview with herself when Dick had gone down to his office next morning. She told herself that what she was afraid of was nothing more than her own fear. How many times had that ill-omened face come to her in dreams, and what significance had it ever proved to possess? Absolutely none at all, except to make her afraid. She was afraid where no fear was: she was guarded, sheltered, prosperous, and what if a nightmare of childhood returned? It had no more meaning now than it had then, and all those visitations of her childhood had passed away without trace . . . And then, despite herself, she began thinking over that vision again. It was grimly identical with all its previous occurrences, except . . . And then, with a sudden shrinking of the heart, she remembered that in earlier years those terrible lips had said: 'I shall come for you when you are older,' and last night they had said: 'I shall soon come for you now.' She remembered, too, that in the warning dream the sea had encroached, and it had now demolished the body of the church. There was an awful consistency about these two changes in the otherwise identical visions. The years had brought their change to them, for in the one the encroaching sea had brought down the body of the church, in the other the time was now near . . .

It was no use to scold or reprimand herself, for to bring her mind to the contemplation of the vision meant merely that the grip of terror closed on her again; it was far wiser to occupy herself, and starve her fear out by refusing to bring it the sustenance of thought. So she went about her household duties, she took the children out for their airing in the park, and then, determined to leave no moment unoccupied, set off with the card of invitation to see the pictures in the private view at the Walton Gallery. After that her day was full enough; she was lunching out, and going on to a matinée, and by the time she got home Dick would have returned, and they would drive down to his little house at Rye for the weekend. All Saturday and Sunday she would be playing golf, and she felt that fresh air and physical fatigue would exorcise the dread of these dreaming fantasies.

The gallery was crowded when she got there; there were friends among the sightseers, and the inspection of the pictures was diversified by cheerful conversation. There were two or three fine Raeburns, a couple of Sir Joshuas, but the gems, so she gathered, were three Vandycks that hung in a small room by themselves. Presently she strolled in there, looking at her catalogue. The first of them, she saw, was a portrait of Sir Roger Wyburn. Still chatting to her friend she raised her eyes and saw it . . .

Her heart hammered in her throat, and then seemed to stand still altogether. A qualm as of some mental sickness of the soul overcame her, for there in front of her was he who would soon come for her. There was the reddish hair, the projecting ears, the greedy eyes set close together, and the mouth smiling on one side, and on the other gathered up into the sneering menace that she knew so well. It might have been her own nightmare rather than a living model which had sat to the painter for that face.

'Ah, what a portrait, and what a brute!' said her companion. 'Look Hester, isn't that marvellous?'

She recovered herself with an effort. To give way to this over-mastering dread would have been to allow nightmares to invade her waking life, and there, for sure, madness lay. She forced herself to look at it again, but there were the steady and eager eyes regarding her; she could almost fancy the mouth began to move. All round her the crowd bustled and chattered, but to her own sense she was alone there with Roger Wyburn.

And yet, so she reasoned with herself, this picture of him – for it was he and no other – should have reassured her. Roger Wyburn, to have been painted by Vandyck, must have been dead near on two hundred years; how could he be a menace to her? Had she seen that portrait by some chance as a child; had it made some dreadful impression on her, since over-scored by other memories, but still alive in the mysterious subconsciousness, which flows eternally, like some dark underground river, beneath the surface of human life? Psychologists taught that these early impressions fester or poison the mind like some hidden abscess. That might account for this dread of one, nameless no longer, who waited for her.

That night down at Rye there came again to her the prefatory dream, followed by the nightmare, and clinging to her husband as the terror began to subside she told him what she had resolved to keep to herself. Just to tell it brought a measure of comfort, for it was so outrageously fantastic, and his robust common sense upheld her. But when, on their return to London, there was a recurrence of these visions, he made short work of her demur, and took her straight to her doctor.

'Tell him all, darling,' he said. 'Unless you promise to do that, I will. I can't have you worried like this. It's all nonsense, you know, and doctors are wonderful people for curing nonsense.'

She turned to him.

'Dick, you're frightened,' she said quietly.

He laughed.

'I'm nothing of the kind,' he said, 'but I don't like being awakened by your screaming. Not my idea of a peaceful night. Here we are.'

The medical report was decisive and peremptory. There was nothing whatever to be alarmed about; in brain and body she was perfectly healthy, but she was run down. These disturbing dreams were, as likely as not, an effect, a symptom of her condition, rather than the cause of it, and Dr Baring unhesitatingly recommended a complete change to some bracing place. The wise thing would be to send her out of this stuffy furnace to some quiet place, to where she had never been. Complete change; quite so. For the same reason her husband had better not go with her; he must pack her off to, let us say, the East coast. Sea air and coolness and complete idleness. No long walks; no long bathings; a dip, and a deck-chair on the sands. A lazy soporific life. How about Rushton? He had no doubt that Rushton would set her up again. After a week or so, perhaps, her husband might go down and see her. Plenty of sleep – never mind the nightmares – plenty of fresh air.

Hester, rather to her husband's surprise, fell in with this suggestion at once, and the following evening saw her installed in solitude and tranquillity. The little hotel was still almost empty, for the rush of summer tourists had not yet begun, and all day she sat out on the beach with the sense of a struggle over. She need not fight the terror any more; dimly it seemed to her that its malignancy had been relaxed. Had she in some way yielded to it and done its secret bidding? At any rate no return of its nightly visitations had occurred, and she slept long and dreamlessly, and woke to another day of quiet. Every morning there was a line for her from Dick, with good news of himself and the children, but he and they alike seemed somehow remote, like memories of a very distant time. Something had driven in between her and them, and she saw them as if through glass. But equally did the memory of the face of Roger Wyburn, as seen on the master's canvas or hanging close in front of her against the crumbling sand-cliff, become blurred and indistinct, and no return of her nightly terrors visited her. This truce from all emotion reacted not on her mind alone, lulling her with a sense of soothed security, but on her body also, and she began to weary of this day-long inactivity.

The village lay on the lip of a stretch of land reclaimed from the sea. To the north the level marsh, now beginning to glow with the pale bloom of the sea-lavender, stretched away featureless till it lost itself in the distance, but to the south a spur of hill came down to the shore ending in a wooded promontory. Gradually, as her physical health increased, she began to wonder what lay beyond this ridge which cut short the view, and one afternoon she walked across the intervening level and strolled up its wooded slopes. The day was close and windless, the invigorating sea breeze, which till now had spiced the heat with freshness, had died, and she looked forward to finding a current of air stirring when she had topped the hill. To the south a mass of dark cloud lay along the horizon, but there was no immi-nent threat of storm. The slope was easily surmounted, and presently she stood at the top and found herself on the edge of a tableland of wooded pasture, and following the path, which ran not far from the edge of the cliff, she came out into more open country. Empty fields, where a few sheep were grazing, mounted gradually upwards. Wooden stiles made a communication in the hedges that bounded them. And there, not a mile in front of her, she saw a wood, with trees growing slantingly away from the push of the prevalent sea winds, crowning the upward slope, and over the top of it peered a grey church tower.

For the moment, as the awful and familiar scene identified itself, Hester's heart stood still: the next a wave of courage and resolution poured in upon her. Here, at last, was the scene of that prefatory dream, and here was she presented with the opportunity of fathoming and dispelling it. Instantly her mind was made up, and under the strange twilight of the shrouded sky she walked swiftly on through the fields she had so often traversed in sleep, and up to the wood, beyond which he was waiting for her. She closed her ears against the clanging bell of terror, which now she could silence for ever, and unfalteringly entered that dark tunnel of wood. Soon in front of her the trees began to thin, and through them, now close at hand, she saw the church tower. In a few yards farther she came out of the belt of trees, and round her were the monuments of a graveyard long disused. The cliff was broken off close to the church tower: between it and the edge there was no more of the body of the church than a broken arch, thick-hung with ivy. Round this she passed and saw below the ruin of fallen masonry, and the level sands strewn with headstones and disjected rubble, and at the edge of the cliff were graves already cracked and toppling. But there was no one here, none waited for her, and the churchyard where she had so often pictured him was as empty as the fields she had just traversed.

A huge elation filled her; her courage had been rewarded and all the terrors of the past became to her meaningless phantoms. But there was no time to linger, for now the storm threatened, and on the horizon a blink of lightning was followed by a crackling peal. Just as she turned to go her eye fell on a tombstone that was balanced on the very edge of the cliff, and she read on it that here lay the body of Roger Wyburn.

Fear, the catalepsy of nightmare, rooted her for the moment to the spot; she stared in stricken amazement at the moss-grown letters; almost she expected to see that fell terror of a face rise and hover over his resting-place. Then the fear which had frozen her lent her wings, and with hurrying feet she sped through the arched pathway in the wood and out into the fields. Not one backward glance did she give till she had come to the edge of the ridge above the village, and, turning, saw the pastures she had traversed empty of any living presence. None had followed; but the sheep, apprehensive of the coming storm, had ceased to feed, and were huddling under shelter of the stunted hedges.

Her first idea, in the panic of her mind, was to leave the place at once, but the last train for London had left an hour before, and besides, where was the use of flight if it was the spirit of a man long dead from which she fled? The distance from the place where his bones lay did not afford her safety; that must be sought for within. But she longed for Dick's sheltering and confident presence; he was arriving, in any case, tomorrow, but there were long dark hours before tomorrow, and who could say what the perils and dangers of the coming night might be? If he started this evening instead of tomorrow morning, he could motor down here in four hours, and would be with her by ten o'clock or eleven. She wrote an urgent telegram:

Come at once (she said). *Don't delay.*

The storm which had flickered in the south now came quickly up, and soon after it burst in appalling violence. For preface there were but a few large drops that splashed and dried on the roadway as she came back from the post-office, and just as she reached the hotel again the roar of approaching rain sounded, and the sluices of heaven were opened.

Through the deluge flared the fire of the lightning, the thunder crashed and echoed overhead, and presently the street of the village was a torrent of sandy, turbulent water, and sitting there in the dark, one picture leapt floating before her eyes – that of the tombstone of Roger Wyburn, already tottering to its fall at the edge of the cliff of the church tower. In such rains as these, acres of the cliffs were loosened; she seemed to hear the whisper of the sliding sand that would precipitate those perished sepulchres and what lay within to the beach below.

By eight o'clock the storm was subsiding, and as she dined she was handed a telegram from Dick, saying that he had already started and sent this off *en route*. By half-past ten, therefore, if all was well, he would be here, and somehow he would stand between her and her fear. Strange how a few days ago both it and the thought of him had become distant and dim to her; now the one was as vivid as the other, and she counted the minutes to his arrival. Soon the rain ceased altogether, and looking out of the curtained window of her sitting-room where she sat watching the slow circle of the hands of the clock, she saw a tawny moon rising over the sea. Before it had climbed to the zenith, before her clock had twice told the hour again, Dick would be with her.

It had just struck ten when there came a knock at the door, and the pageboy entered with the message that a gentleman had come for her. Her heart leaped at the news; she had not expected Dick for half an hour yet, and now the lonely vigil was over. She ran downstairs, and there was the figure standing on the step outside. His face was turned away from her; no doubt he was giving some order to his chauffeur. He was outlined against the white moonlight, and in contrast with that, the gas-jet in the entrance just above his head gave his hair a warm, reddish tinge.

She ran across the hall to him.

'Ah, my darling, you've come,' she said. 'It was good of you. How quick you've been!' Just as she laid her hand on his shoulder he turned. His arm was thrown out round her, and she looked into a face with eyes close-set, and a mouth smiling on one side, the other thick and gathered together as by some physical deformity, sneered and lusted.

The nightmare was on her; she could neither run nor scream, and supporting her dragging steps, he went forth with her into the night.

Half an hour later Dick arrived. To his amazement he heard that a man had called for his wife not long before, and that she had gone out with him. He seemed to be a stranger here, for the boy who had taken his message to her had never seen him before, and presently surprise began to deepen into alarm; inquiries were made outside the hotel, and it appeared that a witness or two had seen the lady whom they knew to be staying there walking, hatless, along the top of the beach with a man whose arm was linked in hers. Neither of them knew him, but one had seen his face and could describe it.

The direction of the search thus became narrowed down, and though with a lantern to supplement the moonlight they came upon footprints which might have been hers, there were no marks of any who walked beside her. But they followed these until they came to an end, a mile away, in a great landslide of sand, which had fallen from the old churchyard on the cliff, and had brought down with it half the tower and a gravestone, with the body that had lain below.

The gravestone was that of Roger Wyburn, and his body lay by it, untouched by corruption or decay, though two hundred years had elapsed since it was interred there. For a week afterwards the work of searching the landslide went on, assisted by the high tides that gradually washed it away. But no further discovery was made.

A CHILD CRYING

James Saunders

*James Saunders has been writing radio plays since the early
1950s. One of them, MENOCCHIO, won a Giles Cooper Award.
Another, THE MAGIC BATHROOM, was a BBC Radio Drama
entry for the Prix Italia. He has also written extensively for
television and for theatre. His stage plays include
NEXT TIME I'LL SING TO YOU and BODIES.*

I'd hardly spoken to him before that night, though he'd
moved into the flat below ours some months earlier.
Now and then I'd pass him on the stairs, with a greeting he
barely acknowledged, looking ahead with a frown as if he
had better things to do than pass the time of day with strangers. I decided he was a shy man.

He was some kind of writer. I had that from old Mrs
Finch, who took it upon herself to act as jungle-drums for
the block, hanging about her landing with a duster to pass
on block gossip to whoever she met. He wrote books, she
said – as if that was at best suspect and probably shameful –
and kept himself to himself. (In other words, I thought, he
wouldn't be pumped.) But there *was* something funny about
him. When I asked what, she said my guess was as good as
hers, but she'd once known someone who'd been in prison
who looked like that.

I had no wish to make guesses about his 'funniness'; I
have my own reasons for believing in live-and-let-live. He
could be as funny as he liked in his flat so long as he didn't
make too much noise (like his radio did sometimes). I gave
him a mental plus for jamming old Mrs Finch's
investigative radar, and forgot about him, apart from the
occasional moment of annoyance when his music came

through our floor.

That evening, my partner Paul was out with a potential client. I'd knocked up something to eat – pork marinaded in garlic, coriander, white wine and walnut oil, with tagliatelle verde and a green salad – and after the meal, with Paul's waiting in the microwave and the washing-up done, I was listening to some music when the doorbell rang.

'I wonder if you could help me.'

He seemed diffident and belligerent at the same time, as if challenging me to reject him. In the sitting-room he sat straight on the edge of the chair in his suit (I guessed he put his trousers under the mattress at night), accepted a whisky and drank it surprisingly quickly. Turning the music down, I said I hoped it hadn't been disturbing him (wondering if I could broach the subject of *his* radio).

'*Music* doesn't worry me. Oh no.'

His name was Guy Gooding. I tried a few pleasantries to break the ice, but he seemed not to be listening. His eyes moved about the room, as if he'd called to value it.

'Nice flat. Very nice.'

It sounded like an accusation. I pointed out that his must be identical in layout.

'Mine's a mess. No, it's nothing to do with how long I've been there. Things don't fit for me, nothing fits, everything looks wrong.'

I confessed to having an unfair advantage, Paul being an interior decorator.

'Your, erm, flat-mate?'

I recognised the tone. He began to ask questions: whether Paul was easy to live with – a sore point at that moment – who did the cooking, did we have a cleaning-lady, did we share clothes? . . . I waited for questions about sleeping arrangements, so that I could get angry. But he changed direction.

'I can't cook. I have things out of packets, you'd laugh at

my food. I'm a writer, you know, I write.'

I said I'd heard as much from old Mrs Finch.

'Oh her, yes, poking her nose in. I hate that kind of thing.'

'Writing must be a lonely occupation.'

'Yes. I'm on my own, as that busybody no doubt told you. Except for . . . Not that it bothers me, I believe in being self-sufficient. People can clutter you up, clutter up your life.'

I thought it time to cut things short.

'So what can I do for you?'

He gave me an odd, fixed look.

'Just a question. Is there a child living in the block? A small child?'

'Not that I know of.'

'So you don't hear anything up here, a child's voice, a child crying? No, of course you don't, it was stupid of me, I just had to make sure. I've had no sleep, you see, she won't let me sleep any more. Forget it. I'll leave you to enjoy your nice flat in peace. Your – flat-mate won't want to find *me* here. Sorry to bother you.'

He seemed suddenly in a rage. He got up, blundering into a table, and opened the door. I called him back. He turned, his eyes staring, sweat on his forehead. I sat him down and gave him another whisky, which he gulped down as quickly as the first. I waited till he'd calmed a little.

'You'd better tell me about it. Do you mean you're – *hearing* things in your flat? A child?'

'Hearing things, yes. An odd expression. "You must be hearing things." What they mean is, you must be hearing things that aren't there, in other words you're not hearing anything at all, it's all imagination and you're probably a bit mad. Only it's getting into my sleep now and I – Damn!'

He stopped, listening.

'Yes, she's realised I've gone. She won't let me escape, she's crying for me.'

I was afraid he was going to break down, and didn't relish

the idea.

'Have you told anyone else about this?'

'You think I need to see a psychiatrist?'

'I only meant –'

'I did see one if you must know. Useless, I soon gave that up. She went on about something traumatic that must have happened when I was a child, absolute rubbish, I told her so. I was an only child, I had a very happy childhood. *I* never cried. Not after my father left anyway, and I was very young then.'

'So it can't have been *all* that happy. Not having a father around.'

'I'm telling you it was. He was a brute, he used to knock us about, my mother and I were glad to see the back of him. If he was a trauma, his going cured it. We lived an idyllic life after he left. I took his place.'

He seemed very far away for a moment; then he turned his peculiarly expressionless eyes on me.

'I want to show you something. Downstairs.'

His flat was dull and characterless: nothing to take exception to, but nothing to give a second glance either. It was spotlessly clean.

'Sorry about the mess.'

Writers' desks are usually cluttered; his was not. The telephone was precisely squared in one corner. Precisely central was a word-processor monitor, the screen lit – I carefully took no interest in what was on it, afraid he might be going to ask me to read his work in progress. Precisely in front of the monitor was the keyboard, precisely to one side the printer, and on the other side, so neatly aligned as to look like a solid block, a pile of paper, the top sheet – and presumably all the others – closely printed: single-spaced, small typeface, and not a paragraph in sight.

'What did you want to show me?'

'Read that.'

My heart sank; but I dutifully read out the last lines on the screen as he indicated: 'help me let me out let me go wrong like this wrong inside be what I am let me go don't –'

'Yes, and so on and so on, absolute drivel. I see she's put some more on while I was upstairs'

'She's *what*?'

'You don't believe me. Why should you? It started about a month ago – the crying, I mean. The writing had been getting more and more difficult, there was something missing, something wrong, and I couldn't put my finger on it, I was getting in quite a state about it. One morning I decided to take the day off from writing. Then the crying started, this child. I went out to complain, but I could only hear her in my flat. I thought I might as well try and do some work after all, and as soon as I sat at the desk she stopped. That's how it's been ever since, getting worse all the time. Finally I couldn't even stop for a coffee or she'd start. Then she found a way into my sleep. I'd dream she was crying and wake up and she *was*. Now she's started *this* – putting messages on my machine. This morning I decided I'd had enough. I thought, "I'll give her something to cry about." I stayed in bed all morning with the radio on loud, my God you should have heard her!'

He gave a loud, rather unpleasant laugh.

'This evening I couldn't stand any more, I was afraid I'd – do something violent. That's when I decided to go up and ask your advice. She's at it again, listen. No, you can't hear it, it's only for me! Shut up, shut up, shut up!'

He turned to me, his face screwed up. I imagined the shrill noise filling his head.

'You don't know how pitiful she can be, how she can wrench at your heartstrings. She makes me think of all the other children crying, this is the only one I hear but all over the world, if we had the ears for it, there are children crying, they started when mankind began and they'll go on till we're wiped off the face of the earth. Can you imagine having ears that could hear all that crying? Is that what she's trying to tell me? I think I might kill myself if it goes on. Do you think that's what she wants?'

I was suddenly desperate to get out of that flat, with its atmosphere of meanness and repression. I didn't take his talk of killing himself seriously, but I couldn't leave him in the state he was in. Neither did I want him back in our flat; Paul was in a bad enough mood that day without coming home to a raving paranoic.

I took him to the pub on the corner, still quiet at that time of the evening. He bought us both a large whisky, downed his at the bar and bought another. Then we sat at a table. I noticed his hand was shaking.

I said, 'Let me get this straight. Do you actually believe someone or something, not you, is leaving messages on your word processor?'

'Oh yes. How crazy can you get, eh?'

'And that there's a real child somewhere, persecuting you?'

'My body believes it. My eyes and ears believe it, how can they not?'

'And your mind?'

'Of course not, I'm not completely mad!'

'But you can't have it both ways. Either you're suffering from certain . . . delusions, or some supernatural agency is getting at you. Now which do you think it is?'

But he wasn't listening. 'I just wish she'd go away. She's here, you know, she's found me, I can almost feel her arms round my neck, she's past crying now, just breathing the words into my ear: help me, help me, help me . . . Go away,' he said softly. 'Go away, go away, please go away . . .'

I decided to try another tack. 'What is it you're writing?'

'A novel.'

'What about?'

'It's about a child.'

'Ah.'

'I know what you're thinking,' he said. 'You're wrong. It's not the same child.'

'How do you know?'

'I know because I'm writing about a boy. This one is a girl. Look, I can't stand this, I'm going back. She won't stop till I sit at my desk.'

And he got up and blundered out, leaving me to follow. On the way back I had an idea.

'Look,' I said, 'This – disturbance is obviously something to do with the novel you're writing . . .'

'I know that, that's obvious. I wish to God I'd never started it. But I've got to finish it now, she won't let me stop.'

'Exactly. You've got some unconscious doubt about what you're doing. Why not try changing this boy character into a girl? Maybe that's the problem.'

He snarled. 'How can I do that! It's about me!'

'You?'

'As a boy, yes. So how can I change him?'

'Does *he* cry? In your novel?'

'Of course not. I *never* cried. I told you, we were happy together, my mother and I. Idyllically happy.'

Outside the door of his flat he paused with the key in his hand, as if listening.

'All right,' he said, 'I'm coming.' Then he turned those strange dead eyes on me and smiled crookedly.

'I suppose I ought to thank you for putting up with my ravings.'

'Will you be all right?'

'Don't worry, I shan't kill myself. I'll have a large scotch and take a few pills, that might get me a little sleep. Go back to your nice flat and your nice flat-mate.'

I gave him our telephone number, in case things got too

bad – hoping to God he wouldn't use it. I suggested he go back to the psychiatrist, give it another try. He said he'd think about it. Then he said:

'I'd better go in, she's getting frantic. You want to go too. You see, we've both got people waiting for us.'

He gave an odd laugh and went in.

Paul was back, and still in a filthy mood. He accused me of bothering more about some anonymous nut than about our relationship, and when I let out that I'd given Gooding our phone number he called me a bloody fool.

'He'll never be off our backs now!'

Then Gooding's music came on loud through the floor – trying to drown out the crying, I assumed. We finished with a shouting match and Paul went to bed leaving his food untouched.

I woke from a confused dream of crying, shouting, a confusion of noises, to find it was no dream. From downstairs I could hear a voice shouting hysterically – Gooding's voice. It sounded as if he were throwing things about the room. There was a final bang, a crash of glass, a scream – and silence. I looked at my watch; it was a little after three. I listened, but could hear nothing. I wanted just to turn over and go back to sleep, but I knew I couldn't. I went to the phone and rang the number of the previous occupants of Gooding's flat, hoping it hadn't been changed, and then hoping it had. The ringing tone went on for some time, then the phone was picked up but there was no voice, just a harsh breathing.

'Hallo? . . . Gooding? Are you there?'

'It's all right,' he said. 'I've let her out.' His voice was slurred, I could hardly make out what he was saying.

'You've what?'

'I've . . . what she wanted . . . know what she wanted. Let her out. Let her in. Now she's in . . . It's all right. She's in now . . .'

He began to sob, the heart-rending sobs of a man come to the end of his limits. I thought about waking Paul; but I guessed what his reaction would be. Then, as I listened, I suddenly realised something weird was happening. The crying was changing, becoming higher, shriller; the voice of a man at the end of his tether had become the bitter, inconsolable crying of a lost and terrified child. I suddenly felt unreasonably, childishly frightened. I wanted to shout, 'Go away, please go away!'

I went downstairs. I could hear Gooding – if it was Gooding – faintly through the door. I rang the bell, hammered on the door, to no effect, the crying went on, though fainter now, little whines and whimpers like a child exhausted by crying. Then I called the police.

Gooding was sprawled across the glass- and blood-covered desk, one hand still holding the telephone, the other fist a red mess through the shattered screen of the word-processor monitor. The blood had almost stopped. He raised his head slightly and looked at me piteously. I crouched down beside him and put a hand against his cheek. He smiled – the smile of a child after a nightmare, comforted at last by its parents. He let his head fall, and with one last little sob closed his eyes. He could have been peacefully asleep.

When they'd taken him away I took a quick look through the pile of paper, the unfinished novel. It was arid stuff; flat and featureless like a monotonous landscape. Above all, it had no style, no sense of personality. It could have been written by an emotionless, sexless machine. One thing struck me, and I checked a number of sheets to make sure: on almost every page was the same phrase:

'He felt so happy . . . It was such a happy day . . . It was an idyllically happy time . . .'

133

THE HORN

Stephen Gallagher

Stephen Gallagher was born in Salford in 1954. He worked first as a documentary researcher and then for a television company before becoming a full-time freelance writer with the sale of his first novel in 1980. CHIMERA has now been adapted for television. Other novels include VALLEY OF LIGHTS, OKTOBER, DOWN RIVER, RAIN and his latest, THE BOAT HOUSE. His stories have been published in numerous magazines both in Britain and the US.

'We've got heat, we've got light, we've got shelter,' Mick said. 'The lads even left us some dirty books. We've got everything we'll need to ride out the bad weather, so why don't we just sit tight until it all blows over?'

It was just then that the lights flickered and failed and the coal effect on the two-bar electric fire went terminally dark. The bars themselves went more slowly, and the three of us could only watch their fading glow with a kind of bleak desperation. Sub-zero winds were still hammering at the walls of the little roadside hut, and I felt about as well-protected as a mouse under a shoebox in the middle of a stampede. I was cold already. It was quickly going to get worse.

The single flame of Mick's gas lighter put giants' shadows onto the walls and ceiling. 'Winds must've brought the line down,' he said.

The other man, whose name was David something or other, said, 'Anything we could fix?'

'Not me, pal. I'd rather live.'

'What do we do, then? Burn the furniture?'

'Then we'd have nowhere to sit.' The big man who'd told us to call him Mick held the flame higher, and our shadows dived for cover. 'Look, there's still candles and a gas ring.

Nothing's altered. We can even have a brew.'

'The kettle's electric and the water pipes are frozen,' David said promptly. Mick looked at him, hard.

'I could really go off you,' he said. 'D'you know that?'

The candles were the dim, slow-burning kind in small tin dishes, and they'd been used before. The gas ring ran from a bottle under the table, and a kinked hose gave us a momentary problem in getting it going. The candles burned yellow, the gas burned blue, and our faces were white and scared-looking in the light that resulted.

Mick, David, me. Three separate stories of blizzard and breakdown and abandoned vehicles, three lifelines that probably wouldn't otherwise have crossed but which had come together in this fragile cabin at the side of a snowbound motorway.

'Well, here goes nothing,' Mick said, and he grabbed a pan and went outside to get us some snow. The one called David went over to try the dead phone yet again.

I'd been the last to find the place, and I'd known immediately on entering that these two hadn't been travelling together. They were an unmatched, and probably unmatchable, pair. Mick weighed in at around eighteen stone and had the look of – well, there's no kind way of putting it – a slob, however you might dress and groom him. If you had to guess his line of work you might well place him as one of those vendors who stand with their push-along wagons near to football grounds, selling hamburgers and hotdogs that have the look of having been poached in bodily fluids.

David (he'd told me his second name but it hadn't stuck in my mind) was more like one of those people you'll often see driving a company car with a spare shirt on a hanger in the back; he'd said that he was 'in sales', which I took to mean that he was a salesman. He was about my own age, and had reddish-blond hair so fine that he seemed to have no eyelashes. The story, as I understood it, was that Mick had been aiming for the big service area about two miles further along the road, but had found his way blocked and had been forced to abandon his vanload of rubber hose in order to walk back to the only light that he'd seen in miles. When he'd made it to the hut he'd found David already there, crouched before the electric fire with a workman's donkey jacket that he'd found and thrown around his shoulders. I'd joined them about half an hour after that, and no one had arrived since; the weather was worsening by the minute and it seemed unlikely that anybody else was going to make it through. The motorway must have been closed for some time now.

'Jesus wept!' Mick gasped when he'd fallen back in through the door three or four minutes later.

I'd thought that he'd simply intended to take two steps out to fill the pan and then return, and so I said, 'What kept you?'

Some of the colour started to seep back into him as he stood over the heat of the gas ring, hands spread as if he was making a blessing. He'd have made a pretty rough-looking priest. 'I went down for a look at the road,' he said, 'just in case there was any sign of a gritter going through.'

'See anything?'

'I'm lucky I even found the way back. I didn't get more than twenty yards, and it blew up so hard that I might as well have been blind. Nothing else is moving out there. Looks like we're in for the duration.'

'Oh, great,' David said heavily.

'You want to stick your nose outside before you say that,' Mick suggested. 'It's worse than before – it's like walking into razor blades, and I'll tell you something else. When the wind gets up in those wires, it's just like voices. You listen long enough and honest to God, you start hearing your own name. You know what I reckon?'

'What?' I said.

'It's all the dead people they've scraped up. They're all cold and lonely out there.' And he winked at me as he said this, I suspect because his back was turned to David and David couldn't see.

'For Christ's sake,' David muttered darkly, and he went over to the other side of the hut and started rummaging around in the cupboards for mugs and tea-bags.

Mick was grinning happily now, but I wasn't exactly sure why. Lowering my voice so that David wouldn't hear me – he'd half-disappeared headfirst into one of the cupboards by now – I said, 'What's all that about?'

'Haven't you seen the noticeboard?' Mick said, and he pointed to the wall behind me. 'Take a look. We've found a right little Happy House to get ourselves snowed into. Desmond was reading all about it when I got here.'

'It's David,' corrected a muffled voice from somewhere inside the furniture and Mick said, unruffled:

'Of course it is.'

I picked up one of the candles and took it over to the wall where the space alongside some lockers had been papered with old newspaper clippings. There were a few yellowing Page Three girls, but the rest of them were news stories. Some had photographs, and the photographs were all of mangled wreckage. It took me a moment to realise that they were all motorway crashes, and that the stretch of motorway where they'd taken place was the one that ran by under three feet of snow right outside.

'This must be where the lads wait for a callout when there's something nasty,' Mick said from just behind me. He'd come around and was inspecting the collection over my shoulder. 'Some of the things they must have seen, eh? Rather them than me.'

Amen to that, I thought, although even in the dim and unsteady candlelight I found that I was browsing through the details in some of the pieces with the kind of detached fascination that I always seem to be able to manage when it's a question of someone else's misery. Entire families wiped out. A teenaged girl decapitated. Lorry drivers crushed when their cabs folded around them like stepped-upon Coke cans. An unwanted mistress – this one really got me looking twice – an unwanted mistress dumped, Jimmy Hoffa-style, into the wire skeleton of a bridge piling that had been boxed-up ready to take concrete the next morning. ENTOMBED ALIVE! the headline said, but even that looked kind of pale next to the disaster involving the old folks' outing and the petfood truck full of offal.

I gathered from the collection that this hut was the base for the clean-up team who worked the road for some distance in either direction, and that they took an honest pride in their gruesome occupation; I imagined them trooping out to their breakdown wagon, whistling as they pulled on their jackets and thinking about next year's holidays. And then, at the other end of the drive, getting out with their bags and shovels to give their professional attention to the loved ones of some cheapskate who'd saved the cost of a cabin on the car ferry or skipped a night in a hotel to drive on through and get an extra half-day out of the holiday flat. Where the team would be right now, I could only guess; I imagined that they'd have moved their base along to the service area as soon as the weather had started to clamp down, because the hut was no place to be marooned out of choice. The services would probably be starting to resemble a refugee centre by now, cut off but reasonably self-sufficient, and I wished that I could be there instead of here. The gas ring behind us was running with the valve wide-open, and still I could see my breath in the air in front of me.

David, over by the table, said, 'Did you fill this?'

I tore myself away from the interesting stuff on the wall and followed Mick over to the ring, where David was peering into the aluminium pan. Where before it had been so overfilled with snow that it had looked like a big tub of ice cream, now it held about an inch of water.

Mick observed, 'It melts down to nothing, doesn't it?' And then the silence that followed was like the slow race in a restaurant to reach for the bill.

But then, finally, I said, 'I'll get us some more.'

I don't know how to describe the way the cold hit me as I stepped out of the hut. It was almost like walking into a wall, much worse than it had been when I'd made my way up there. The wind was the most disorienting factor, filling my eyes with hail and battering me around so hard that I could barely draw breath; but then, thankfully, it dropped a little, and the air cleared enough for me to see without being blinded.

Visibility was somewhere between fifty and a hundred yards, beyond which everything just greyed-out as if reality couldn't hold together any further. I could see about half a dozen of the overhead sodium lights marching off in either direction, their illumination blanketed and diffused by the amount of snow clouding the air; of the motorway itself I could make out the parallel lines of the crash barriers as hardly more than pencilmarks sketched onto the snow, and that was it. A few of the lightweight plastic cones that had been used earlier to close off lanes had been blown around and had lodged themselves here and there like erratic missiles, but nothing else broke the even cover.

I didn't see what Mick had been talking about. I didn't hear any voices, just the wind in the wires somewhere off the road and out of sight. The sound meant nothing special to me.

I had a baked bean can, catering size and the only other clean-looking container that I'd been able to find. I stooped and tried to fill it with snow. The newly-fallen stuff was too fine, it just streamed away as I tried to load it in, but then I tried wedging it into snowball nuggets and did rather better.

I was already starting to shake with the cold. I paused for a moment to wipe at my nose with the back of my glove, and realised with a kind of awe that I couldn't even feel the contact.

I fell back into the hut like a drowning man plucked from an icy sea. I'd been outside for less than a minute.

David looked up from the phone. I wouldn't have believed how welcoming the place could look with its candlelight and comparative warmth and the road gang's mugs set out ready, each with the name of an absent person written on the side in what looked like nail varnish. I did my best to make it look as if I had a grip on myself, and went over to set the rest of the snow to melt as Mick secured the door behind me.

'Still dead?' I said to David, with a nod at the phone.

'It's not exactly dead,' he said, jiggling the cradle for about the hundredth time. 'It's more like an open line with nothing on the other end.'

'It'll be like a field telephone,' Mick said from over by the door. 'If nobody's plugged in, then there's no one to hear. How's it looking outside?'

'I'd still rather be in here than out there,' I said.

Mick made the tea with a catering bag and some of that non-dairy whitener that looks and smells like paint. It was the worst I'd ever tasted, and the most welcome. The three of us pulled our chairs in close to get into the circle of warmth around the gas ring, and we grew heady on the monoxide fumes. Inevitably, the conversation returned to the clippings on the wall.

'You want to see it from their point of view,' Mick said. 'It'll be like working in a morgue. You get bad dreams for the first few weeks and then after that, it's just another job.'

'How would *you* know?' David said.

'I've got a brother-in-law who's a nurse, he's just about seen it all. I mean, the likes of me and you, we don't know the half of what it's about.'

David didn't comment, but I suspect that by then he was starting to read something personal into everything that Mick was saying. I believed that I'd recognised his type by now. Some people's reaction to pressure is to look around for someone convenient to dump on; they get angry, they get sarcastic, and if you pull through it tends to be in spite of them, rather than with much in the way of help. I knew what Mick was talking about. I could imagine the team sitting there, patiently reading or playing cards while waiting for carnage. They were one up on us . . . we'd go through life telling ourselves that it was never going to happen, but they knew that it was and the knowledge wasn't even anything special to them.

Mick seemed to be the one who was holding us together, here. I'm not sure that right then I'd have wanted to rely on David for anything. He was frowning at the floor, his borrowed donkey jacket sitting uneasily on his shoulders. Had he really struggled from his car to the cabin with just a suit jacket and no overcoat? He must have seen the way that the weather was going before he set out, but he didn't look as if he'd taken any account of the possibility that he might have to step much beyond the warmth of a heated building or a moving car. Some people have too much faith in everything. I'm the opposite – I reckon that God intended few things to be immutable and that such things as designer luggage, golf shoes and the new shape of Volvo aren't among them.

I'd been heading for my girlfriend's place over in the next county when I'd come to my own unscheduled journey's end. She was with a big retail chain who were moving her around and paying her peanuts and I was just about holding down one of those jobs that they kept telling me might or might not turn out to be something permanent The only way that we could ever get together was at weekends, hiding out from the landlady in her one-roomed flat. Mine must have been one of the last cars to get on to the road before they'd closed it. I'd had to stop as a jack-knifed articulated lorry had been cleared from the sliproad, and then it took two policemen to get me rolling again because my tyres wouldn't grip on the icy surface. They advised me to stay in low gear and to keep my revs down, and I remembered their last words to me as I managed to get moving again – *Rather you than me, pal.* It got worse as I went on. After half an hour in first gear, following the crash barrier like a blind man following a rail, the temperature needle crept up into the red zone and then finally both hoses blew. I stopped and taped them and topped up the water, but the engine seized soon after that.

Mick was the only one who seemed to be listening as I told them the story. He said, 'I've been driving this route since they opened it. I've never known it this bad. It looks like the end of the world.'

'You've got the knack of seeing the bright side, Mick,' I told him.

'You won't have seen that road train about half a mile on,' he said. 'A big new wagon and two trailers. It was blocking the road all the way across, that's why I had to give up and walk back to the last light I'd seen. Those things are like dinosaurs, they'll go on through anything. But it couldn't get through this. What do you reckon, Desmond?'

'It's *David*! David!' His sudden shout was startling in the enclosed space of the cabin, and I think even Mick was surprised by the reaction he got.

'All right,' he said. 'I'm sorry.'

'Well, bloody get it right, then!'

'I said I'm sorry. I was only asking what you thought.'

'I just want to get home,' David said miserably, looking down at the floor as if he was embarrassed by his sudden outburst.

And then Mick said, with unexpected gentleness, 'Nothing to argue with there, Dave.'

It was then that the gas ring began to make a popping sound. We all turned to look and I heard somebody say *Oh, shit*, and then I realised that it had been me.

The flame didn't exactly go out, not right away, but it was obviously into some kind of terminal struggle. Mick reached under the table and heaved out the squat metal cylinder; when he raised it two-handed and gave it a shake, it sounded as if there was about a cupful of liquid sloshing around in the bottom.

'There's some left,' David said hopefully.

'You always get some in the bottom,' Mick said. 'Still means it's empty.'

There was another cylinder under the table and right at the back, but this one sounded just about the same. By now the ring was giving out no heat at all and making such a racket that nobody objected when Mick turned the valve to shut it off.

The silence got to us before the cold did. But the cold started getting to us a couple of minutes later.

We broke open the lockers in the hope of finding more coats or blankets, but all that we found were tools and empty lunch buckets and mud-encrusted work boots. David's earlier remark about burning the furniture no longer seemed like a joke, but the truth of it was that there wasn't much about the furniture that was combustible; the chairs were mostly tubular steel and the table was some kind of laminate over chipboard, which left a stack of soft-core porno magazines and a few paperbacks and one deck of cards. By now, the hut had turned from a haven into an ice-box.

David was the one who put it into words:

'We're going to have to go out and find somewhere else, aren't we?' He made it sound as if the place itself had done a number and betrayed us. 'This is great,' he said bitterly. 'This really puts the bloody tin lid on it.'

Possibly we could have stayed put, jogged on the spot a little, done our best to keep going in the sub-zero air until the worst of the weather receded and rescue came pushing through. But Mick was already going through the lockers for a second time, as if looking again for something that he'd already seen.

'The way I see it,' he said, 'there's only one thing we can do.'

'The services?' I hazarded.

'We'd never make it that far. It's more than two miles and it might as well be twenty. I reckon we can do maybe a quarter of that, at the most.'

'Which gets us nowhere,' David said.

'It gets us as far as that big road train that's blocking the carriageway.' So saying, Mick reached into the third locker and came out with a short, hooked wrecking bar. Holding up the jemmy he went on, 'If we can get into that and get its engine running, we can sit tight in the cab with the heater on.'

'Until the fuel runs out,' I said, probably a touch too pessimistically.

'Those things never run out. They've got tanks like swimming pools. We can either wait for the snowplough to find us or else strike out again as the weather improves. What do you think?'

'It'll have a radio,' David said, with a sense of discovery that seemed to surprise even him.

We both looked at him.

'A CB radio,' he said. 'Don't most of these big trucks carry them? We can tell someone where we are.'

'That we can, Dave,' Mick said with a note of approval, and then he looked from him to me. 'Are you game?'

'Let's go,' I said, sounding about four hundred per cent more eager than I felt. But Mick raised a warning hand.

'Just wait on a minute,' he said. 'There's no point in all of us scrambling out together. What I reckon is, one of us strikes out and does the necessary, and then he leans on the horn as a signal for the others to follow.'

'I wouldn't know what to do,' David said bleakly.

'Me neither,' I said.

'Well,' Mick said, 'since we're talking about breaking and entering and a little creative rewiring, I'd say that I'm the only one with the education in the appropriate subjects around here. Am I right?'

He was right, and as far as I was concerned he could make all the jibes about education that he wanted as long as he got us out of this. He turned up his collar and buttoned up his coat, and he pulled on his sheepskin gloves as I moved with him to the door. David decided to give the phone yet another try as I made ready to let Mick out into the unwelcoming night.

I said, 'You're mad, you know that?'

'I had my brain surgically removed,' Mick said. 'I've been feeling much better without it.' Then he turned serious. 'I'm going to get down to the crash barrier and follow it along, otherwise there's no knowing where I may end up. Keep listening for the horn.' He glanced at David. 'And keep an eye on him.'

'He'll be all right.'

'If he starts messing about, dump him. I mean it.'

There was a blast of cold air for the brief second or so between Mick going out and me getting the door closed after him, and this time it stayed in there with us like some unwelcome dog that had dashed in and was standing its ground. David had slammed the phone down with a curse, as if its non-cooperation was a matter of deliberate choice, before settling on one of the chairs with his hands thrust deep into the pockets of his borrowed coat and the collar up over his nose to recirculate the heat of his breath. He looked like some odd kind of animal retreating into its blue worsted shell.

'I heard what he said, you know.' David's voice was muffled by the thick material, and sounded distant.

'He didn't mean anything by it.'

'Yeah, I bet. And who does he think *he* is? Scott of the Antarctic?'

'I don't care if he thinks he's Scotty of the Starship Enterprise. If he gets us out of trouble he'll be okay by me.'

He settled in deeper. 'Well, don't go worrying about me. I'm no deadweight.'

'Never said I thought you were.'

There was silence for a while.

Then he said, 'Pretty serious, though, isn't it?'

Yes, I was thinking, it *was* pretty serious . . . but it could have been worse. Worse was being sliced in two at a combined speed of a hundred and fifty miles an hour, just because someone else chose the day of your trip to cross the central reservation and come looking for suicide in the oncoming traffic. Worse was being buried alive in concrete, so deep that even X-rays couldn't find you. It was sitting with your hands on the wheel while your head lay on the back seat. It was any one of the fifty or so examples of a messy and uncontrolled exit to be found in the road gang's private black museum over there on the wall.

'We've still got options,' I said. 'That puts us one step ahead.'

'As long as he makes it,' David said.

The next twenty or thirty minutes seemed to last forever. David wasn't great company, particularly after the way that Mick's parting words had stung him. I wondered what I ought to expect; more of the ball-and-chain act, or would he become dangerously gung-ho? If the latter, then I was going to be happy to let him go out first.

Finally, the wind dropped a little and we heard the distant

sound of a horn.

I said, with some relief, 'Our call, I think.'

David said that he was ready. I asked him if he wanted to take one last shot at the phone, but he said no.

'The greaseball was right in one thing,' he said. 'You listen for long enough, and you *do* start to hear them calling your name.'

I let him go out ahead of me.

My spirit of optimism took an instant hammering as the door was banging shut behind us; compared to this brutal storm, the wind that had set the wires keening on my last excursion had been a precise and delicate instrument. All sound and sense was destroyed on contact, and I was beginning to panic when I felt David's rough grip on my arm, shoving me forward into the blind haze. The snow had drifted high in places, masking the contours of the ground beneath and making progress even more difficult; we stumbled and floundered downhill towards the road surface, and as we descended from the more exposed slopes the wind mercifully lessened. We got across to the central crash barrier, a constant mist of snow streaming from its knife-edged top, but by then I'd become as disoriented as if I'd been popped into a box and shaken.

'*Which way*?' I shouted, and David had to put his face right up to my ear to make himself heard.

'*Northbound!*' he roared.

'*What?*'

'*This way!*' And he gave me a hard push to get me moving.

I wouldn't have believed how heavy the going could be. It went from thigh-deep to waist-deep and then back to thigh deep again, and the barrier disappeared for entire stretches so that we had to navigate by the yellow sodium lights above us. I'd break the trail for a while, and then David would move up and replace me. Any tracks that Mick might have left had been obliterated, but then there was the sound of the distant horn to lead us on whenever the storm took out a beat to let it through.

He'd made it. So would I.

I reckoned that we'd been going for about three hours, although a more rational part of my mind knew that it had actually been closer to fifteen minutes, when we reached the first place where we could stop and rest. It was a flyover bridge, too high and too wide to feel like much of a shelter but offering a respite from the cutting edge of the wind. We staggered in so all-over numb that we might as well have been on Novocaine drips for the last quarter of an hour, and we collapsed against the wall like footsoldiers in some forgotten war.

'Are you okay?' I said to David, my voice oddly flattened by the carpet of snow that had blown in under the bridge.

'You must be bloody joking,' he gasped, and that was all I could get out of him.

I tried to knock off some of the dry snow that had crusted onto my clothing. I didn't want to risk any of it melting and soaking through only to refreeze as we pushed on. It came off in chunks. David was hunkered down and hugging himself, presenting as small an area for heat loss as he could. If we stayed here for too long, we might end up staying here for good.

I listened for the horn.

Even though the bridge was open at the sides there was an enclosed, somehow isolated feeling about that few yards of shelter. It was brighter here than outside because there was nothing clouding the air between the sodium lights and the reflecting snow and, as I'd already noticed when I'd spoken to David, sounds went dead as if they'd run into something soft. There was scaffolding around the bridge support across the carriageway, but I could still make out the spraycanned graffiti in amongst the repair work behind it as if through a grid; it read ROBSON YOUR DEAD WHEN YOU GET OUT, and it had been written in red.

The wind outside must have dropped a little because a
snatch of the horn came through, and it sounded closer than
ever. It acted on David like a goad. He suddenly lurched to
his feet and set out again, stumbling and flailing his arms as
if he hadn't quite brought his limbs under control yet.
Wearily, I wondered if I'd ever be able to raise the energy to
follow; but even as I was wondering, I was starting to move.
David was muttering as he went, but I couldn't hear anything of what he was saying.

I stumbled, because there seemed to be all kinds of
jumbled crap under the snow here; my foot hooked up what
looked like a length of compressor hose, and I had to kick it
off. Over on what would normally be the hard shoulder I
could see the half-buried shapes of machinery, big genera-
tors with tow-hitches and a small dumper that might have
been the answer to our prayers if it hadn't been jacked up
with a wheel missing. It looked as if, until the bad weather
had intervened, they'd been drilling out the concrete like a
bad tooth. Canvas on the scaffolding had concealed the
work, but the material had been ripped by a through-wind to
leave only a few flapping shreds around the hole. The cage
of reinforcing wire inside the piling had been exposed, and
the wire had been burst outward as if by a silent explosion. It
looked as if they'd gone so far, and then the freeze-up had
enlarged the hole further.

I suppose I could have thought about it harder. But there
are some things, you can think about them as hard as you
like but you'll never anticipate what you're actually going to
see.

And the sight that I was concentrating on, to the exclusion
of just about everything else, was that of the road train firm-
ing-up in the blizzard about a hundred yards ahead.

The first details that I made out were its hazard lights, and
there were plenty of them; almost enough to define its

shape, rather like those diagrams that take a scattered handful of stars and connect them up into some improbable-looking constellation. They were flashing on and off in time with the horn, and they were about the most welcome warning that I'd ever seen. Ahead of me, David was striding out like a wind-up toy that nothing could stop.

It was a big Continental articulated rig in three jack-knifed sections, a true monster of the road that would look like a landslide on the move. The distant *parp-parp* that had led us so far had now become a deep, regular airhorn bellow as we'd drawn closer. David tried to break into a run for the cab, but he had to be close to exhaustion by now.

We helped each other up and in. An alarm beeper was sounding off inside the cab and in synchronisation with the horn and the lights. There was no sign of Mick anywhere.

I said, 'Where is he?'

'God knows,' David said, studying a dash that looked like a piece of the space shuttle. 'He might at least have left the engine running.'

'Maybe he didn't get that far.'

But David pointed to a bunch of wires that had been pulled out to hang behind the steering column. 'What's that, then?' he said. 'Heinz spaghetti? You check the radio.'

I checked the radio.

'I don't think it's working,' I said.

Sixty seconds after our entry, the alarms cut and the horn stopped. The silence almost hurt.

David had found the starter by now, and he was trying it; the first couple of times it stayed dead, but he jiggled the hanging wires like a child patting a balloon into the air and this must have helped some weak connection, because on the third attempt the engine somewhere beneath the cab floor turned over without any hesitation at all. After a few seconds, it caught; but then, almost immediately, it faded away and died again.

'Bastard thing,' David said, and tried again; but there was no persuading it to catch for a second time.

He flopped back heavily in the driver's seat. I said, 'Maybe we can just stay here anyway.'

'There's still no heat,' he said. 'It may seem warmer, but that's just the comparison with being outside. If we can't get the blowers going, I don't see any advantage over being back in the hut.'

He tried the starter again, but still nothing.

'There's your reason why,' he said suddenly, and pointed to a part of the dashboard display. If what he was pointing to was the fuel level readout, it was reading something like empty.

'These things never run out,' he said bitterly, in what I assume he intended to be mimicry of Mick's voice. 'They've got tanks like swimming pools.' And he punched the steering wheel hard, and flopped back in the driver's seat again with a face as dark as a bruised plum.

And somewhere out in the night, another horn began to sound.

We both listened, lost it for a while as the wind howled, and then heard it again. Our signal was being repeated from somewhere further along the road.

'Here we go,' David said wearily, and he opened the door on the far side of the cab to climb down. This time he didn't even flinch when the hail hit him. *All right*, I wanted to say, *case proven, you're no deadweight, now why don't we just try sticking it out here a while longer*, but instead I levered myself up and clambered awkwardly across the cab. I could have dropped and slept, right there. And probably died, ready-chilled and prepared for the morgue, but at that moment I hardly felt as if it would matter.

Mick's sheepskin gloves were on the cab floor.

I reached down and picked them up. I wasn't hallucinating them, they were real enough. He must have taken them off for the delicate work of hotwiring . . . but how come he'd allowed himself to be parted from them? I was wearing my clumsy ski gloves, and even inside these my hands were feeling dead from the knuckles out. If Mick had gone the distance to the next stranded lorry, as the sounding of this second horn seemed to suggest, then I reckoned that he'd better not be planning any piano practice for a while.

I slid out of the cab and hit the snow again. I was now on the northern side of the big vehicle. David had launched off without me, hooked by the call like some deep-sea fish being drawn up to the gaff. The horn wasn't so regular this time, but it was coming through more clearly.

And me, I wasn't happy.

The forgotten gloves were only one part of it. Another part of it was the fact that you didn't put a rig and its cargo, total value anything from a quarter of a million up, into the hands of a driver who's going to be walking the hard shoulder with a can to get some diesel because he let the tanks get empty. And the radio – the radio should have been working, even if only to give out white noise to match the scene on the other side of the glass.

I was looking around the side of the road train when I fell over Mick's body in the snow. He was lying face-down and already he was half-covered by drift, which for a moment gave me the absurd hope that he might have been insulated from the chilling effect of the wind and might be basically okay. But when I tried to turn him over he was as stiff as a wet sheet hung out in winter, and when I finally got him onto his back I could see that there was a spike of reinforcing wire from the concrete flyover driven right up under his chin. I could see it passing up through his open mouth as if his head were something spitted for a barbecue. His eyes were half-open, but plugged with ice. The short jemmy was still in his ungloved hand, held tightly like a defensive weapon that he'd never managed to use.

This had happened right by the big diesel tanks behind the cab. The tanks themselves had been slashed open so that all the oil had run out and gone straight down into the snow. And when I say slashed, I mean raked open in four parallel lines as if by fingernails, not just spiked or holed by something sharp.

David had stopped, and was looking back; but he was too far away to see anything and only just on the verge of being seen, a smudgy ghost painted in smoke. He beckoned me on with a big, broad gesture that looked like he was trying to hook something out of the air, and even though I yelled 'No! Don't go! It isn't him!' he simply shouted back something inaudible and turned away. He walked on, and the blizzard sucked him in.

And from somewhere beyond him came the sound of the horn, the mating call of some dark mistress of nightmares with her skin oiled and her back arched and her long silver knives at the ready.

I started to run after him.

I call it running, although it wasn't much in the way of progress. I reckon you could have lit up a small town with the energy that I burned just to close up the distance between David and me. Close it up I did, but not enough. He didn't even glance back. I saw him duck at a near-miss from something windborne and I felt my heart stop for a moment, but I think it was only one of the plastic cones or some other piece of road debris. David couldn't have been distracted by nuns dancing naked in the air by that stage, because he was now within sight of the next truck.

The truck.

It was much older than the first one, and not so much of a giant. It was over on the far side of the barrier and facing my way; it looked as if it had come to a long, sliding halt before being abandoned and half-buried where it stood. It had a crouched, malevolent look, its engine running and breathing steam, pale headlamps like sick-bed eyes. David reached the cab and pounded on the side to be let in, and I stopped at the crash barrier and could only watch.

The horn ceased. The door opened. The cab's interior light blinked on, but the insides of the windows were all steamed up and runny and there was only the vague shape of someone visible. David had already hoisted himself halfway up with his foot in the stirrup over the wheel, but now I saw him hesitate. The door had swung out and was screening whatever confronted him . . . and then suddenly he was gone, jerked in at an impossible speed, and the door was slammed and the light went out. I winced at the loud, long and intense muffled screaming that began to come from the cab, but I knew there was nothing that I could do. I thought about those long slashes in the diesel tank and, for David's sake, I could only hope that whatever was happening would be over quickly.

It wasn't.

And when it finally ended, and after the long silence that followed, I saw the door opening out a crack like a trap being reset. Light streamed out into the snow-mist, a narrow slice falling like a rain of something solid. I looked up at the truck's windows and saw that the now-lit windshield had been sprayed red on the inside like the jug of a blender, and it was just starting a slow wash-down as the cab sweat began to trickle through it. I watched a while longer, but I couldn't see anything moving.

I was calculating my chances of making it through to the service area. What had seemed like a complete impossibility before now had the look of the most attractive available option. I had to have covered a good part of the distance already, hadn't I? And having just had a glimpse of the alternative, I was suddenly finding that the prospect of pressing on had a certain appeal.

The first move would be to cross the carriageway and put

as much distance as possible between me and the truck. There was nothing that I could do for David now, and it made no sense to stay out where the overhead lights made a tunnel of day through the blizzard. It was as I was striking out at an angle across a field of white that had once been the fast lane, a stumbling and deep-frozen body with a white-hot core of fear, that the horn began again.

That was okay, that suited me fine. As long as somebody was leaning on the button then they weren't out here with me, and that was exactly the way that I wanted it. I was trying to remember the route from the times that I'd driven it before; my guess was that I was just about to come to an exposed and elevated curve that would swing out to overlook a reservoir before entering the hills where the service area would be sheltered. I wouldn't be able to see much, if any, of this, but I'd know it because the intensity of the wind was bound to increase; high-sided vehicles took a battering on this stretch at the best of times, and this certainly wasn't one of those. I'd have to watch my footing. On a clear night I'd have been able to see right out to the lights of some mill town several miles out and below, but for now all that I could see was a dense white swirling. In my mind I could see myself holding one of those Christmas-scene paperweights, the kind that you shake and then watch as the contents settle, but in mine there was a tiny figure of David hammering on the glass and calling soundlessly to be let out. I saw myself shaking the globe once, and I saw the storm turn pink.

Stupid, I know – I wasn't responsible for anybody, and I certainly hadn't got behind him and boosted him up into the arms of whatever had been waiting in the cab. But I suppose that when you've just seen somebody meet an end roughly comparable to the act of walking into an aircraft propeller, it's bound to overheat your imagination just a little. Maybe that could explain some of what came later.

But somehow, I don't think so.

The truck horn was starting to recede behind me. The notes were longer now, like the moan of some trapped beast tiring of its struggles. Great, fine, I was thinking, you just stay there and keep at it, when the storm brightened and a dark figure suddenly rose before me.

It was my own shadow, cast forward into the blizzard way out beyond the edge of the road so that it seemed to stand in the air over nothing. I looked back and saw that there was some kind of a spotlight being operated from the cab of the truck, the kind that turns on a mount fixed to the body and stays however you leave it. This one was pointing straight at me; it went on past, and I realised that I was too small and too far away to spot with any ease. And there was probably so much snow sticking to me on the windward side that I'd be tough to spot even at close range.

Any relief that I felt was short-lived, though, because just a few seconds later the spotlight picked up the line of my trail through the snowfield. The bright light and the low angle exaggerated it and left no room for any doubt. The light stopped roving, and the horn stopped sounding only a moment later.

There followed a silence that I didn't like, filled with unstated menace.

And then the cab door opened, and its occupant stepped down to the road.

I don't know what I'd been expecting. Anything but this. She was small, and slight. Her light summer dress was torn and soiled and her hair was lank and dusty and blowing across her face. Her arms were bare, but she seemed oblivious to the cold and the wind. She started out towards the point where my trail angled out across the road, and I knew that I ought to be turning and running but I couldn't come unglued. She was walking barefoot on the snow and leaving no mark; I saw her bend to touch the barrier as she stepped over, and it might have been a stile out in the countryside somewhere in the warmest part of the spring.

I finally turned to run. I got a brief impression of another of those plastic cones tumbling by in the wind, and then it bopped me as I walked right into it. I went down. I tried to struggle to get up but it was as if I'd had my wires pulled and crossed so that none of the messages were getting through in the right order.

I could hear her light tread over the wind as she approached.

She came up and stood right over me. Her skin was as white as marble, and veined with blue; I couldn't see her face for the halo of light from the cab spotlight behind her. All I could see was her ruined hair blowing around a pitiless darkness in which something was watching me.

Louie, she whispered.

Louie? I thought. Who the hell's Louie? Because listen, lady, it sure isn't me. I opened my mouth to say something similar and I think I made one tiny, almost inaudible croak. The wind dropped and the night grew still, and then her eyes turned on like blazing torches in the ravaged pit of her face as she bent down towards me, and I could feel their heat and the breath of corruption warming my frost-bitten skin. I could see now that her hair was matted with concrete, and that patches of it had been torn out. The exposed skin was like that of a plucked grouse that had been hanging in a cellar for far too long a time.

Louie, she said again, this time with a kind of nightmare tenderness, and she took hold of my dead-feeling face in her dead-looking hands and I realised with terror that she was raising me up for a kiss. I saw the darkness roaring in like an airshaft straight down to hell and I wanted to scream, but instead I think I just peed myself.

She stopped only inches away. She lowered me again. I think she'd just realised that I wasn't the one she was looking for.

Then she raised her hand and I saw the state of her fingers, and I knew how she'd caused the damage that she'd done to the diesel tank. I shut my eyes and I waited and I waited, and after I'd waited for what seemed like the entire running time of *Conan the Barbarian* I managed to unstick one eye and look up.

She was still there, but she wasn't looking at me. She seemed to be listening for something. I listened too, but all I could hear was wind in the wires overhead.

And then, only once and very faintly, the single blast of a horn.

Louie? she said. And she started to rise.

Most of what I know now is what I've learned since. Louis Robson was a construction services manager who drove a Mercedes, and she was a supermarket checkout trainee. How she ever believed that he'd desert his wife and run away with her will be one of those eternal mysteries like, why do old cars run better when they've been washed and waxed. But he must have made the promise one time and she must have replayed it over and over until finally, he told her to meet him one night with her bags packed and a goodbye letter ready to mail. The place where she was to wait was one of his company's site offices by the new motorway; he'd pull in outside and sound the all clear on the car's horn. Except that it was a signal that she would have to wait a long time to hear because when she got there, he was already waiting in the dark with a lug wrench. He dropped her unconscious body into a prepared mould for a bridge piling and threw her cardboard suitcase after, and then he put the sealed letter into the post without realising that it mentioned him by name. This was all five years before.

I don't know if it was just the signal, or whether there was room for anything beyond obsession in the dark, tangled worm-pit of what was left of her mind; but she lurched stiffly upright and then, like a dead ship drawn to some distant beacon, she set off in what she thought was the direction of the sound.

The blade of the snowplough hit her square-on as she stepped out into the road.

She wasn't thrown; it was more like she exploded under gas pressure from within, a release of the bottled-up forces of five years' worth of corruption. She went up like an eyeball in a vacuum chamber, and the entire blade and windshield of the plough were sprayed with something that stuck like tar and stank like ordure. Rags of foul hide were flung over a hundred-yard radius, showering down onto the snow with a soft pattering sound. The destruction was so complete that nothing would ever be pieced together to suggest anything remotely human. The plough had stopped and I could see men in orange Day-Glo overjackets climbing out, stunned and uncertain of what they'd seen, and I managed to get up to my knees and to wave my arms over my head.

'Anybody else with you?' they asked me when we were all inside and I was holding a thermos cup of coffee so hot that it could have blanched meat. 'No sign of anybody?'

I told them that I'd seen some kind of a bird fly into the blade, and it had all happened so fast that nobody had a better story to offer. They'd told me their names, and I'd recognised them from the tea mugs back in the hut that they'd been forced to abandon as a base for a while. I said that I hadn't seen anybody else. Then one of them asked me how long I'd been out there and I said, it seemed like forever.

'You know the police have jacked it in and closed the road for the night,' one of them said. 'We wouldn't have come out at all if it hadn't been for somebody hearing your horn solo one time when the wind dropped. You've got no idea how lucky you are.'

I raised my face out of the steam. We all swayed as the big chained wheels turned the snow into dirt beneath us as we swung around for the return journey, and somebody put a hand out to the seat in front to steady himself. They'd find Mick and David when the thaw set in, and I'd say that I didn't know a damn thing about either of them. And did I really have no idea of how lucky I was?

'No,' I said pleasantly. 'I don't expect I do.'

And I thought, *You really want to bet?*

THE MONKEY'S PAW

W. W. Jacobs

William Jacobs (1863–1943) resigned from his job as a clerk in the Civil Service after the success of his first collection of short stories, MANY CARGOES, in 1896. Although he also wrote novels – AT SUNWICH PORT (1902) and DIALSTONE LANE (1904) – it was principally his short stories which brought him fame. These also included humorous tales of sailors and country characters, as well as those of a more macabre nature.

I

Without, the night was cold and wet, but in the small parlour of Laburnum Villa the blinds were drawn and the fire burned brightly. Father and son were at chess; the former, who possessed ideas about the game involving radical changes, putting his king into such sharp and unnecessary perils that it even provoked comment from the white-haired old lady knitting placidly by the fire.

'Hark at the wind,' said Mr White, who, having seen a fatal mistake after it was too late, was amiably desirous of preventing his son from seeing it.

'I'm listening,' said the latter, grimly surveying the board as he stretched out his hand. 'Check.'

'I should hardly think that he'd come tonight,' said his father, with his hand poised over the board.

'Mate,' replied the son.

'That's the worst of living so far out,' bawled Mr White, with sudden and unlooked-for violence; 'of all the beastly, slushy, out-of-the-way places to live in, this is the worst. Path's a bog, and the road's a torrent. I don't know what people are thinking about. I suppose because only two

161

houses in the road are let, they think it doesn't matter.'

'Never mind, dear,' said his wife soothingly; 'perhaps you'll win the next one.'

Mr White looked up sharply, just in time to intercept a knowing glance between mother and son. The words died away on his lips, and he hid a guilty grin in his thin grey beard.

'There he is,' said Herbert White, as the gate banged to loudly and heavy footsteps came toward the door.

The old man rose with hospitable haste, and opening the door, was heard condoling with the new arrival. The new arrival also condoled with himself, so that Mrs White said, 'Tut, tut!' and coughed gently as her husband entered the room, followed by a tall, burly man, beady of eye and rubicund of visage.

'Sergeant-Major Morris,' he said, introducing him.

The sergeant-major shook hands, and taking the proffered seat by the fire, watched contentedly while his host got out whisky and tumblers and stood a small copper kettle on the fire.

At the third glass his eyes got brighter, and he began to talk, the little family circle regarding with eager interest this visitor from distant parts, as he squared his broad shoulders in the chair and spoke of wild scenes and doughty deeds; of wars and plagues and strange peoples.

'Twenty-one years of it,' said Mr White, nodding at his wife and son. 'When he went away he was a slip of a youth in the warehouse. Now look at him.'

'He don't look to have taken much harm,' said Mrs White politely.

'I'd like to go to India myself,' said the old man, 'just to look round a bit, you know.'

'Better where you are,' said the sergeant-major, shaking his head. He put down the empty glass, and sighing softly, shook it again.

'I should like to see those old temples and fakirs and jugglers,' said the old man. 'What was that you started telling me the other day about a monkey's paw or something, Morris?'

'Nothing,' said the soldier hastily. 'Leastways nothing worth hearing.'

'Monkey's paw?' said Mrs White curiously.

'Well, it's just a bit of what you might call magic, perhaps,' said the sergeant-major offhandedly.

His three listeners leaned forward eagerly. The visitor absent-mindedly put his empty glass to his lips and then set it down again. His host filled it for him.

'To look at,' said the sergeant-major, fumbling in his pocket, 'it's just an ordinary little paw, dried to a mummy.'

He took something out of his pocket and proffered it. Mrs White drew back with a grimace, but her son, taking it, examined it curiously.

'And what is there special about it?' inquired Mr White as he took it from his son, and having examined it, placed it upon the table.

'It had a spell put on it by an old fakir,' said the sergeant-major, 'a very holy man. He wanted to show that fate ruled people's lives, and that those who interfered with it did so to their sorrow. He put a spell on it so that three separate men could each have three wishes from it.'

His manner was so impressive that his hearers were conscious that their light laughter jarred somewhat.

'Well, why don't you have three, sir?' said Herbert White cleverly.

The soldier regarded him in the way that middle age is wont to regard presumptuous youth. 'I have,' he said quietly, and his blotchy face whitened.

'And did you really have the three wishes granted?' asked Mrs White.

'I did,' said the sergeant-major, and his glass tapped

against his strong teeth.

'And has anybody else wished?' persisted the old lady.

'The first man had his three wishes. Yes,' was the reply; 'I don't know what the first two were, but the third wish was for death. That's how I got the paw.'

His tones were so grave that a hush fell upon the group.

'If you've had your three wishes, it's no good to you now, then, Morris,' said the old man at last. 'What do you keep it for?'

The soldier shook his head. 'Fancy, I suppose,' he said slowly. 'I did have some idea of selling it, but I don't think I will. It has caused enough mischief already. Besides, people won't buy. They think it's a fairy tale, some of them; and those who do think anything of it want to try it first and pay me afterward.'

'If you could have another three wishes,' said the old man, eyeing him keenly, 'would you have them?'

'I don't know,' said the other. 'I don't know.'

He took the paw, and dangling it between his forefinger and thumb, suddenly threw it upon the fire. White, with a slight cry, stooped down and snatched it off.

'Better let it burn,' said the soldier solemnly.

'If you don't want it, Morris,' said the other, 'give it to me.'

'I won't,' said his friend doggedly. 'I threw it on the fire. If you keep it, don't blame me for what happens. Pitch it on the fire again like a sensible man.'

The other shook his head and examined his new possession closely. 'How do you do it?' he inquired.

'Hold it up in your right hand and wish aloud,' said the sergeant-major, 'but I warn you of the consequences.'

'Sounds like the *Arabian Nights*,' said Mrs White, as she rose and began to set the supper. 'Don't you think you might wish for four pairs of hands for me?'

Her husband drew the talisman from his pocket, and then all three burst into laughter as the sergeant-major, with a look of alarm on his face, caught him by the arm.

'If you must wish,' he said gruffly, 'wish for something sensible.'

Mr White dropped it back in his pocket, and placing chairs, motioned his friend to the table. In the business of supper the talisman was partly forgotten, and afterward the three sat listening in an enthralled fashion to a second instalment of the soldier's adventures in India.

'If the tale about the monkey's paw is not more truthful than those he has been telling us,' said Herbert, as the door closed behind their guest, just in time to catch the last train, 'we shan't make much out of it.'

'Did you give him anything for it, Father?' inquired Mrs White, regarding her husband closely.

'A trifle,' said he, colouring slightly. 'He didn't want it, but I made him take it. And he pressed me again to throw it away.'

'Likely,' said Herbert, with pretended horror. 'Why, we're going to be rich, and famous, and happy. Wish to be an emperor, father, to begin with; then you can't be henpecked.'

He darted round the table, pursued by the maligned Mrs White armed with an antimacassar.

Mr White took the paw from his pocket and eyed it dubiously. 'I don't know what to wish for, and that's a fact,' he said slowly. 'It seems to me I've got all I want.'

'If you only cleared the house, you'd be quite happy, wouldn't you!' said Herbert, with his hand on his shoulder. 'Well, wish for two hundred pounds, then; that'll just do it.'

His father, smiling shamefacedly at his own credulity, held up the talisman, as his son, with a solemn face, somewhat marred by a wink at his mother, sat down at the piano and struck a few impressive chords.

'I wish for two hundred pounds,' said the old man distinctly.

A fine crash from the piano greeted the words, interrupted

by a shuddering cry from the old man. His wife and son ran toward him.

'It moved,' he cried, with a glance of disgust at the object as it lay on the floor. 'As I wished, it twisted in my hand like a snake.'

'Well, I don't see the money,' said his son, as he picked it up and placed it on the table, 'and I bet I never shall.'

'It must have been your fancy, Father,' said his wife, regarding him anxiously.

He shook his head. 'Never mind, though; there's no harm done, but it gave me a shock all the same.'

They sat down by the fire again while the two men finished their pipes. Outside, the wind was higher than ever, and the old man started nervously at the sound of a door banging upstairs. A silence unusual and depressing settled upon all three, which lasted until the old couple rose to retire for the night.

'I expect you'll find the cash tied up in a big bag in the middle of your bed,' said Herbert, as he bade them good night, 'and something horrible squatting up on top of the wardrobe watching you as you pocket your ill-gotten gains.'

He sat alone in the darkness, gazing at the dying fire, and seeing faces in it. The last face was so horrible and so simian that he gazed at it in amazement. It got so vivid that, with a little uneasy laugh, he felt on the table for a glass containing a little water to throw over it. His hand grasped the monkey's paw, and with a little shiver he wiped his hand on his coat and went up to bed.

II

In the brightness of the wintry sun next morning as it streamed over the breakfast table he laughed at his fears. There was an air of prosaic wholesomeness about the room which it had lacked on the previous night, and the dirty, shrivelled little paw was pitched on the sideboard with a carelessness which betokened no great belief in its virtues.

'I suppose all old soldiers are the same,' said Mrs White. 'The idea of our listening to such nonsense! How could wishes be granted in these days? And if they could, how could two hundred pounds hurt you, Father?'

'Might drop on his head from the sky,' said the frivolous Herbert.

'Morris said the things happened so naturally,' said his father, 'that you might if you so wished attribute it to coincidence.'

'Well, don't break into the money before I come back,' said Herbert as he rose from the table. 'I'm afraid it'll turn you into a mean, avaricious man, and we shall have to disown you.'

His mother laughed, and following him to the door, watched him down the road; and returning to the breakfast table, was very happy at the expense of her husband's credulity. All of which did not prevent her from scurrying to the door at the postman's knock, nor prevent her from referring somewhat shortly to retired sergeant-majors of bibulous habits when she found that the post brought a tailor's bill.

'Herbert will have some more of his funny remarks, I expect, when he comes home,' she said, as they sat at dinner.

'I dare say,' said Mr White, pouring himself out some beer; 'but for all that, the thing moved in my hand; that I'll swear to.'

'You thought it did,' said the old lady soothingly.

'I say it did,' replied the other. 'There was no thought about it; I had just – What's the matter?'

His wife made no reply. She was watching the mysterious movements of a man outside, who, peering in an undecided fashion at the house, appeared to be trying to make up his mind to enter. In mental connexion with the two hundred pounds, she noticed that the stranger was well dressed, and wore a silk hat of glossy newness. Three times he paused at the gate, and then walked on again. The fourth time he stood with his hand upon it, and then with sudden resolution flung it open and walked up the path. Mrs White at the same moment placed her hands behind her, and hurriedly unfastening the strings of her apron, put that useful article of apparel beneath the cushion of her chair.

She brought the stranger, who seemed ill at ease, into the room. He gazed at her furtively, and listened in a preoccupied fashion as the old lady apologised for the appearance of the room, and her husband's coat, a garment which he usually reserved for the garden. She then waited as patiently as her sex would permit, for him to broach his business, but he was at first strangely silent.

'I – was asked to call,' he said at last, and stooped and picked a piece of cotton from his trousers. 'I come from Maw and Meggins.'

The old lady started. 'Is anything the matter?' she asked breathlessly. 'Has anything happened to Herbert? What is it? What is it?'

Her husband interposed. 'There, there, Mother,' he said hastily. 'Sit down, and don't jump to conclusions. You've not brought bad news, I'm sure, sir;' and he eyed the other wistfully.

'I'm sorry –' began the visitor.

'Is he hurt?' demanded the mother wildly.

The visitor bowed in assent. 'Badly hurt,' he said quietly, 'but he is not in any pain.'

'Oh, thank God!' said the old woman, clasping her hands. 'Thank God for that! Thank –'

She broke off suddenly as the sinister meaning of the assurance dawned upon her and she saw the awful confirmation of her fears in the other's averted face. She caught her breath, and turning to her slower-witted husband, laid her trembling old hand upon his. There was a long silence.

'He was caught in the machinery,' said the visitor at length in a low voice.

'Caught in the machinery,' repeated Mr White, in a dazed fashion, 'yes.'

He sat staring blankly out at the window, and taking his wife's hand between his own, pressed it as he had been wont to do in their old courting days nearly forty years before.

'He was the only one left to us,' he said, turning gently to the visitor. 'It is hard.'

The other coughed, and rising, walked slowly to the window. 'The firm wished me to convey their sincere sympathy with you in your great loss,' he said, without looking round. 'I beg that you will understand I am only their servant and merely obeying orders.'

There was no reply; the old woman's face was white, her eyes staring and her breath inaudible; on the husband's face was a look such as his friend the sergeant might have carried into his first action.

'I was to say that Maw and Meggins disclaim all responsibility,' continued the other. 'They admit no liability at all, but in consideration of your son's services, they wish to present you with a certain sum as compensation.'

Mr White dropped his wife's hand, and rising to his feet, gazed with a look of horror at his visitor. His dry lips shaped the words, 'How much?'

'Two hundred pounds,' was the answer.

Unconscious of his wife's shriek, the old man smiled faintly, put out his hands like a sightless man, and dropped, a senseless heap, to the floor.

III

In the huge new cemetery, some two miles distant, the old people buried their dead, and came back to the house steeped in shadow and silence. It was all over so quickly that at first they could hardly realise it, and remained in a state of expectation as though of something else to happen – something else which was to lighten this load, too heavy for old hearts to bear.

But the days passed, and expectation gave place to resignation – the hopeless resignation of the old, sometimes miscalled apathy. Sometimes they hardly exchanged a word, for now they had nothing to talk about, and their days were long to weariness.

It was about a week after that the old man, waking suddenly in the night, stretched out his hand and found himself alone. The room was in darkness, and the sound of subdued weeping came from the window. He raised himself in bed and listened.

'Come back,' he said tenderly. 'You will be cold.'

'It is colder for my son,' said the old woman, and wept afresh.

The sound of her sobs died away on his ears. The bed was warm, and his eyes heavy with sleep. He dozed fitfully, and then slept until a sudden wild cry from his wife awoke him with a start.

'*The paw!*' she cried wildly. 'The monkey's paw!'

He started up in alarm. 'Where? Where is it? What's the matter?'

She came stumbling across the room toward him. 'I want it,' she said quietly. 'You've not destroyed it?'

'It's in the parlour, on the bracket,' he replied, marvelling. 'Why?'

She cried and laughed together, and bending over, kissed his cheek.

'I only just thought of it,' she said hysterically. 'Why didn't I think of it before? Why didn't *you* think of it?'

'Think of what?' he questioned.

'The other two wishes,' she replied rapidly. 'We've only had one.'

'Was not that enough?' he demanded fiercely.

'No,' she cried triumphantly; 'we'll have one more. Go down and get it quickly, and wish our boy alive again.'

The man sat up in bed and flung the bedclothes from his quaking limbs. 'Good God, you are mad!' he cried, aghast.

'Get it,' she panted; 'get it quickly, and wish – Oh, my boy, my boy!'

Her husband struck a match and lit the candle. 'Get back to bed,' he said unsteadily. 'You don't know what you are saying.'

'We had the first wish granted,' said the old woman feverishly; 'why not the second?'

'A coincidence,' stammered the old man.

'Go and get it and wish,' cried his wife, quivering with excitement.

The old man turned and regarded her, and his voice shook. 'He has been dead ten days, and besides he – I would not tell you else, but – I could only recognise him by his clothing. If he was too terrible for you to see then, how now?'

'Bring him back,' cried the old woman, and dragged him toward the door. 'Do you think I fear the child I have nursed?'

He went down in the darkness, and felt his way to the parlour, and then to the mantelpiece. The talisman was in its place, and a horrible fear that the unspoken wish might bring his mutilated son before him ere he could escape from the room seized upon him, and he caught his breath as he found that he had lost the direction of the door. His brow cold with sweat, he felt his way round the table, and groped along the walls until he found himself in the small passage with the unwholesome thing in his hand.

Even his wife's face seemed changed as he entered the room. It was white and expectant, and to his fears seemed to have an unnatural look upon it. He was afraid of her.

'*Wish!*' she cried, in a strong voice.

'It is foolish and wicked,' he faltered.

'*Wish!*' repeated his wife.

He raised his hand. 'I wish my son alive again.'

The talisman fell to the floor, and he regarded it fearfully. Then he sank trembling into a chair as the old woman, with burning eyes, walked to the window and raised the blind.

He sat until he was chilled with the cold, glancing occasionally at the figure of the old woman peering through the window. The candle-end, which had burned below the rim of the china candlestick, was throwing pulsating shadows on the ceiling and walls, until, with a flicker larger than the rest, it expired. The old man, with an unspeakable sense of relief at the failure of the talisman, crept back to his bed, and a minute or two afterward the old woman came silently and apathetically beside him.

Neither spoke, but lay silently listening to the ticking of the clock. A stair creaked, and a squeaky mouse scurried noisily through the wall. The darkness was oppressive, and after lying for some time screwing up his courage, he took the box of matches, and striking one, went downstairs for a candle.

At the foot of the stairs the match went out, and he paused to strike another; and at the same moment a knock, so quiet and stealthy as to be scarcely audible, sounded on the front door.

The matches fell from his hand and spilled in the passage. He stood motionless, his breath suspended until the knock was repeated. Then he turned and fled swiftly back to his room, and closed the door behind him. A third knock sounded through the house.

'*What's that?*' cried the old woman, starting up.

'A rat,' said the old man in shaking tones '– a rat. It passed me on the stairs.'

His wife sat up in bed listening. A loud knock resounded

through the house.

'It's Herbert!' she screamed. 'It's Herbert!'

She ran to the door, but her husband was before her, and catching her by the arm, held her tightly.

'What are you going to do?' he whispered hoarsely.

'It's my boy; it's Herbert!' she cried, struggling mechanically. 'I forgot it was two miles away. What are you holding me for? Let go. I must open the door.'

'For God's sake don't let it in,' cried the old man, trembling.

'You're afraid of your own son,' she cried, struggling. 'Let me go. I'm coming, Herbert; I'm coming.'

There was another knock, and another. The old woman with a sudden wrench broke free and ran from the room. Her husband followed to the landing, and called after her appealingly as she hurried downstairs. He heard the chain rattle back and the bottom bolt drawn slowly and stiffly from the socket. Then the old woman's voice, strained and panting.

'The bolt,' she cried loudly. 'Come down. I can't reach it.'

But her husband was on his hands and knees groping wildly on the floor in search of the paw. If he could only find it before the thing outside got in. A perfect fusillade of knocks reverberated through the house, and he heard the scraping of a chair as his wife put it down in the passage against the door. He heard the creaking of the bolt as it came slowly back, and at the same moment he found the monkey's paw, and frantically breathed his third and last wish.

The knocking ceased suddenly, although the echoes of it were still in the house. He heard the chair drawn back, and the door opened. A cold wind rushed up the staircase, and a long loud wail of disappointment and misery from his wife gave him courage to run down to her side, and then to the gate beyond. The street lamp flickering opposite shone on a quiet and deserted road.

WILLIAM AND MARY

Roald Dahl

Born in 1916, Roald Dahl began writing in 1942. Among his bestsellers are, SOMEONE LIKE YOU, SWITCH BITCH, TALES OF THE UNEXPECTED, and his highly praised novel, MY UNCLE OSWALD. Now in his seventies, he continues to dominate the children's bestseller list with such favourites as JAMES AND THE GIANT PEACH, CHARLIE AND THE CHOCOLATE FACTORY and THE WITCHES. Many of his short stories have been translated into other languages and have received world-wide acclaim.

William Pearl did not leave a great deal of money when he died, and his will was a simple one. With the exception of a few small bequests to relatives, he left all his property to his wife.

The solicitor and Mrs Pearl went over it together in the solicitor's office, and when the business was completed, the widow got up to leave. At that point, the solicitor took a sealed envelope from the folder on his desk and held it out to his client.

'I have been instructed to give you this,' he said. 'Your husband sent it to us shortly before he passed away.' The solicitor was pale and prim, and out of respect for a widow he kept his head on one side as he spoke, looking downward. 'It appears that it might be something personal, Mrs Pearl. No doubt you'd like to take it home with you and read it in privacy.'

Mrs Pearl accepted the envelope and went out into the street. She paused on the pavement, feeling the thing with her fingers. A letter of farewell from William? Probably, yes. A formal letter. It was bound to be formal – stiff and formal. The man was incapable of acting otherwise. He had never

174

done anything informal in his life.

> *My dear Mary, I trust that you will not permit my departure from this world to upset you too much, but that you will continue to observe those precepts which have guided you so well during our partnership together. Be diligent and dignified in all things. Be thrifty with your money. Be very careful that you do not . . . et cetera, et cetera.*

A typical William letter.

Or was it possible that he might have broken down at the last moment and written her something beautiful? Maybe this was a beautiful tender message, a sort of love letter, a lovely warm note of thanks to her for giving him thirty years of her life and for ironing a million shirts and cooking a million meals and making a million beds, something that she could read over and over again, once a day at least, and she would keep it for ever in the box on her dressing-table together with her brooches.

There is no knowing what people will do when they are about to die, Mrs Pearl told herself, and she tucked the envelope under her arm and hurried home.

She let herself in the front door and went straight to the living-room and sat down on the sofa without removing her hat or coat. Then she opened the envelope and drew out the contents. These consisted, she saw, of some fifteen or twenty sheets of lined white paper, folded over once and held together at the top left-hand corner by a clip. Each sheet was covered with the small, neat, forward-sloping writing that she knew so well, but when she noticed how much of it there was, and in what a neat businesslike manner it was written, and how the first page didn't even begin in the nice way a letter should, she began to get suspicious.

She looked away. She lit herself a cigarette. She took one puff and laid the cigarette in the ash-tray.

If this is about what I am beginning to suspect it is about,

175

she told herself, then I don't want to read it.

Can one refuse to read a letter from the dead?

Yes.

Well . . .

She glanced over at William's empty chair on the other side of the fireplace. It was a big brown leather armchair, and there was a depression on the seat of it, made by his buttocks over the years. Higher up, on the backrest, there was a dark oval stain on the leather where his head had rested. He used to sit reading in that chair and she would be opposite him on the sofa, sewing on buttons or mending socks or putting a patch on the elbow of one of his jackets, and every now and then a pair of eyes would glance up from the book and settle on her, watchful but strangely impersonal, as if calculating something. She had never liked those eyes. They were ice blue, cold, small, and rather close together, with two deep vertical lines of disapproval dividing them. All her life they had been watching her. And even now, after a week alone in the house, she sometimes had an uneasy feeling that they were still there, following her around, staring at her from doorways, from empty chairs, through a window at night.

Slowly she reached into her handbag and took out her spectacles and put them on. Then, holding the pages up high in front of her so that they caught the late afternoon light from the window behind, she started to read:

THIS NOTE, *my dear Mary*, is entirely for you, and will be given you shortly after I am gone.

Do not be alarmed by the sight of all this writing. It is nothing but an attempt on my part to explain to you precisely what Landy is going to do to me, and why I have agreed that he should do it, and what are his theories and his hopes. You are my wife and you have a right to know these things. In fact you *must* know them. During the past few days I have tried very hard to speak with you about Landy, but you have steadfastly refused to give me a hearing. This, as I have already told you, is a very foolish attitude to take, and I find it not entirely an unselfish one either. It stems mostly from ignorance, and I am absolutely convinced that if only you were made aware of all the facts, you would immediately change your view. That is why I am hoping that when I am no longer with you, and your mind is less distracted, you will consent to listen to me more carefully through these pages. I swear to you that when you have read my story, your sense of antipathy will vanish, and enthusiasm will take its place. I even dare to hope that you will become a little proud of what I have done.

As you read on, you must forgive me, if you will, for the coolness of my style, but this is the only way I know of getting my message over to you clearly. You see, as my time draws near, it is natural that I begin to brim with every kind of sentimentality under the sun. Each day I grow more extravagantly wistful, especially in the evenings, and unless I watch myself closely my emotions will be overflowing on to these pages.

I have a wish, for example, to write something about you and what a satisfactory wife you have been to me through the years, and I am promising myself that if there is time, and I still have the strength, I shall do that next.

I have a yearning also to speak about this Oxford of mine where I have been living and teaching for the past seventeen years, to tell something about the glory of the place and to explain, if I can, a little of what it has meant to have been allowed to work in its midst. All the things and places that I loved so well keep crowding in on me now in this gloomy bedroom. They are bright and beautiful as they always were, and today, for some reason, I can see them more clearly than ever. The path around the lake in the gardens of Worcester College, where Lovelace used to walk. The gateway at Pembroke. The view westward over the town from Magdalen Tower. The great hall at Christchurch. The little rockery at St John's where I have counted more than a dozen varieties of campanula, including the rare and dainty *C. Waldsteiniana*. But there, you see! I haven't begun and already I'm falling into the trap. So let me get started now; and let you read it slowly, my dear, without any of that sense of sorrow or disapproval that might otherwise embarrass your understanding. Promise me now that you will read it slowly, and that you will put yourself in a cool and patient frame of mind before you begin.

The details of the illness that struck me down so suddenly in my middle life are known to you. I need not waste time upon them – except to admit at once how foolish I was not to have gone earlier to my doctor. Cancer is one of the few remaining diseases that these modern drugs cannot cure. A surgeon can operate if it has not spread too far; but with me, not only did I leave it too late, but the thing had the effrontery to attack me in the pancreas, making both surgery and survival equally impossible.

So here I was with somewhere between one and six months left to live, growing more melancholy every hour – and then, all of a sudden, in comes Landy.

That was six weeks ago, on a Tuesday morning, very early, long before your visiting time, and the moment he entered I knew there was some sort of madness in the wind. He didn't creep in on his toes, sheepish and embarrassed, not knowing what to say, like all of my other visitors. He came in strong and smiling, and he strode up to the bed and stood there looking down at me with a wild bright glimmer in his eyes, and he said, 'William, my boy, this is perfect. You're just the one I want!'

Perhaps I should explain to you here that although John Landy has never been to our house, and you have seldom if ever met him, I myself have been friendly with him for at least nine years. I am, of course, primarily a teacher of philosophy, but as you know I've lately been dabbling a good deal in psychology as well. Landy's interest and mine have therefore slightly overlapped. He is a magnificent neurosurgeon, one of the finest, and recently he has been kind enough to let me study the results of some of his work, especially the varying effects of prefrontal lobotomies upon different types of psychopath. So you can see that when he suddenly burst in on me on Tuesday morning, we were by no means strangers to one another.

'Look,' he said, pulling up a chair beside the bed. 'In a few weeks you're going to be dead. Correct?'

Coming from Landy, the question didn't seem especially unkind. In a way it was refreshing to have a visitor brave enough to touch upon the forbidding subject.

'You're going to expire right here in this room, and then they'll take you out and cremate you.'

'Bury me,' I said.

'That's even worse. And then what? Do you believe you'll go to heaven?'

'I doubt it,' I said, 'though it would be comforting to think so.'

'Or hell, perhaps?'

'I don't really see why they should send me there.'

'You never know, my dear William.'

'What's all this about?' I asked.

'Well,' he said, and I could see him watching me carefully, 'personally, I don't believe that after you're dead you'll ever hear of yourself again – unless . . .' and here he paused and smiled and leaned closer . . . unless, of course, you have the sense to put yourself into my hands. Would you care to consider a proposition?'

The way he was staring at me, and studying me, and appraising me with a queer kind of hungriness, I might have been a piece of prime beef on the counter and he had bought it and was waiting for them to wrap it up.

'I'm really serious about it, William. Would you care to consider a proposition?'

'I don't know what you're talking about.'

'Then listen and I'll tell you. Will you listen to me?'

'Go on then, if you like. I doubt if I've got very much to lose by hearing it.'

'On the contrary, you have a great deal to gain – especially *after you're dead*.'

I am sure he was expecting me to jump when he said this, but for some reason I was ready for it. I lay quite still, watching his face and that slow white smile of his that always revealed the gold clasp of an upper denture curled around the canine on the left side of his mouth.

'This is a thing, William, that I've been working on quietly for some years. One or two others here at the hospital have been helping me, especially Morrison, and we've completed a number of fairly successful trials with laboratory animals. I'm at the stage now where I'm ready to have a go with a man. It's a big idea, and it may sound a bit far-fetched at first, but from a surgical point of view there doesn't seem to be any reason why it shouldn't be more or less practicable.'

Landy leaned forward and placed both hands on the edge of my bed. He has a good face, handsome in a bony sort of way, with none of the usual doctor's look about it. You know that look, most of them have it. It glimmers at you out of their eyeballs like a dull electric sign and it reads *Only I can save you*. But John Landy's eyes were wide and bright and little sparks of excitement were dancing in the centres of them.

'Quite a long time ago,' he said, 'I saw a short medical film that had been brought over from Russia. It was a rather gruesome thing, but interesting. It showed a dog's head completely severed from its body, but with the normal blood supply being maintained through the arteries and veins by means of an artificial heart. Now the thing is this: that dog's head, sitting there all alone on a sort of tray, was *alive*. The brain was functioning. They proved it by several tests. For example, when food was smeared on the dog's lips, the tongue would come out and lick it away; and the eyes would follow a person moving across the room.

'It seemed reasonable to conclude from this that the head and the brain did not need to be attached to the rest of the body in order to remain alive – provided, of course, that a supply of properly oxygenated blood could be maintained.

'Now then. My own thought, which grew out of seeing this film, was to remove the brain from the skull of a human and keep it alive and functioning as an independent unit for an unlimited period after he is dead. *Your* brain, for example, after *you* are dead.'

'I don't like that,' I said.

'Don't interrupt, William. Let me finish. So far as I can tell from subsequent experiments, the brain is a peculiarly self-supporting object. It manufactures its own cerebrospinal fluid. The magic processes of thought and memory which go on inside it are manifestly not impaired by the absence of limbs or trunk or even of skull, provided, as I say, that you keep pumping in the right kind of oxygenated blood under the proper conditions.

'My dear William, just think for a moment of your own brain. It is in perfect shape. It is crammed full of a lifetime of learning. It has taken you years of work to make it what it is. It is just beginning to give out some first-rate original ideas. Yet soon it is going to have to die along with the rest of your body simply because your silly little pancreas is riddled with cancer.'

'No, thank you,' I said to him. 'You can stop there. It's a repulsive idea, and even if you could do it, which I doubt, it would be quite pointless. What possible use is there in keeping my brain alive if I couldn't talk or see or hear or feel?

Personally, I can think of nothing more unpleasant.'

'I believe that you *would* be able to communicate with us,'
Landy said. 'And we might even succeed in giving you a certain amount of vision. But let's take this slowly. I'll come to
all that later on. The fact remains that you're going to die
fairly soon whatever happens; and my plans would not
involve touching you at all until *after* you are dead. Come
now, William. No true philosopher could object to lending
his dead body to the cause of science.'

'That's not putting it quite straight,' I answered. 'It seems
to me there'd be some doubts as to whether I were dead or
alive by the time you'd finished with me.'

'Well,' he said, smiling a little, 'I suppose you're right
about that. But I don't think you ought to turn me down
quite so quickly before you know a bit more about it.'

'I said I don't want to hear it.'

'Have a cigarette,' he said, holding out his case.

'I don't smoke, you know that.'

He took one himself and lit it with a tiny silver lighter that
was no bigger than a shilling piece. 'A present from the
people who make my instruments,' he said. 'Ingenious, isn't
it?'

I examined the lighter, then handed it back.

'May I go on?' he asked.

'I'd rather you didn't.'

'Just lie still and listen. I think you'll find it quite interesting.'

There were some blue grapes on a plate beside my bed. I
put the plate on my chest and began eating the grapes.

'At the moment of death,' Landy said, 'I should have to be
standing by so that I could step in immediately and try to
keep your brain alive.'

'You mean leaving it in the head?'

'To start with, yes. I'd have to.'

'And where would you put it after that?'

'If you want to know, in a sort of basin.'

'Are you really serious about this?'

'Certainly I'm serious.'

'All right. Go on.'

'I suppose you know that when the heart stops and the brain is deprived of fresh blood and oxygen, its tissues die very rapidly. Anything from four to six minutes and the whole thing's dead. Even after three minutes you may get a certain amount of damage. So I should have to work rapidly to prevent this from happening. But with the help of the machine, it should all be quite simple.'

'What machine?'

'The artificial heart. We've got a nice adaptation here of the one originally devised by Alexis Carrel and Lindbergh. It oxygenates the blood, keeps it at the right temperature, pumps it in at the right pressure, and does a number of other little necessary things. It's really not at all complicated.'

'Tell me what you would do at the moment of death,' I said. 'What is the first thing you would do?'

'Do you know anything about the vascular and venous arrangements of the brain?'

'No.'

'Then listen. It's not difficult. The blood supply to the brain is derived from two main sources, the internal carotid arteries and the vertebral arteries. There are two of each, making four arteries in all. Got that?'

'Yes.'

'And the return system is even simpler. The blood is drained away by only two large veins, the internal jugulars. So you have four arteries going up – they go up the neck, of course – and two veins coming down. Around the brain itself they naturally branch out into other channels, but those don't concern us. We never touch them.'

'All right,' I said. 'Imagine that I've just died. Now what would you do?'

'I should immediately open your neck and locate the four arteries, the carotids and the vertebrals. I should then perfuse them, which means that I'd stick a large hollow needle into each. These four needles would be connected by tubes to the artificial heart.

'Then, working quickly, I would dissect out both the left and right jugular veins and hitch these also to the heart machine to complete the circuit. Now switch on the machine, which is already primed with the right type of blood, and there you are. The circulation through your brain would be restored.'

'I'd be like that Russian dog.'

'I don't think you would. For one thing, you'd certainly lose consciousness when you died, and I very much doubt whether you would come to again for quite a long time – if indeed you came to at all. But, conscious or not, you'd be in a rather interesting position, wouldn't you? You'd have a cold dead body and a living brain.'

Landy paused to savour this delightful prospect. The man was so entranced and bemused by the whole idea that he evidently found it impossible to believe I might not be feeling the same way.

'We could now afford to take our time,' he said.'And believe me, we'd need it. The first thing we'd do would be to wheel you to the operating-room, accompanied of course by the machine, which must never stop pumping. The next problem . . .'

'All right,' I said. 'That's enough. I don't have to hear the details.'

'Oh, but you must,' he said. 'It is important that you should know precisely what is going to happen to you all the way through. You see, afterwards, when you regain consciousness, it will be much more satisfactory from your point of view if you are able to remember exactly *where* you are and *how* you came to be there. If only for your own peace of mind you should know that. You agree?'

I lay still on the bed, watching him.

'So the next problem would be to remove your brain, intact and undamaged, from your dead body. The body is useless. In fact it has already started to decay. The skull and face are also useless. They are both encumbrances and I don't want them around. All I want is the brain, the clean beautiful brain, alive and perfect. So when I get you on the table I will take a saw, a small oscillating saw, and with this I shall proceed to remove the whole vault of your skull. You'd be unconscious at that point so I wouldn't have to bother with anaesthetic.'

'Like hell you wouldn't,' I said.

'You'd be out cold, I promise you that, William. Don't forget you died just a few minutes before.'

'Nobody's sawing off the top of my skull without an anaesthetic,' I said.

Landy shrugged his shoulders. 'It makes no difference to me,' he said. 'I'll be glad to give you a little procaine if you want it. If it will make you any happier I'll infiltrate the whole scalp with procaine, the whole head, from the neck up.'

'Thanks very much,' I said.

'You know,' he went on, 'it's extraordinary what sometimes happens. Only last week a man was brought in unconscious, and I opened his head without any anaesthetic at all and removed a small blood clot. I was still working inside the skull when he woke up and began talking.

'"Where am I?" he asked.

'"You're in hospital."

'"Well," he said. "Fancy that."

'"Tell me," I asked him, "is this bothering you, what I'm doing?"

'"No," he answered. "Not at all. What *are* you doing?"

'"I'm just removing a blood clot from your brain."

'"You *are*?"

'"Just lie still. Don't move. I'm nearly finished."

'"So that's the bastard who's been giving me all those headaches," the man said.'

Landy paused and smiled, remembering the occasion.

'That's word for word what the man said,' he went on, 'although the next day he couldn't even recollect the incident. It's a funny thing, the brain.'

'I'll have the procaine,' I said.

'As you wish, William. And now, as I say, I'd take a small oscillating saw and carefully remove your complete calvarium – the whole vault of the skull. This would expose the top half of the brain, or rather the outer covering in which it is wrapped. You may or may not know that there are three separate coverings around the brain itself – the outer one called the dura mater or dura, the middle one called the arachnoid, and the inner one called the pia mater or pia. Most laymen seem to have the idea that the brain is a naked thing floating around in fluid in your head. But it isn't. It's wrapped up neatly in these three strong coverings, and the cerebrospinal fluid actually flows within the little gap between the two inner coverings, known as the subarachnoid space. As I told you before, this fluid is manufactured by the brain and it drains off into the venous system by osmosis.

'I myself would leave all three coverings – don't they have lovely names, the dura, the arachnoid, and the pia? – I'd leave them all intact. There are many reasons for this, not least among them being the fact that within the dura run the venous channels that drain the blood from the brain into the jugular.

'Now,' he went on, 'we've got the upper half of your skull off so that the top of the brain, wrapped in its outer covering, is exposed. The next step is the really tricky one: to release the stubs of the four supply arteries and the two veins hanging underneath ready to be re-connected to the machine. This is an immensely lengthy and complicated business involving the delicate chipping away of much bone, the severing of many nerves, and the cutting and tying of numerous blood vessels. The only way I could do it with any hope of success would be by taking a rongeur and slowly biting off the rest of your skull, peeling it off downward like an orange until the sides and underneath of the brain covering are fully exposed. The problems involved are highly technical and I won't go into them, but I feel fairly sure that the work can be done. It's simply a question of surgical skill and patience. And don't forget that I'd have plenty of time, as much as I wanted, because the artificial heart would be continually pumping away alongside the operating-table, keeping the brain alive.

'Now, let's assume that I've succeeded in peeling off your skull and removing everything else that surrounds the sides of the brain. That leaves it connected to the body only at the base, mainly by the spinal column and by the two large veins and the four arteries that are supplying it with blood. So what next?

'I would sever the spinal column just above the first cervical vertebra, taking great care not to harm the two vertebral arteries which are in that area. But you must remember that the dura or outer covering is open at this place to receive the spinal column, so I'd have to close this opening by sewing the edges of the dura together. There'd be no problem there.

'At this point, I would be ready for the final move. To one side, on a table, I'd have a basin of a special shape, and this would be filled with what we call Ringer's Solution. That is a special kind of fluid we use for irrigation in neuro-surgery. I would now cut the brain completely loose by severing the supply arteries and the veins. Then I would simply pick it up in my hands and transfer it to the basin. This would be the only other time during the whole proceeding when the blood flow would be cut off; but once it was in the basin, it wouldn't take a moment to re-connect the stubs of the arteries and veins to the artificial heart.

'So there you are,' Landy said. 'Your brain is now in the basin, and still alive, and there isn't any reason why it shouldn't stay alive for a very long time, years and years perhaps, provided we looked after the blood and the machine.'

'But would it *function*?'

'My dear William, how should I know? I can't even tell you whether it would ever regain consciousness.'

'And if it did?'

'There now! That would be fascinating!'

'Would it?' I said, and I must admit I had my doubts.

'Of course it would! Lying there with all your thinking processes working beautifully, and your memory as well ...'

'And not being able to see or feel or smell or hear or talk,' I said.

'Ah!' he cried. 'I knew I'd forgotten something! I never told you about the eye. Listen. I am going to try to leave one of your optic nerves intact, as well as the eye itself. The optic nerve is a little thing about the thickness of a clinical thermometer and about two inches in length as it stretches between the brain and the eye. The beauty of it is that it's not really a nerve at all. It's an out-pouching of the brain itself, and the dura or brain covering extends along it and is attached to the eyeball. The back of the eye is therefore in very close contact with the brain, and cerebrospinal fluid flows right up to it.

'All this suits my purpose very well, and makes it reasonable to suppose that I could succeed in preserving one of your eyes. I've already constructed a small plastic case to contain the eyeball, instead of your own socket, and when the brain is in the basin, submerged in Ringer's Solution, the

188

eyeball in its case will float on the surface of the liquid.'

'Staring at the ceiling,' I said.

'I suppose so, yes. I'm afraid there wouldn't be any muscles there to move it around. But it might be sort of fun to lie there so quietly and comfortably peering out at the world from your basin.'

'Hilarious,' I said. 'How about leaving me an ear as well?'

'I'd rather not try an ear this time.'

'I want an ear,' I said. 'I insist upon an ear.'

'No.'

'I want to listen to Bach.'

'You don't understand how difficult it would be,' Landy said gently. 'The hearing apparatus, the cochlea, as it's called – is a far more delicate mechanism than the eye. What's more, it is encased in bone. So is a part of the auditory nerve that connects it with the brain. I couldn't possibly chisel the whole thing out intact.'

'Couldn't you leave it encased in the bone and bring the bone to the basin?'

'No,' he said firmly. 'This thing is complicated enough already. And anyway, if the eye works, it doesn't matter all that much about your hearing. We can always hold up messages for you to read. You really must leave me to decide what is possible and what isn't.'

'I haven't said yet that I'm going to do it.'

'I know, William, I know.'

'I'm not sure I fancy the idea very much.'

'Would you rather be dead, altogether?'

'Perhaps I would. I don't know yet. I wouldn't be able to talk, would I?'

'Of course not.'

'Then how would I communicate with you? How would you know that I'm conscious?'

'It would be easy for us to know whether or not you regain consciousness,' Landy said. 'The ordinary electroencephalograph could tell us that. We'd attach the electrodes directly to the frontal lobes of your brain, there in the basin.'

'And you could actually tell?'

'Oh, definitely. Any hospital could do that part of it.'

'But I couldn't communicate with *you*.'

'As a matter of fact,' Landy said, 'I believe you could. There's a man up in London called Wertheimer who's doing some interesting work on the subject of thought communication, and I've been in touch with him. You know, don't you, that the thinking brain throws off electrical and chemical discharges? And that these discharges go out in the form of waves, rather like radio waves?'

'I know a bit about it,' I said.

'Well, Wertheimer has constructed an apparatus somewhat similar to the encephalograph, though far more sensitive, and he maintains that within certain narrow limits it can help him to intercept the actual things that a brain is thinking. It produces a kind of graph which is apparently decipherable into words or thoughts. Would you like me to ask Wertheimer to come and see you?'

'No,' I said. Landy was already taking it for granted that I was going through with this business, and I resented his attitude. 'Go away and leave me alone,' I told him. 'You won't get anywhere by trying to rush me.'

He stood up at once and crossed to the door.

'One question,' I said.

He paused with a hand on the doorknob. 'Yes, William?'

'Simply this. Do you yourself honestly believe that when my brain is in that basin, my mind will be able to function exactly as it is doing at present? Do you believe that I will be able to think and reason as I can now? And will the power of memory remain?'

'I don't see why not,' he answered. 'It's the same brain. It's alive. It's undamaged. In fact, it's completely untouched. We haven't even opened the dura. The big difference, of course, would be that we've severed every single nerve that leads into it – except for the one optic nerve – and this means that your thinking would no longer be influenced by your senses. You'd be living in an extraordinarily pure and detached world. Nothing to bother you at all, not even pain. You couldn't possibly feel pain because there wouldn't be any nerves to feel it with. In a way, it would be an almost perfect situation. No worries or fears or pains or hunger or thirst. Not even any desires. Just your memories and your thoughts, and if the remaining eye happened to function, then you could read books as well. It all sounds rather pleasant to me.'

'It does, does it?'

'Yes, William, it does. And particularly for a Doctor of Philosophy. It would be a tremendous experience. You'd be able to reflect upon the ways of the world with a detachment and a serenity that no man had ever attained before. And who knows what might not happen then! Great thoughts and solutions might come to you, great ideas that could revolutionise our way of life! Try to imagine, if you can, the degree of concentration that you'd be able to achieve!'

'And the frustration,' I said.

'Nonsense. There couldn't be any frustration. You can't have frustration without desire, and you couldn't possibly have any desire. Not physical desire, anyway'

'I should certainly be capable of remembering my previous life in the world, and I might desire to return to it.'

'What, to this mess! Out of your comfortable basin and back into this madhouse!'

'Answer one more question,' I said. 'How long do you believe you could keep it alive?'

'The brain? Who knows? Possibly for years and years. The conditions would be ideal. Most of the factors that cause deterioration would be absent, thanks to the artificial heart. The blood-pressure would remain constant at all times, an impossible condition in real life. The temperature would also be constant. The chemical composition of the blood would be near perfect. There would be no impurities in it, no virus, no bacteria, nothing. Of course it's foolish to guess, but I believe that a brain might live for two or three hundred years in circumstances like these. Good-bye for now,' he said. 'I'll drop in and see you tomorrow.' He went out quickly, leaving me, as you might guess, in a fairly disturbed state of mind.

My immediate reaction after he had gone was one of revulsion towards the whole business. Somehow, it wasn't at all nice. There was something basically repulsive about the idea that I myself, with all my mental faculties intact, should be reduced to a small slimy blob lying in a pool of water. It was monstrous, obscene, unholy. Another thing that bothered me was the feeling of helplessness that I was bound to experience once Landy had got me into the basin. There could be no going back after that, no way of protesting or explaining. I would be committed for as long as they could keep me alive.

And what, for example, if I could not stand it? What if it turned out to be terribly painful? What if I became hysterical?

No legs to run away on. No voice to scream with. Nothing. I'd just have to grin and bear it for the next two centuries.

No mouth to grin with either.

At this point, a curious thought struck me, and it was this: Does not a man who has had a leg amputated often suffer from the delusion that the leg is still there? Does he not tell the nurse that the toes he doesn't have any more are itching like mad, and so on and so forth? I seemed to have heard something to that effect quite recently.

Very well. On the same premise, was it not possible that my brain, lying there alone in that basin, might not suffer from a similar delusion in regard to my body? In which case, all my usual aches and pains could come flooding over me and I wouldn't even be able to take an aspirin to relieve them. One moment I might be imagining that I had the most excruciating cramp in my leg, or a violent indigestion, and a few minutes later, I might easily get the feeling that my poor bladder – you know me –was so full that if I didn't get to emptying it soon it would burst.

Heaven forbid.

I lay there for a long time thinking these horrid thoughts. then quite suddenly, round about midday, my mood began to change. I became less concerned with the unpleasant aspect of the affair and found myself able to examine Landy's proposals in a more reasonable light. Was there not, after all, I asked myself, something a bit comforting in the thought that my brain might not necessarily have to die and disappear in a few weeks time? There was indeed. I am rather proud of my brain. It is a sensitive, lucid, and uberous organ. It contains a prodigious store of information, and it is still capable of producing imaginative and original theories. As brains go, it is a damn' good one, though I say it myself. Whereas my body, my poor old body, the thing that Landy wants to throw away – well, even you, my dear Mary, will have to agree with me that there is really nothing about *that* which is worth preserving any more.

I was lying on my back eating a grape. Delicious it was, and there were three little seeds in it which I took out of my mouth and placed on the edge of the plate.

'I'm going to do it,' I said quietly. 'Yes, by God, I'm going to do it. When Landy comes back to see me tomorrow I shall tell him straight out that I'm going to do it.'

It was as quick as that. And from then on, I began to feel very much better. I surprised everyone by gobbling an enormous lunch, and shortly after that you came in to visit me as usual.

But how well I looked, you told me. How bright and well

and chirpy. Had anything happened? Was there some good news?

Yes, I said there was. And then, if you remember, I bade you sit down and make yourself comfortable, and I began immediately to explain to you as gently as I could what was in the wind.

Alas, you would have none of it. I had hardly begun telling you the barest details when you flew into a fury and said that the thing was revolting, disgusting, horrible, unthinkable, and when I tried to go on, you marched out of the room.

Well, Mary, as you know, I have tried to discuss this subject with you many times since then, but you have consistently refused to give me a hearing. Hence this note, and I can only hope that you will have the good sense to permit yourself to read it. It has taken me a long time to write. Two weeks have gone since I started to scribble the first sentence, and I'm now a good deal weaker than I was then. I doubt whether I have the strength to say much more. Certainly I won't say good-bye, because there's a chance, just a tiny chance, that if Landy succeeds in his work I may actually *see* you again later, that is if you can bring yourself to come and visit me.

I am giving orders that these pages shall not be delivered to you until a week after I am gone. By now, therefore, as you sit reading them, seven days have already elapsed since Landy did the deed. You yourself may even know what the outcome has been. If you don't, if you have purposely kept yourself apart and have refused to have anything to do with it – which I suspect may be the case – please change your mind now and give Landy a call to see how things went with me. That is the least you can do. I have told him that he may expect to hear from you on the seventh day.

Your faithful husband,

William

P.S. Be good when I am gone, and always remember that it is

harder to be a widow than a wife. Do not drink cocktails. Do not waste money. Do not smoke cigarettes. Do not eat pastry. Do not use lipstick. Do not buy a television apparatus. Keep my rose beds and my rockery well weeded in the summers. And incidentally I suggest that you have the telephone disconnected now that I shall have no further use for it.

W.

Mrs Pearl laid the last page of the manuscript slowly down on the sofa beside her. Her little mouth was pursed up tight and there was a whiteness around her nostrils.

But really! You would think a widow was entitled to a bit of peace after all these years.

The whole thing was just too awful to think about. Beastly and awful. It gave her the shudders.

She reached for her bag and found herself another cigarette. She lit it, inhaling the smoke deeply and blowing it out in clouds all over the room. Through the smoke she could see her lovely television set, brand new, lustrous, huge, crouching defiantly but also a little self-consciously on top of what used to be William's worktable.

What would he say, she wondered, if he could see that now?

She paused, to remember the last time he had caught her smoking a cigarette. That was about a year ago, and she was sitting in the kitchen by the open window having a quick one before he came home from work. She'd had the radio on loud playing dance music and she had turned round to pour herself another cup of coffee and there he was standing in the doorway, huge and grim, staring down at her with those awful eyes, a little black dot of fury blazing in the centre of each.

For four weeks after that, he had paid the housekeeping bills himself and given her no money at all, but of course he wasn't to know that she had over six pounds salted away in a soap-flake çarton in the cupboard under the sink.

'What is it?' she had said to him once during supper. 'Are you worried about me getting lung cancer?'

'I am not,' he had answered.

'Then why can't I smoke?'

'Because I disapprove, that's why.'

He had also disapproved of children, and as a result they had never had any of them either.

Where was he now, this William of hers, the great disapprover?

Landy would be expecting her to call up. Did she *have* to call Landy?

Well, not really, no.

She finished her cigarette, then lit another one immediately from the old stub. She looked at the telephone that was sitting on the worktable beside the television set. William had asked her to call. He had specifically requested that she telephone Landy as soon as she had read the letter. She hesitated, fighting hard now against the old ingrained sense of duty that she didn't quite yet dare to shake off. Then, slowly, she got to her feet and crossed over to the phone on the worktable. She found a number in the book, dialled it, and waited.

'I want to speak to Mr Landy, please.'

'Who is calling?'

'Mrs Pearl. Mrs William Pearl.'

'One moment, please.'

Almost at once, Landy was on the other end of the wire.

'Mrs Pearl?'

'This is Mrs Pearl.'

There was a slight pause.

'I am so glad you called at last, Mrs Pearl. You are quite well, I hope?' The voice was quiet, unemotional, courteous. 'I wonder if you would care to come over here to the hospital? Then we can have a little chat. I expect you are very eager to know how it all came out.'

She didn't answer.

'I can tell you now that everything went pretty smoothly, one way and another. Far better, in fact, than I was entitled to hope. It is not only alive, Mrs Pearl, it is conscious. It recovered consciousness on the second day. Isn't that interesting?'

She waited for him to go on.

'And the eye is seeing. We are sure of that because we get an immediate change in the deflections on the encephalograph when we hold something up in front of it. And now we're giving it the newspaper to read every day.'

'Which newspaper?' Mrs Pearl asked sharply.

'*The Daily Mirror*. The headlines are larger.'

'He hates *The Mirror*. Give him *The Times*.'

There was a pause, then the doctor said, 'Very well, Mrs Pearl. We'll give it *The Times*. We naturally want to do all we can to keep it happy.'

'*Him*,' she said. 'Not *it*. *Him!*'

'Him,' the doctor said. 'Yes, I beg your pardon. To keep him happy. That's one reason why I suggested you should come along here as soon as possible. I think it would be good for him to see you. You could indicate how delighted you were to be with him again – smile at him and blow him a kiss and all that sort of thing. It's bound to be a comfort to him to know that you are standing by.'

There was a long pause.

'Well,' Mrs Pearl said at last, her voice suddenly very meek and tired. 'I suppose I had better come on over and see how he is.'

'Good. I knew you would. I'll wait here for you. Come straight up to my office on the second floor. Good-bye.'

Half an hour later, Mrs Pearl was at the hospital.

'You mustn't be surprised by what he looks like,' Landy said as he walked beside her down a corridor.

'No, I won't.'

'It's bound to be a bit of a shock to you at first. He's not very prepossessing in his present state, I'm afraid.'

'I didn't marry him for his looks, Doctor.'

Landy turned and stared at her. What a queer little woman this was, he thought, with her large eyes and her sullen, resentful air. Her features, which must have been quite pleasant once, had now gone completely. The mouth was slack, the cheeks loose and flabby, and the whole face gave the impression of having slowly but surely sagged to pieces through years and years of joyless married life. They walked on for a while in silence.

'Take your time when you get inside,' Landy said. 'He won't know you're in there until you place your face directly above his eye. The eye is always open, but he can't move it at all, so the field of vision is very narrow. At present we have it looking straight up at the ceiling. And of course he can't hear anything. We can talk together as much as we like. It's in here.'

Landy opened a door and ushered her into a small square room.

'I wouldn't go too close yet,' he said, putting a hand on her arm. 'Stay back here a moment with me until you get used to it all.'

There was a biggish white enamel bowl about the size of a washbasin standing on a high white table in the centre of the room, and there were half a dozen thin plastic tubes coming out of it. These tubes were connected with a whole lot of glass piping in which you could see the blood flowing to and from the heart machine. The machine itself made a soft rhythmic pulsing sound.

'He's in there,' Landy said, pointing to the basin, which was too high for her to see into. 'Come just a little closer. Not too near.'

He led her two paces forward.

By stretching her neck, Mrs Pearl could now see the surface of the liquid inside the basin. It was clear and still, and on it there floated a small oval capsule, about the size of a pigeon's egg.

'That's the eye in there,' Landy said. 'Can you see it?'

'Yes.'

'So far as we can tell, it is still in perfect condition. It's the right eye, and the plastic container has a lens on it similar to the one he used in his own spectacles. At this moment he's probably seeing quite as well as he did before.'

'The ceiling isn't much to look at,' Mrs Pearl said.

'Don't worry about that. We're in the process of working out a whole programme to keep him amused, but we don't want to go too quickly at first.'

'Give him a good book.'

'We will, we will. Are you feeling all right, Mrs Pearl?'

'Yes.'

'Then we'll go forward a little more, shall we, and you'll be able to see the whole thing.'

He led her forward until they were standing only a couple of yards from the table, and now she could see right down into the basin.

'There you are,' Landy said. 'That's William.'

He was far larger than she had imagined he would be, and darker in colour. With all the ridges and creases running over his surface, he reminded her of nothing so much as an enormous pickled walnut. She could see the stubs of the four big arteries and the two veins coming out from the base of him and the neat way in which they were joined to the plastic tubes; and with each throb of the heart machine, all the tubes gave a little jerk in unison as the blood was pushed through them.

'You'll have to lean over,' Landy said, 'and put your pretty face right above the eye. He'll see you then, and you can smile at him and blow him a kiss. If I were you I'd say a few

199

nice things as well. He won't actually hear them, but I'm sure he'll get the general idea.'

'He hates people blowing kisses at him,' Mrs Pearl said. 'I'll do it my own way if you don't mind.' She stepped up to the edge of the table, leaned forward until her face was directly over the basin, and looked straight down into William's eye.

'Hallo, dear,' she whispered. 'It's me – Mary.'

The eye, bright as ever, stared back at her with a peculiar, fixed intensity.

'How are you, dear?' she said.

The plastic capsule was transparent all the way round so that the whole of the eyeball was visible. The optic nerve connecting the underside of it to the brain looked like a short length of grey spaghetti.

'Are you feeling all right, William?'

It was a queer sensation peering into her husband's eye when there was no face to go with it. All she had to look at was the eye, and she kept staring at it, and gradually it grew bigger and bigger, and in the end it was the only thing that she could see – a sort of face in itself. There was a network of tiny red veins running over the white surface of the eyeball, and in the ice-blue of the iris there were three or four rather pretty darkish streaks radiating from the pupil in the centre. The pupil was large and black, with a little spark of light reflecting from one side of it.

'I got your letter, dear, and came over at once to see how you were. Dr Landy says you are doing wonderfully well. Perhaps if I talk slowly you can understand a little of what I am saying by reading my lips.'

There was no doubt that the eye was watching her.

'They are doing everything possible to take care of you, dear. This marvellous machine thing here is pumping away all the time and I'm sure it's a lot better than those silly old hearts all the rest of us have. Ours are liable to break down at any moment, but yours will go on for ever.'

She was studying the eye closely, trying to discover what there was about it that gave it such an unusual appearance.

'You seem fine, dear, simply fine. Really you do.'

It looked ever so much nicer, this eye, than either of his eyes used to look, she told herself. There was a softness about it somewhere, a calm, kindly quality that she had never seen before. Maybe it had to do with the dot in the centre, the pupil. William's pupils used always to be tiny black pin-heads. They used to glint at you, stabbing into your brain, seeing right through you, and they always knew at once what you were up to and even what you were thinking. But this one she was looking at now was large and soft and gentle, almost cowlike.

'Are you quite sure he's conscious?' she asked, not looking up.

'Oh yes, completely,' Landy said.

'And he *can* see me?'

'Perfectly.'

'Isn't that marvellous? I expect he's wondering what happened.'

'Not at all. He knows perfectly well where he is and why he's there. He can't possibly have forgotten that.'

'You mean he *knows* he's in this basin?'

'Of course. And if only he had the power of speech, he would probably be able to carry on a perfectly normal conversation with you this very minute. So far as I can see, there should be absolutely no difference mentally between this William here, and the one you used to know back home.'

'Good *gracious* me,' Mrs Pearl said, and she paused to consider this intriguing aspect.

You know what, she told herself, looking behind the eye now and staring hard at the great grey pulpy walnut that lay so placidly under the water. I'm not at all sure that I don't

201

prefer him as he is at present. In fact, I believe that I could live very comfortably with this kind of a William. I could cope with this one.

'Quiet, isn't he?' she said.

'Naturally he's quiet.'

No arguments and criticisms, she thought, no constant admonitions, no rules to obey, no ban on smoking cigarettes, no pair of cold disapproving eyes watching me over the top of a book in the evenings, no shirts to wash and iron, no meals to cook – nothing but the throb of the heart machine, which was a rather soothing sound anyway and certainly not loud enough to interfere with television.

'Doctor,' she said, 'I do believe I'm suddenly getting to feel the most enormous affection for him. Does that sound queer?'

'I think it's quite understandable.'

'He looks so helpless and silent lying there under the water in his little basin.'

'Yes, I know.'

'He's like a baby, that's what he's like. He's exactly like a little baby.'

Landy stood still behind her, watching.

'There,' she said softly, peering into the basin. 'From now on Mary's going to look after you *all* by herself and you've nothing to worry about in the world. When can I have him back home, Doctor?'

'I beg your pardon?'

'I said when can I have him back – back in my own house?'

'You're joking,' Landy said.

She turned her head slowly around and looked directly at him. 'Why should I joke?' she asked. Her face was bright, her eyes round and bright as two diamonds.

'He couldn't possibly be moved.'

'I don't see why not.'

'This is an experiment, Mrs Pearl.'

'It's my husband, Doctor Landy.'

'A funny little nervous half-smile appeared on Landy's mouth. 'Well . . .' he said.

'It *is* my husband, you know.' There was no anger in her voice. She spoke quietly, as though merely reminding him of a simple fact.

'That's rather a tricky point,' Landy said, wetting his lips. 'You're a widow now, Mrs Pearl. I think you must resign yourself to that fact.'

She turned away suddenly from the table and crossed over to the window. 'I mean it,' she said, fishing in her bag for a cigarette. 'I want him back.'

Landy watched her as she put the cigarette between her lips and lit it. Unless he were very much mistaken, there was something a bit odd about this woman, he thought. She seemed almost pleased to have her husband over there in the basin.

He tried to imagine what his own feelings would be if it were *his* wife's brain lying there and *her* eye staring up at him out of that capsule.

He wouldn't like it.

'Shall we go back to my room now?' he said.

She was standing by the window, apparently quite calm and relaxed, puffing her cigarette.

'Yes, all right.'

On her way past the table she stopped and leaned over the basin once more. 'Mary's leaving now, sweetheart,' she said. 'And don't worry about a single thing, you understand? We're going to get you right back home where we can look after you properly just as soon as we possibly can. And listen dear . . .' At this point she paused and carried the cigarette to her lips, intending to take a puff.

Instantly the eye flashed.

She was looking straight into it at the time, and right in

the centre of it she saw a tiny but brilliant flash of light, and the pupil contracted into a minute black pinpoint of absolute fury.

At first she didn't move. She stood bending over the basin, holding the cigarette up to her mouth, watching the eye.

Then very slowly, deliberately, she put the cigarette between her lips and took a long suck. She inhaled deeply, and she held the smoke inside her lungs for three or four seconds; then suddenly, *whoosh*, out it came through her nostrils in two thin jets which struck the water in the basin and billowed out over the surface in a thick blue cloud, enveloping the eye.

Landy was over by the door, with his back to her, waiting. 'Come on, Mrs Pearl,' he called.

'Don't look so cross, William,' she said softly. 'It isn't any good looking cross.'

Landy turned his head to see what she was doing.

'Not any more it isn't,' she whispered. 'Because from now on, my pet, you're going to do just exactly what Mary tells you. Do you understand that?'

'Mrs Pearl,' Landy said, moving towards her.

'So don't be a naughty boy again, will you, my precious,' she said, taking another pull at the cigarette. 'Naughty boys are liable to get punished most severely nowadays, you ought to know that.'

Landy was beside her now, and he took her by the arm and began drawing her firmly but gently away from the table.

'Good-bye, darling,' she called. 'I'll be back soon.'

'That's enough, Mrs Pearl.'

'Isn't he sweet?' she cried, looking up at Landy with big bright eyes. 'Isn't he heaven? I just can't wait to get him home.'

EVERY DETAIL
BUT ONE

Bert Coules

*Bert Coules, who lives on the Kent coast within whistling distance
of the Romney, Hythe and Dymchurch Railway, produced his first
creepy story at the age of seven and has been horrifying people
with his writing ever since. He describes himself as six foot four,
craggily handsome, stupendously fit and an inveterate liar.*

From *The Complete Handbook of the Occult* by Jonathan Weiss:

The most important thing to realise about this field is that it's far
wider than most people imagine; there's a lot more to the para-
normal than ghoulies and ghosties and long-leggedy beasties.

Bump! It wasn't the most satisfying sound in the world –
the damn door just wouldn't slam, no matter how hard
you kicked it – but it served to get rid of some of the frustra-
tions of the day. Jenny Waterman relaxed. 'We're home, Bas.
Home again, home again, jiggety-jig.'

Basil said nothing.

Jenny, who hadn't expected him to, threw off her coat and
switched the answering machine to replay. Beep. After the
opening two words she was able to join in the first message:
Don't get excited, it's only Lesley said the tape. Les reminded her
about their lunch date tomorrow and signed off with a
cheery hallo to Bas and the parting thought that he was
probably a girl. Beep. Next was Jenny's mother with some
endless message about a TV special involving Anneka Rice
who's been through it herself, so she knows what she's talking about.

Beep. Jenny gave the machine a knowing smile. 'OK Mother, what have you forgotten?'

Silence.

'Oh come on, Mum, there's always something. Beef tea? Eating for two? Don't go out when there's a full moon?'

The message, when it came, wasn't any of those things. In fact, it wasn't boring old Mum at all. In *fact* it wasn't exactly a message. And – Jenny instantly (and fairly convincingly) told herself – it was more annoying than upsetting. 'Oh wonderful. It's an event, Bas. Our first heavy breather.'

Jenny listened for a moment to the breathy half-words. Was the creep actually saying anything? She couldn't decide. 'Listen, freak,' she threw at the Panasonic, 'you can moan as long as you like, see if we care. C'mon, Bas, it's kettle time.'

It was while she was making the tea that the words finally began to form.

Jenny . . . Jenny . . . Help me.

But by then she was out of earshot.

Ghosts, as such, are pretty rare. But there are lots of other things . . .

At their corner table in the Tomorrow We Diet Lesley was stuffing herself with chocolate fudge cake and being sympathetic. 'I don't care what you say, it made you a bit jumpy, I can tell. And you can do without that sort of thing. Particularly at the moment.'

'Oh please. Next thing, you'll be telling me to put my feet up and start eating for two.'

'I seem to have hit a nerve.'

'It's called "mother".'

'Sorry. It's my envy showing.'

Jenny was immediately contrite. 'Oh, Les . . .'

'I'm all right. Tell me more about your heavy breather.'

She shook her head. 'No, let's forget it. I'm OK, we both are. And it's never going to happen again.'

Associated areas would include telepathy, divination, telekinesis, distant viewing, that sort of thing. There are an awful lot of highly obscure phenomena.

There were no messages waiting when Jenny and Basil got home that evening, but Jenny's private sigh of relief was abruptly interrupted by the phone ringing.

But it wasn't the breather; it was Lesley, checking up.

'How are the two of you?'

'We're fine. Mind you, one of us nearly jumped out of –'

Thinking about it afterwards, Jenny could never decide exactly how she knew that there was someone else on the line. There was no sound – not at first – no obvious change at all. But there was someone there, all right.

'Jen? Jenny?'

For a brief moment Lesley didn't exist. Every sensory nerve in Jenny's body was connected to the new presence. Somehow, she spoke to it. 'Who's there?'

'What? Have you got a crossed line?'

And the moment was over and Jen was back in the real world again. 'Les, can't you hear it?'

'I can't hear anything. Not a thing.'

But Jenny could.

Jenny . . .

'No!'

Lesley was shouting down the phone. 'What can you hear? Tell me! Is it him again?'

Jenny. Jenny.

'Les, he knows my name. He knows who I am!'

Help me, Jenny . . .

'Lesley!'

'I'm listening, Jen. But I can't hear anyone. Are they still there?'

You've got to help me . . .

'What do you mean, help you? Who are you? Yes, yes! Still here.' Part of Jenny's brain was telling her that poor old Les must be terminally confused by all this crosstalk.

And so she was. But not too confused to do something about it. 'Right. Listen to me, you bastard. If you're not off this line in ten seconds dead, I'll have the law onto you faster than you can say "Cagney and Lacey". Got that?'

Jenny . . .

Was the voice weaker? Uncertain?

'Go away. Leave me alone!'

Lesley again, authoritative: 'Jenny, hang up. Hang up!'

But the voice had gone.

And Jenny hardly heard her friend urging her to take the phone off the hook and sit tight, she'd be straight round.

It's important to remember that ninety-nine per cent of all the cases investigated turn out to be a complete blank.

It was cold in the street by Jenny's front door. Les had calmed her down, made her some warm milk (Warm milk! How could she even look at the stuff?) and now was on her way home. 'You're sure you're going to be all right?'

'Yes! Stop fussing.' Jenny was back to normal.

'Right. Now get in, it's freezing.'

'Yes, mother. Bye.'

Lesley grinned. 'Bye. Bye, Basil.'

'Idiot. And Les . . .'

'That's me.'

'Thanks.'

Back in the flat, Jenny lifted the phone from its cradle and laid it on the table. 'OK, Bas, so I'm a coward. Now – what we need is a mindless evening's entertainment; feet up in front of the telly.' Not caring what was on – just so long as it didn't prove to be Anneka Rice – Jenny clicked the remote.

It wasn't Anneka Rice.

Help me, Jenny!

Her own voice, when she finally found it, was a cruel, breathless mirror-image of what she'd just heard. 'No. Please, no . . .'

Next day in the Tomorrow We Diet, Jenny looked full into Lesley's sticky face. 'OK, suppose you're right and I'm not going mad. What the hell *is* happening to me?'

Lesley put down her spoon. 'Simple.'

'Simple?'

'Simple. You've had a couple of damn stupid phone calls from some idiot man with all the intellectual capacity of a washing-machine, and you quite naturally got upset. Then you fell asleep in front of the telly and your subconscious did the rest.'

'You're saying I dreamt it?'

'Got it in one.'

And, as Lesley reattacked her sponge-pudding-with-treacle, Jenny tried very hard to believe her.

There are lots of well-authenticated cases where people have seen an individual when he or she was miles away. Quite often, the distant person gives – or tries to give – some kind of important information. Sometimes a warning.

Jenny's bedroom, that night. She pulled up the duvet and forced a smile. Good old Les, rock-solid as ever. She turned off the bedside lamp.

And knew, instantly, something that simply could not be true.

There was someone else in the bedroom.

Fear is a strange emotion, it leaves room round the edges for all sorts of other random thoughts. How did he get in?

Why here? All the stuff worth stealing is in the other room. It's not a burglar, it's someone who's followed me, some pervert who gets off on pregnant women, some –

Help me, Jenny.

She'd never screamed before and part of her was surprised to be doing it now, and then the darkness in the room was in her eyes and in her brain and she stopped worrying about it.

'Drink this. Careful, it's hot.'

'Les!'

'The very same.'

'But how . . . ?'

'Ssh. Drink your milk.'

Jenny drank. Then she told her friend what had happened. Lesley listened, an unreadable expression on her face. When she finally spoke, it was to complain.

'Typical, isn't it? A strange man rings me up in the middle of the night and all he says is "can you come round and see your friend? I think there's something wrong."'

'Michael called you?'

'If that's his name. Why can't my neighbours look like that? Come on, let's get you back to bed.'

'No!'

'What?'

'I'm not going back in that room.'

'Jen, be reasonable. It was a dream. The old subconscious.'

For the first time, tears. 'Why won't you believe me? I'm telling the truth.'

'Hey, ssh, I'm sorry. You've had a hell of a shock.'

Slowly, the crying subsided. 'You believe me?'

'Come on, get up.'

Panic. 'No! I can't!'

'Not back in there. You're coming home with me.'

When someone has a psychic or paranormal experience it often

210

affects them very deeply. Their whole picture of the world is suddenly turned completely upside-down. Coming to terms with that is frequently more traumatic than the experience itself.

In their expensively-fitted kitchen, tidy in a way that only a room in a child-free house can be, Lesley and her husband Tim exchanged whispers.

'She's asleep at last.'

'She was in a hell of a state.'

'It does that to you. I'm told.'

Tim sighed. 'Come on, love.'

'I'm sorry. I really thought I'd come to terms with it – you know.'

'I know. Me too.'

'But I've sort of been living through it with her, and now she's practically about to have the thing . . .'

'I wish there was something I could do.'

'There isn't.'

A silence. 'Yeah, I know.'

Lesley looked at him. 'I said she could stay here for a while.'

Tim tried to make it sound sincere. 'Good. Good idea.'

The idea of a fate or destiny that's mapped out for you, whatever you try to do to change it, is something that you find in the myths and legends of every race on earth.

This visit, they both had the fudge cake. Celebration time. They'd just come from the doctor's, and a verdict of mother and offspring both doing fine. Lesley beamed at the sight of good old Jen, back again.

'You know, you look so much better.'

A fudge-filtered reply. 'It's amazing what a couple of days of normal company can do to a person.'

'I don't know about "normal".'

Jen laughed. 'I was being polite.'

'Good grief, you have changed.'

'You haven't.'

'It's too late for that. And a lot of other things.' Lesley was wincing inside even before the words were out. Damn! Why did she have to drag that up now?

Jenny was suddenly a picture of misery. 'Oh God, Les. I'm really sorry about all this. The way I've been pushing myself down your throat.'

'Rubbish!'

'It's not rubbish. I know how much having a family means to you and Tim. So whammo, there goes yours truly, with all the tact of an expectant elephant, taking over your lives day and night.'

'Shut up, you idiot. I'm glad we were there to help.'

'So am I – or rather so are we, aren't we Bas?'

A genuine grin. 'It's great the way you talk to him all the time. Any day now he'll surprise you and answer back.'

A heavily pregnant young woman turning over a table in her haste to leave a restaurant is not something you see every day. So it was hardly surprising that a frozen, shocked silence framed Jenny's next words.

'Drive me home! I've got to get home!'

Some of these things inevitably sound extremely far-fetched. Well, a little scepticism is a healthy thing.

'I'm not leaving you alone.'

'Oh yes you are. You must.'

'Look – just a couple of days ago –'

'Will you please get out!'

A pause. 'If anything should happen to you –'

'Go! Just go, for Christ's sake! I don't want you here!'

Lesley held the frantic woman's stare for as long as she could. Then she turned and walked away.

For some people, the intensity of a psychic experience, the feeling of unique insight, becomes desperately linked to the fear that the link – whatever it is – is something amazingly fragile and tenuous, something that could be irretrievably and permanently broken at any moment.

'Talk to me! Talk to me, damn you! Bas!'

Nothing.

'The phone. Like before!' Jenny clawed at the receiver, heard nothing but dialling tone, slammed it back.

'Come on! I don't know what you need!' On a sudden thought she moved to the television, clicked it on. The shouting wasn't working; she dropped her voice to a whisper. 'You can use the TV. You've done it before. Please!'

Nothing. Just the afternoon drone of cosy Australian domesticity.

'Well, what do you want? Darkness? Shall I shut my eyes? What? *Talk to me!*'

The silence that followed was absolute. The TV sound had died, no traffic noise filtered in through the windows, no clock ticked. Total silence.

Except for the voice.

It was hardly audible. *Jenny* . . .

'Yes! Yes, I'm here. I can hear you.'

Help me . . .

'How? Tell me how!'

The words had gone. Was that breathing? Tortured breathing?

'Is it . . . Is it really you? Are you – my baby?'

This time the effort behind the single word was painfully clear. *Yes* . . .

Jenny missed the next word. 'What? I can't hear you!'

Dying.

'No!'

Even weaker now. *Dying* . . .

'You said I could help! You said so! What can I do?'
Silence.
'Tell me!'
Too late . . .
And it was gone.

One final case: NASA, the space people in America, had a series of phone calls from a woman who warned them that their next space shuttle flight was going to crash and everyone on board was going to be killed. She'd seen it in a vision.

'Is she going to die?'
   'That's no way to think, miss.'
   'Tell me!'
   He wouldn't, of course. Ambulance men aren't allowed to be honest.

NASA get a lot of crank calls, but something about this woman stopped them from just dismissing her out of hand. She told them technical details that an ordinary member of the public shouldn't have known.

When Tim arrived at the hospital, Lesley was standing in a corridor. Just standing there, eyes blank. She didn't see him until he stepped right in front of her. And she didn't wait for him to ask the question.
   'Jenny's dead.'
   'Oh Jesus. Are you all right?'
   'They're trying to save the baby.'

This woman's vision had apparently shown her one of the main fuel tanks on the shuttle rupturing on takeoff. You're probably thinking 'But that's incredible. That's exactly what happened.' But you're wrong. It isn't. They took her seriously enough to check the tank. It was in perfect condition. The shuttle lifted off with no problems and the flight was a text-book success.

Lesley and Tim's bedroom, that night. The night of the day that Jenny Waterman died and her baby – her little girl – lived. Lesley, who had been Jenny's closest friend and who had left her alone to kill herself, was standing by the window in the darkness.

'Come to bed, love.'

'Yes.'

But she didn't move. Tim came over to her. 'She was still alive when I broke in, did you know that?'

Tim knew. 'Les, try to stop thinking about it.'

'When I found her, I thought at first it was the baby, you know? And then I realised what she'd done. But she was still alive. She spoke to me. I had to get right down beside her to hear. I got her blood all over my dress. She said "My baby's dead." Over and over again. "My baby's dead. My baby's dead." I shouldn't have left her!'

'You mustn't blame yourself.'

She wasn't hearing him.

There was one thing he could try. One thing that might just snap her out of this guilt. 'I've been thinking . . .'

Eventually: 'Yes?'

'About. . . Well, we've never really talked about adopting.'

A monotone. 'No.'

'Perhaps we should.'

Again. 'Adopt?'

'Talk about it at least. We ought to find out about the requirements.'

He turned her face to his. Blank, nothing. One last shot! Tentatively. 'Do you think . . .'

'What?'

Tim gave up. 'We'll talk about it in the morning.'

And then, at last, from deep inside, a glimmer of light. 'You don't mean . . . Jenny's baby?'

He'd broken through. And now it was safe to let it rest. 'In the morning.'

She moved closer. 'Right.'

They both slept surprisingly well.

The point is this: the woman's vision was in January 1985; a whole year *before* the shuttle disaster. What she experienced – and it's by no means an isolated case – was so vivid, so real, that she took it for granted that she was seeing the present. But she wasn't – totally without realising it, she was seeing the future. If you like, the paranormal was playing with her: she was allowed to get it right in every detail – every detail but one.

Time passed. But eventually, Lesley and Tim Pargeter could have been found gazing fondly down at a beautiful baby. Jenny's baby. Their baby.

Lesley shook her head in disbelief, not for the first time. 'You know, I never really thought it would happen. I still can't believe it.'

Tim smiled down. 'She believes it. Don't you, eh? Yes.'

'I can see so much of Jen in her.'

'She's beautiful.'

'She certainly is. She's everything we've ever wanted: a beautiful, healthy baby.'

The baby said nothing.

THE SNOWMAN KILLING

J. C. W. Brook

James Brook failed as a teacher. Decided to become rich and famous as a writer. Failed. Went into computers for job satisfaction. Sort of made it. Went into marriage and fatherhood for happiness. Succeeded. Worries in case becoming smug.

I t was turning out to be a miserable winter. Cold, wet and soul-destroying. Ann sighed as she looked through the kitchen window. Outside a thin aimless drizzle drifted down from an overcast sky. The garden seemed grey and lifeless.

'Mummy – can I play outside?' Colin spoke from right beside her elbow, making her jump.

'Darling – I've asked you before not to do that.'

'Do what, Mummy?' His blue eyes were completely guileless, his expression blank. She hated it when he looked like that. It made him seem somehow old, old far beyond his seven years.

Ann took off her rubber gloves. 'I don't like it when you creep up on me like that.'

'I wasn't creeping, Mummy.' He said and then, quickly: 'Can I go and play outside?'

'Outside? But it's horribly cold.' With a kind of blank certainty she knew what he was going to say next.

'I want to build a snowman.' He smiled. 'A big one. As big as me. Bigger.'

Ann took a deep breath. He was just a child. Children see things differently. He probably thought the whole thing was a joke. But then it might easily be that anyway, a joke the

217

two of them had created in an idle moment. The snowman. The dreams. The fear.

'Darling,' she said as levelly and logically as she could, 'You can't build a snowman. There's no snow.'

He went to the back door, and pressed his nose against the cold, frosted glass, his voice obstinate and stubborn. 'I'm going to build a snowman. With bits of coal, for eyes.'

Ann became brisk and matter of fact. 'Well you can't and that's all there is to it. What's Alex doing?'

At the mention of his twin, Colin turned round. 'Oh, he's reading. He's always reading. He's wet. I hate him.'

'Don't be silly. Of course you don't.' Ann switched on the kettle. 'I'm not going to get involved in some stupid childish argument between you two. Tea in ten minutes, all right?'

Colin went to the kitchen door, then stopped, smiled. A thin smile. 'He's not really reading.' He paused for effect. 'He's asleep. He's dreaming. He's dreaming of the snowman.'

'What?' A stream of ice seemed to trickle down Ann's spine. 'What did you say?'

'He's ever so cold, Mummy.'

Ann moved to the door. She tried not to run. 'Darling, what are you on about?' She was glad her voice came out reasonably level. It was all stupid and irrational: there was nothing really wrong. It was just the children playing one of their macabre games.

'He's as cold as ice.' He backed away, then repeated, 'As cold as ice.'

In the living-room Alex was lying in front of the gas fire. he looked very white and very still. Ann was beside him in an instant. His hand felt cold. As cold as ice.

'Told you, didn't I?' Colin spoke triumphantly. He had followed her in. His eyes glanced first at his brother and then to her. 'Told you.'

Ann flared. 'Go to your room and go now!'

218

He stuck his hands deep in his pockets. 'I only told you the truth, Mummy.'

'Alex, are you all right?' She rubbed his hands and lifted his head. 'Are you all right?' Colour and warmth came back, came back so fast that afterwards she half wondered if she'd dreamt it all.

His eyes opened. 'I was dreaming,' were the first words he said. 'I was dreaming about the snowman.'

'Told you, didn't I?' said Colin triumphantly.

That evening after supper and the twins' bedtime, she and Henry sat drinking coffee. He folded his newspaper into neat precise rectangles, an article at a time.

'There's something I have to talk to you about,' Ann began awkwardly. She had been waiting for this time of day, rehearsing the words to herself.

'They've given Sanders a cavalier,' he said. She looked at him blankly. 'A cavalier. A car. He's only been with the firm a year and they go and give him a car. A car. I ask you.'

'Henry, Alex had that dream again today.' She blurted.

'What dream?' he said exasperated.

'What dream? The dream about the snowman, of course. And he was ever so cold. But the point is, Colin knew what Alex was dreaming, he came and told me.' She'd said it, but it hadn't made much sense, it was all mixed up and wrong.

Predictably, Henry said 'Ann, what are you talking about?'

She took a deep breath. 'He's had the dream about the snowman again. That's twice. Twice in the last month. It's creepy Henry – really creepy. It frightens me. And Colin doesn't help either, he's . . .' she paused, lost for words.

'He's what?'

'I don't know, it's difficult to describe. He says these stupid things –'

'What things?'

'I'm trying to tell you!' she snapped.

He drank his coffee and smoothed his paper, every action precise and economical. She knew precisely what he was thinking, knew what a martyr he was feeling. 'You don't know what it's like here,' she said. 'I don't like this house. It gets on my nerves. The whole place is claustrophobic. It comes in on you.'

'Ann,' he said reasonably, 'ever since we moved you've been preoccupied about the boys or the house or both. We must have had this conversation hundreds of times and quite frankly –' his annoyance finally came through '– and quite frankly I'm sick of it!'

Later, she tried again. The bedroom was dark and quiet. Ann knew he was not asleep, although his breathing was regular and light. She reached out and touched his back.

'Darling, we have to stay together on this. You have to help me.' He said nothing. 'All right, so it might be all my imagination, maybe I'm making a lot out of nothing, but . . .' she bit her lip, 'it's very real to me and I'm rather scared. You weren't there. You didn't see him.'

He sighed and turned over. 'D'you know what I think?' he said. 'I think the same as I've always thought.' Against the soft light coming through the curtains his profile was set and stubborn. 'I think you should get out more. Meet more people. There's no need for you to stay in all day. There must be clubs or something you can join.'

'You don't understand –' she began, but he cut her off.

'I'll tell you what I'll do. I'll leave you the car tomorrow and go in by train. You get Mrs Macpherson in to look after the boys and take yourself into town. Do some shopping – buy yourself a new dress, go to the hairdressers. Anything to get you out of this rut.'

'Darling, that's not what I need –'

'Yes it is. He rolled over away from her. 'It is but you just

220

don't realise it. Believe me, I know.'

The next day was cold with a biting chill wind. Henry backed the car from the garage and left it on the drive. Then he made a big business of finding his thicker coat and ringing the station to check train times. Finally he left. 'I'll probably be back late,' were his parting words. 'I'll be in late and have to make up the time.' A perfunctory kiss and he was gone.

Ann decided to blitz the house. The car could stay where it was, and it would give her an obscure pleasure to see it sitting there unused all day. She banned the twins from upstairs and set to. As she worked she felt better. This is what she needed. Activity – useful sensible everyday activity. She turned on the radio. Familiar songs and music. She found herself humming, then singing.

'Mummy . . . Mummy!'

Ann turned off the vacuum cleaner. 'Colin, I told both of you to stay downstairs.'

He ran over to the window. They were in the front bedroom. 'He's back!'

'Colin, what are you talking about?'

'The snowman, of course. The snowman's back. Can I go and play with him?' He stood on tiptoe pointing down. 'There he is, Mummy.'

Ann stood motionless for a long moment. The radio was playing 'When You Wish Upon a Star'. The lightness of heart she'd been feeling had gone. Her legs felt like lead.

'He's there, right by the tree. He's scaring the birds. Can't you see him?'

With a dreadful premonition of what she was going to see Ann went over to him. As she moved, the lower edge of the window seemed to paint the scene beyond, almost as if outside reality was being created second by second just for her. Time crystalised and became timeless.

For an instant – a single clear sane instant, she saw it. The snowman. White, by the tree, scaring the birds. She closed her eyes. This could not be happening.

'Told you, didn't I, Mummy!'

She turned her back to the window. 'There is no snowman,' she said firmly. 'There is no snow and therefore there is no snowman.'

'Yes there is, and I want to play with him.'

She whirled round, kneeling at the same time. 'Look –' she said, and stopped.

Outside, where she thought she'd seen the snowman, was Alex. He was lying on his back on the cold damp grass, his arms spread in a disjointed, asymmetric manner, his face upturned to the sky, his eyes closed.

At the other end of the line Henry's phone rang precisely twice before it was answered. 'Henry Makepeace,' he said in his steady measured way.

'Henry, it's me.' Ann shifted her grip on the receiver slightly. She mustn't sound panicked. 'Henry, it's happened again.'

She heard a small sigh of exasperation from him. 'Ann –'

'I don't know what's happening, Henry. It was awful. He was outside lying on the lawn. He looked all awkward –' Henry said something, but she carried on '– and when I touched him he was as cold as ice. Henry, it was really frightening –'

Again he spoke 'Ann – listen – are the boys all right? Are they all right now?'

Guiltily she stopped. 'I'm sorry. Yes, of course – they're all right now.' She glanced over her shoulder. Both Alex and Colin were glued to the television, watching a cartoon. They looked perfectly healthy and normal. 'They're fine.'

'What was he doing outside? Had he slipped? Was he hurt at all?'

For a moment she paused. 'I think it's a game. I don't know. When I touched him he was cold, but when he woke up he said he'd been dreaming.' A deep breath. 'Henry, can you come home please?'

He was silent for a moment, then said: 'Come home? When nothing's wrong? When the boys are all right?'

'Please Henry.' She lowered her voice. 'I need you.'

There was another pause. Desperately she tried again. 'I don't know what's going on, Henry, and I'd like you here.'

Eventually he spoke. 'I can't come home. It really is impossible. I'm up to my neck. Look – I take it you haven't gone into town yet?'

'No. Of course not.'

'Then for heaven's sake go. Buy yourself a new dress and an iced bun and you'll feel heaps better.'

The call over, Ann stared angrily at the receiver. New dresses! Iced buns! She wasn't a child. Well, if that was all he thought of her then she'd show him! Determinedly, Ann grabbed her address book.

As she drove into town Ann started to relax. Mrs Macpherson had been able to come straight away, and she'd even offered to provide lunch for the boys.

'You get yourself off,' she'd said in her soft Scottish accent: 'you look like you need a break.' Her presence was large and comforting and extremely normal. 'Don't you worry about the boys. I'll look after them.'

Their local town was about five miles away. The centre had recently been rebuilt and now featured a large covered shopping mall. Inside it was warm, colourful, bustling and full of noise. There were several shops she had not seen before and others she'd never had a chance to look around. It'd been ages since she'd been out without the boys or Henry. Just on her own. On her own with time to spare and money to spend. She caught sight of her reflection in a shop window. Depressingly, she looked exactly what she was: a hassled and rather harried thirty-year-old mum, wearing last year's clothes from some anonymous department store.

Ann turned and straightened. Well – he had said she should buy a new dress, hadn't he? She checked her credit card and glanced at her watch. 12.30. She'd look in a couple of shops and then find somewhere to have lunch.

'Ann . . . Ann – is it really you?' The voice was tantalisingly familiar, a voice from the past. Ann looked up, was puzzled for a moment and then smiled.

'Good God!' She stood and grinned at the tall dark woman standing beside her table. 'Helen!'

'The very same,' said Helen. She put down tea things and sat. 'I can hardly believe it's you.'

Later – much later, when the world had steadied and things were again as normal as they could ever be – Ann came to believe that her meeting with Helen had nothing to do with chance. It was the malignant hand of fate. If she hadn't met Helen then she might not have noticed the man, and if she hadn't noticed the man then she wouldn't have made the phone call, and if she hadn't made the phone call then . . .

But at the time she was overjoyed to see an old friend. Fate seemed to be smiling on her at long last.

After they had both agreed it had been simply years, far too long, Helen said, 'So, how's married life?'

'Oh well, y'know . . . boring at times, not too bad at others.' Ann shrugged and looked away. 'Tell me about you – did you get into journalism?'

'Oh yes. In fact you're talking to the local rag's leading investigator.'

'Really? I'm impressed.'

Helen smiled. 'It sounds a lot grander than it is, believe me.' She pushed a wedge of dark hair from her eyes – a characteristic gesture Ann remembered well. 'And you? Did you go on with your writing?'

'No. I got submerged in marriage and children.'

'It's a swap I'd gladly make,' Helen said flatly. Ann noticed the long elegant, ringless fingers. She immediately felt ashamed.

'I suppose it's not too bad,' she said. Then with a rush: 'but it's not a bed of roses. Take Henry. Henry told me to come along here and spend some money to make myself feel better. Typical man. Thinks everything can be solved with money. Buy yourself a new dress, he said and an iced bun. An iced bun!' Ann glanced down at the expensively wrapped parcels by her feet. 'I've shown him!'

Helen reached over, touched her hand. 'Steady on.'

Ann took a deep breath and let it out slowly. 'I'm sorry. You've caught me at a particularly bad time.'

'No worry,' said Helen. 'We're going to stay in touch this time.' She sipped some tea. 'So – where exactly are you living now?'

'Over at Knowlewater – Maple Drive.'

Helen paused for a split second and then said 'Maple Drive?'

'Why do you say it like that?' said Ann, and sealed her fate.

Helen paused and shrugged, 'Oh, it's just a name from the past, that's all.'

'Go on. You know something, don't you – something about it.'

She realised Helen was looking curiously at her. 'It's just I've heard rumours,' she improvised. 'What happened?'

Helen stared at her steadily for a few seconds and then said. 'It made the nationals. My first and only big story.' A pause. 'Are you sure you really want to know?' Ann nodded. Beyond Helen a man came in. There was something about him that tweaked at her mind, nudged her subconscious, but

225

she ignored it.

'Please tell me,' she said, sounding calm.

'There was a family lived there,' said Helen, 'when the estate was first built. The Osbornes I think they were called. That's right, the Osbornes. Nothing remarkable about them at all. Mum, Dad, a couple of boys – twins as it happens.' She stopped. 'Look, it was a long time ago –'

'Please,' said Ann desperately '– please.' The man behind Helen was sitting down. Her subconscious was screaming at her.

'All right,' said Helen. 'There was an accident. Between the two boys. They were outside playing in the snow, and one of them got hurt.'

'Hurt? How hurt? How badly hurt?'

'Remember – you asked me,' said Helen steadily. The man had risen and was taking off his coat. 'He was hurt as badly as anyone could be hurt. He fell over or something and his neck got twisted. It was very sad, but . . . the reason why we got interested – why it was in the papers, why I remember it so well.' Helen stopped. 'Ann, are you all right?'

'Yes. Go on, you have to go on.' The man was brushing something from the shoulders of his coat, brushing something off his coat with great fat slaps of his hand, chuckling as he did so.

'Well,' Helen continued, 'the other boy panicked and built a snowman.'

'What?' To Ann, it seemed her voice came from very, very far away. The man was sitting down again, studying the menu.

'A snowman,' repeated Helen. 'Over his brother's body, to hide it.'

And then everything fell into place, and the nightmare began. The man had been outside. He'd come in and brushed snow from his coat. Thick white snow. It must have been snowing all afternoon.

*   *   *

'Hello,' Mrs Macpherson said at last: '687456, no, wait a moment it's 66 –'

'Mrs Macpherson,' said Ann. 'It's me, Mrs Makepeace. Where are the twins?'

'I'm not wearing my proper glasses,' came the reply, 'I think it's 6674 –'

'Where are the boys?' said Ann. 'Just tell me where they are please.' There was a brief pause. The electric silence was loud in her ears.

Finally Mrs Macpherson said, 'That's better, I've got my proper ones now. It is 667456. Who did you say you were?'

'It's Mrs Makepeace. Where are the boys? What are they doing?'

'Oh, hallo, dear – are you having a nice time?'

Ann felt her fingers whiten. 'Just tell me where the boys are, please. Just tell me where they are. Are they inside or where?'

'The boys . . . ?' came the slow reply. 'Why outside of course, enjoying the snow. It's all right, I made them wear their wellie boots. Is it snowing where you are?'

As she turned on the ignition Ann became aware of a knocking on the side window. Helen.

'What's the mad rush?' she said. 'I saw you running away from the 'phone and came after. What's happened?'

Ann switched on the wipers and snatched at the gears. The car lurched forward. 'I've got to get home.'

'I'll come with you.' Once in the car she said, 'Now take it easy. These roads are treacherous.'

Ann pressed her foot down. The car slewed round a corner and accelerated. The wipers moved hypnotically from side to side, brushing the fat, soft flakes first one way and then the next. The street lights were on. Dim, dark huddled figures hurried along the pavements. The red rear lights of a car appeared in front of them. Ann wrenched the steering wheel wildly.

'Oh God!' said Helen. The car disappeared behind. The street lights suddenly stopped. The headlights lit up nothing but falling snow. They were driving through some cold limbo.

'Please God slow down,' said Helen. 'For God's sake slow down!' Ann said nothing. Her eyes were unblinking, staring forward. More lights. The blast of a horn. A distant voice shouted, but it was outside and gone, gone and left behind before it was heard. Helen was whimpering. 'Please, please, please, please slow down!'

Then, suddenly, a street sign. MAPLE DRIVE. Ann turned the wheel, the steering went light for a moment and the back wheels spun wildly before the car found a grip and leapt forward.

'We're here!' said Ann. She slowed to take the drive, steered carefully through the open gate. She didn't want to spoil it now.

The car gently and inexorably slid sideways across the lawn. She glimpsed a small figure throwing himself from their path and then they stopped with a rendering, sickening crunch against something white and cold that toppled over.

Outside it was cold. Bitter. The car engine was still ticking over and the windscreen wipers whirred backwards and forwards. The headlights defined the world. And there he was. For a moment she wasn't sure, she couldn't tell, but when she swept him up in her arms and felt that distinct weight and the way he was put together, she knew.

'Alex. Oh thank God it's you. Alex!'

He seemed strangely unresponsive. 'I'm all right Mummy,' he said.

She kissed him. His cheeks were cold. 'Alex, I've been so worried,' she said. 'I was getting things all twisted in my mind, but it's all right now, it's all right now.'

There was a hand on her arm. 'Ann,' said Helen distinctly

and gently.

'It's all right,' said Ann. 'He's all right.'

'Ann,' said Helen again. 'Ann.'

Ann put Alex down. Her back was to the car. She turned stiffly, feeling like a marionette.

It was curious the way the snowman had shattered. The scattered pieces remained somehow connected and all in proportion, all of a size – a small boy's size. From the end of one leg, one white leg, protruding quite naturally, seeming so normal that at first she didn't notice what it was, was a foot. A human foot. And from the head, the shattered flaking head, the head that was set at a peculiar, awkward angle to the rest of the body, she could see the eyes.

Not black pieces of coal but blue and familiar, staring and dead.

HIS LAST CARD

Nick Warburton

*Nick Warburton was born in 1947 and is married with one son.
He gave up teaching in primary schools after ten years to try
writing (also doing part-time work in libraries and selling on craft
stalls). He writes children's books, radio, stage and television
scripts and in 1985 was joint winner of the BBC/Radio Times
Drama Award for CONVERSATION FROM THE ENGINE ROOM.*

It was while they were putting up decorations in the
lounge that they came across that first, unsigned card.
Charles was standing on the steps when Laura handed it to
him.

'What's this?' he asked, treading carefully down.

He held the card out for Laura to see. It was a photograph
of a bench on the Embankment, overlooking the Thames. It
annoyed him that it wasn't a particularly Christmassy scene
and didn't fit in with his plans for the lounge.

'I don't know why I bother,' he said. 'Look at this wall
here. It's supposed to be a coherent group. A square. Fifteen
humorous cards . . . and a river scene!'

He looked up at Laura and saw her shrink back from him
a little. And he was immediately ashamed at the sound of
his own voice, so ridiculously angry. So ridiculous. He shook
his head and, glancing down at the card again, recognised
something in it he ought to have seen before.

'Oh Laura,' he said. 'I am sorry. I am so sorry.'

'Why? What's the matter?' said Laura.

'The Embankment,' he said. 'It's from you, isn't it? The
bench by the river. Where we met . . .'

But Laura's face was blank.

'No,' she told him. 'It's not my card.'

He felt the irritation rise again, like a tickle in his throat.

'Then where the hell has it come from?'

He flicked it open to read the message and was silenced by its starkness.

'Remember, remember,' it said.

Laura knew that the card had upset Charles. It was unsigned and he couldn't understand it. She decided it was best to avoid further mention of it that evening. After all, the poor boy had enough to contend with. Laura couldn't forget the card, however, or its strange message.

'Remember, remember.'

She was sure that she did remember. That place, where she sometimes took her lunch. And a name.

The following day the snow came, catching London by surprise, as it always does. As Laura was leaving the office, Richard, one of the clerks, offered to run her home. He hesitated on the steps into the street, looking up at her without quite catching her eye.

'I mean, what with the snow and everything,' he said.

Laura smiled and accepted. He seemed to make such a muddle of the invitation, as if he was afraid that she might misunderstand his motives.

It was an awkward journey. The windscreen wipers batted against the snow and Richard puffed on his pipe, trying to think of things to talk about.

When they reached the house Laura glanced at him and hesitated before getting out of the car.

'Is anything the matter?' he asked.

'No. No, I don't think so. It's just that . . .'

'What?'

'It's probably silly but I thought the house was being watched.'

'Watched?'

'Yes. There was someone hanging about by that street

231

lamp last night. Just watching. It's probably nothing but, well, you know.'

Richard walked to the corner of the street and looked around but saw no sign of anyone. He offered to see her into the house. Just to be on the safe side. In the hall Laura held onto his arm as she slipped out of her shoes.

'Please,' she said. 'I've held you up long enough. It was very kind of you to see me in.'

As he drove home Richard made up his mind not to tell his sister why he was late. The snow was a good enough excuse. No need to say anything about Laura.

The second card arrived at breakfast the next morning. Charles brought in the post and tossed it on the table.

'Here,' he said. 'Two for you. One's from Chester so I expect it's from what's-her-name.'

There was a cold edge to his voice. He didn't like the occasional contact that Laura kept up with Alex's mother. It seemed to him that the woman was trying to keep Alex alive in Laura's memory. A morbid clinging to the past. And he didn't like to think of himself as Laura's second husband. His love for her was precious and unique. It could do without reminders from the past.

'Who's the other one from?' he asked as he sat down.

For a second the familiar scene – the bench and the Embankment wall – was exposed on the kitchen table. Then Laura slipped it into her jacket pocket and busied herself with the breakfast things.

'It's . . . from a girl I used to work with,' she said. 'Carol. I don't think you knew her.'

It's not bad news, is it?'

'Of course not. Why should it be?'

'Hiding it away like that.'

'No, she's just catching up on the gossip, Charles. I'll read it at the office.'

'Not another of your lame ducks, I hope,' said Charles.

'Lame ducks?'

'Looking for a shoulder to cry on. They seem to seek you out.'

'No,' said Laura, taking the plates and cups over to the sink. 'Not Carol.'

'Leave those,' he said. 'I'll see to them. I haven't got anything else to do.'

She paused at the kitchen door, watching Charles as he turned his coffee cup in his unsteady fingers.

'Charles,' she said, 'shall we get a tree?'

'A what?'

'A Christmas tree. To mark our first Christmas together.'

'Of course,' he said smiling. 'Of course we must.'

And she left him with the card still in her pocket.

'Do not forget my love,' it said. 'Nor let this become the last of all our Christmasses.'

The card sat on Laura's desk throughout the morning. After lunch she returned to the office and found Richard looking at it. He jumped and fumbled with it at the sound of the closing door.

'I'm sorry, Laura,' he said. 'I didn't mean to . . .'

She ignored his discomfort, keeping him there while she sat down behind the desk and looked at him.

'Do you remember taking me home the other night?' she asked at last.

'Yes, of course I do.'

'And I said I thought there was someone in the street.'

'Yes.'

'I believe this card is from the man who is watching my house.'

'Oh?'

'He worked here some years ago. His name is Frank Blackwell.'

233

'Yes,' stammered Richard. 'I remember him. He took a posting overseas.'

'Frank and I were very close. Did you know that?'

He nodded briefly. His neck had reddened and Laura guessed that he wanted to leave. She had started to tell her story, though, and could not stop now.

'When Alex, my first husband, died Frank was a great comfort to me. We worked closely together and I suppose it was inevitable that I should lean on him for support. Everything seemed so bleak and I needed someone to talk to. One Christmas Eve he came round to my flat and . . .'

Laura paused and studied Richard's face deliberately. He cleared his throat as if he thought he should say something but she carried on before he could speak.

'The Far East posting was Frank's idea. He said we needed time to be sure of ourselves. He didn't know how right he was about that, poor boy. He expected us to marry when he returned but, well, time passed and I felt better, as if I was coming out of a kind of tunnel. And then, of course, there was Charles.'

'So you called it off,' said Richard.

'Not exactly. My letters became more infrequent, more cool, I suppose. I couldn't bear to hurt him but I think that's just what I have done. By being such a coward.'

'And now he's come back to see you?'

'I'm sure he has. I can never quite see his face but I'm sure it's him out there watching me. He sent me this card. A picture of the Embankment where I . . .'

'Where you take your lunch. I know.'

'You know?'

'Well, I've noticed,' said Richard, looking at the floor.

'Unfortunately it's where I met Charles as well. Charles doesn't know anything about all this . . .'

'But if Frank is watching your house . . . well, he's bound to find out soon, isn't he?'

234

'Yes, Richard. That's what I'm so afraid of.'

Richard drove home through a second fall of snow and found himself wondering about these two men in Laura's life. He remembered Frank as a dark, secretive man, difficult to talk to. He'd only met Charles once and found him quick and nervy. Very different from Frank, in fact. And yet they had both loved and been loved by Laura.

He stopped the car in the drive and saw his sister's face at the window. She was holding the curtain aside and looking out for him.

'Yes,' he thought. 'That's what she saw in them. Vulnerability.'

The third card was on the kitchen table for two hours before Charles snatched it up and opened it. He'd returned to it time and again throughout the morning. Laura's name printed neatly in ink. A London post-mark. He wasn't surprised to see the photograph of the Embankment. Nevertheless he felt a pang of outrage at the sight of it and screwed it tightly in his fist. Then, breathing deeply, he smoothed it flat and looked at the message.

'Remember Christmas Eve. If the past means anything at all, we must meet.'

And this time it was signed, not with a full name but an initial: F.

When Laura got home from work he placed the card before her and asked her about it. He didn't give her time to take her coat off. Of course, she said. It was from Carol. Carol Francis who was too scatty to remember whether she'd already sent a card and who signed herself with the initial of her surname. Charles wasn't even sure that he wanted to believe her.

'Tell me,' he said. 'That smell in the hall the other day. 'Pipe smell. You must've noticed it. Carol smoke a pipe, does she?'

Laura reached out and touched his cheek but he twisted his head away.

'Charles,' she said, 'there's no need to be so afraid. You think I'm seeing someone else? Is that it?'

'I don't know what to think, Laura,' he said, turning his face to hers.

She smiled and took his head between her hands. He remained motionless as she kissed his forehead.

'The pipe was Richard's,' she smiled. 'He gave me a lift home when the snow started.'

'Richard?'

'From the office.'

'Richard the rabbit, you mean?' he said, almost laughing.

'Oh, Charles, it's naughty to call him that, poor old Richard. He's not a rabbit. He's just very shy.'

They laughed together at the idea that Charles should be jealous of Richard. But, as their laughter died, Laura pursed her lips and frowned.

'About the card,' she said. 'Will you trust me, Charles?'

He nodded.

'And, if I were in danger,' she added, 'you would be strong, wouldn't you? You wouldn't let me come to harm?'

'Of course I wouldn't,' Charles answered quietly. 'I'd do anything . . . anything to protect you.'

Several times over the next few days Richard drifted into Laura's office, hoping perhaps that she would speak to him again. She sat distractedly at her desk, though, staring out of the window and hardly noticing him. Once he came in with some papers to sign and found her on the phone. Her head was bowed and her face obscured by a curtain of honey-coloured hair. Sensing that he was in the room, she dropped the receiver back in its place, softly and carefully.

'Can't you knock?' she snapped.

'I'm sorry, Laura,' he mumbled. 'I was worried . . .'

She was looking at him as if she intended to shout. Then she stood and moved close to him. She lowered her voice and held up her hands in a little gesture of hopelessness. For a second he thought she was going to touch him lightly on the chest.

'There's been another card,' she said. 'Four cards. I can't sit around and think about this all day, Richard.'

'But what can you do?'

'I think I must go home and sort it out somehow.'

'What about Frank? Is he still around?'

'I see his shadow almost every night. Maybe Charles has seen him too. I just don't know.'

'Look, maybe there's something I can do . . .'

'You?' she asked and he detected a faint note of incredulity in her voice.

'Yes, why not me? You know, for a moment, Laura, you sounded like my sister. She always assumes I'm not capable of . . .'

'No, Richard, of course I didn't mean that,' she said and this time she did rest her finger tips against his chest. 'Of course you're capable but this is my problem and I have to sort it out alone.'

'Then she hurried past him and on through the bustle of activity in the outer office. Richard held his breath and watched her disappear. It would take her, he calculated, almost an hour to get home.

Charles sat in the lounge with the cards spread before him. He picked up the last one and looked again at its message.

'23rd December: one day to death.'

He noticed that his pulse had calmed and that the card no longer shook in his hand. And he was pleased. I can face what I have to face, he thought. I know I will be strong enough. He replaced the card carefully on the floor. His last card. Whoever he is. Then he leaned back in his armchair, pressed the tips of his fingers together and waited.

At some point in the afternoon – he wasn't sure exactly when – there was an urgent ringing on the doorbell. It shattered the silence of the house but it didn't startle him. He'd been expecting it. He smiled to himself as he got to his feet.

As soon as Laura let herself in she knew that the house was not empty. There was an unmistakeable sense of someone being in another room. She pushed open the door to the lounge. The curtains were closed and she waited a moment till her eyes were used to the gloom. Then she saw a figure in the armchair, facing away from her, shoulders hunched inside a dark raincoat.

'Frank?' she whispered.

The figure half-turned. Thin light from the curtains lit his cheekbone.

'No,' said Charles. 'But this is his coat. It got rather chilly in here.'

'What's going on, Charles?'

'You should've destroyed the cards,' he said, still without looking at her. 'Or made a better job of hiding them. We've had a visitor,' he added, 'I'm sure that won't surprise you. Perhaps you ought to go and see.'

And suddenly he was standing and had grasped her arm. He pulled her into the kitchen. The breakfast cups and plates were scattered over the floor. A wall of chill air struck Laura. There was a jagged hole in the glass of the back door. Outside in the garden she saw the twisted legs of a man face-down in the snow. And smears of pink blood on the step, as if he'd tried to claw his way back into the kitchen.

'He said you were expecting him,' said Charles. 'Were you, Laura?'

He stooped and picked the bread-knife from the floor, holding it up to her between his thumb and finger, like a child showing his treasures.

'It's over now,' he said, pulling Laura towards him. 'I couldn't do anything else, could I? Be weak or strong. I had to be strong.'

'Yes,' she whispered. 'You had to be strong.'

'It's what you made me. I wanted to be strong for you.'

'You poor, poor boy . . .'

'No. Don't call me that. Not any more.'

He kissed her on the mouth and she dared not resist. He threw down the knife and pulled the coat from her shoulders. A shudder of fear passed through her as her fingers dug into his back. Fear and something other than fear. Something like excitement.

The kitchen became dark around them. Laura held onto Charles, concentrating on his face, for her life's sake. His eyes were wide open and he stared at the ceiling.

'When they come for me, Laura,' he said, 'you'll be with me, won't you? And you will wait for me?'

'Of course, my darling. Of course I will.'

Richard didn't know how he managed to get through the rest of that evening. Nothing in his experience had prepared him for what he found when he got to the house. Laura, her face silent and white with shock, her blouse open and flecked with blood. Charles crouching in a corner of the kitchen, moving his lips but saying nothing. And the body. The body contorted in the snow outside.

It was well into January before Laura could forget Charles enough to go back to the house. Richard drove her there and they busied themselves taking down the decorations. Laura said it would be easier to cope if they kept themselves busy. They lit a fire in the lounge and for some time they managed to hold back the air of oppression that still clung to the place.

When Richard hauled the Christmas tree into the garden he saw her watching him through the kitchen window. He grinned and waved to her.

'You've been so sweet to me,' she said to him when he came in, rubbing his hands against the cold.

She brushed his cheek with the back of her hand. He didn't know what to say and took half a step towards her. She stopped him by holding up some cards and tapping him on the chin with them. He recognised them at once. Four cards, each with the same river scene.

'I'd like you to burn these for me,' she said softly. 'You know what they are?'

'Yes,' he said. 'Frank's cards.'

'Hmm. The first one was Frank's. Perhaps, one day, I'll explain about the others.'

He kept his eyes fixed on her and Laura knew he would do exactly as she asked.

'I'd very much like it if *you* burned them for me, Richard,' she said.

'Of course. If it's what you want.'

He tossed the cards onto the fire and she could see that he knew he was, in some way, implicating himself. She watched him as he knelt on the rug, staring into the fire.

The cards curled and flared. It was impossible to tell which was the one Frank had sent. They all looked the same in the fire. Hers burned just as well. It seemed a pity to see her careful work go up in flames like that. And his last card, with its pitiful message: 'Remember, remember.'

Poor, poor Frank. He had sounded so anxious about her on the phone, so very eager to come to the house on Christmas Eve. To see if he could help. Because, of course, he still loved her, very much.

And so had Alex . . .

And so did Charles. Quite surprisingly, in fact.

And so does Richard . . .

Such a timid boy, she thought, lightly touching the top of his head. Your time will come. But not just yet, perhaps.

THE JUDGE'S HOUSE

Bram Stoker

*Abraham Stoker, born in Dublin in 1847, wrote a number of
novels and short stories, but is chiefly remembered for DRACULA
(1897). Stoker acted as touring manager for Sir Henry Irving for
twenty-seven years and produced PERSONAL REMINISCENCES
OF HENRY IRVING. He died in 1912.*

When the time for his examination drew near
Malcolm Malcolmson made up his mind to go
somewhere to read by himself. He feared the attractions of
the seaside, and also he feared completely rural isolation, for
of old he knew its charms, and so he determined to find
some unpretentious little town where there would be nothing to distract him. He refrained from asking suggestions
from any of his friends, for he argued that each would
recommend some place of which he had knowledge, and
where he had already acquaintances. As Malcolmson
wished to avoid friends he had no wish to encumber himself
with the attention of friends' friends, and so he determined
to look out for a place for himself. He packed a portmanteau
with some clothes and all the books he required, and then
took a ticket for the first name on the local time-table which
he did not know.

When at the end of three hours' journey he alighted at
Benchurch, he felt satisfied that he had so far obliterated his
tracks as to be sure of having a peaceful opportunity of pursuing his studies. He went straight to the one inn which the
sleepy little place contained, and put up for the night.
Benchurch was a market town, and once in three weeks was
crowded to excess, but for the remainder of the twenty-one
days it was as attractive as a desert. Malcolmson looked

around the day after his arrival to try to find quarters more isolated than even so quiet an inn as 'The Good Traveller' afforded. There was only one place which took his fancy, and it cerainly satisfied his wildest ideas regarding quiet; in fact, quiet was not the proper word to apply to it – desolation was the only term conveying any suitable idea of its isolation. It was an old rambling, heavy-built house of the Jacobean style, with heavy gables and windows, unusually small, and set higher than was customary in such houses, and was surrounded with a high brick wall massively built. Indeed, on examination, it looked more like a fortified house than an ordinary dwelling. But all these things pleased Malcolmson. 'Here,' he thought, 'is the very spot I have been looking for, and if I can only get opportunity of using it I shall be happy.' His joy was increased when he realised beyond doubt that it was not at present inhabited.

From the post-office he got the name of the agent, who was rarely surprised at the application to rent a part of the old house. Mr Carnford, the local lawyer and agent, was a genial old gentleman, and frankly confessed his delight at anyone being willing to live in the house.

'To tell you the truth,' said he, 'I should be only too happy, on behalf of the owners, to let anyone have the house rent free for a term of years if only to accustom the people here to see it inhabited. It has been so long empty that some kind of absurd prejudice has grown up about it, and this can be best put down by its occupation – if only,' he added with a sly glance at Malcolmson, 'by a scholar like yourself, who wants it quiet for a time.'

Malcolmson thought it needless to ask the agent about the 'absurd prejudice'; he knew he would get more information, if he should require it, on that subject from other quarters. He paid his three months' rent, got a receipt, and the name of an old woman who would probably undertake to 'do' for him, and came away with the keys in his pocket. He then went to the landlady of the inn, who was a cheerful and most kindly person, and asked her advice as to such stores and provisions as he would be likely to require. She threw up her hands in amazement when he told her where he was going to settle himself.

'Not in the Judge's House!' she said, and grew pale as she spoke. He explained the locality of the house, saying that he did not know its name. When he had finished she answered:

'Aye, sure enough – sure enough the very place! It is the Judge's House sure enough.' He asked her to tell him about the place, why so called, and what there was against it. She told him that it was so called locally because it had been many years before – how long she could not say, as she was herself from another part of the country, but she thought it must have been a hundred years or more – the abode of a judge who was held in great terror on account of his harsh sentences and his hostility to prisoners at Assizes. As to what there was against the house itself she could not tell. She had often asked but no one could inform her; but there was a general feeling that there was *something*, and for her own part she would not take all the money in Drinkwater's Bank and stay in the house an hour by herself. Then she apologised to Malcolmson for her disturbing talk.

'It is too bad of me, sir, and you – and a young gentleman, too – if you will pardon me saying it, going to live there all alone. If you were my boy – and you'll excuse me for saying it – you wouldn't sleep there a night, not if I had to go there myself and pull the big alarm bell that's on the roof!' The good creature was so manifestly in earnest, and was so kindly in her intentions, that Malcolmson, although amused, was touched. He told her kindly how much he appreciated her interest in him, and added:

'But, my dear Mrs Witham, indeed you need not be concerned about me! A man who is reading for the Mathematical Tripos has too much to think of to be disturbed by any of these mysterious "somethings", and his work is of too exact and prosaic a kind to allow of his having any corner in his mind for mysteries of any kind. Harmonical Progression, Permutations and Combinations, and Elliptic Functions have sufficient mysteries for me!' Mrs Witham kindly undertook to see after his commissions, and he went himself to look for the old woman who had been recommended to him. When he returned to the Judge's House with her, after an interval of a couple of hours, he found Mrs Witham herself waiting with several men and boys carrying parcels, and an upholsterer's man with a bed in a cart, for she said, though tables and chairs might be all very well, a bed that hadn't been aired for mayhap fifty years was not proper for young bones to lie on. She was evidently curious to see the inside of the house; and though manifestly so afraid of the 'somethings' that at the slightest sound she clutched on to Malcolmson, whom she never left for a moment, went over the whole place.

After his examination of the house, Malcolmson decided to take up his abode in the great dining-room, which was big enough to serve for all his requirements; and Mrs Witham, with the aid of the charwoman, Mrs Dempster, proceeded to arrange matters. When the hampers were brought in and unpacked, Malcolmson saw that with much kind fore-thought she had sent from her own kitchen sufficient provisions to last for a few days. Before going she expressed all sorts of kind wishes; and at the door turned and said:

'And perhaps, sir, as the room is big and draughty it might be well to have one of those big screens put round your bed at night – though, truth to tell, I would die myself if I were to be so shut in with all kinds of – of "things", that put their heads round the sides, or over the top, and look on me!' The image which she had called up was too much for her nerves and she fled incontinently.

Mrs Dempster sniffed in a superior manner as the

landlady disappeared, and remarked that for her own part she wasn't afraid of all the bogies in the kingdom.

'I'll tell you what it is, sir,' she said: 'bogies is all kinds and sorts of things – except bogies! Rats and mice, and beetles; and creaky doors, and loose slates, and broken panes, and stiff drawer handles, that stay out when you pull them and then fall down in the middle of the night. Look at the wainscot of the room? It is old – hundreds of years old! Do you think there's no rats and beetles there! And do you imagine, sir, that you won't see none of them! Rats is bogies, I tell you, and bogies is rats; and don't you get to think anything else!'

'Mrs Dempster,' said Malcolmson gravely, making her a polite bow, 'you know more than a Senior Wrangler! And let me say, that, as a mark of esteem for your indubitable soundness of head and heart, I shall, when I go, give you possession of this house, and let you stay here by yourself for the last two months of my tenancy, for four weeks will serve my purpose.'

'Thank you kindly, sir!' she answered, 'but I couldn't sleep away from home a night. I am in Greenhow's Charity, and if I slept a night away from my rooms I should lose all I have got to live on. The rules is very strict; and there's too many watching for a vacancy for me to run any risks in the matter. Only for that, sir, I'd gladly come here and attend on you altogether during your stay.'

'My good woman,' said Malcolmson hastily, 'I had come here on purpose to obtain solitude; and believe me that I am grateful to the late Greenhow for having so organised his admirable charity – whatever it is – that I am perforce denied the opportunity of suffering from such a form of temptation! Saint Anthony himself could not be more rigid on the point!'

The old woman laughed harshly. 'Ah, you young gentlemen,' she said, 'you don't fear for naught; and belike you'll get all the solitude you want here.' She set to work with her cleaning; and by nightfall, when Malcolmson returned from his walk – he always had one of his books to study as he walked – he found the room swept and tidied, a fire burning in the old hearth, the lamp lit, and the table spread for supper with Mrs Witham's excellent fare. 'This is comfort, indeed,' he said, as he rubbed his hands.

When he had finished his supper, and lifted the tray to the other end of the great oak dining-table, he got out his books again, put fresh wood on the fire, trimmed his lamp, and set himself down to a spell of real hard work. He went on without pause till about eleven o'clock, when he knocked off for a bit to fix his fire and lamp, and to make himself a cup of tea. He had always been a tea-drinker, and during his college life had sat late at work and had taken tea late. The rest was a great luxury to him, and he enjoyed it with a sense of delicious, voluptuous ease. The renewed fire leaped and sparkled, and threw quaint shadows through the great old room; and as he sipped his hot tea he revelled in the sense of isolation from his kind. Then it was that he began to notice for the first time what a noise the rats were making.

'Surely,' he thought, 'they cannot have been at it all the time I was reading. Had they been, I must have noticed it!' Presently, when the noise increased, he satisfied himself that it was really new. It was evident that at first the rats had been frightened at the presence of a stranger, and the light of fire and lamp; but that as the time went on they had grown bolder and were now disporting themselves as was their wont.

How busy they were! and hark to the strange noises! Up and down behind the old wainscot, over the ceiling and under the floor they raced, and gnawed, and scratched! Malcolmson smiled to himself as he recalled to mind the saying of Mrs Dempster, 'Bogies is rats, and rats is bogies!' The tea began to have its effect of intellectual and nervous stimulus, he saw with joy another long spell of work to be done before the night was past, and in the sense of security which it gave him, he allowed himself the luxury of a good look around the room. He took his lamp in one hand, and went all around, wondering that so quaint and beautiful an old house had been so long neglected. The carving of the oak on the panels of the wainscot was fine, and on and round the doors and windows it was beautiful and of rare merit. There were some old pictures on the walls, but they were coated so thick with dust and dirt that he could not distinguish any detail of them, though he held his lamp as high as he could over his head. Here and there as he went round he saw some crack or hole blocked for a moment by the face of a rat with its bright eyes glittering in the light, but in an instant it was gone; and a squeak and a scamper followed.

The thing that most struck him, however, was the rope of the great alarm bell on the roof, which hung down in a corner of the room on the right-hand side of the fireplace. He pulled up close to the hearth a great high-backed carved oak chair, and sat down to his last cup of tea. When this was done he made up the fire, and went back to his work, sitting at the corner of the table, having the fire to his left. For a while the rats disturbed him somewhat with their perpetual scampering, but he got accustomed to the noise as one does to the ticking of a clock or to the roar of moving water; and he became so immersed in his work that everything in the world, except the problem which he was trying to solve, passed away from him.

He suddenly looked up, his problem was still unsolved, and there was in the air that sense of the hour before the dawn, which is so dread to doubtful life. The noise of the rats had ceased. Indeed it seemed to him that it must have ceased but lately and that it was the sudden cessation which had disturbed him. The fire had fallen low, but still it threw out a deep red glow. As he looked he started in spite of his *sang froid*.

There on the great high-backed carved oak chair by the right side of the fireplace sat an enormous rat, steadily glaring at him with baleful eyes. He made a motion to it as though to hunt it away, but it did not stir. Then he made the motion of throwing something. Still it did not stir, but showed its great white teeth angrily, and its cruel eyes shone in the lamplight with an added vindictiveness.

Malcolmson felt amazed, and seizing the poker from the hearth ran at it to kill it. Before, however, he could strike it, the rat, with a squeak that sounded like the concentration of hate, jumped upon the floor, and, running up the rope of the alarm bell, disappeared in the darkness beyond the range of the green-shaded lamp. Instantly, strange to say, the noisy scampering of the rats in the wainscot began again.

By this time Malcolmson's mind was quite off the problem; and as a shrill cock-crow outside told him of the approach of morning, he went to bed and to sleep.

He slept so sound that he was not even waked by Mrs Dempster coming in to make up his room. It was only when she had tidied up the place and got his breakfast ready and tapped on the screen which closed in his bed that he woke. He was a little tired still after his night's hard work, but a strong cup of tea soon freshened him up, and, taking his book, he went out for his morning walk, bringing with him a few sandwiches lest he should not care to return till dinner time. He found a quiet walk between high elms some way outside the town, and here he spent the greater part of the day studying his Laplace. On his return he looked in to see Mrs Witham and to thank her for her kindness. When she saw him coming through the diamond-paned bay-window of her sanctum she came out to meet him and asked him in. She looked at him searchingly and shook her head as she said:

'You must not overdo it, sir. You are paler this morning than you should be. Too late hours and too hard work on the brain isn't good for any man! But tell me, sir, how did you pass the night? Well, I hope? But, my heart! sir, I was glad when Mrs Dempster told me this morning that you were all right and sleeping sound when she went in.'

'Oh, I was all right,' he answered, smiling, 'the "some-things" didn't worry me, as yet. Only the rats; and they had a circus, I tell you, all over the place. There was one wicked looking old devil that sat up on my own chair by the fire, and wouldn't go till I took the poker to him, and then he ran up the rope of the alarm bell and got to somewhere up the wall or the ceiling – I couldn't see where, it was so dark.'

'Mercy on us,' said Mrs Witham, 'an old devil, and sitting on a chair by the fireside! Take care, sir! take care! There's many a true word spoken in jest.'

'How do you mean? 'Pon my word I don't understand.'

'An old devil! The old devil, perhaps. There! sir, you needn't laugh,' for Malcolmson had broken into a hearty peal. 'You young folks thinks it easy to laugh at things that makes older ones shudder. Never mind, sir! never mind! Please God, you'll laugh all the time. It's what I wish you myself!' and the good lady beamed all over in sympathy with his enjoyment, her fears gone for a moment.

'Oh, forgive me!' said Malcolmson presently. 'Don't think me rude; but the idea was too much for me – that the old devil himself was on the chair last night!' And at the thought he laughed again. Then he went home to dinner.

This evening the scampering of the rats began earlier; indeed it had been going on before his arrival, and only ceased whilst his presence by its freshness disturbed them. After dinner he sat by the fire for a while and had a smoke; and then, having cleared his table, began to work as before. Tonight the rats disturbed him more than they had done on the previous night. How they scampered up and down and under and over! How they squeaked, and scratched, and gnawed! How they, getting bolder by degrees, came to the mouths of their holes and to the chinks and cracks and crannies in the wainscoting till their eyes shone like tiny lamps as the firelight rose and fell. But to him, now doubtless accustomed to them, their eyes were not wicked; only their playfulness touched him. Sometimes the boldest of them made sallies out on the floor or along the mouldings of the wainscot. Now and again as they disturbed him Malcolmson made a sound to frighten them, smiting the table with his hand or giving a fierce 'Hsh, hsh,' so that they fled straightway to their holes.

And so the early part of the night wore on; and despite the noise Malcolmson got more and more immersed in his work.

All at once he stopped, as on the previous night, being overcome by a sudden sense of silence. There was not the faintest sound of gnaw, or scratch or squeak. The silence was as of the grave. He remembered the odd occurrence of the previous night, and instinctively he looked at the chair standing close by the fireside. And then a very odd sensation thrilled through him.

There, on the great old high-backed carved oak chair beside the fireplace sat the same enormous rat, steadily glaring at him with baleful eyes.

Instinctively he took the nearest thing to his hand, a book of logarithms, and flung it at it. The book was badly aimed and the rat did not stir, so again the poker performance of the previous night was repeated; and again the rat, being closely pursued, fled up the rope of the alarm bell. Strangely too, the departure of this rat was instantly followed by the renewal of the noise made by the general rat community. On this occasion, as on the previous one, Malcolmson could not see at what part of the room the rat disappeared, for the green shade of his lamp left the upper part of the room in darkness, and the fire had burned low.

On looking at his watch he found it was close on midnight; and, not sorry for the *divertissement*, he made up his fire and made himself his nightly pot of tea. He had got through a good spell of work, and thought himself entitled to a cigarette; and so he sat on the great carved oak chair before the fire and enjoyed it. Whilst smoking he began to think that he would like to know where the rat disappeared to, for he had certain ideas for the morrow not entirely disconnected with a rat-trap. Accordingly he lit another lamp and placed it so that it would shine well into the right-hand corner of the wall by the fireplace. Then he got all the books he had with him, and placed them handy to throw at the vermin. Finally he lifted the rope of the alarm bell and placed the end of it on the table, fixing the extreme end under the lamp. As he handled it he could not help noticing how pliable it was, especially for so strong a rope, and one not in use. 'You could hang a man with it,' he thought to himself. When his preparations were made he looked around, and said complacently:

'There now, my friend, I think we shall learn something of you this time!' He began his work again, and though as before somewhat disturbed at first by the noise of the rats, soon lost himself in his propositions and problems.

Again he was called to his immediate surroundings suddenly. This time it might not have been the sudden silence only which took his attention; there was a slight movement of the rope, and the lamp moved. Without stirring, he looked to see if his pile of books was within range, and then cast his eye along the rope. As he looked he saw the great rat drop from the rope on the oak armchair and sit there glaring at him. He raised a book in his right hand, and taking careful aim, flung it at the rat. The latter, with a quick movement, sprang aside and dodged the missile. He then took another book, and a third, and flung them one after another at the rat, but each time unsuccessfully. At last, as he stood with a book poised in his hand to throw, the rat squeaked and

251

seemed afraid. This made Malcolmson more than ever eager to strike, and the book flew and struck the rat a resounding blow. It gave a terrified squeak, and, turning on its pursuer a look of terrible malevolence, ran up the chair-back and made a great jump to the rope of the alarm bell and ran up it like lightning. The lamp rocked under the sudden strain, but it was a heavy one and did not topple over. Malcomson kept his eyes on the rat, and saw it by the light of the second lamp leap to a moulding of the wainscot and disappear through a hole in one of the great pictures which hung on the wall, obscured and invisible through its coating of dirt and dust.

'I shall look up my friend's habitation in the morning,' said the student, as he went over to collect his books. 'The third picture from the fireplace; I shall not forget.' He picked up the books one by one, commenting on them as he lifted them. '*Conic Sections* he does not mind, nor *Cycloidal Oscillations*, nor the *Principia*, nor *Quaternions*, nor *Thermodynamics*. Now for the book that fetched him!' Malcolmson took it up and looked at it. As he did so he started, and a sudden pallor overspread his face. He looked round uneasily and shivered slightly, as he murmured to himself:

'The Bible my mother gave me! What an odd coincidence.' He sat down to work again, and the rats in the wainscot renewed their gambols. They did not disturb him, however; somehow their presence gave him a sense of companionship. But he could not attend to his work, and after striving to master the subject on which he was engaged gave it up in despair, and went to bed as the first streak of dawn stole in through the eastern window.

He slept heavily but uneasily, and dreamed much; and when Mrs Dempster woke him late in the morning he seemed ill at ease, and for a few minutes did not seem to realise exactly where he was. His first request rather surprised the servant.

'Mrs Dempster, when I am out today I wish you would get

252

the steps and dust or wash those pictures – specially that one the third from the fireplace – I want to see what they are.'

Late in the afternoon Malcolmson worked at his books in the shaded walk, and the cheerfulness of the previous day came back to him as the day wore on, and he found that his reading was progressing well. He had worked out to a satisfactory conclusion all the problems which had as yet baffled him, and it was in a state of jubilation that he paid a visit to Mrs Witham at 'The Good Traveller'. He found a stranger in the cosy·sitting-room with the landlady, who was introduced to him as Dr Thornhill. She was not quite at ease, and this combined with the Doctor's plunging at once into a series of questions, made Malcolmson come to the conclusion that his presence was not an accident, so without preliminary, he said:

'Dr Thornhill, I shall with pleasure answer you any question you may choose to ask me if you will answer me one question first.'

The Doctor seemed surprised, but he smiled and answered at once. 'Done! What is it?'

'Did Mrs Witham ask you to come here and see me and advise me?'

Dr Thornhill for a moment was taken aback, and Mrs Witham got fiery red and turned away; but the Doctor was a frank and ready man, and he answered at once and openly:

'She did: but she didn't intend you to know it. I suppose it was my clumsy haste that made you suspect. She told me that she did not like the idea of your being in that house all by yourself, and that she thought you took too much strong tea. In fact, she wants me to advise you if possible to give up the tea and the very late hours. I was a keen student in my time, so I suppose I may take the liberty of a college man, and without offence, advise you not quite as a stranger.'

Malcolmson with a bright smile held out his hand. 'Shake! as they say in America,' he said. 'I must thank you for your kindness and Mrs Witham too, and your kindness deserves a return on my part. I promise to take no more strong tea – no tea at all till you let me – and I shall go to bed tonight at one o'clock at the latest. Will that do?'

'Capital,' said the Doctor. 'Now tell us all that you noticed in the old house,' and so Malcolmson then and there told in minute detail all that had happened in the last two nights. He was interrupted every now and then by some exclamation from Mrs Witham, till finally when he told of the episode of the Bible the landlady's pent-up emotions found vent in a shriek; and it was not till a stiff glass of brandy and water had been administered that she grew composed again. Dr Thornhill listened with a face of growing gravity, and when the narrative was complete and Mrs Witham had been restored he asked:

'The rat always went up the rope of the alarm bell?'

'Always.'

'I suppose you know,' said the Doctor after a pause, 'what the rope is?'

'No!'

'It is,' said the Doctor slowly, 'the very rope which the hangman used for all the victims of the Judge's judicial rancour!' Here he was interrupted by another scream from Mrs Witham, and steps had to be taken for her recovery. Malcolmson, having looked at his watch and found that it was close to his dinner hour, had gone home before her complete recovery.

When Mrs Witham was herself again she almost assailed the Doctor with angry questions as to what he meant by putting such horrible ideas into the poor young man's mind. 'He has quite enough there already to upset him,' she added. Dr Thornhill replied:

'My dear madam, I had a distinct purpose in it! I wanted to draw his attention to the bell rope, and to fix it there. It may be that he is in a highly overwrought state, and has been studying too much, although I am bound to say that he seems as sound and healthy a young man, mentally and bodily, as ever I saw – but then the rats – and that suggestion of the Devil.' The doctor shook his head and went on. 'I would have offered to go and stay the first night with him but that I felt sure it would have been a cause of offence. He may get in the night some strange fright or hallucination; and if he does I want him to pull that rope. All alone as he is it will give us a warning, and we may reach him in time to be of service. I shall be sitting up pretty late tonight and shall keep my ears open. Do not be alarmed if Benchurch gets a surprise before morning.'

'Oh, Doctor, what do you mean? What do you mean?'

'I mean this; that possibly – nay, more probably – we shall hear the great alarm bell from the Judge's House tonight,' and the Doctor made about as effective an exit as could be thought of.

When Malcolmson arrived home he found that it was a little after his usual time, and Mrs Dempster had gone away – the rules of Greenhow's Charity were not to be neglected. He was glad to see that the place was bright and tidy with a cheerful fire and a well-trimmed lamp. The evening was colder than might have been expected in April, and a heavy wind was blowing with such rapidly-increasing strength that there was every promise of a storm during the night. For a few minutes after his entrance the noise of the rats ceased; but so soon as they became accustomed to his presence they began again. He was glad to hear them, for he felt once more the feeling of companionship in their noise, and his mind ran back to the strange fact that they only ceased to manifest themselves when that other – the great rat with the baleful eyes – came upon the scene. The reading-lamp only was lit and its green shade kept the ceiling and the upper part of the room in darkness, so that the cheerful light from the hearth spreading over the floor and shining on the white cloth laid over the end of the table was warm and cheery. Malcolmson sat down to his dinner with a good appetite and a buoyant spirit. After his dinner and a cigarette he sat steadily down to work, determined not to let anything disturb him, for he remembered his promise to the doctor, and made up his mind to make the best of the time at his disposal.

For an hour or so he worked all right, and then his thoughts began to wander from his books. The actual circumstances around him, the calls on his physical attention, and his nervous susceptibility were not to be denied. By this time the wind had become a gale, and the gale a storm. The old house, solid though it was, seemed to shake to its foundations, and the storm roared and raged through its many chimneys and its queer old gables, producing strange, unearthly sounds in the empty rooms and corridors. Even the great alarm bell on the roof must have felt the force of the wind, for the rope rose and fell slightly, as though the bell were moved a little from time to time, and the limber rope fell on the oak floor with a hard and hollow sound.

As Malcolmson listened to it he bethought himself of the doctor's words, 'It is the rope which the hangman used for the victims of the Judge's judicial rancour,' and he went over to the corner of the fireplace and took it in his hand to look at it. There seemed a sort of deadly interest in it, and as he stood there he lost himself for a moment in speculation as to who these victims were, and the grim wish of the Judge to have such a ghastly relic ever under his eyes. As he stood there the swaying of the bell on the roof still lifted the rope now and again; but presently there came a new sensation – a sort of tremor in the rope, as though something was moving along it.

Looking up instinctively Malcolmson saw the great rat coming slowly down towards him, glaring at him steadily. He dropped the rope and started back with a muttered curse, and the rat, turning, ran up the rope again and disappeared, and at the same instant Malcomson became conscious that the noise of the rats, which had ceased for a while, began again.

All this set him thinking, and it occurred to him that he had not investigated the lair of the rat or looked at the pictures, as he had intended. He lit the other lamp without the shade, and, holding it up, went and stood opposite the third picture from the fireplace on the right hand side where he had seen the rat disappear on the previous night.

At the first glance he started back so suddenly that he almost dropped the lamp, and a deadly pallor overspread his face. His knees shook, and heavy drops of sweat came on his forehead, and he trembled like an aspen. But he was young and plucky, and pulled himself together, and after the pause of a few seconds stepped forward again, raised the lamp, and examined the picture which had been dusted and washed, and now stood out clearly.

It was of a judge dressed in his robes of scarlet and ermine. His face was strong and merciless, evil, crafty, and vindictive, with a sensual mouth, hooked nose of ruddy colour, and shaped like the beak of a bird of prey. The rest of the face was of a cadaverous colour. The eyes were of peculiar brilliance and with a terribly malignant expression. As he looked at them, Malcolmson grew cold, for he saw there the very counterpart of the eyes of the great rat. The lamp almost fell from his hand, he saw the rat with its baleful eyes peering out through the hole in the corner of the picture, and noted the sudden cessation of the noise of the other rats. However, he pulled himself together, and went on with his examination of the picture.

The Judge was seated in a great high-backed carved oak chair, on the right-hand side of a great stone fireplace where, in the corner, a rope hung down from the ceiling, its end lying coiled on the floor. With a feeling of something like horror, Malcolmson recognised the scene of the room as it stood, and gazed around him in an awe-struck manner as though he expected to find some strange presence behind him. Then he looked over to the corner of the fireplace – and with a loud cry he let the lamp fall from his hand.

There, in the Judge's armchair, with the rope hanging behind, sat the rat with the Judge's baleful eyes, now intensified and with a fiendish leer. Save for the howling of the storm without there was silence.

The fallen lamp recalled Malcolmson to himself. Fortunately it was of metal, and so the oil was not spilt. However, the practical need of attending to it settled at once his nervous apprehensions. When he had turned it out, he wiped his brow and thought for a moment.

'This will not do,' he said to himself. 'If I go on like this I shall become a crazy fool. This must stop! I promised the Doctor I would not take tea. Faith, he was pretty right! My nerves must have been getting into a queer state. Funny I did not notice it. I never felt better in my life. However, it is all right now, and I shall not be such a fool again.'

Then he mixed himself a good stiff glass of brandy and water and resolutely sat down to his work.

It was nearly an hour later when he looked up from his book, disturbed by the sudden stillness. Without, the wind howled and roared louder than ever, and the rain drove in sheets against the windows, beating like hail on the glass; but within there was no sound whatever save the echo of the wind as it roared in the great chimney, and now and then a hiss as a few raindrops found their way down the chimney in a lull of the storm. The fire had fallen low and had ceased to flame, though it threw out a red glow. Malcolmson listened attentively and presently heard a thin, squeaking noise, very faint. It came from the corner of the room where the rope hung down, and he thought it was the creaking of the rope on the floor as the swaying of the bell raised and lowered it. Looking up, however, he saw in the dim light the great rat clinging to the rope and gnawing it. The rope was already nearly gnawed through – he could see the lighter colour where the strands were laid bare. As he looked the job was completed, and the severed end of the rope fell clattering on the oaken floor, whilst for an instant the great rat remained like a knob or tassel at the end of the rope, which now began to sway to and fro. Malcolmson felt for a moment another pang of terror as he thought that now the possibility of calling the outer world to his assistance was cut off, but an intense anger took its place, and seizing the book he was reading he hurled it at the rat. The blow was well aimed, but before the missile could reach it the rat dropped off and struck the floor with a soft thud. Malcolmson instantly rushed over towards it, but it darted and disappeared in the darkness of the shadows of the room. Malcolmson felt that his work was over for the night, and determined then and there to vary the monotony of the proceedings by a hunt for the rat, and took off the green shade of the lamp so as to ensure a wider spreading light. As he did so the gloom of the upper part of the room was relieved, and in the new flood of light, great by comparison with the previous darkness, the pictures on the wall stood out boldly. From where he stood, Malcolmson saw right opposite to him the third picture on the wall from the right of the fireplace. He rubbed his eyes in surprise, and then a great fear began to come upon him.

In the centre of the picture was a great irregular patch of brown canvas, as fresh as when it was stretched on the frame. The background was as before, with chair and chimney-corner and rope, but the figure of the Judge had disappeared.

Malcolmson, almost in a chill of horror, turned slowly round, and then he began to shake and tremble like a man in a palsy. His strength seemed to have left him, and he was incapable of action or movement, hardly even of thought.

He could only see and hear.

There, on the great high-backed carved oak chair sat the Judge in his robes of scarlet and ermine, with his baleful eyes glaring vindictively, and a smile of triumph on the resolute, cruel mouth, as he lifted with his hands a *black cap*. Malcolmson felt as if the blood was running from his heart, as one does in moments of prolonged suspense. There was a singing in his ears. Without, he could hear the roar and howl of the tempest, and through it, swept on the storm, came the striking of midnight by the great chimes in the market place. He stood for a space of time that seemed to him endless, still as a statue and with wide-open, horror-struck eyes, breathless. As the clock struck, so the smile of triumph on the Judge's face intensified, and at the last stroke of midnight he placed the black cap on his head.

Slowly and deliberately the Judge rose from his chair and picked up the piece of rope of the alarm bell which lay on the floor, drew it through his hands as if he enjoyed its touch, and then deliberately began to knot one end of it, fashioning it into a noose. This he tightened and tested with his foot, pulling hard at it till he was satisfied and then making a running noose of it, which he held in his hand. Then he began to move along the table on the opposite side to Malcolmson, keeping his eyes on him until he had passed him, when with a quick movement he stood in front of the door. Malcolmson then began to feel that he was trapped, and tried to think of what he should do. There was some fascination in the Judge's eyes, which he never took off him, and he had, perforce, to look. He saw the Judge approach – still keeping between him and the door – and raise the noose and throw it towards him as if to entangle him. With a great effort he made a quick movement to one side, and saw the rope fall beside him, and heard it strike the oaken floor. Again the Judge raised the noose and tried to ensnare him, ever keeping his baleful eyes fixed on him, and each time by a mighty effort the student just managed to evade it. So this went on for many times, the Judge seeming never discouraged nor discomposed at failure, but playing as a cat does with a mouse. At last in despair, which had reached its climax, Malcolmson cast a quick glance round him. The lamp seemed to have blazed up, and there was a fairly good light in the room. At the many ratholes and in the chinks and crannies of the wainscot he saw the rats' eyes; and this aspect, that was purely physical, gave him a gleam of comfort. He looked around and saw that the rope of the great alarm bell was laden with rats. Every inch of it was covered with them, and more and more were pouring through the small circular hole in the ceiling whence it emerged, so that with their weight the bell was beginning to sway.

Hark! it had swayed till the clapper had touched the bell. The sound was but a tiny one, but the bell was only beginning to sway, and it would increase.

At the sound the Judge, who had been keeping his eyes fixed on Malcolmson, looked up, and a scowl of diabolical anger overspread his face. His eyes fairly glowed like hot coals, and he stamped his foot with a sound that seemed to make the house shake. A dreadful peal of thunder broke overhead as he raised the rope again, whilst the rats kept running up and down the rope as though working against time. This time, instead of throwing it, he drew close to his victim, and held open the noose as he approached. As he came closer there seemed something paralysing in his very presence, and Malcolmson stood rigid as a corpse. He felt the Judge's icy fingers touch his throat as he adjusted the rope. The noose tightened – tightened. Then the Judge, taking the rigid form of the student in his arms, carried him over and placed him standing in the oak chair, and stepping up beside him, put his hand up and caught the end of the swaying rope of the alarm bell. As he raised his hand the rats fled, squeaking, and disappeared through the hole in the ceiling. Taking the end of the noose which was round Malcolmson's neck he tied it to the hanging bell-rope, and then, descending, pulled away the chair.

When the alarm bell of the Judge's House began to sound a crowd soon assembled. Lights and torches of various kinds appeared, and soon a silent crowd was hurrying to the spot. They knocked loudly at the door, but there was no reply. Then they burst in the door, and poured into the great dining-room, the Doctor at the head.

There at the end of the rope of the great alarm bell hung the body of the student, and on the face of the Judge in the picture was a malignant smile.

DREAMING OF THEE

Gwen Cherrell

*Actress Gwen Cherrell wrote her first play for BBC Radio in 1957.
Since then she has written screenplays for film and television,
scripts for radio and theatre plays. Her book publications include
101 THINGUMAJIGS and HOW MOVIES ARE MADE. She has
continued her acting career, which began in 1944 with SCANDAL
AT BARCHESTER in London's West End. A Clarence Derwent
Award winner for Best Supporting Actress, she has also appeared
in many roles on television; more recently she was a member of
the BBC Radio Drama Rep company. She is a member of the
Executive Council and of the Radio Committee of the Writers'
Guild of Great Britain.*

She had to get to the house.

*It lay ahead across the field and she could feel her heart pounding
as she ran towards it, hear the gravel rasping under her feet as she
reached the door.*

*'Let me in,' she cried desperately. And then, overcome with sad-
ness, she sank to her knees and sobbed.*

'Oh, you're awake', said Cass. 'I've been thumping the
door for the last ten minutes.'

Cass had moved into the flat first, sharing with another
girl, leaving the single room for Lorna.

'I've had a card from Joanna. Used to rent your room,' Cass
said. '"Why don't you come and stay with me and Eddie for
a weekend" she says. "Bring Lorna."'

'Where do they live?' asked Lorna.

'Shropshire. You drive off the motorway and suddenly it's
really rustic. All ploughed fields and . . . what's the matter?'

Lorna shook her head. 'I was dreaming. I dreamt I was

walking across a ploughed field and beyond it there was a house. As soon as I saw it I knew I had to get into it.' She shivered as she recalled her feeling of desolation.

'I'll be late back tonight,' said Cass. 'Sweet dreams if I don't see you.'

Lorna was within sight of the house again. This time when she hammered on the door she heard footsteps. They were coming from inside the house. Then they stopped. She banged again, more urgently now. She heard the sound of a chain being loosed, of a bolt being drawn back, a key being turned in the lock. Then, as the door slowly began to open, she heard a terrible wailing cry. . .

Cass was opening the curtains, letting in the drone of a police siren from the street outside. She nodded towards the bedside table. 'I've brought you a cup of tea. Oh, yes, do you think I could borrow your red jacket?'

Lorna lay, half in, half out of her dream. 'I must get into that house,' she said in a perplexed voice. 'This time the door nearly opened, Cass.'

'Wow!' said Cass jokily. But Lorna shivered. 'My hands feel like ice.'

The next few nights were undisturbed and Lorna began to stop worrying that the dream might come back. But a week or so later, she and Cass went to an early music concert together and she could feel herself sliding into sleep.

She was running towards the house again. Now, as before, she pounded on the door, heard the footsteps, the bolt being drawn back, the key turning in the lock . . . and, as the door swung open, she started to move across the threshold.

Suddenly she saw the man.

He was standing beside the door. The look on his face froze her in her tracks with horror. Opening her mouth to scream, she was terrified to find that she could make no sound.

'For God's sake!' muttered Cass as Lorna woke up abruptly, trembling. She looked round and was unnerved to see people staring at her.

'Cass? What happened?'

'Let's get out of here,' said Cass. 'Are you all right?'

'I must have fallen asleep.' said Lorna. Then, recalling the dream, she pushed her way to the end of the row of seats and ran out of the building. Cass caught up with her near the park.

'It's so real, Cass, it's so real!'

Ordinarily Cass would have made a joke but, seeing Lorna's anguished face, she said nothing until they were both drinking coffee in the nearest café. 'It's only a dream,' she said.

'Then why do I go on dreaming it?' said Lorna. 'Tonight the door opened.'

'Is that why you screamed?'

Lorna looked at her blankly. 'What?'

'You screamed, Lorna,' said Cass.

Lorna looked puzzled. 'In the concert?'

'Yes, in the concert. Why do you think everybody was staring? You screamed bloody murder!'

Lorna caught her breath. 'But I couldn't have. I couldn't.'

'OK,' said Cass. 'The door opened. Who opened it?' She wanted to get through it as briskly as possible.

'A man.'

'What sort of man?'

'Sort of . . . my age, tall, good-looking.'

'But frightening.'

'No,' said Lorna. 'That's what's so odd. He just opened the door and . . . he looked at me as if I was dead.'

'Dead?'

'He looked sad. And there was that awful icy feeling again. As if I knew I was dead.' Lorna stared wretchedly at Cass. 'Is that what's going to happen, do you think? If I go on

265

dreaming the same dream. That I'll end up dead?'

The following weekend the two of them were on their way to Shropshire in Cass's car. The weather had been wonderful but now the windshield wipers were working flat out to clear a view through driving rain. They had left the motorway and Cass was trying to navigate the lanes from memory.

'There should be a right turn in a minute, keep your eyes open for a finger-post,' she said. Lorna peered out of the window.

'Slow down a minute.' Lorna wiped her hand over the misted side-window. 'Stop the car!'

The tone of her voice was so urgent that Cass put on the brakes. Lorna rolled down the window and looked across the fields.

'I think I must have been here before,' she said. 'That house. I know it. Behind that door there's a paved hall and . . .' her voice tailed away. 'Cass, it's the house in my dreams.'

Since the evening of the concert Lorna's dream had not been mentioned and Cass had hoped to hear no more about it. Now here was Lorna tugging on her wellies and apparently intending to go off in the sheeting rain.

'I'm not going to try and get in or anything. I must have a squint at it. Shan't be long.'

'You're crazy,' Cass said. Lorna shook her head.

'Must,' she said. 'I'll be back in a minute.' She got out of the car and started off across the field.

'I hope so,' Cass called after her as she rolled up the window. And then she paused. 'Now why did I say that?' she thought.

As she started to run towards the house, Lorna could feel her heart pounding . . . hear the rasp of gravel under her feet . . . and when she reached the door she knew that she had to knock.

Unbelievably, footsteps were coming towards her, the

same footsteps as those in her dream . . . the chain being loosed . . . the bolt drawn back . . . the key turning in the lock. The door opened and a man stood beside it. Lorna lurched slightly in the sickening shock of recognition – it was the same man.

Pulling herself together, Lorna said that she was sorry to trouble him but – she faltered and then gave him the lie direct – 'but I used to live here.'

The man said quietly, 'I live here now.'

'I know,' said Lorna. 'I know you do.'

'Go away,' he said.

'Oh, please –' Lorna heard the yearning from the dream creep into her voice now '– would it be possible for me to come in for a moment?'

'No,' he said. 'Go away.'

But she couldn't. She had to get inside.

'Nobody comes inside this house,' he said.

Lorna faced him. 'Why not?'

'Because it's haunted.'

She felt as if her body had been drained of blood. She saw again the look in his eyes which had chilled her to the bone when she had dreamed of him. Almost fainting with fear, she made herself ask the question.

'Who is it haunted by?'

'By you,' said the man. 'By you.'

Cass had been watching Lorna from the car as best she could through the rain and from a distance; suddenly Lorna was no longer in sight. Cursing her, Cass got out and stumped off after her. She found her collapsed over the front doorstep – inert and deathly white. She was soaked to the skin. Seeing her stir, Cass said, 'I'm going inside to use their telephone.'

'No!'

Lorna clawed Cass with stiffened fingers and begged her not to. She struggled to stand and somehow the two girls managed to get back to the car together.

Later, in front of Joanna's fire, warmed with coffee and brandy, Lorna was beginning to recover, when Eddie began to rationalise her dreams.

'You must have met him before. Good-looking guy – you clock him, later you dream about him, happens all the time.'

'How do you know he's good-looking?' asked Cass.

'I've met him in the pub.'

Eddie went on to explain how people often rented the house while they searched for something to buy.

'So he doesn't live there?' said Cass.

Eddie shrugged. 'Nobody seems to want to.'

They could all feel Lorna tense up again. 'Because it's haunted, that's why,' she said. Her voice grew shrill and she began to tremble. Joanna rescued her by bringing out a photograph of the three girls taken outside their flat.

'I was moving out, Lorna was moving in and Cass was playing landlady,' she said. And for a while they talked of other things until Joanna, looking at the time, said, 'I hope you and Cass don't mind sharing a room tonight, Lorna.'

Lorna looked up and said 'I'm glad, actually. I'm rather dreading going to bed.'

The church clock was striking three when Cass woke up to find the light on and Lorna sitting upright in bed.

'You're not going to stay awake all night?' she protested.

'Suppose I dream again. Suppose I get into the house this time. Suppose he's waiting for me. Like today.'

Cass had had enough. 'Listen,' she hissed, 'today you met the bloke. He shut the door on you – right? Finish. Whatever you dream, it'll only be a dream.'

As she humped her back towards Lorna, Cass could hear her murmuring 'I'm sorry. You're right.'

The next morning a shattering scream brought Joanna rushing into the girls' bedroom. Cass was on her knees beside Lorna's bed begging her to wake up. Lorna was lying on her back, her eyes wide in stark terror. By the time Eddie reached them, both girls were weeping. One look told him that Lorna was dead.

The local doctor's report found that the only outward manifestations of disorder lay in the contortion of the facial muscles commonly associated with acute terror but for which there was no accountable cause. There was no evidence on the body that violence had been inflicted. The coroner's opinion was of heart failure due to vagal inhibition. His verdict was death from natural causes.

After the inquest, the three friends moved over to the pub. They had given in evidence their accounts of the events that had actually taken place on the previous Saturday, but Cass was feeling uneasy.

'Yet how could I have told them about her dreams? She might have been making them up.'

'Brandy for Cass, your vermouth, Joanna . . .' Eddie came back to the table with the drinks and Cass noticed that he wasn't alone.

Beside him stood a man of around their age. He was unsmiling. Without introduction he said, 'This is probably not the time but . . .' he hesitated, 'I just wanted to say that I'm terribly sorry about your friend. My name's Bob Cadenyer.'

Cass went straight into the attack. 'Did you open the door to Lorna?' Again he hesitated and then he said, 'Yes.'

Joanna gasped. 'But you told the police that you didn't. That you'd never seen her. That's why you weren't called to give evidence.'

The man hadn't taken his eyes off Cass. 'Is there anywhere we can talk?' he said.

Back in the cottage, Cass grew impatient with Joanna's social offering of drinks. 'Why did you lie?' she asked Cadenyer.

'I heard her knocking,' Cadenyer said. 'I opened the door. I

269

told her to go away. When she wouldn't, I slammed the door on her. I heard no more and I thought she'd gone. The next day the police came. They showed me a photograph of the three of you and told me she was dead. That shook me.'

'You recognised her,' said Cass.

Cadenyer gave a shuddering sigh. 'Oh, I recognised her all right. I'd seen her the night before. And the night before that. And –'

'Where?' demanded Cass.

'I'd seen her in my dreams.'

Not even Eddie could dismiss the frisson that Cadenyer's words created.

'From the day I moved into the house. Always the same dream. A girl – walking round and round the house trying to get in. And me – desperate to keep her out. Then one night I dreamed that I'd opened the door. I was convinced that if I ever had the same dream again something ghastly might happen.'

Cadenyer seemed to be talking to Cass alone now. 'Last Saturday there was knocking at the front door. When I opened it I got the shock of my life. There was the girl. It was like my worst nightmare. But she was real. And she was begging to come in.'

Cadenyer sat down shakily, Eddie moved to get him a drink but Cass wasn't to be put off. 'Why did you tell her that she was haunting you?' she said.

Cadenyer's voice rose at her accusing tone. 'I was frantic to get rid of her,' he shouted. Then, more quietly, he continued, 'That night I dreamed what had actually happened in the afternoon, that the girl came to the door. But in the dream I didn't slam the door on her. She came in.'

Cass leaned forward. 'Lorna went into your house? *In your dream?*'

'Yes.'

'What happened?' They all waited for his reply.

'I murdered her,' said Cadenyer simply. 'That's why I went to the inquest today. Time of death, cause of death – I had to know.'

He was talking to Cass again.

'She died of heart failure,' said Joanna.

It was Eddie who asked, 'In your dream, how did you . . .?' Cadenyer sighed again.

'With an axe . . . horrible . . . there was blood everywhere.' He got up and moved towards the window. Looking out, he said, 'I feel that in some way I'm responsible for her death.'

Eddie handed him a glass of whisky. 'She died ten hours after your meeting. She was with us when she died,' he said.

'But she died at exactly the time I was killing her in my dream.'

'*Her* dream,' said Cass flatly.

Cadenyer looked puzzled. 'I'm sorry?' he said.

'She was in your dream, you were in hers.'

'What are you talking about?' he said.

'You and Lorna shared the same dream. She died of fright.'

Cadenyer stared at Cass. 'That night,' she said, 'after she'd met you, she was terrified of falling asleep, because of what might happen.'

'But so was I!' cried Cadenyer. 'The awful thing is – I still am. Lorna died. What scares me now is suppose it happens again. Suppose I dream that I'm killing someone else?'

Cass turned away. 'I didn't believe her,' she said with remorse.

'There was nothing you could have done. The power of evil . . .'

'And I won't believe you,' Cass said fiercely. 'I can't believe that people move in and out of other people's dreams.'

Cadenyer looked at her. 'Can't you?' he said. 'Do you really not believe me?'

Three months later, Joanna and Eddie spent the night

with Cass in the flat. They had her large room and Cass went into Lorna's old room. They all went to bed around midnight.

Cass could see the house across the fields, with its curving drive and heavy door. She could feel her heart pounding as she knocked, begging to be let in. Then she heard footsteps . . . the chain being loosed . . . the key turning in the lock . .

When Cadenyer opened the door and he said he'd been waiting for her, she knew that what she had been dreading was happening. And when she opened her mouth to scream, she was terrified to find that she could make no sound.

BY THE RIVER, FONTAINEBLEAU

Stephen Gallagher

Stephen Gallagher was born in Salford in 1954. He worked first as a documentary researcher and then for a television company before becoming a full-time freelance writer with the sale of his first novel in 1980. CHIMERA has now been adapted for television. Other novels include VALLEY OF LIGHTS, OKTOBER, DOWN RIVER, RAIN and his latest, THE BOAT HOUSE. His stories have been published in numerous magazines both in Britain and the US.

We sheltered under the great oak for more than an hour, watching as the rain came down in sheets. The sky was as dark as old lead, and when the thunder came it seemed to shake the very soil of the forest. Even Antoine couldn't pretend that this was nothing more than a brief spring shower, and so we sat together in a bleak silence with our packs at our feet and our oilskin coats over our heads. It was then, I suppose, that I really came to my decision.

When the rain finally stopped, we shouldered our baggage and walked on. The lane had now mostly turned to mud, and a weak sun showed through the trees and raised a mist from the sodden ground. I wasn't in much of a mood to appreciate it, but after a while Antoine started to whistle. Ten minutes or so later we came to a shallow, fast-running river where the lane disappeared and re-emerged over on the far side, and so wet and miserable was I by this time that I waded in to make the crossing without hesitation or complaint. Every step was taking me nearer to home, and this was all that I cared for.

But it soon became obvious that the track would take us

no further than the farm which stood on the opposite bank, as it led straight into a yard which had no exit. It was a mean-looking place, charmless and squalid even in the late-afternoon sunlight, and my immediate impulse was to turn around and walk away. But Antoine, ever an optimist, said:

'Do you think they'll take pity and feed us?'

'They're more likely to hit us over the head and rob us,' I told him. 'You stay here and look after the gear. I'll ask the way.'

I left him and went on into the yard, looking for some sign of life. A few hens were picking over the barren ground close to where four scrawny goats stood in a makeshift pen, and a dog was barking somewhere over beyond the barn. The corner of the yard to my left was shaded by a large chestnut tree, and it was on the dry beaten earth in the shelter of this that I saw a terrible sight.

It was an underweight pig, trussed and made ready for slaughter; this was obviously the farm's regular spot for killing, because hooks had been fixed to the tree's lower branches for carcasses to be hung as they bled. What made the sight so terrible was the way in which the pig had been prepared. Each of its feet had been cut at the knuckle, sliced right back so that the bone showed bloodless and white. Those bound-together limbs were almost severed, but still the pig squirmed as it tried to stand.

I turned my head aside, and went on by. In the open on the far side of the barn I finally found the people who lived there; and an unwashed, surly crowd they turned out to be, a father and four brothers with narrow faces and a dark, piercing stare. They were hauling logs for cutting, but all work stopped when they saw me. As I addressed myself to the older man the others simply stood and watched, their mouths open and their hands hanging by their sides whilst a dim spark of intelligence burned in each pair of eyes. It went badly until I realised that money was the key that would unlock their patient and persistent misunderstanding, and then at the end of the process I learned nothing more than that the only way to regain the Paris road would be to return along the track by which we'd arrived. I thanked the farmer – feeling defeated and foolish, because really I ought to have been cursing him – and trudged back to Antoine.

Antoine was where I'd left him. The packs with our easels, brushes and sketchbooks were at his feet, and he was leaning on the wall with a distant, thoughtful expression on his face. He was looking towards the chestnut tree. This was something that I'd avoided doing on my way back, but now I had to turn and see what it was that was affecting him so; and it was then that I realised that the trussed pig had been taken away at some time during my short absence, and that a different scene was now before him.

'I'm staying, Marcel,' he said.

I didn't understand. 'Staying where?'

'Right here. They must have a room or a loft or a barn, and they're not going to turn down good money. And it's late, and I'm tired . . .'

'Any other reason?' I said, and I gave a pointed glance across to where, under the chestnut tree, a young girl was now standing and unselfconsciously brushing her hair. She was looking into a broken old mirror that she'd hung from one of the butchery-hooks, and she didn't seem to be aware of us at all. She was barefoot, and in a cotton shift so damp and clinging that it was plain she wore nothing underneath. To my eyes she was nothing more than an ordinary farm girl, too heavy for grace and probably too dull for conversation . . . but who could say what she was to Antoine? I'd already learned, during the weeks of our walking tour, that his eyes and mine often seemed to see by a different light. Now, in answer to my question, he was smiling and saying nothing more.

'Then,' I said, 'you stay alone, Antoine.'

This surprised him. 'Are we going to argue over this?'

'No,' I said, leaning on the wall beside him, 'not an argument. I simply don't want to get in your way. It's over for me, Antoine, and there's no point in me pretending otherwise. I've had enough of walking and sketching and being face-to-face with nature. I've yawned through sunrises and I've shivered through the rain, and if I died without ever seeing another tree or village or field of wheat, I'd be dying happy. What I'm trying to say is that I'm not an artist, Antoine. If these last few weeks have been the test, then I'm admitting that I've failed. I'm footsore and I'm aching, and I've got nothing left to prove. I'm going back to Paris tonight.'

This had been my decision back in the forest and under the oak. The excursion that had seemed so appealing to two young would-be painters had turned into a drudgery of patchy weather and draughty inns and a yearning for home; I'd carried on sketching only as a kind of dogged duty, something that I wouldn't have bothered with if Antoine hadn't been there. I hadn't looked back through the pages, and didn't care to. My artistic talent, I'd realised, wasn't strong enough to survive outside the most pampered of drawing-room conditions – which, I suppose, meant that it wasn't a real talent at all. A useful way of persuading young women to undress for me, perhaps, but not art.

'Oh, Marcel,' Antoine said with sympathy. 'Has it really been hell for you?'

'I'm going to be a dull citizen, Antoine,' I told him. 'I was *born* to be a dull citizen. It took a trip like this to make me realise how much I'd been looking forward to it.'

He glanced across the yard again, to where the plain farm girl stood beneath the chestnut tree. For a moment it seemed that her eyes strayed from the mirror and met his, but her face betrayed nothing at all.

'I can't come with you,' he said.

'I understand that.'

I told him where to find the farmer, and while he was gone I transferred all of the pastels, paints and charcoal sticks from my luggage into his own. It was a strange feeling; the feeling of letting go of a dream. It was relief and regret, inextricably mixed. I also gave him my two untouched canvases in their carrying frame, and my fixing atomiser. When Antoine returned, he told me of the terms that the farmer had fixed for him to stay on; put simply, they were giving him two weeks in their barn with whatever meals the family could spare, in return for every franc that he carried. I was horrified, but Antoine was unruffled. He made me promise that I would go to his father and collect his monthly allowance, and that before the two weeks expired I would return with the money. Although I wouldn't have cared if I never saw the forest of Fontainebleau again, I was uneasy about leaving Antoine completely at the mercy of his new obsession. This way, at least, I'd be able to check on him.

He walked with me back to the river. There was little more than an hour of daylight left, and I had some way to go. Before I set out across the ford, I said, 'What shall I tell your father?'

'Whatever you like,' he said. 'Whatever you think he needs to hear. But do it for me, Marcel.'

I'd have said more, but he was already casting a longing look back towards the yard. A half-hour's familiarity made it seem no less squalid to me than it had been at first sight . . . but, as I said, Antoine often seemed to see things with a different eye. An artist's eye perhaps. My test had come and gone; and the next two weeks would be his.

I stayed that night in Barbizon, and made it back to Paris by the next evening. I entered the family home by the back door, partly because I was ashamed of what I saw as my failure, but mostly because I was aware that I looked like a tramp. The next few days saw the beginning of the process of my absorption into the family's business dealings, a strange world of ledger entries and manifests that somehow bore a relation to real ships that sailed somewhere out on real oceans. I was given a position as an apprentice clerk, in order that I should be able to learn from the most fundamental of basic principles.

Even though I'd known what to expect, the long hours and the rigid timekeeping came as something of a shock to me. I'd sent out a note to Antoine's parents assuring them of his safety as soon as I'd arrived home, but it wasn't until the Friday that I was able to go and see them in the evening with his request.

The news was not good. My own father, to his credit, had been willing to let my preoccupations run themselves out; it was as if he'd foreseen the final result and quietly made his preparations for when that time came around. Antoine's father had no such patience. All that he gave me was a message; there would be no allowance until Antoine abandoned his games and returned home.

Saturday was a half-day, and as soon as my work was finished I set out for the railway station. It was late in the afternoon before I finally came into sight of the farm again. The place was much as I remembered it, although I dare say that I had changed in its eyes; I now wore my one decent suit and overcoat, and came prepared for the shallow river crossing.

It was a warm day. Spring was slipping towards summer, and the breeze no longer cut. The broken looking-glass was still hanging under the chestnut tree, and it swung lightly back and forth as I stood in the doorway to the barn and called Antoine's name. He'd been sleeping *here*? Half of the place was taken up with hay, all the way to the upper loft, and there was nothing in the way of furniture. The slatted walls were badly fitted, and some of the gaps in the planking were a hand's width. But this was his lodging, all right, because over on the clear part of the floor I saw his easel and a stool and some of his materials laid out. Antoine's possessions, but no Antoine. I set out to search.

I finally found him in a clearing no more than two hundred metres from the barn. The girl, as I'd half-expected, was with him. She was sitting on the ground with her hands clasped around her knees as Antoine sketched her; but on seeing me, with a cry of 'Marcel!', he threw aside his pad and jumped up to greet me.

I confess that I was shocked, although I hid it well. In the space of less than a week, he'd deteriorated like a man in the grip of a serious illness. He seemed thinner, and there were dark rings around his eyes that made them seem sunken and staring; but his manner was lively enough, and he seemed pleased to see me . . . although how much of this was a genuine eagerness and how much of it was due to the money that he assumed I'd brought with me, I couldn't say.

They had a basket with them, and together we dined on cheese and rough wine and bread that had the texture of damp thatch. Antoine introduced the girl as Lise, short for Anneliese; I knew within a moment of hearing her speak that she was no native French girl, although her accent was one that I couldn't place. She seemed shy and ate nothing, and only took a little of the wine.

Antoine gave me his sketchbook to look through, just as we'd done at the end of each of our days together. As I'd expected, he'd been spending all of his time on the girl, switching between head studies and full-length portrayals, some of them hardly more than a few swift lines depicting the essence of some moment of motion. Although I didn't show it, I was disappointed. I was hoping that there would be some sign here, some showing-through of the vision that had motivated him, but each drawing seemed little more than a technical exercise. Perhaps there was nothing to envy here after all, I thought. Nothing other than a casual infatuation made practical by the artist–model relationship – a situation that I, at least, could understand, although I was strangely disappointed that I found nothing more.

Lise asked if Antoine was finished with his sketching for the day, and then excused herself. I noted a certain pain in Antoine's eyes as he watched her go.

'Who is she?' I said as soon as she was decently out of earshot.

'I don't know. She's an orphan, I think. The family just ignores her.'

'Does she work on the farm?'

'I don't think so,' he said, his face reflecting some of his uncertainty as if it was a question that he'd thought over a number of times in the past few days. 'I can't be sure. She disappears for hours at a time, but . . . it's not important, anyway. Did you speak to my father?'

I had no choice then but to give him the hard news. I saw his face fall, and the air of vague contentment that had offset the wasting of his features was replaced by a kind of desperation.

'Then I don't know what to do,' he said. 'They won't let me stay here without money. They've bled me white already. You don't understand these people.'

'Not half as well as they seem to understand you,' I told him. 'It *is* because of the girl, isn't it?'

He looked down, and didn't answer.

'Then,' I went on, 'why don't you simply take her away?'

But he was dismissing the idea even before I'd finished suggesting it. 'That's not possible,' he said. 'It pains her to walk any distance.' And then, going on as if this minor quibble had been enough to put an end to the entire argument, he was getting to his feet and saying, 'I can see only one way out. You'd better come with me.'

He said nothing more as he led the way back towards the

barn. Over by another of the outbuildings, I saw one of the four sons watching us as we passed. He made no sign towards us, and Antoine didn't even glance his way.

Lise wasn't there when we arrived, nor did Antoine seem to expect her to be. He went over to the easel, and I followed; and then I waited as he hesitated for a moment before drawing away the paint-splashed cloth that had been draped to protect the canvas.

It was a painting, in full oils. I stood amazed. It was wonderful.

It showed that vision of the first moment in which Antoine had seen Lise under the chestnut tree. It was every detail that I'd seen, but transformed; I now realised that I'd been so preoccupied with my own discomfort that I'd been aware of almost nothing, nothing at all. Lise stood, brush in hand, dappled in late-afternoon sunlight with soft blue shadows behind her. In her plain features was a kind of quiet beauty as she studied her image in the glass; I knew instinctively that it was a sad picture, a celebration of the brevity of all experience and of life itself.

And as I looked, I felt something within me die. I thought of my own pretty, nondescript Fontainebleau landscapes, and finally knew for sure that my decision had been a right one. My technique was as good as Antoine's, if not slightly better, but technique was only half of the story. To paint, one first had to see. And I didn't, until led to it.

'You have to take it to Paris for me,' he said. 'Sell it for whatever you can get.'

I nodded slowly. There was no question about it now, I would help him however I could. 'I'm envious, you know,' I said.

'Don't be,' he said, staring at his own canvas as if it disturbed him, somehow. 'The things we want most aren't always the things that make us happy.'

I gave him most of the money that I had with me,

including what I had set aside for a night's lodging before returning to the town. I sensed a certain reluctance in Antoine as we climbed a ladder and he showed me the upper loft where I could sleep, but I took it as a natural aversion to charity between friends. I didn't see it that way; if I was going to be a *bourgeois*, I thought ruefully, I might as well go the whole hog and become a patron of the arts.

A blanket in the hay was not my idea of comfort, but it was all that was available. I was warm enough, but the hay stuck at me through the thin wool from every angle; and though my overcoat, rolled, made a reasonable pillow, I couldn't help wondering what it would look like when I came to shake it out in the morning. No wonder Antoine was looking such a wreck, I thought, after a week of this.

I don't know what time it was when I awoke, but it must have been somewhere around two or three o'clock. I lay uneasy, looking at where the cloudy moonlit sky showed through the spaces in the walls, and I heard voices from below. They were whispering, but the night was so still that it was impossible not to hear.

'I remember leaving you and your friend,' Lise was saying. 'I was so tired after sitting for you this morning. But I don't remember where I went.'

'You went where you always go,' I heard Antoine say. 'To the big stack of straw, behind the house. You made yourself a space and you burrowed down inside.'

But the next thing that I knew, it was dark and I was standing out under the tree again. I was exhausted, and it was as if I'd been running. What had I been *doing*?'

'You were sleeping, that's all. Like you always do.'

But Lise seemed scared, unable to accept so simple an explanation. 'But you *know* this?' she said insistently. 'You've seen me?'

There was a long silence from Antoine. And then he said, 'Yes.'

I heard her moving slightly, making the hay rustle. She said, 'I sometimes feel as if you're the only one who really sees me. As I am, I mean. As if, when you close your eyes, I no longer exist . . . because I didn't, in a way, before you came along.'

Antoine said, 'That's just foolish talk.'

Her next question was one that I wouldn't have expected. She said, 'Who am I, Antoine?' And she sounded lost and miserable, as if the answer would never be known.

'Sleep, now,' he told her.

It was a good suggestion, and one that I wished I could follow; but further sleep seemed to elude me, and all that I could do was to squirm miserably in that itchy byre. Antoine's breathing became deep and noisy. And after a while I heard the sound below of somebody rising and making their way towards the door of the barn.

Moving as silently as I could, I crawled over to the trap by which I'd entered the loft and peered down. Lise was at the doorway, framed in moonlight, and she was looking back at Antoine. I could not make out her expression, but her general attitude suggested a regretful leave-taking. Of Antoine himself, I could see little more than the creamy blur of his shirt in the darkness. Then Lise turned, and walked out into the yard.

A board creaked as I moved across to the unglazed window from where I'd be able to see down into the yard, but Antoine didn't stir. She was moving quickly now, a faint shape in a simple dress, and she was heading towards the back of the house as Antoine had said; and then, as I watched, I saw another form rise from the shadows to meet her. This was, I guessed from his brutish outline, either the farmer or one of his four sons, and he seemed to have been waiting; I saw him raise a rod or a switch of some kind, and to swipe at the air with it as if to speed her in the direction in which she was already going. He followed her through the

283

gap between the buildings, and then bent to something that I couldn't see; but then I heard the scrape of a wooden gate across the rutted dirt, and the bang of it falling shut.

When they were gone from sight, Lise being casually driven ahead like some common farm animal, I returned to my blanket. It was obvious that she'd been expected, up and away the moment that Antoine was fully asleep like a sheep being called to the fold at the end of the day. And having seen the way in which she'd been treated, I could only reflect that perhaps she'd been right; that Antoine's vision of her differed so much from theirs that it was almost as if he'd actually created her beauty out of some more basic stuff, to which she could only revert when Antoine's attention moved elsewhere, as in sleep.

And sleep, unexpectedly, was what these idle and speculative thoughts led me to.

Breakfast was left outside for us in the morning. It was meagre, but decent. Antoine carefully packed the picture, wary of the paint which was still soft in patches; he called it *La Jeune Fille au Miroir*, The Looking-Glass Girl. Lise sat aside and watched us; she'd returned to the barn at some time before I'd woken, I didn't know when. She said little, and ate nothing. I now found it difficult to imagine how I could ever have thought her plain.

I suppose that, to develop my fanciful line of thought from the night before, I now saw her as through Antoine's eyes. My own first impression now counted for nothing; it was not that I had simply changed an opinion to acquiesce to the views of another, but more that I'd found the actual fabric of my world transformed by the intensity of his vision. But it was an intensity that was draining him, I could see; he looked no better physically now than he had when I'd arrived, and seemed perhaps even a little worse. I wondered if a taste of success from the sale of the painting might nourish him.

I was on my way before ten, knowing that I had a long walk and a carriage drive ahead of me before I'd even reach the railway. My toughest boots had leaked a little during the river crossing the previous day, but they'd dried out overnight and Antoine went out to negotiate a ride of some kind so that I wouldn't be restarting the journey with a squelch. I didn't hear what was said or what was promised, but after ten minutes a dilapidated trap pulled by an even more dilapidated pony came rattling into the yard.

The morning sun struck a shimmering light from the river as we waved our good-byes and the trap jarred its way into the rutted crossing. My driver was one of the four brothers. I wondered if he might have been the one who had waited in the yard for Lise in the moonlight. I thought about asking . . . but he hadn't said one word to me so far, and seemed unlikely to. He sat with his shoulders hunched, and his eyes apparently fixed on the horse's rear end. I was half expecting to be set down on the opposite bank, but it soon became clear that Antoine's bargaining would take me further as we continued, wheels dripping, down the lane. I turned for one last wave to Antoine's solitary figure, and then I faced front with *La Jeune Fille au Miroir* held protectively by my side.

I had a strange feeling of loss, as if I'd left a world that I might never be sure of re-entering. The river was its boundary, the banks its borderland.

Ten minutes later, as we came into sight of the main crossroads, my coachman spoke.

'We've told your friend,' he said suddenly and without any preamble, 'we can't eat his pictures. When his money's gone, so's he.'

It was a moment before I could be certain that I was the one being addressed; he hadn't lifted his eyes from the mare's backside. But when I was sure, I said, 'Would you consider letting Lise come away with him?'

I watched for a reaction, but saw none. He simply said, 'Why?'

'She doesn't work for you, she isn't one of you . . . there's no future for her here. Antoine's family is very rich. He could set her up in apartments of her own and give her an income. She could send you money.'

It was my boldest stroke, but it was having little effect; he was shaking his head slowly, and this angered me.

'It's rather late to start considering her moral welfare, isn't it?' I demanded. 'Since you see fit to send her out to sleep in a barn with strangers.'

'That doesn't matter,' he said, reining the nag in so that we came to a halt at the empty crossroads. 'She can't leave, that's all.'

Such were my initial efforts on Antoine's behalf. I had little more success in my new role as artist's agent. I gave my choice of dealer a lot of thought, and settled on one who I believed would be sympathetic to the picture's fresh and quite modern approach to its subject; he had, I knew, recently made a buying trip to England and returned with several works of Constable that were considered to be almost revolutionary in their treatment of nature. I left the painting in his hands for several days, and then called on him to check on progress.

He'd found a buyer. But when I heard the sum on offer, my initial excitement died and went cold within me.

'So little?' I said. 'But . . .'

'You might get more if you let it hang in the gallery for a few weeks, but I doubt it,' he said. 'And I wouldn't want to get a reputation for handling this kind of material.' But then he conceded, 'I'm not saying it isn't good.'

'But if it's good, it *must* bring more.'

'Not so. Good isn't what sells . . . fashionable is what sells. We're talking about classical characters in idealised landscapes. Nature rearranged in the studio. Now, you tell me. How do I sell this little farm girl in a market like that?'

It was a good piece of work, I *knew* it; knew it with a greater confidence than I had ever brought to any work of my own. I said, 'Are you telling me that this painting is at fault because there's too much of the truth in it?'

He shrugged delicately. 'If you like. For what it's worth, I think your friend's very brave. But I can't sell his nerve, either . . . I just sell pictures.'

What could I do? Antoine's tenure at the farm would last only as long as his ability to pay matched the greed of his landlords. The sum I'd been offered wouldn't buy him more than a few days' grace at current rates, but any effort to find a better price for the picture would take time. Even then, there were no guarantees of any greater success. With a sense of defeat, I accepted the offer.

There had to come a point, I'd decided, where Antoine would have to get his obsession into some kind of perspective. He'd found himself in a situation which had made a conceptual breakthrough possible, but now it was time to give some consideration to the strategy of his new career. After all, hadn't he already made his first commercial sale? And if I was beginning to sound like his father in this way of thinking I didn't dwell on the fact long enough for it to bother me.

I went out to the farm again on the following Sunday. Antoine was waiting for me, on the wrong side of the river.

He was sitting on a rock by the crossing, staring into the fast-running current. If I'd been shocked by his appearance before, I was horrified now. He was filthy and wretched, his skin grey with ill-health under its ingrained surface of dirt; his hair was like old straw, and his entire body was hunched and bent. I saw what looked like dried wounds on his hands, and when he looked up at my approach it was with the eyes of the starving.

For a moment, I was unable to speak. To see a friend reduced so far, so fast! His bags, easel and paints were beside him; they lay as if thrown there, the easel broken and the paints scattered and trampled into the riverside mud.

'Antoine!' I finally managed to say. 'What happened here?'

'The money was gone, so they threw me out,' he said simply. His voice was rough and weak. 'I've been here for two days. When I tried to go back in, they set the dogs on me.'

This, I assumed, would explain the wounds on his hands. 'That's outrageous,' I said. 'I'm going to speak to them. Let them set the dogs on *me*, if they dare.'

I stormed across the ford, not caring how much noise I made nor how much spray I created. Antoine, after rising unsteadily from his rock, hesitated for a while and then began to follow me at a distance.

The yard was in silence, and to me seemed just as grim as it had on that first day. Lise's mirror no longer hung under the chestnut tree, and from the dark stains on the ground I guessed that the butchery hooks had been put to recent use. With Antoine still trailing along behind, I took a look in the barn; some of the hay had been carted out, but there was no sign of anyone around.

'We're too late,' Antoine said, but I paid him no attention and went out through the back doors of the barn. Out here, at least, I found a sign of life in the form of the remains of a recent fire; it was smoking still, and as I drew closer I saw that the smoke actually came from a scattering of almost-extinct coals in the bottom of a shallow pit. They lay on a bed of deep ash. Even without extending my hand, I could feel the heat.

I was not to be stopped. Antoine started to speak again, but I didn't wait to listen; I was already on my way towards the stone house with its steeply-pitched roof and its inch-thick doors, as stolid and resistant to enquiry as I knew the people inside it to be. I strode across a kitchen garden where almost nothing grew, and hesitated at the side-entrance; I could hear noises from inside, the sounds of a number of people together, and so without knocking I threw back the unbolted door before me and stepped through.

The noise ended as I entered, as sharply as if it had been cut by a blade. I saw a plain, whitewashed room with a broad table down its centre, around which at least a dozen people sat; if seemed that the same face turned towards me in twelve or thirteen slightly differing forms, from a child of three to a woman so old and pale that she seemed bloodless. One of them, a man of around thirty years, was bibbed like a baby and being fed with a spoon. All of their eyes save his were on me; he continued to look eagerly at his plate.

I'd interrupted a feast, and a strange feast it was; on the table stood nothing but meat and dishes of liquid fat, and more of this in one spread than such a family might normally expect to see in a year. I saw joints and ribs and bones already picked clean, and at the far end of the table a plate piled high with roasted offal. This, I didn't doubt, was all the product of the cooking-pit that I'd seen behind the barn. The sight and the smell made me queasy at the excess on display; the faces that now studied me blankly were bloated and smeared with grease.

Nobody spoke. But in my mind I heard that voice from days before; *Tell your friend, we can't eat his pictures.*

And then came something that terrified me, as if the hooks that held the backcloth of my world had suddenly slipped in their holes and allowed a corner to fall revealing the dark machinery that usually stood concealed. My gaze came to rest on one of the smaller serving-dishes, runny with juices and melted fat. The joint that lay on it was charred around the edges, the skin scored and crisp; but for no more than a second it was recognisable, nails and all, as a human hand. I blinked and stared, and even as I did so the joint seemed to shimmer and to change, becoming indistinct for a moment before being restored to my sight in a less obvious form. I might have called it an illusion, but I knew that it was not; it was, I am certain, the final demise of Antoine's vision, crushed by the presence of the same poverty and ignorance and need that had given it birth.

The retarded thirty-year-old began to wail and to drum on the table with his fists, and I took three halting steps back and grabbed at the door handle to pull it closed on that terrible scene.

Antoine hadn't followed me to the house. He'd stayed back, and now waited at some distance. He seemed to be hugging himself, his left arm holding his right as if he was nursing some half-healed bruise. I went across to him, turned him and began to usher him out of the yard. He complied without protest. On the other side of the river, we gathered up such of his things as were worth taking away; I gave him a few small pieces to carry, but the heaviest baggage I carried myself.

It was in this way that we walked down the lane, myself well-laden and Antoine allowing himself to be hastened along. I couldn't take him by train, not in a public compartment in his present state and condition, but there was enough money from the sale of the painting to be able to afford a horse and carriage to take us all of the way back to Paris. We would arrive late and in darkness, but that would be no disadvantage.

I spoke on the subject only once, as we left Corbeil after a half-hour's rest. Antoine was huddled by the window, looking like a bundle of miserable sticks.

'I said, 'When you slept. Do you know where she went to?'

Antoine slowly turned his head, so that his bleak eyes met mine. 'I never wondered,' he said.

And although I knew that he lied, I never asked him again.

290

HAND IN GLOVE

Elizabeth Bowen

*Elizabeth Bowen published her first collection of short stories,
ENCOUNTERS, in 1923. Though born in Dublin and brought up
in County Cork, she spent much of her life in London. The most
well known of her novels are probably THE DEATH OF THE
HEART (1938) and THE HEAT OF THE DAY (1949). Many of
her stories deal with the supernatural and she has also been
described as one of the great writers of the blitz.*

Jasmine Lodge was favourably set on a residential,
prettily-wooded hillside in the south of Ireland, overlooking a river and, still better, the roofs of a lively garrison
town. Around 1904, which was the flowering period of the
Miss Trevors, girls could not have had a more auspicious
home – the neighbourhood spun merrily round the military.
Ethel and Elsie, a spirited pair, garnered the full advantage –
no ball, hop, picnic, lawn tennis, croquet or boating party
was complete without them; in winter, though they could
not afford to hunt, they trimly bicycled to all meets, and on
frosty evenings, with their guitars, set off to *soirées*, snug
inside their cab in their fur-tipped capes.

They possessed an aunt, a Mrs Varley, *née* Elysia Trevor, a
formerly notable local belle, who, drawn back again in her
widowhood to what had been the scene of her early tri-
umphs, occupied a back bedroom in Jasmine Lodge. Mrs
Varley de Grey had had no luck: her splashing match, in its
time the talk of two kingdoms, had ended up in disaster –
the well-born captain in a cavalry regiment having gone so
far as to blow out his brains in India, leaving behind him
nothing but her and debts. Mrs Varley de Grey had returned
from India with nothing but seven large trunks crammed

291

with recent finery; and she also had been impaired by shock. This had taken place while Ethel and Elsie, whose father had married late, were still unborn – so it was that, for as long as the girls recalled, their aunt had been the sole drawback to Jasmine Lodge. Their parents had orphaned them, somewhat thoughtlessly, by simultaneously dying of scarlet fever when Ethel was just out and Elsie soon to be – they were therefore left lacking a chaperone and, with their gift for putting everything to some use, propped the aunt up in order that she might play that role. Only when her peculiarities became too marked did they feel it necessary to withdraw her: by that time, however, all the surrounding ladies could be said to compete for the honour of taking into society the sought-after Miss Trevors. From then on, no more was seen or heard of Mrs Varley de Grey. ('Oh, just a trifle unwell, but nothing much!') She remained upstairs, at the back: when the girls were giving one of their little parties, or a couple of officers came to call, the key of her room would be turned in the outer lock.

The girls hung Chinese lanterns from the creepered veranda, and would sit lightly strumming on their guitars. Not less fascinating was their badinage, accompanied by a daring flash of the eyes. They were known as the clever Miss Trevors, not because of any taint of dogmatism or book-learning – no, when a gentleman cried, 'Those girls have brains!' he meant it wholly in admiration – but because of their accomplishments, ingenuity and agility. They took leading parts in theatricals, lent spirit to numbers of drawing-room games, were naughty mimics, and sang duets. Nor did their fingers lag behind their wits – they constructed lampshades, crêpe paper flowers and picturesque hats; and, above all, varied their dresses marvellously – no one could beat them for ideas, nipping, slashing or fitting. Once more allowing nothing to go to waste, they had remodelled the trousseau out of their aunt's trunks, causing sad old tulles

and tarlatans, satins and *moiré* taffetas to appear to have
come from Paris only today. They re-stitched spangles,
pressed ruffles crisp, and revived many a corsage of
squashed silk roses. They went somewhat softly about that
task, for the trunks were all stored in the attic immediately
over the back room.

They wore their clothes well. 'A pin on either of those
would look smart!' declared other girls. All that they were
short of was evening gloves – they had two pairs each, which
they had been compelled to buy. *What* could have become of
Mrs Varley de Grey's presumably sumptuous numbers of
this item, they were unable to fathom, and it was too bad.
Had gloves been overlooked in her rush from India? – or,
were they here, in that *one* trunk the Trevors could not get at?
All other locks had yielded to pulls or pickings, or the sisters
found keys to fit them, or they had used the tool-box; but this
last stronghold defied them. In that sad little soiled silk sack,
always on her person, Mrs Varley de Gray, they became
convinced, hoarded the operative keys, along with some
frippery rings and brooches – all true emeralds, pearls and
diamonds having been long ago, as they knew, sold. Such
contrariety on their aunt's part irked them – meanwhile,
gaities bore hard on their existing gloves. Last thing at nights
when they came in, last thing in the evenings before they
went out, they would manfully dab away at the fingertips.
So it must be admitted that a long whiff of benzine pursued
them as they whirled round the ballroom floor.

They were tall and handsome – nothing so soft as pretty,
but in those days it was a vocation to be a handsome girl;
many of the best marriages had been made by such. They
carried themselves imposingly, had good busts and
shoulders, waists firm under the whalebone, and straight
backs. Their features were striking, their colouring high; low
on their foreheads bounced dark mops of curls. Ethel was,
perhaps, the dominant one, but both girls were pronounced

to be full of character.

Whom, and still more when, did they mean to marry? They had already seen regiments out and in; for quite a number of years, it began to seem, bets in the neighbourhood had been running high. Sympathetic spy-glasses were trained on the conspicuous gateway to Jasmine Lodge; each new cavalier was noted. The only trouble might be, their promoters claimed, that the clever Trevors were always so surrounded that they had not a moment in which to turn or choose. Or otherwise, could it possibly be that the admiration aroused by Ethel and Elsie, and their now institutional place in the local scene, scared out more tender feeling from the masculine breast? It came to be felt, and perhaps by the girls themselves, that, having lingered so long and so puzzlingly, it was up to them to bring off (like their aunt) a *coup*. Society around this garrison town had long plumed itself upon its romantic record; summer and winter, Cupid shot his darts. Lush scenery, the oblivion of all things else bred by the steamy climate, and perpetual gallivanting – all were conducive. Ethel's and Elsie's names, it could be presumed, were by now murmured wherever the Union Jack flew. Nevertheless, it was time they should decide.

Ethel's decision took place late one spring. She set her cap at the second son of an English marquess. Lord Fred had come on a visit, for the fishing, to a mansion some miles down the river from Jasmine Lodge. He first made his appearance, with the rest of the house party, at one of the more resplendent military balls, and was understood to be a man-about-town. The civilian glint of his pince-nez, at once serene and superb, instantaneously wrought, with his great name, on Ethel's heart. She beheld him, and the assembled audience, with approbation, looked on at the moment so big with fate. The truth, it appeared in a flash, was that Ethel, though so condescending with her charms, had not from the first been destined to love a soldier; and that here, after long attrition, her answer was. Lord Fred was, by all, at once signed over to her. For his part, he responded to her attentions quite gladly, though in a somewhat dazed way. If he did not so often dance with her – indeed, how could he, for she was much besought? – he could at least be perceived to gaze. At a swiftly organised river picnic, the next evening, he by consent fell to Ethel's lot – she had spent the foregoing morning snipping and tacking at a remaining muslin of Mrs Varley de Grey's, a very fresh forget-me-not-dotted pattern. The muslin did not survive the evening out, for when the moon should have risen, rain poured into the boats. Ethel's good-humoured drollery carried all before it, and Lord Fred wrapped his blazer around her form.

Next day, more rain; and all felt flat. At Jasmine Lodge, the expectant deck chairs had to be hurried in from the garden, and the small close rooms, with their greeneried windows and plentiful bric-à-brac, gave out a stuffy, resentful, indoor smell. The maid was out; Elsie was lying down with a migraine; so it devolved on Ethel to carry up Mrs Varley de Grey's tea – the invalid set very great store by tea, and her manifestations by door rattlings, sobs and mutters were apt to become disturbing if it did not appear. Ethel, with the not particularly dainty tray, accordingly entered the back room, this afternoon rendered dark by its outlook into a dripping uphill wood. The aunt, her visage draped in a cobweb shawl, was as usual sitting up in bed. '*Aha*,' she at once cried, screwing one eye up and glittering round at Ethel with the other, 'so what's all this in the wind today?'

Ethel, as she lodged the meal on the bed, shrugged her shoulders, saying: 'I'm in a hurry.'

'No doubt you are. The question is, will you get him?'

'Oh drink your tea!' snapped Ethel, her colour rising.

The old wretch responded by popping a lump of sugar into her cheek, and sucking at it while she fixed her wink on her niece. She then observed: '*I* could tell you a thing or two!'

'We've had enough of *your* fabrications, Auntie.'

'Fabrications!' croaked Mrs Varley de Grey. 'And who's been the fabricator, I'd like to ask? Who's so nifty with the scissors and needle? Who's been going a-hunting in my clothes?'

'Oh, what a fib!' exclaimed Ethel, turning her eyes up. 'Those old musty miserable bundles of things of yours – would Elsie or I consider laying a finger on them?'

Mrs Varley de Grey replied, as she sometimes did, by heaving up and throwing the tray at Ethel. Nought, therefore, but cast-off kitchen china nowadays was ever exposed to risk. And the young woman, not trying to gather the debris up, statuesquely, thoughtfully stood with her arms folded, watching tea steam rise from the carpet. Today, the effort required seemed to have been too much for Aunt Elysia, who collapsed on her pillows, faintly blue in the face. 'Rats in the attic,' she muttered. '*I've* heard them, rats in the attic! Now where's my tea?'

'You've had it,' said Ethel, turning to leave the room. However, she paused to study a photograph in a tarnished, elaborate silver frame. 'Really quite an Adonis, poor Uncle Harry. From the first glance, you say, he never looked back?'

'My lovely tea,' said her aunt, beginning to sob.

As Ethel slowly put down the photograph, her eyes could be seen to calculate, her mouth hardened and a reflective cast came over her brow. Step by step, once more she approached the bed, and, as she did so, altered her tune. She suggested, in a beguiling tone: 'You said you could tell me a thing or two . . ?'

Time went on; Lord Fred, though forever promising, still failed to come quite within Ethel's grasp. Ground gained one hour seemed to be lost the next – it seemed, for example, that things went better for Ethel in the afternoon, in the open air, than at the dressier evening functions. It was when she swept down on him in full plumage that Lord Fred seemed to contract. Could it be that he feared his passions? – she hardly thought so. Or, did her complexion not light up well? When there was a question of dancing, he came so late that her programme already was black with other names, whereupon he would heave a gallant sigh. When they did take the floor together, he held her so far at arm's length, and with his face turned so far away, that when she wished to address him she had to shout – she told herself this must be the London style, but it piqued her, naturally. Next morning, all would be as it was before, with nobody so completely assiduous as Lord Fred – but, through it all, he still never came to the point. And worse, the days of his visit were running out; he would soon be back in the heart of the London Season. 'Will you ever get him, Ethel, now, do you think?' Elsie asked with trying solicitude, and no doubt the neighbourhood wondered also.

She conjured up all her fascinations. But was something further needed, to do the trick?

It was now that she began to frequent her aunt.

In that dank little back room looking into the hill, proud Ethel humbled herself, to prise out the secret. Sessions were close and long. Elsie, in mystification outside the door, heard the dotty voice of their relative rising, falling, with, now and then, blood-curdling little knowing laughs. Mrs Varley de Grey was back in the golden days. Always, though, of a sudden it would break off, drop back into pleas, whimpers and jagged breathing. No doctor, though she constantly asked for one, had for years been allowed to visit Mrs Varley de Grey – the girls saw no reason for that expense, or for the interference which might follow. Aunt's affliction, they swore, was confined to the head; all she required was quiet, and that she got. Knowing, however, how gossip spreads, they would let no servant near her for more than a minute or two, and then with one of themselves on watch at the door.

They had much to bear from the foetid state of her room.

'You don't think you'll kill her, Ethel?' the out-of-it Elsie asked. 'Forever sitting on top of her, as you now do. Can it be healthy, egging her on to talk? What's this attraction, all of a sudden? – whatever's this which has sprung up between you two? She and you are becoming quite hand-in-glove.'

Elsie merely remarked this, and soon forgot: she had her own fish to fry. It was Ethel who had cause to recall the words – for, the afternoon of the very day they were spoken, Aunt Elysia whizzed off on another track, screamed for what was impossible and, upon being thwarted, went into a seizure unknown before. The worst of it was, at the outset her mind cleared – she pushed her shawl back, reared up her unkempt grey head and looked at Ethel, unblinkingly studied Ethel, with a lucid accumulation of years of hate. 'You fool of a gawk,' she said, and with such contempt! 'Coming running to me to know how to trap a man. Could *you* learn, if it was from Venus herself? Wait till I show you beauty. Bring down those trunks!'

'Oh, Auntie.'

'Bring them down, I say. I'm about to dress myself up.'

'Oh, but I cannot; they're heavy; I'm single-handed.'

'Heavy? – they came here heavy. But there've been rats in the attic. *I* saw you, swishing downstairs in my *eau-de-nil*!'

'Oh, you dreamed that!'

'Through the crack of the door. Let me up, then. Let us go where they are, and look – we shall soon see!' Aunt Elysia threw back the bedclothes and began to get up. 'Let's take a look,' she said, 'at the rats' work.' She set out to totter towards the door.

'Oh, but you're not fit!' Ethel protested.

'And when did a doctor say so?' There was a swaying: Ethel caught her in time and, not gently, lugged her back to the bed – and Ethel's mind the whole of this time was whirling, for tonight was the night upon which all hung. Lord Fred's last local appearance was to be, like his first, at a ball:

tomorrow he left for London. So it must be tonight, at this ball, or never! How was it that Ethel felt so strangely, wildly confident of the outcome? It was time to begin on her coiffure, lay out her dress. Oh, tonight she would shine as never before! She flung back the bedclothes over the helpless form, heard a clock strike, and hastily turned to go.

'I will be quits with you,' said the voice behind her.

Ethel, in a kimono, hair half done, was in her own room, in front of the open glove drawer, when Elsie came in – home from a tennis party. Elsie acted oddly; she went at once to the drawer and buried her nose in it. 'Oh, my goodness,' she cried, 'it's all too true, and it's awful!'

'What is?' Ethel carelessly asked.

'Ethel dear, would you ever face it out if I were to tell you a certain rumour I heard today at the party as to Lord Fred?'

Ethel turned from her sister, took up the heated tongs and applied more crimps to her natural curliness. She said: 'Certainly; spit it out.'

'Since childhood, he's recoiled from the breath of benzine. He wilts away when it enters the very room!'

'Who says that's so?'

'He confided it to his hostess, who is now spitefully putting it around the country.'

Ethel bit her lip and put down the tongs, while Elsie sorrowfully concluded: 'And your gloves stink, Ethel, as I'm sure do mine.' Elsie then thought it wiser to slip away.

In a minute more, however, she was back, and this time with a still more peculiar air. She demanded: 'In what state did you leave Auntie? She was sounding so very quiet that I peeped in, and I don't care for the looks of her now at all!' Ethel swore, but consented to take a look. She stayed in there in the back room, with Elsie biting her thumb-nail outside the door, for what seemed an ominous length of time – when she did emerge, she looked greenish, but held her head high. The sisters' eyes met. Ethel said, stonily: 'Dozing.'

'You're certain she's *not* . . ? She *couldn't* ever be – you
know?'

'Dozing, I tell you.' Ethel stared Elsie out.

'If she *was* gone,' quavered the frailer sister, 'just think of it
– why, we'd never get to the ball! And a ball that everything
hangs on,' she ended up, with a scared but conspiratorial
glance at Ethel.

'Reassure yourself. Didn't you hear me say?'

As she spoke Ethel, chiefly from habit, locked her late
aunt's door on the outside. The act caused a sort of secret
jingle to be heard from inside her fist, and Elsie asked:
'What's that you've got hold of, now?'

'Just a few little keys and trinkets she made me keep,'
replied Ethel, disclosing the small bag she had found where
she'd looked for it, under the dead one's pillow. 'Scurry on
now, Elsie, or you'll never be dressed. Care to make use of
my tongs while they're so splendidly hot?'

Alone at last, Ethel drew in a breath, and, with a gesture of
resolution, retied her kimono sash tightly over her corset.
She shook the key from the bag and regarded it, murmuring,
'Providential!' then gave a glance upward, towards where
the attics were. The late spring had set, but an apricot after-
glow, not unlike the light cast by a Chinese lantern, crept
through the upper storey of Jasmine Lodge. The cessation of
all those rustlings, tappings, whimpers and moans from
inside Mrs Varley de Grey's room had set up an unfamiliar,
somewhat unnerving hush. Not till a whiff of singeing hair
announced that Elsie was well-employed did Ethel set out
on the quest which held all her hopes. Success was impera-
tive – she *must* have gloves. Gloves, gloves . . .

Soundlessly, she set foot on the attic stairs.

Under the skylight, she had to suppress a shriek, for a rat –
yes, of all things! – leaped at her out of an empty hatbox; and
the rodent gave her a wink before it darted away. Now Ethel
and Elsie knew for a certain fact that there never *had* been
rats in Jasmine Lodge. However, she continued to steel her

nerves, and to push her way to the one inviolate trunk.

All Mrs Varley de Grey's other Indian luggage gaped and. yawned at Ethel, void, showing its linings, on end or toppling, forming a barricade around the object of her search – she pushed, pitched and pulled, scowling as the dust flew into her hair. But the last trunk, when it came into view and reach, still had something select and bridal about it: on top, the initials E. V. de G. stared out, quite luminous in a frightening way – for indeed how dusky the attic was! Shadows not only multiplied in the corners but seemed to finger their way up the sloping roof. Silence pierced up through the floor from the room below – and, worst, Ethel had the sensation of being watched by that pair of fixed eyes she had not stayed to close. She glanced this way, that way, backward over her shoulder. But, Lord Fred was at stake! – she knelt down and got to work with the key.

This trunk had two neat brass locks, one left, one right, along the front of the lid. Ethel, after fumbling, opened the first – then, so great was her hurry to know what might be within that she could not wait but slipped her hand in under the lifted corner. She pulled out one pricelessly lacy tip of what must be a bride-veil, and gave a quick laugh – must not this be an omen? She pulled again, but the stuff resisted, almost as though it were being grasped from inside the trunk – she let go, and either her eyes deceived her or the lace began to be drawn back slowly, in again, inch by inch. What was odder was that the spotless fingertip of a white kid glove appeared for a moment, as though exploring its way out, then withdrew.

Ethel's heart stood still – but she turned to the other lock. Was a giddy attack overcoming her? – for, as she gazed, the entire lid of the trunk seemed to bulge upward, heave and strain, so that the E. V. de G. upon it rippled.

Untouched by the key in her trembling hand, the second lock tore itself open.

She recoiled, while the lid slowly rose – of its own accord.

She should have fled. But oh, how she craved what lay there exposed! – layer upon layer, wrapped in transparent paper, of elbow-length, magnolia-pure white gloves, bedded on the inert folds of the veil. 'Lord Fred,' thought Ethel, 'now you're within my grasp!'

That was her last thought, nor was the grasp to be hers. Down on her knees again, breathless with lust and joy, Ethel flung herself forward on to that sea of kid, scrabbling and seizing. The glove she had seen before was now, however, readier for its purpose. At first it merely pounced after Ethel's fingers, as though making mock of their greedy course; but the hand within it was all the time filling out . . . With one snowy flash through the dusk, the glove clutched Ethel's front hair, tangled itself in her black curls and dragged her head down. She began to choke among the sachets and tissue – then the glove let go, hurled her back, and made its leap at her throat.

It was a marvel that anything so dainty should be so strong. So great, so convulsive was the swell of the force that, during the strangling of Ethel, the seams of the glove split.

In any case, the glove would have been too small for her.

The shrieks of Elsie, upon the attic threshold, began only when all other sounds had died down . . . The ultimate spark of the once-famous cleverness of the Miss Trevors appeared in Elsie's extrication of herself from this awkward mess – for, who was to credit how Ethel came by her end? The sisters' reputation for warmth of heart was to stand the survivor in good stead – for, could those affections nursed in Jasmine Lodge, extending so freely even to the unwell aunt, have culminated in Elsie's setting on Ethel? No. In the end, the matter was hushed up – which is to say, is still talked about even now. Ethel Trevor and Mrs Varley de Grey were interred in the same grave, as everyone understood that they would have wished. What conversation took place under the earth, one does not know.

THE JOURNEY HOME

Bert Coules

*Bert Coules, who lives on the Kent coast within whistling distance
of the Romney, Hythe and Dymchurch Railway, produced his first
creepy story at the age of seven and has been horrifying people
with his writing ever since. He describes himself as six foot four,
craggily handsome, stupendously fit and an inveterate liar.*

George Morstan watched anxiously as Doctor McKay
peered into Felicity's unseeing eyes, listened to her
shallow, regular breathing and sat back, satisfied. 'She's
gone into a secure trance. She'll respond to my questions but
she won't say anything unless I prompt her.'

At which point the unconscious Felicity mumbled,
'Nineteen'.

The doctor frowned. 'What's the significance of nineteen?'

George replied immediately. 'I don't know.'

McKay turned back to his patient. 'Felicity, can you hear
me?'

A pause. Then: 'Yes, I can.'

'Good. Why nineteen?'

Instantly this time. 'Number nineteen. I said nineteen and
George said Twelve. No; eleven.' He nodded with great certainty.

Felicity was amused. George turned his head, quietly enjoying how good she looked. A long day at work, a hectic party in
the evening and there she was, fresh as ever, happily arguing
over Mozart symphony numbers and handling the car better
than he ever could. The music played on.

She smiled sideways at him. 'Well? Which?'

'Fourteen.'

She laughed out loud as he knew she would.

They both relaxed. The road was clear, the music was soothing. Happiness isn't a constant state, thought George, it's a condition encountered in specific, fleeting moments. Like this one. Enjoy it.

'You stupid fool!'

'Why can't you look where you're driving?'

'Yelling at me like that!'

It was a full-scale row. Another car had appeared from nowhere, its lights full in their eyes, and now they were at each other's throats. And I've got one hell of a headache, thought George, and that damn whine on the radio isn't helping, it's like nails on a blackboard. He stretched forward to turn it off, succeeded only in making it deafening. He could feel it vibrating the bones of his skull. Felicity reached down and roughly pushed his hand away from the set.

'Leave it alone! For God's sake leave it alone!' She stirred uneasily in her chair, her face taut. The doctor leaned towards her, his voice reassuring.

'All right, Felicity, relax, relax. You're completely calm. Rest for a moment.' The doctor turned to her husband. 'Well, Mr Morstan? That was an extremely vivid recollection. Why should that incident be so important?'

'It wasn't. She just dredged it up at random.'

The doctor regarded him closely. 'The music suddenly gave way to a high-pitched whistle. The car radio broke down?'

'Cheap Japanese rubbish.'

'And you had a row. What exactly sparked it off?'

'We were both tired out.'

The doctor didn't look satisfied. But he let it drop and turned back to the woman in the chair. 'Felicity, can you hear me?'

A mumbled monotone. 'Yes, I can.'

'Good. I want you to go on a short while. It's a little later now, after the car journey. You're home now.'

'Yes.'

'Good. Where are you?'

She stirred. 'In the hall. With George.'

'What are you doing?'

'I'm saying it can't be half-past two in the morning!'

George spun round to face her. He was angry and his head was hammering. 'This is ridiculous.'

She wouldn't let it go. 'What time did we leave Tim and Maureen's?'

He couldn't believe this. 'Good God, I don't know. Thirty, forty minutes ago.'

'It was eleven thirty.'

'Don't be stupid.' He stared at her.

She was unshakeable. 'I'm telling you it was eleven thirty!' In the frozen moment that followed he saw for the first time that she was also scared. Very scared. 'George, it's taken us three hours to do a half-hour drive.'

There was nothing he could say. He turned and went up to bed.

'George has gone to bed.'

'And what are you thinking?'

'I'm thinking, why isn't George worried?'

'Are you worried?'

Her hands clenched compulsively. 'I'm terrified. What happened? Something happened! Why can't I remember?'

And, to the amazement of her doctor and the horror of her husband, Felicity Morstan howled in agony and fell writhing to the floor.

Both men knelt beside her. The doctor's voice was low, insistent. 'Felicity, listen to me. Listen! This pain is not real. It isn't happening. There is no pain.' Slowly, she relaxed and they helped her back into the chair. The doctor turned to George. 'Did that seem like a typical attack?'

His eyes hadn't left his wife. 'Yes. The sudden pain, the

loss of control . . .' He looked up. 'What do you mean, "seem like"? That *was* another one.'

'No. If it had been I wouldn't have been able to erase the pain so easily. That was just the recollection of an earlier attack, presumably just after you'd gone to bed.'

'I'd no idea . . .'

'I'm going to talk her through it.'

George flared. 'I don't want her to go through that again!'

'She won't. Felicity, listen to me.'

He told the still unconscious woman that she was now back, back just before the onset of the attack, and this time there would be no pain, no discomfort at all. He asked Felicity to describe what was happening to her, and – her voice barely a whisper – she told them that she couldn't see a thing. Where the hell were they?

'George? What's happening?'

'Tell me what you see.'

It was like plunging your hands into rotting flesh, the sound of that voice. She choked back the impulse to vomit.

'Who are you? Where's George?'

'That's not important.'

'Tell me, damn you! Tell me!'

George grabbed the doctor's arm. 'Who's she supposed to be talking to? I thought you were trying to find out about the attack.'

'This is the attack. Her unconscious is giving the pain a concrete form.' But for the first time, a tiny crack had appeared in the professional cool. 'Felicity, who are you talking to?'

She shuddered, but the trance was still firm. 'I can't see him.'

'Can you see anything at all? Tell me what you see.'

She wanted that voice to go away. She wanted to ignore it. But she couldn't. She looked around. 'I can see a man and a woman.'

'Good.' It was the sound of fatted maggots sated on a corpse.

'Do you know them?'

Did she? She wasn't sure. She looked again. And yelled 'Look out!'

'It's all right, relax, relax. What can you see?'

A pause. Then: 'I can see our hallway.'

The pain had gone, she was through it. The doctor suddenly asked: 'What about the man and the woman?'

'Who?' But she was struggling with some elusive image.

'Never mind, it doesn't matter.'

George broke in, his voice cold. 'Look, this isn't getting us anywhere.'

'Then let's see if we can't force the pace a little. When was the first attack you were aware of?'

'That same night. She was in the bathroom when the smell of the antiseptic hit her. Funny how a smell can be so instantly evocative. Antiseptic, freshly-laundered sheets, starched uniforms, these places always smell the same. Safe, comforting. Then the rotting stink of that voice cutting through it all, spoiling it. And the same insistent demand: tell me what you see. This time she resisted: I'm dreaming, she said, this is a dream, it isn't real. And then a pause, and then the laughing, the filthy, mocking laughing. And then the words.

'Look over there, Felicity. Look on the bed.'

And, her thin wall of resistance gone, she looked. She looked and she screamed.

And the doctor let her scream herself out. Then McKay turned to George, nodding in satisfaction.

'Excellent. We're getting somewhere.'

'What?'

The doctor ignored his astonishment. 'So, she screamed and you rushed into the bathroom.'

'And she was fine. Except for the trifling fact that she'd put her fist through the bathroom cabinet. And couldn't remember doing it.'

*   *   *

Several more recollected attacks later, they reached that morning's final, devastating seizure, at the height of which Felicity was frantically clawing at him, her fingers held like rigid steel spikes. George tried to grab her wrists but she pushed him back as though he weighed nothing. In blind desperation he roughly knocked her hands to one side and slapped her face with all the strength he could summon.

She didn't waver for a second. Her fingers dug into his flesh as though she were kneading pastry. Blood was running freely down his cheeks, thin strips of skin were flapping loose.

Again and again George hit her. And finally, mercifully, she froze, fixed her eyes full on her husband's and pleaded in a terrifying whisper: 'George! Help me!'

She was still fully in the trance.

'I'm going to take her back to the car journey.'

'That again? But I've told you –'

'Yes, that again. It's clearly at the core of the trauma. Felicity, can you hear me?'

George sat stone-faced as his wife was regressed once again to the journey home after that damned party. Why the hell did they go? He hadn't wanted to, she knew that. And they were her friends really, hers, not his. He snapped back as Felicity moaned softly, clearly in distress.

McKay said, 'I don't understand this. Her recollection of events seems to be different this time. I can't home her in on the row, or the radio breaking down.'

George said nothing.

The doctor's voice was smooth. 'OK, Felicity, remember that nothing can harm or hurt you. What's happening?'

George looked at her. 'I don't know, love. Is this the right road?'

She was really scared, he could sense it in the darkness. 'Of course it's not the right bloody road! Do you remember a tunnel being here before?'

'We must have taken a wrong turn in the fog.'

'That's another thing! Where the hell did – what's that light? Up ahead?'

George could see it too, now. 'Stop the car.' I think we should stop this.'

The doctor pushed George back. 'Mr Morstan. I know what I'm doing. Felicity, don't be scared. Tell me what you see.'

'No!' She loathed that voice. Why wouldn't it leave her alone? And where was George? The voice was all around her, inside her, everywhere. She had to answer. Perhaps if she answered it would go away. 'I can see a man and a woman.'

'What are they doing?'

'I don't want to see!'

'Everything's fine, nothing can harm you. What are they doing? Tell me!'

She had to. She had to look. The voice had the power. She looked. She screamed.

'Felicity!' It was the sharpest the doctor had allowed his voice to be all through the session. She stopped shaking. 'I'm going to ask you to look at the man and the woman again. You will be quite calm and relaxed. Do you understand?'

'Yes.' She was sitting perfectly still, her breathing even.

'Good. Tell me what is happening.'

She was beyond shock. 'The man is trying to kill the woman.'

'No!' George was up out of his chair, reaching for her. The doctor shoved him back.

'This is it. The core of the psychosis.' Was that pride in his voice? A job well done? 'Felicity, where are you now?'

A long pause. Then: 'These places always smell the same. She's here.'

'You're where she is? The woman?'

'Yes.' The flat voice had taken on a puzzled tone.

'Felicity, do you know this woman?'

'I can't see her face.'

309

Go closer, said the graveyard voice, go closer. And she obeyed, everything else forgotten in the compulsion to do as she was bidden. And, knowing it had won, the voice became enticing, smooth, almost loving.

'Look at her now.'

Felicity shook her head. 'She's dead. How can she be dead?'

The doctor smiled, actually smiled. Back on the textbook course again. 'Yes she's dead. It's important that you accept that. Vitally important.'

Animation snapped back into Felicity's whole body. 'Don't say that!'

The voice laughed. It was an indulgent laugh, an adult's amusement at an endearing child.

'Stop it! Don't say it again!' She was shaking, terrified. A thin sliver of blood ran reluctantly out of one clenched fist.

George was shouting. 'Bring her round. Get her out of it.' The doctor ignored him, bending his face close to Felicity's.

'What is he saying, Felicity? What are the words?'

The voice dripped dead flesh. 'Destiny, Felicity,' it said. 'Fate. Karma. Things to come.'

Felicity slumped, unseeing eyes staring.

McKay was whispering, inches from her ear. 'All right Felicity, it's nearly over. I want you to look at the dead woman. I want you to tell me who she is.'

She couldn't force her voice above a croak. 'I can't! Don't make me!'

George had his hands on the doctor's shoulders. 'Stop this!'

'I can't. This is essential if she's to free herself. This projection has to be exorcised. Now sit down.'

He didn't sit down. But he did take his hands away.

McKay's voice was hard. 'You must look. Just one look and then it'll all be over.'

'No!'

'Yes! Do as I say.'

310

No more than a breath. 'No! Please!'

It was a voice accustomed to being obeyed. 'Who is that woman?'

'Don't look! Don't do it!' George was close to hysterical.

She looked.

She found her voice.

'Me! She's me! Me . . .'

She was sobbing. George was pulling her out of the chair, shaking her viciously. The doctor tried to push him away and George slammed him into a corner.

Felicity's eyes focused, deep with the recollection of what she had seen and heard and told.

George's voice was soft. 'Come on love. We're going home.'

They were sitting in their car, outside the hospital. And, since someone had to say something, he began.

'How much do you remember, love?'

'Everything.' She shuddered. 'God, that voice!'

He persisted, gently. 'Exactly what?'

Her voice was still the monotone of the trance. 'I remember us driving along. And everything being all right. The music ending. And then the fog.'

George heard himself prompting her. 'Coming up from nowhere.'

A flicker of surprise. 'Yes. Then . . . Then there was . . .'

'Then there was the tunnel. It was very dark. And then we saw the light at the end.'

She was staring at him. '*We* saw? You too?'

Slowly, he nodded. 'Me too.'

'But – you said nothing happened. You kept saying nothing happened.'

'I know.'

'You forgot? Like I did?'

'No love. I didn't forget.'

311

'You mean you knew all the time? Right from the start?'

George had rehearsed this moment a hundred times. But that didn't make it any easier. 'At first I thought maybe I was going mad. Hallucinations or something. I couldn't believe it had been real. After all, you didn't seem to remember any of it.' *That's right!* he thought. *Put the blame on her, why don't you? Just what she needs!*

He took a deep breath. 'Then you started having the attacks. Some of the things you said. . . it was as if something was trying to break through, get out into the open.'

She shook her head. 'That's why you made them try the hypnosis?'

'I had to be sure. You must see that!'

She didn't respond to his outburst. 'But what does it mean?'

'It means that you were right. Something did happen to us on the journey home. Something that took two and a half hours.'

There was a faint echo of the dead voice when she spoke. 'Destiny. Fate. Things to come.'

He nodded. 'The future. We were shown the future.'

Suddenly, there was concern for him in her eyes and her voice. It was the most heartening thing he'd seen since this whole business had begun. 'What I saw – you saw it too? You heard that voice?'

'I saw exactly what you saw.'

'Someone's going to kill me.'

'Yes.'

'But who? Did you see who it was?'

He reached out for her hands. He could feel the caked blood where the nails had penetrated. 'Oh, my love. It was me.'

It took a long time for it to sink in. But she believed him, he could see it.

'Why do you think I've been half out of my mind? I was shown it, just the same as you. But I saw a little more detail. And I was – what's the right word? – *permitted* to remember everything.'

'You're going to kill me.' It was a simple statement of fact.

'And there's nothing we can do about it. He told me. And I believe it.'

'Yes. Yes, so do I. God, I'll never forget that voice, not as long as – George!'

And suddenly whatever barrier had been holding back the reaction wasn't there any more, and the tears came and the shaking and they held each other in silence for a very long time.

When he was able to, George said: 'I love you.' And he thought, *As if that's going to solve anything*.

And Felicity said: 'I know you do. But it's still going to happen.'

'Yes. But for God's sake – why?'

Thinking about it afterwards, he found it hard to believe that it hadn't come to him before that moment. But it genuinely was a totally new thought when she said:

'Why? Why isn't really important, is it? The real question is – when?'

He stared at her. Then, without a word, he switched on the car and drove them home.

ST AUSTIN FRIARS

Robert Westall

Art master, critic and award-winning writer, Robert Westall
was born in Newcastle-upon-Tyne in 1929. Westall's work,
predominantly stories for older children, broadly embraces
thriller, fantasy and the supernatural. He won the Carnegie
Medal for THE MACHINE GUNNERS in 1975. His other
popular children's books include THE WATCH HOUSE (1977),
FATHOM FIVE (1979), THE SCARECROWS (1981), THE
FUTURETRACK FIVE (1983) and URN BURIAL (1987).

The church of St Austin Friars stands in an inner suburb
of Muncaster. It is huge for a parish church, beautiful in
the Perpendicular style, and black as coal from the smoke of
the city. It stands on a hill, amidst its long-disused
graveyard, and its only near companion is the Greek Revival
rectory, like a temple with chimneys, also coal-black. It is
really St Margaret's, but Muncastrians always call it St Austin Friars, in memory of the Augustinian Canons who had
their monastery there in the Middle Ages.

Then, it stood in fair countryside, amidst its own rich
demesne. Muncaster was no more than the houses of the
monastic servants. But the Industrial Revolution came to
Muncaster and it grew, covering all the green fields and hills
with soot and sweat and money. By the time that the Reverend Martin Williams was appointed rector in 1970 the only
traces of the monastery, apart from the church, were a mean
street called Fishponds and another called Cloister Lane.

Martin Williams came when the Industrial Revolution
was departing, having had its way with Muncaster. The day
after he moved into the rectory, the houses of Fishponds
were being demolished. The dust from falling brick and the

smoke from the scrap-wood fires were so engulfing that the demolition-foreman, a decent man, came up to the rectory to apologise.

'You'll soon be shot of us,' he said, sitting down to a mug of tea that Sheila, as a well-trained clergy wife, immediately laid before him. 'Trouble is, you'll soon be shot o' your parish, too. It's all going, you know!'

'Yes, I know,' said Martin, sticking his hands into the pockets of long thin trousers and staring out of the window. 'It's a shame.'

'Shame nothing!' said the foreman. 'Seen a mort o' suffering, this place. Bringing up fo'teen bairns on a pound a week in a room no bigger nor your pantry. Beggin' yer pardon, missus. But me dad an' me grandad told me about it. Had an evil name, round here. Cholera – typhoid – afore they got the drains right. Four hundred dead in one week, they say; one long hot summer. Good riddance to bad rubbish, *I* say.'

'Aren't they going to build multi-storey flats instead?' asked Sheila.

'Not that *I* heard,' said the foreman. 'Not that they tell the likes of us anything. Other parts, people are crying their hearts out 'cause they're having to leave, not in Fishponds. They can't wait to get out to the overspill. What you aiming to do wi' yerself, then?'

Martin gave a violent start; he still could not get used to the sudden bluntness of the North, after his last curacy in Kent. Here, people asked you the most intimate questions the moment they'd shaken hands. This chap would be asking next when they were going to start a family.

'What am I going to do with myself? Well, it just so happens that the city centre is also part of this parish. So I'll be down there a lot . . .'

'*They're* a right queer push an' all,' opined the forcman, drinking deep into his mug and, to Sheila's fascination, actually wiping his moustache with the back of his hand.

'Pimps, prostitutes, homosexuals, actors – what's the difference? Beggin' yer pardon, missus.'

'Jesus mixed with prostitutes and sinners,' said Martin, giving him a look of sharp blue charity that had the foreman on his feet in a second.

'Thank you for the tea, missus. And –' he gave Martin a sharp look in return – 'best o' luck wi' the city centre. Yer might just do something down *there* – wi' luck. All the best.' And he wiped his hands on the seat of his trousers, shook both their hands, and departed. His boots, crunching down the long drive, left that peculiar silence that lay like the black dust all over the rectory, and that Martin and Sheila were to come to know so well.

'I don't like this place,' said Sheila, washing up the mug to break the silence.

'I know you don't,' said Martin. 'But it's a good living, and a good city – think of all the concerts we can go to. And you'll be out teaching most of the time. And out in the evenings. We'll hardly be in the place – just camping out.'

The kitchen was large and fully fitted. Equipped down to a Kenwood mixer, and not a thing in it was theirs. Pity the main areas of formica were in a spirit-lowering shade of browny-purple . . .

All the many rooms were the same: beautifully decorated, beautifully furnished. The sitting-room had leather settees and couches, hardly touched. The whole house was recently wired, totally weatherproof and structurally immaculate. There wasn't a bit of do-it-yourself for Martin or Sheila to lay their fingers on.

'Canon Maitland must have been awfully well-off, to afford all this,' said Sheila. 'And no one to leave it all to when he died.'

'He was *very* old,' said Martin. 'Ninety-four.'

'But they're supposed to retire at seventy.'

'This place was special. Very little work, even before the

316

demolition. The Bishop told me.' The Bishop had told him many things.

The Bishop was an old-school-tie friend of Martin's previous Bishop in Kent. The Bishop had wanted a bright young man, willing to try unorthodox methods in a city-centre parish. And to be one of the Bishop's Chaplains, which mainly involved marking high-level clergy exam-papers. And to be a one-day-a-week lecturer in Christian Social Work at the Church of England college. 'Plenty of interesting things to fill your week, young man. Don't you worry your head about Fishponds and Cloister Lane,' the Bishop had said, hand on Martin's shoulder, when Martin finally accepted the job, without consulting Sheila first (a sore point).

But in spite of this, for a year they were happy. Sheila enjoyed her school, and Martin his college. Three days a week he worked his city-centre parish, using the back rooms of ornate Edwardian pubs such as The Grapes, drinking half-pints of shandy carefully, and eating a lot of curious pub-grub. He knew enough to wear a sports-coat and cover his clergyman's dog-collar with a poloneck sweater (except when a clergyman was actually required, when he would roll down the neck of the sweater to reveal all). By the time the pimps and prostitutes, actors and homosexuals found out he was a clergyman, they'd also found out that he was a good sort, a good listener, a good shoulder to cry on, and good for a bed for the night in a crisis. He was *quite* wise, but he was *very* nice; he helped a number of people to avoid committing suicide, simply because, in the moment of the act, they thought how upset he would be, how disappointed if they really did it. A lot of the men kept his card and phone number in their pocket; a lot of the girls brought him home-knitted sweaters and jars of jam their mums had made. A certain number of the girls tried to persuade him into bed with them, in the cause of the New Theology, but he always

317

got away by saying, 'Not while on duty.' He was always on duty. Sheila stored the pullovers (most of which didn't fit, but none of which he would throw away) in a large cupboard, and lined the shelves of the pantry with the jars of jam. They weren't for eating, Martin said, they were for looking at. Sheila was pretty philosophical; anybody who'd married Martin would have had to be philosophical.

They went to lots of concerts; threw lots of parties, full of drunken radical social-workers, militant black leaders, manic-depressive pimps and nymphomaniac Liberal débutantes. The isolated rectory kept their secrets; there was no complaint to the Bishop. But when the last of the guests had gone, the rectory returned to its own secrets.

Meanwhile, the demolition continued. Cloister Lane went, and Infirmary Street, and Boundary Road. Every time Martin looked out of the window, the battered gable-ends of the houses, defiantly flaunting their tattered wallpaper through wind and rain, seemed to get further away. Martin got the strange idea that the whole city was recoiling from St Austin Friars, like the crowd at a circus when the tiger gets loose. He told himself not to be silly. Sheila told him not to be silly. They were living in clover.

The congregation at Sunday service was three: Sheila, and the two churchwardens. One warden, Mr Phillips, was also verger and caretaker. The other, Mr Rubens, was said to be the city's last big pawnbroker. Dark, solid, formal and sleek, he wasn't the kind of man you could ask that kind of question. The congregation on Wednesday morning was nil; Martin said the service alone in the great, dark, hollow church. He would have liked to sing it, but there were too many echoes answering, and he soon gave it up. He recognised this as his first defeat.

It was all defeats, as far as the church services were concerned. He went round the poor houses and corner shops that were left, beyond Fishponds and Cloister Lane. The people were respectful, sickeningly respectful. He tried to be friendly, but they treated him as if he were a pope, and not a jolly pope, either. If there was a crowd in a shop, they stood aside deferentially to let him buy his cigarettes, then listened silently, hushed to his remarks about the weather or the football team. Waiting for him to go, so they could resume their whispering, scurrying, mouse-like lives. If he called at a house, he was sat in the tiny, freezing, front parlour, while the housewife sent out for expensive cakes and the children peeped round the door at him, and fled when he spoke to them. They gave him horrifying amounts of money, 'for the church'. One pensioner gave him a five-pound note, though her stockings were darned and her shoes cracked. When he tried to refuse it, she burst into tears, pleading with him to take it, and would not be pacified until he did. He thought, bitterly, that they never saw *him* at all; they saw another Canon Maitland, or some other Victorian tyrant-priest. He was walking in another man's shoes. He hated that man; he would have strangled that man if he could. But that man was invisible; close to him as his own skin. None of the local people came to church; they were paying him to go away and leave them in peace.

He had better luck with his city-centre people; sometimes they came to church for love of him: a group of actors from the Library Theatre, theatrically muffled in long scarves and wide-brimmed black hats; once, a bunch of the girls, in fun-furs, mini-skirts and suede boots. They hadn't a clue how to take part in the service, and they caused an explosion at the churchwardens' meeting afterwards. Mr Phillips, whose house now stood out of the flat, spreading clearances like a decaying Gothic tooth, said that the likes of them were not fit to be seen in church. His bitten grey moustache and his pendulous jowls wobbled in hideous indignation. But the smooth Mr Rubens cut him short.

'Father Williams is entitled to have anyone he likes in his

church. Your job is to keep it clean and ring the bell.' Mr
Phillips came to heel like a whipped cur; which taught Martin a lot. Mr Rubens cracked the whip. Mr Rubens got things
done.

Like the strange matter of the choir. Martin had discovered a moth-balled oak wardrobe, full of red and white choir
vestments. He said wistfully at one meeting that he *would*
like to have a choir . . . The next Sunday, he was amazed to
find he had a choir, of total strangers, complete with
organist-and-choirmaster. They sang beautifully. But in
conversation with one child in the vestry afterwards, he
found they were a school choir, bussed-in from a distance at
considerable expense, and quite obviously doing it for the
money. When he pointed out to Mr Rubens that this was not
what he had meant at all, Mr Rubens looked at him very
sharply and said he wouldn't be bothered with them again.
Just as long as he made up his mind what he wanted. Martin
began to feel like somebody's pampered mistress. But he was
growing a little afraid of Mr Rubens. For one thing, Mr
Rubens had never given his address or phone number. He
always rang Martin; he was the one that fixed the church-wardens' meetings.

Afterwards, Martin realised he should have got out of St
Austin's then. But the Bishop was pleased with all the work
he was doing; and Mr Rubens had told the Bishop that he
was *delighted* with all the work Martin was doing. And
everything but St Austin's was going so well.

St Austin's got worse and worse. Martin loved churches,
but he couldn't love St Austin's. It wasn't spooky exactly,
just infinitely old and cold and dark. It rejected him. He had
the vestry redecorated in contemporary style, installed a
vinyl-topped desk and telephone, hung framed prints of the
Turin Shroud and Dali's modern crucifixion on the wall. He
would make that, at least, a place where people came, for
coffee and a chat when they had a problem. Nobody came.

Still, Martin bravely persisted in his church, like an occupying army, for three hours every Wednesday morning. After the service, he drifted up the aisles reading the epitaphs of long-dead Muncastrians, engraved on Georgian and Regency marble on the walls.

> *Near this spot are buried the Mortal Remains of Jonathan Appleby Esq, who died on the 14th day of February, 1828, aetat 17 yeers.*
>
> *For those who never knew him, no words can convey his Infinite Excellence of Character.*
>
> *As for his grieving Friends, who had the Infinite Privilege of his Acquaintanceship, they are silenced by Greefe.*
>
> *Therefore, no word Further is Uttered.*

Tactful, that, thought Martin with a wry grin. But grave-humour is thin gruel to feed the human heart, and on the whole the epitaphs did not console him. He did, however, notice a preponderance of odd names. *Canzo. Frederick Canzo, William Ewart Canzo, Joshua Canzo.* And *Betyl.* And *Morsk.* But especially the name *Drogo* cropped up. There must be more Drogos buried in the crypt under the church than all the rest put together. Funny, how these odd names had died out. He had never met a Canzo or a Betyl or a Morsk or a Drogo in his life.

One Wednesday morning he was amazed to hear the phone ringing, at the far end of the church. He ran so eagerly, he arrived quite out of breath. The only person who had ever rung him until now was Sheila from the rectory, to tell him lunch was ready. But at this moment she would be hard at it, teaching.

'St Margaret's church. Can I help you?'

'That St Austin Friars?'

'Yes.'

'Why didn't you say so? We've got a funeral for you.'

'Wait, let me find the diary and a pencil. Now where did I

– ah good. Right.' Martin was practically gabbling, at the idea of actually being useful for a change. 'Who's speaking?'

'This is Bettle's the undertakers. Deceased's name is William Henry Drogo. Yes, that's right, D-R-O-G-O. Friday morning, 28th March at 10.30 a.m.'

Martin glanced over his shoulder at the Mowbray's calendar on the wall. Today was Wednesday the 26th. 'Fine,' he said. 'Will you want the bell rung?'

'Old Phillips knows how we like it. Leave it to him.'

'And your telephone number?'

'Muncaster 213245.' The voice sounded grudging. 'Phillips will fill you in.' There was a click and the speaker was gone.

Martin looked down at the details in his diary. Strange, the name Drogo cropping up, just when he'd been telling himself that such names must be dead and gone. Usual kind of service, he supposed. No request for a special sermon.

It was then that he realised that today was not Wednesday the 26th of March.

It was only Wednesday the 26th of February. Somebody had booked a funeral a month in advance.

Martin rang the number back.

'Excuse me, I think you've made some mistake. I think you want Mr Drogo buried on the 28th February. You said the 28th March. It's a mistake that's easily made – I often make it – '

'When I say the 28th of March,' said the voice, very Muncastrian, 'I *mean* the 28th of March.'

'But – '

'Ask old Phillips.' The phone went down with an extra-loud click, and when Martin re-dialled, the other end didn't answer.

At first, he was sure it was a practical joker. Especially as he went through the telephone directory and could find no undertaker called Bettle. Or Beddle. Or Bethel, for that matter. Nor Bettell, nor Bettall. So then he looked up Drogo.

To his surprise, there were quite a lot of Drogos – eight in all, including *Drogo's, Pharmaceutical Suppliers and Wholesalers.* And a *Drogo, William H.*, at a very lush address in Willington, out in the fresh air in the foothills of the Pennines.

Martin paced up and down the vestry in a rare taking. Of course, he could always ask old Phillips, as he'd been told. But he had a certain reluctance to be laughed at by old Phillips. There must be other ways to check . . .

William H. Drogo was a man of importance – perhaps the chairman of Drogo Pharmaceuticals? Heart pounding, he rang Drogo Pharmaceuticals and asked for William H. Drogo. Yes, a very expensive female voice answered, Mr William H. Drogo was chairman. Yes, Mr William *Henry* Drogo. But unfortunately he was not available, being out all day at a meeting in London. If Mr . . ? – Mr Williams would care to ring back tomorrow . . ?'

'Are there any other William Henry Drogos?'

No. The expensive voice allowed itself to sound faintly offended. There was only one Mr William Henry Drogo. And she knew the *whole* family. There *was* only one Drogo family, at least in Britain. The voice curved upwards, making the Drogos sound more distinctive than the Royal Family.

Martin rang off, before he was reduced to sounding a complete blithering idiot.

He took to pacing up and down again. That expensive voice . . . that imperturbable voice . . . would be quite calm enough to effect a cover-up. Why a cover-up? Perhaps for commercial reasons. Some firms were pretty vulnerable when the big bossman suddenly died. But you couldn't cover-up a death for a month, for God's sake . . . Feeling even more of an idiot, but rather cross just the same, he rang the Drogo home number. This time a deep female voice answered; a voice so rich and exotic, it made the other female voice sound plastic.

'I'm sorry, Mr . . . Williams. My grandfather is away in London all day today. If you rang his office in the morning, I'm sure he'd be delighted to speak to you.'

He hung up. That was certainly no house of mourning, no house shaken to the roots by a death. That house was smug, rich, utterly certain of itself, full of the careless decency that comes from years without pain. It was a hoax. He wouldn't ask old Phillips. It was probably old Phillips who had made the hoax call. Who else knew all about the Drogos lining the aisles of his church with their memorials? Drogos and Canzos and Morsks and Betyls.

Betyl. Not Bettle the undertaker, but Betyl the undertaker.

Oh, don't be crazy. Whoever heard of anyone called Betyl?

Whoever had heard of anyone called Drogo? He reached for the telephone directory.

No *Betyl*.

Then he realised that the current directory was held up by a pile of other directories, well-nibbled by the church mice and rather damp towards the bottom of the heap.

In the rotting, falling-apart 1953 directory, he found it. *Betyl, Georg & Son, Funeral Directors, 4 Albert St, Hathershaw, Muncaster 213245.* Hathershaw was the next inner suburb, only two miles away.

Feeling slightly unreal, he got out the car and drove over.

Hathershaw was in the throes of demolition, too. It was like fleeing through a doomed city. Houses first slateless, then roofless, then windowless. Streets that were only pavements and cobbles and solitary lamp-posts on corners; streets pressed flat like wild flowers in a book. Streets with no names, just old Victorian manhole covers. Fires on every mound of fallen brick. Bulldozers; sweating, filthy, rejoicing demolition men.

'Albert Street?' yelled Martin, winding down his window and trying to compete against another wall falling down.

'You'll be lucky, squire. If you're quick, you might just catch it before it goes. Third right, second left. Mind yer head.'

He caught it. The slates were just coming off the roof of Number 4. The bulldozers were three houses away.

Georg Betyl and Son. Funeral Directors. Established 1832.

The shop window was still draped in faded ecclesiastical purple. There were three black urns, tastelessly arranged, and a squat marble box for flowers, labelled *From friends and neighbours.*

'Stop!' shouted Martin, leaping from his car. The demolition team was facetious, but not unsympathetic.

Yeah,' said the gaffer, to his request for admittance. 'Why not? It won't be here by five o'clock.' They smashed in the black, rather nice Georgian front door with a sledgehammer, while Martin winced.

Inside, the place felt odd already, with half the roof stripped. There was the phone; dead when Martin picked it up.

'GPO was here an hour ago, to cut it off,' said the gaffer. 'If you want that phone, you can have it,' he added generously. 'Cost you a quid – you don't get many like that, these days.' There was also an ancient iron safe, door hanging open, some cremation urns in white plastic, and a tin wastebucket full of empty envelopes addressed to *Georg Betyl and Son, Funeral Directors, 4 Albert Street, Hathershaw* and going back sixty years. Two old wooden chairs, and nothing else at all.

The next day, Martin rang GPO telephones. They were unable to help; all communications and bills for Mr Betyl had always been sent to 4 Albert Street. As far as they were concerned, Mr Betyl had paid his terminal bill and ceased to exist. There had certainly been no application for a new telephone number at a new address. Muncaster Corporation also did their best; yes, they had purchased the shop from Mr Betyl; and had sent all correspondence and the final purchase cheque to 4 Albert Street. No, he was only on their rolls of electors at the Albert Street address. Perhaps he had lived above the shop?

Feeling the boldness of despair, Martin rang Drogo Pharmaceuticals again. The expensive voice (who knew something more about him than she had known the previous day) put him straight through to Mr William Henry Drogo.

'I don't know how to start,' said Martin, suddenly helpless.

'You sound rather upset,' Drogo's voice had the same richness as his granddaughter's.

'I am a little upset. There's something I have to tell you.'

'You are the new rector of St Austin Friars.'

'Yes. How did you know that?'

'I've always had an interest in St Austin's,' said Mr Drogo. 'Perhaps you would honour my granddaughter and me with your company at dinner tomorrow night.'

Martin gasped audibly. Did anybody still talk like that?

'We have our own ways,' said Mr Drogo. Martin had the idea that he was gently laughing at him.

Martin drove over to Willington in a fair state of resentment; he had had to lie to Sheila; had made up a story of church business and the offer of funds. It was the first time he'd ever seriously lied to her. But the whole business was so crazy . . . He'd tell her everything once he'd cleared it up.

The Drogo house was large, modern, but rather ugly, standing well clear of its neighbours among mature decorative conifers. The granddaughter answered the door and took his coat.

'I'm the housekeeper tonight. It's the servants' night off.' Her appearance went with her voice; she was tall, about thirty, very much the confident businesswoman. Her looks could only be described as opulent: a mass of blue-black hair, swept up on top of her head, a figure that curved richly, but with the utmost discretion, in a dark-grey business suit with white lace at throat and wrists drawing attention to the plump, creamy beauty of her face and hands. No wedding ring. Her dark eyes surveyed him with a frank female interest that was disconcerting. It was the way certain rich men eyed a new woman . . . he flashed up in his mind a vision of Sheila, thin, red-haired and freckled. Ashamedly, he thought she made the vision of Sheila seem very thin indeed. She walked ahead of him, the powerful hips and calves moving discreetly, expensively, arrogantly.

The man who rose from the dark-red leather armchair could not possibly be the grandfather. He could be no more than fifty. The same blue-black hair and dark, amused eyes, the same sombre and wealthy solidity that could never be described as fat.

'Oh,' said Martin. 'I'd hoped to speak to Mr Drogo.'

'I *am* Mr Drogo.'

'Mr William Henry Drogo?'

'The same.'

'But . . .'

'Let me get you a drink. What will you have?' He moved to a highly polished mahogany sideboard. With its brass handles, Martin thought it looked like the most expensive kind of coffin. Desperately, he fought to get hold of himself. But his hand still trembled, and the sherry ran down over his fingers. For some reason he began to worry because he hadn't told Sheila exactly where he was going.

'Do sit down, Mr Williams. How can I help you?'

Martin glanced at the girl, sitting listening intently. She got up at once, saying, 'I must see to the dinner.' Fascinated, Martin watched her as she left the room. At his next confession, he was going to have to confess the sin of lechery. It was not a sin he had had to confess before.

'My granddaughter interests you.' It was not a question, it was a statement. There was no disapproval in it. Blindly, Martin lunged into the reason he had come: the phone call from the vanishing undertaker, the funeral of William Henry Drogo, booked a month ahead. Mr Drogo listened, nodding sympathetically, without a hint of surprise or disbelief. Martin finished up, lamely:

'I wouldn't have bothered you, only it's been preying on my mind. Is it just some ridiculous practical joke, or is it a – a threat of some kind? Against your life, or something? I mean, it sounds like something the Mafia would do – if we had anything like the Mafia in Muncaster.' He forced himself to smile and shrug at his own childishness.

'Oh,' said Mr Drogo. 'We *had* the Mafia in Muncaster, a couple of years ago. On a very small scale. They tried to take over an interest in one or two rather second-rate gambling clubs. Very small beer. We had a quiet word in the Chief Constable's ear, and they went away peacefully enough.'

The muffled note of a small dinner-gong echoed through the house. 'Come and eat,' said Mr Drogo, putting a fatherly hand on Martin's shoulder.

The meal was good, though a little strange and spicy. So was the wine. The daughter – no, the granddaughter – whose name was Celicia, moved about serving it as silently as a cat on the thick red carpet. The rest of the time, from the side, she watched Martin as he talked. Or rather, listened.

Mr Drogo talked. In between eating with the most exquisite manners, he talked about Muncaster; he talked about St Austin's, right back to the time of the Augustinian Canons. He talked with the authority of an historian. Martin was fascinated, the way he showed one thing growing out of another. He made it sound as if he'd lived right through it. Martin stopped trembling eventually. But if he listened to the grandfather, he secretly watched the girl. The girl watched him, too, a slight smile playing about the corners of her mouth.

'About that phone call.' Martin's voice, almost a shout, broke through the smooth flow of Mr Drogo's talk. 'Was I *meant* to come and tell you?'

'Yes, you were meant to come and tell me.' Mr Drogo pulled a grape from a bunch that lay on a dish near him and popped it into his mouth with evident enjoyment.

'But . . . *why*?'

'I am going to die – on March 26th.' He helped himself, unhurriedly, to another grape.

'Oh, I see. The doctor's told you. I'm so sorry.' Then reality broke in like a blizzard. 'But . . . but he can't have told you the exact date!'

'I chose the date.' Mr Drogo extracted a grape pip from the back of his excellent teeth, with the delicacy of a cat. He looked as healthy as any man Martin had ever seen.

'But what –'

'Do you know how old I am?' asked Mr Drogo. He might have been asking the right time. 'I am one hundred and ninety-two years old, on March 26th. I thought that made it rather neat.'

Martin stared wildly at the girl, as if assessing how much help she would be against this madman.

'And I am eighty-four next birthday,' said the girl. She smiled, showing all her perfect white teeth. Martin noticed that the canines were slightly, very slightly, longer than usual. But not more than many people's were . . .

Martin leapt to his feet, knocking over his chair behind him with a thud. 'I came here in good faith,' he cried. 'I didn't come here to be made a fool of!'

'We are not making a fool of you. Have you got your birth certificate, my dear?'

The girl disappeared into the hall, returning moments later with the certificate in her hand. She passed it across to

Martin. Even now, in his rage and fear, her perfume was soothing . . . Hands trembling again, he unfolded the paper roughly, tearing it along one fold. It was old and frail and yellow.

Celicia Margaret Drogo. Born July 8th, 1887, to William Canzo Drogo and Margaret Drogo, formerly Betyl.

'Do you want to see her parents' marriage certificate?' asked Mr Drogo gently. 'I want your mind to be absolutely satisfied.'

'I'd like my coat,' shouted Martin, only half hoping he would be given it.

'As you wish,' said Mr Drogo. 'But,' he added, 'it would be easier if you went with my granddaughter now. She could make everything perfectly clear to you. She helped Canon Maitland to see things clearly. We gave Canon Maitland a very contented life for many years. He was almost one of us.'

'Get lost!' shouted Martin, most regrettably. 'All I want from you is my coat!'

They did not try to stop him. Celicia came with him, but only to help him on with his coat. Her fingers were still gentle, pleading, on the nape of his neck. Then he was outside and running for the car. He drove out of the drive like a lunatic, narrowly avoiding a collision with a Rover that hooted at him angrily until it turned a corner. He made himself pull up, then, and sit till he had calmed down. Then he drove home shakily and painfully slowly. Sheila was just standing on the doorstep, pulling on her gloves before going to the pictures; she had a distaste for being in the rectory on her own at night and went to watch whatever film was on, however stupid.

'What's the matter with you?' She took him inside gently. After three whiskies, he plucked up the courage to tell her everything. It said a lot for her love for him that she believed him unquestioningly.

*   *   *

'I tried to ring you on Tuesday,' said the Bishop. 'Tried all day.'

'Tuesday's my day off,' said Martin. 'I was in London.'

'That explains it,' said the Bishop, who always had the last word, however pointless. He shuffled the papers on his desk, as if they were a squad of idle recruits. He had begun life as a major in the war, passed on to be an accountant, and only in later life been drawn to the church. Some spiteful clergy said he remained a major first, an accountant second and a bishop only third. His jutting nose and bristling moustache certainly sat oddly under his mitre on high days and holy days. Every church in his diocese had its accounts scrutinised by his eagle eye, and paid the uttermost farthing. He was brave, honest, loving and as unstoppable as one of his own old tanks when he'd made up his mind.

'I've taken up your complaint with Mr Drogo,' he announced. 'He apologised handsomely, I must say. Said his granddaughter was a great one for practical jokes, and rather a one for the men. More than I'd care to admit about *my* granddaughter. Said he was a fool to go along with her, but he didn't know how far she was going. Damned decent apology, I call that. He's writing to you. Wants you to take your missus over for a meal – make things up.'

Martin gaped. He had not complained about Mr Drogo; he had sent the Bishop a long and detailed report marked *Personal and Confidential*. That Mr Drogo now knew all about it filled him with a nameless dread.

'It wasn't a practical joke,' he said. 'I've been doing some investigating. That's why I went to London – Somerset House: births, deaths and marriages. I spent the whole day checking. There has not been a single Drogo birth since 1887 – that *was* Celicia. But from the electoral rolls, there are at the present time thirty-two Drogos living in Muncaster.'

'Rubbish!' said the Bishop. 'Stuff and nonsense. Of course they were born – I know a lot of them well. Michael Drogo is solicitor to the diocesan board, Giles Drogo was chairman of Rotary last year. Why, in a quiet way, the Drogos *are* Muncaster. Don't know what we'd do without them. Without their generosity, St Austin's would have had to be demolished years ago. Your lectureship at the college is funded by Drogo money –'

'How long have *you* been in Muncaster?' shouted Martin. 'Ever baptised any Drogo babies?'

'I've been here five long years, my lad. And no, I've never baptised a Drogo baby – it's not my line of business. And what's more I won't have young clergymen who are no more than jacked-up curates havin' the vapours on *my* hearthrug. Go away, Martin, before I start revising my good opinion of you. You'll not prosper in Muncaster long if you get the Drogos' backs up. Though why anybody in their senses should want to . . . Stop waving those bits of paper in my face!' Colour was showing in the Bishop's cheeks – what the cathedral clergy referred to as the red warning flags.

'There's something funny going on at St Austin's . . . something against the will of God . . .'

'That,' said the Bishop, 'is my province to decide. If you don't agree with me, you can always resign. *Well*?'

Martin swallowed, and was silent, as the enormity of it hit him. If he resigned the living, Sheila and he had nowhere to go. They'd even sold off their own poor sticks of furniture, because they looked so pathetic in the opulence of the rectory. They could just about exist on Sheila's teaching salary, but if the Bishop passed the word he was an awkward hysterical character . . .

The Bishop pounced on his hesitation; he was never one to miss an opening. He came round the desk and put an arm on Martin's shoulder, in a way horribly reminiscent of Mr Drogo. 'This is racial prejudice, Martin, don't you see? There is foreign blood in the Drogos – touch of the tarbrush there, perhaps. Lot of people think they're Jews, but they're not.

Good old Church of England – among our keenest support-
ers. They have their own funny ways in private, but they do a
lot of damn good work in public. They don't do any *harm* – I
happen to know their chemical workers are the highest-
paid in the city. Live and let live, Martin, live and let live. Go
home and think it over – I don't want to lose you now you're
doing so well. Why, I've just had an invitation for you to give
a talk on your city-centre work to the Social Science department of the university . . .' He picked up a thick, expensive-
looking envelope from his desk, with the university crest on
the back flap. 'Bless you, my boy.' He shook Martin's hand
warmly on the way out.

Martin opened the envelope in the car, his hands shaking
with something which might have been anticipation. There
was the invitation to give the James Drogo Memorial Lecture.

On the twenty-eighth of next month. Friday, 28th March.
At 10.30 a.m.

'They want me out of the church on that morning,' gabbled
Martin. 'Don't you see? They want me out of the way so they
can . . .'

'Can what?' said Sheila, with a brave attempt at briskness.
But her hand shook as she passed Martin another whisky.

'I don't know,' said Martin. 'That's the awful thing. It's
only two weeks off and I don't *know.*'

'Well, they can hardly bury him in the churchyard. It's
been closed how long? A hundred years?'

'More than that.'

'And it's so jam-packed it's practically standing-room
only. And people would notice . . .'

'What people?' said Martin, despondently. 'Anyway, they
wouldn't have to use the churchyard – St Austin's has got a
crypt. All those names on plaques on the church walls – *near
this spot lie the Mortal Remains of* etc. They're down under the

333

floor in coffins on shelves, in a place probably as big as the church itself.'

'Ugh,' said Sheila. 'I didn't know that.'

'Most people don't, or they wouldn't go near some churches. It's a kind of clerical conspiracy of silence. What the eye doesn't see, the heart doesn't grieve over. Tastes have changed. Mind you, some crypts are just coke-holes, even headquarters for Telephone Samaritans or tramps' shelters, like St Martin-in-the-Fields. But a lot . . .'

Sheila glanced round the opulent kitchen and shuddered. 'Where was old Canon Maitland buried?'

'It'll be in the church diary – in the church. Let's go and look.'

Sheila glanced out of the kitchen window. Dusk was just starting to gather around the graceful spire of St Austin Friars.

'We can be there and back in ten minutes,' said Martin. 'It's better than wondering. Better than not knowing.'

The church door was locked, but Martin had his key. He banged his hand down across the massed banks of switches in the vestry and the whole church sprang out into light. Martin hoped the lights at this hour would not attract the eye of Mr Phillips. Old Phillips who knew the ropes, old Phillips who would see to it. Old Phillips who spent a quite extraordinary amount in the betting-shop for a poorly paid church verger.

They opened the church diary, holding their breath. The entry for the burial of William Henry Drogo, in Martin's own handwriting, mocked them.

'That was the *awful* thing,' whispered Martin. 'When he told me he was going to die, he smiled. As if he was looking forward to it, like his summer holidays.'

Sheila firmly turned over the page in the book, because his own handwriting seemed to have paralysed Martin, like a snake hypnotises a rabbit. The previous entry, in old

Phillips' hand, recorded the funeral of Canon Maitland, conducted by a Revd Leonard Canzo, fellow of a minor Cambridge college. The body had been interred in . .

. . . the crypt of St Austin Friars, by special faculty, authorised by the Bishop. Because of his long and faithful service to the church of seventy years . . .

'Where's the door down to the crypt?' whispered Sheila.

'I don't know. There are two I've never been down. One's the boiler-house for the central heating – I left all that to old Phillips.' They looked round nervously, expecting to see old Phillips coming up the aisle at any moment, in his dull overcoat and checked muffler, which he seemed to wear, winter and summer, as a uniform. But he was nowhere in sight. And yet all that stood between the brilliantly illuminated church and the verger's house was a flat stretch of demolition-site . . .

'Probably in the betting-shop,' said Sheila, and giggled, then stopped herself abruptly.

They swiftly found the pair of doors; the door-surrounds were Gothic and crumbling, but the doors were Victorian, oak and very solid. And the hasps and and padlocks on them were even newer and even more solid.

'Have you got keys?'

'Not for these locks.'

'Old Phillips has got them,' said Sheila, grimly. She thought. 'Look, most boiler-rooms have another door to the outside, for the coke-deliveries in the old days – I mean, they didn't want coke all over the aisle-floors and people crunching up to communion. That might be open – it's worth a try.'

Every fibre of his body said no. But some kind of frenetic excitement had seized Sheila. She flew off down the aisle. He didn't dare wait to switch the lights off; besides, they would need them, shining out through the church windows, if they were not to break a leg in the wilderness of tilted table-tombs, leaning urns and tangled brambles in the

graveyard outside. He wished he'd thought to bring a torch
. . . but he caught sight of Sheila's slim figure, in her white
mac, flitting through the tombscape ahead. Halfway round,
he found her waiting for him, outside a low Gothic door.

'It's shut,' she said. 'Locked.'

He felt suddenly flat, and yet glad. 'It'll only be the coke-
hole,' he said. In the semi-dark, they could hear the coke
droppings of centuries crunching beneath their feet. Relief
made him gabby. 'It's funny about this churchyard; disused
urban churchyards are usually a menace: vandals writing on
the tombs with aerosols, or throwing the gravestones over –
even black-magic cranks. But here, there isn't a trace of van-
dalism –'

A hand on his arm stopped him both talking and walking.
She pointed ahead. There was a faint crunching of footsteps
on the coky path. 'Somebody's coming.' They hid in a flurry
behind a miniature Greek temple, black as coal.

It was old Phillips, shabby overcoat and checked muffler.
He kept glancing up at the lighted windows of the church as
he walked; a little uneasy, a little cautious. He passed, and
went as far as the locked door. Without benefit of torch or
light, he fitted a key neatly first time into the keyhole.

'That's not the first time he's done that in the dark,' whispered Sheila.

'Shhh!'

Old Phillips swung the door open; the hinges did not
creak.

'Well oiled,' muttered Sheila.

'*Shhh*! What's he doing?'

But it was all too obvious what old Phillips was doing. He
was returning, leaving the little door not only unlocked but
ajar. He passed again, and faded into the dusk.

'What's he done that for?' whispered Sheila. 'That's
mad – *unlocking* a door at dusk. Shall we look inside?'

Just then, the church window above their heads went

dark. Old Phillips was busy putting off the church lights. Another light went off, and another. It was enough to panic them. They fled across the graveyard, and didn't stop running till they reached the rectory.

'Quick!' said Martin. 'Let's get all the lights on – on the *far* side of the house. Not these. Phillips can see these from the church.' Suddenly it was desperately important that Phillips should not know they'd been anywhere near the church.

They went and sat in the sitting-room, which, fortunately, *was* on the side away from the church. The central heating was on, but low, and the room was too cold. Martin banged on all three bars of the electric fire and the telly. They sat shivering till the room began to warm up. 'Get something to do,' whispered Martin, savagely. 'Get your knitting out. Take your coat off. Get your slippers on . . .' He was just taking off his own coat and hiding it behind the settee, when there came a ring on the doorbell. 'Relax!' screeched Martin, and made himself walk slowly to answer it.

Old Phillips' face was set in that look of joyful censoriousness beloved of caretakers the world over. He held up Martin's bunch of keys.

'Your keys, I believe, Mr Williams. I found the church unlocked and *all* the lights on. Vestry open, *and* the church diary.' He held that up in turn, still open at the page that recorded Canon Maitland's funeral. 'I thought at first it was vandals.'

'Sorry,' said Martin, and his voice didn't shake. 'I've been meaning to go back and lock up, but I got lost in the football on the telly. Won't you come in for a moment? The match is just over.'

Phillips came in; his eyes did not miss the slippers and the knitting, the telly and the warmth of the room. They roamed over everything, making it dirty as if they were a pair of grey slugs. When he was satisfied, *barely* satisfied, he turned to them.

'You want to be careful, Mr Williams. A lot more careful. And you, Mrs Williams. Canon Maitland would never have made a mistake like that. Very happy and well settled here, Canon Maitland was.'

They all knew he wasn't talking about the church keys.

They were careful. They hardly went near the church at all; Martin found he could no longer face his solo Wednesday service. If God was listening above, who was listening down below, beneath the black stone slabs of the nave floor? Martin found his thoughts going downward far more than they ever ascended upward. What was down there? Why did they need their door *opened* at dusk? What was Mr Drogo looking forward to, more than his holidays? Anyway, old Phillips was now round the place practically every hour of the day and night, as the 28th of March approached. None of the crypt doors was ever found unlocked again.

But they planned carefully, too, for the 28th of March; and it worked out well. An actor friend called Larry Harper stayed in the rectory overnight (and they were very glad to have him). He was tall, thin and fair like Martin, and by the time he had donned Martin's rector's garb and a huge pair of horn-rimmed spectacles, he even gave Sheila a fright. His walk was the living image of Martin's lope; he said he'd been practising mimicking it for nearly a year, to get a laugh round The Grapes.

He left for the University at nine-thirty, Sheila with him in her best suit and hat, driving the car. He delivered Martin's talk (from the pages Martin had written out for him) far more convincingly than Martin would ever have done, and got a tremendous round of applause. He fumbled his impromptu questiontime rather badly, but everyone put that down to well-earned exhaustion. Nobody at the university ever dreamed they hadn't seen the real Martin Williams . . .

. . . Who had been up the tower of St Austin Friars since

seven that morning, creeping in through the cobwebbed dewiness of the graveyard with a sergeant from Muncaster Constabulary, summoned by phone with some nasty hints of black-magic activity in the churchyard. They waited behind the uppermost parapet of the tower, well-hidden, so that they saw it all.

At ten-twenty, the overcoated, mufflered figure of old Phillips walked leisurely through the churchyard and unlocked the main door. At ten-twenty-five he began to toll the bell. At ten-twenty-eight, five large black Rolls-Royce limousines started across the huge demolition-plain, following a Rolls-Royce hearse. Thirty-one Drogos, men and women, emerged, sleek in black top-coats, black fur coats and the flash of a black-nyloned leg. All the women were very handsome and looked about thirty, so it was impossible to pick Celicia out. There was the undertaker, Mr Betyl, no doubt, proper in black tail-coat and top-hat swathed in black muslin. The opulent coffin (which looked sickeningly like Mr Drogo's sideboard) vanished into the church.

'Let's go and get a good view inside,' Martin whispered to the sergeant. They went down through the bell-chamber – the bell had stopped tolling but was still swaying in its bed – and down into the ringers' chamber, where a little window gave a good view into the body of the church, from just under the ancient rafters.

Martin looked down, and almost fainted.

Far from a scattering of thirty-one Drogos near the front, the church was full. The door to the crypt was gaping open. And as he looked down, every dark figure turned and looked up at him.

'Come on down, Mr Williams,' called Betyl, the undertaker, with sepulchral joviality. 'We are so glad you could make it after all.'

Martin turned desperately to the policeman.

'Time to go, sir,' said the policeman gently. He got out his

339

warrant card and held it up open for Martin to inspect.

Sergeant Harold Morsk, Muncaster CID.

Like a condemned man, Martin tottered down the stairs and was marched to the front of the congregation.

'We shall only require you to say amen,' said Mr Betyl. 'We are a god-fearing race and have always supported your church. It is the least you can do for us.' Then he began to declaim to the congregation in a harsh, strange tongue, and they replied in the same tongue. And when they all looked at Martin, with their smooth, handsome faces, he knew it was time to say 'Amen'. Twice, they took black books from their pockets and broke out into a hymn. Old Phillips played the organ reasonably well. Then the body was reverently borne, on the shoulders of six pallbearers, down into the crypt. One corner, grating against the door-jamb, lost a sliver of wood and rich varnish, and some flakes of white limestone dropped onto the black floor.

After all was over down there (strange sounds floated up in the silence above) a man who looked incredibly like the late William Henry Drogo came across to Martin and shook him firmly and warmly by the hand.

'I am glad you were here. If *they* are not blessed by the presence of a clergyman, they get out of hand and run wild, and then there is trouble. There are still people cruel enough to sharpen ash-stakes for us – the world gets little better, except on the surface. Now we shall have no trouble in Muncaster . . . thank you.' He paused, and said concernedly, 'You do not look well . . . these things are troubling you . . . you may have had bad dreams. Here is my granddaughter – Celicia, come here, Celicia – she has an affection for you. Go with her now, and she will make all things well and clear for you. No, Celicia, *not* in the crypt – the vestry will do for Mr Williams.' He spoke to her quite sharply, as if he suddenly feared she might go too far.

As in a dream, Martin walked through the open vestry

door, his hand in Celicia's.

When he woke up on the vestry floor, he could never quite remember anything that had happened the morning of the 28th of March, in the church of St Austin Friars.

But it didn't matter, for shortly afterwards he and Sheila left the city, for a small rural living that had fallen vacant in Kent.

SOUL SEARCHING

Martyn Wade

*Martyn Wade has written for radio since 1978. His plays include
adaptations of Greek and Roman comedy and the lives of
composers Percy Grainger and William Baines. Among other
occupations, he has enjoyed several stints as a hospital porter.*

He woke up, remembered where he was, and groaned
to himself.

'Morning, Mr Timmins,' said the man in a white jacket.
Mr Timmins raised his head a little.

'Morning, doctor,' he answered.

He was a young man, the doctor, with a pale face and wiry
hair. Toying the while with his stethoscope, he studied some
notes on a clip-board. 'Chronic stomach pains. Dyspepsia.
Attendant depression. Hmm.' The doctor's voice took on a
tone which was almost threatening. 'It says here your operation's scheduled for Wednesday morning.'

'Yes,' replied Mr Timmins, adding quickly, 'but I'd be prepared to wait a day or two longer if you'd prefer.'

'Oh no, no, no. Let's have you in at the sharp end, eh?' The
young man grinned, glanced around, sat down on the bed,
and looked at the clip-board again. 'You're fifty-five . . .
Hmm. Heart not terribly strong. Do you wet the bed at all?'

Mr Timmins stared at the doctor. 'I do not.'

'Blood pressure normal. Fairly normal. Even so . . .'

Mr Timmins raised his head. 'What do you mean, "even
so"?'

'Mr Timmins, I don't want to alarm you unduly, but to be
frank – and I always like to be frank with my patients – a
choledochotomy can be . . .'

'Yes?'

The doctor sucked in his cheeks. 'Well – a bit tricky. An incision has to be made into the bile duct, you see. Anything might go wrong. And often does.'

Mr Timmins was now almost as pale as the young man. 'But my doctor said –'

'Of course he did,' replied the young man. 'He had to get you in here somehow. In my view, though –'

He broke off suddenly. He shoved the stethoscope into his pocket, and got up from the bed, smiling in a slightly sullen fashion as the ward sister strode past.

'Come along, you,' she boomed at him. 'Time and tide.'

She disappeared from view. 'Now – where was I?' said the young man. 'Oh yes –'

Mr Timmins interrupted him. 'You're not a doctor, are you?'

'No.'

'What is your position in the hospital, exactly?'

'I'm a student.'

'A student. Ah.'

'Name's Tom.'

They shook hands. Tom revealed, in due course, that he would not be involved in Wednesday's operation. The colour began to return to Mr Timmins's cheeks. 'And what are you a student of, Tom?'

'Parapsychology, with particular reference to communication with the dead.'

'Good grief,' exclaimed Mr Timmins. 'They don't do that here, surely?'

'Of course they do,' replied Tom. 'This is a modern hospital.' Mr Timmins dwelt on this remark.

'So – you know who I am,' said Tom. 'Tell me about yourself. What's your job?'

'I'm a teacher.'

'Are you now? Went to university, did you?'

'Yes.'

'Wife? Family?'

'Not now,' replied Mr Timmins. 'She went off. Took the children with her.'

'Well. A life full of incident.' Tom paused. 'Are you ready to leave it, I wonder?' He looked hard at Mr Timmins. 'Are you at all afraid of dying?'

Mr Timmins said nothing. 'I mean, let's face facts, Mr Timmins. Dr Kildare doesn't win every time. So what's your view about the hereafter?'

Mr Timmins shook his head.

'You don't believe in it? Oh, Mr Timmins – you should. You should. Of course, if you had proof, you'd have to believe, wouldn't you?'

'Of course.'

Tom revealed that he had been trying to find that proof for the last three years, as part of his studies. During that time he had encountered so many spiritual manifestations and para-normal phenomena that he himself was absolutely certain that there was a life after death, but what a boon it would be, he declared, and what a scientific breakthrough, if he could actually find conclusive, incontrovertible proof.

Tom sat down on the bed. 'You're a very lucky man, Mr Timmins,' he confided in a half whisper. 'As it happens, I'll have that proof tomorrow night.'

'Tomorrow night?'

'Yes. You see, I devised an experiment, some time ago in fact, but tomorrow night I have the opportunity to carry it out – thanks to Oswald.'

'Who's Oswald?' asked Mr Timmins.

'The venerable piece of parchment in the corner there,' said Tom, pointing. 'He's happy to take part in the experi-ment. We're conducting it in the bathroom. Why don't you come along as an observer?'

Part of Mr Timmins was incredulous. Another was intrigued. Perhaps even excited.

'What kind of experiment is it?'

'It rests on two principles,' explained Tom, 'one, that the soul is a specific entity within the body; and the other, that at the point of death it manages to free itself from its earthly bonds, if I may put it like that, and escape into a new dimension. With me so far?'

'Well, I think I understand what you're saying . . .'

'From there, my reasoning went like this: if I could somehow take hold of the soul before it escaped, if I could prise it from the body, keep it safe and unharmed, then I could demonstrate beyond doubt its ability to continue existing after its body had died.'

'My God! You're going to do this to Oswald? Cut his body up and search for his soul?'

'No, no, no. I tried that. With a rat, that is.'

'What happened?'

'It died. But then I conceived a much neater, less messy experiment.'

There was silence.

'Well?' asked Mr Timmins.

'Come to the bathroom tomorrow night,' said Tom, 'and you'll see it performed. In the meantime, of course, not a word to anyone about this.' He got up. 'Must dash.'

Mr Timmins was not stupid. He knew, or thought he knew, that Tom was not really to be trusted. He was certain, at the very least, that what Tom intended to attempt was unethical, however willing a partner Oswald might be in the experiment. On the other hand, though, Mr Timmins was not a healthy man, and with the operation imminent he was not perhaps totally rational or clear-headed. In particular, he couldn't help telling himself how much more confidently he'd approach the operating table if by some means Tom could convince him that there was a life to come.

Tom returned later that afternoon. Mr Timmins wanted to

question him further about the experiment, but Tom was concerned only to reinforce the need for secrecy, and to advise Mr Timmins that – depending on the movements of the night nurse – he would be woken at approximately midnight tomorrow, and escorted to the bathroom in order to perform his role of observer.

Despite his vow of silence, however, Mr Timmins decided he had every right to question Oswald about the forthcoming experiment. Late the following morning, with some trepidation, he approached Oswald's bed. The old man's eyes were closed.

'Oswald – I want to ask you about Tom.'

The old man's lips parted. 'Tom,' he murmured. He smiled faintly, and then drifted off again into unconsciousness.

Mr Timmins sat up, and drew a deep breath. 'Dressing gown,' whispered Tom, and Mr Timmins put his arms into the sleeves. He was shaking slightly.

'Come on, then,' prompted Tom. 'Night nurse is right up the other end.' Timmins swung his legs out of the blankets. He sat on the edge of the bed. 'No,' he said.

'What do you mean – "no"?'

'I think . . . I think this is all very stupid. Possibly dangerous. I'm not going.'

'But you've got to,' said Tom. 'You can't back out now. Think how disappointed you'll be in the morning.'

'Conduct the experiment without me. Tell me how you got on.'

'Mr Timmins – I can't do that. How would you be certain that I was speaking the truth? You should never take anything on trust, you know.'

Mr Timmins sighed. 'Here are your slippers,' said Tom. 'We don't want you getting cold feet again.'

Tom and Mr Timmins walked down to the bathroom. Breathing heavily, Mr Timmins sat on a chair by the door. It was a sizeable room. Bags of laundry and big boxes of disposable bedpans stood against a wall. In a corner was a set of scales equipped with a seat for disabled or elderly patients.

'What about Oswald?' asked Mr Timmins.

'Oswald? Oh – I'll fetch him in a second.'

'What happens if night nurse comes along during the experiment?'

'I'll hide behind the bedpans. You and Oswald can pop into a cubicle. A separate one each, preferably, to avoid suspicion.'

Mr Timmins felt cold. He stood up. Tom motioned him back down again. Tom went to the laundry bags, rummaged around in one of them, and brought out a black battered briefcase. 'Tell me what you intend to do to Oswald,' blurted out Mr Timmins. 'I must know before you start.'

'All right,' said Tom, sitting down on the scales. He coughed; cleared his throat. 'The basic idea of the experiment, as you'll see, is beautifully simple. But in order for me to be able to implement it, a rather special requirement had to be met. I needed the assistance of someone who was prepared to say good-bye to this world.'

'I thought as much,' said Mr Timmins.

'Yes, the advancement of learning and an act of mercy to one who can no longer enjoy life – both together in one magnificent night.'

'But you do have Oswald's agreement?'

'Of course, of course.' Tom rapidly explained the experiment. Oswald, when he arrived, would be weighed. A fatal cocktail, the elements of which Tom had borrowed from the dispensary, would then be administered, and as soon as Oswald was out of his misery he would be weighed again. 'After making appropriate adjustments for the weight of the lethal dose itself,' continued Tom, 'we will find that Oswald weighs less when he is dead than he did when alive. How, Mr Timmins, will we be able to account for this, except –

quod erat, I believe, *demonstrandum* – that his soul has left his body?' Tom's eyes sparkled. 'Impressive, eh?'

Mr Timmins admitted that it was. He still felt cold. 'I don't think Oswald's coming,' he said, and was unsure whether he was relieved or disappointed.

Tom opened his briefcase, and drew out a notebook, pencil, a syringe and ampoule, a thermos flask, and a package of ham and pickle sandwiches. 'Care for one?' he asked, as he tucked in.

Mr Timmins shook his head. He wanted to discuss with Tom the morality of euthanasia, and the legal consequences, but Tom informed him sharply that he knew exactly what he was letting himself in for. He delved into his case again, and produced a piece of rope and some sticking plaster. Mr Timmins noticed these items, but so casual was Tom's manner in extracting them that it was some seconds before he became alarmed. 'What are they for?' he asked.

'I've dreamt for so long of getting this opportunity, Mr Timmins. Articles in learned journals. Lecture tours. A professorship. To achieve all that – it would be quite something, wouldn't it?'

Mr Timmins stood up. 'I've made a very serious mistake,' he said, more to himself than Tom. His mouth was dry. 'You're not a student at all, are you?'

Tom was indignant. 'I am. I am. Part-time. I've no backing, you see. Got to work to finance the research.' He put the remains of the sandwich back in its bag, and took a step towards Mr Timmins. 'Now – you were asking what the rope and sticking plaster were for . . .'

Mr Timmins was too weak to put up much of a fight. He was gagged, bound, and bundled onto the scales. 'I told you a little fib, I'm afraid,' said Tom. 'About Oswald, I mean.' From behind the wad of plaster, Mr Timmins produced a kind of sad bleating noise. 'As I said, never take anything on trust. I had to get you down here somehow, Mr Timmins, and let's face it: you were reluctant enough to come as an observer, never mind guinea pig. Yes, as far as I know, dear old Oswald has every intention of clinging desperately to his pathetic life. So that's good news, isn't it? You were rather worried about him. Sit still, Mr Timmins – I'm going to weigh you.'

With great care, Tom adjusted the bar of the scales, read off the weight, and jotted it down in his notebook. 'No number ones or number twos now please, Mr Timmins: it'll ruin the whole experiment.'

He took out the syringe from its cellophane wrapper. Mr Timmins trembled as violently as the rope would allow. 'I don't mind portering work,' said Tom. 'How does the hymn go? The trivial round and all that. And it does take me to the mortuary from time to time. I've made that my centre of studies.' He depressed the plunger of the syringe; pulled it out again. 'The thing is, Mr Timmins, what happened was . . . They all refused to help me. All those university people. The bastards. So not only is my research entirely self-funded: it's independent too.' He jabbed the syringe into the air a few times to emphasise his remarks. 'You know, people in this country are so blinkered, so hide-bound. Teachers at school – they couldn't cope. I was different, you see. I questioned things. I had imagination. So they threw me out as soon as they could. No qualifications, no –'

Tom's complaint was interrupted by a burst of noise from the bleep which sat in the pocket of his porter's jacket.

'Oh dear,' he said. 'Damn.' He filled the syringe from the ampoule. 'We'll have to hurry, Mr Timmins. Any last requests?'

Mr Timmins moaned – a desperate plea for an escape from his nightmare world. 'I know what you're trying to tell me,' said Tom. 'It's not fair, why me, and all that. But the way I see it, Mr Timmins, when it comes to something of the magnitude of this experiment, the personal prejudices of a very, very ordinary member of the public really aren't worth a toss. Left arm or right, Mr Timmins?'

Mr Timmins whimpered. 'Oh, Mr Timmins!' said Tom. 'Come now! Don't tell me you're scared of injections.'

The bleep sounded again. Tom grimaced, and pulled up the sleeve of Mr Timmins' dressing gown. 'I'll show them. I'll teach them!' Mr Timmins was very still now. Terror seemed to have frozen him. 'Oh, Mr Timmins,' said Tom. 'I'm very excited. Are you?' He held the syringe close to Mr Timmins's upper arm. 'Now this won't hurt a bit, provided I do it right, and as soon as the needle's gone in, all the way, you'll begin to feel a little drowsy, that's all.'

The bleep sounded once more. The shrill noise continued for some time. When at last it had finished, Tom paused, muttered, 'Oh dear,' and put down the syringe. 'Don't go away,' he said.

Tom walked through the ward. Frustrated as he felt, he knew that if he didn't go looking for night nurse, she would go looking for him – and that might end all hope of the experiment being concluded.

She was in the office. Tom swore that his bleep hadn't made a sound; he'd just happened to be passing. 'What's the problem, anyway?'

'Mr Hutchings has died.'

'Mr Hutchings? Oh – Oswald.'

'I'd like you to take him down to the mortuary.'

'Oswald,' said Tom. 'Well, well, well.'

'Have you done it before?' asked the nurse.

'Removing the body? Oh yes. Not on nights, though.'

He had to leave the main block of the hospital in order to reach the mortuary. There was a breeze. The sky was clear, the moon almost full. Tom wheeled along the trolley as fast as he could, anticipating with enthusiasm his return to Mr Timmins.

The mortuary was a low, brick building. Tom turned the key in the front door and pushed Oswald inside. Just past the *post mortem* area he found the little alcove where he'd been told to leave the body. Two other trolleys were there already.

'Sorry, Oswald,' he said, and his voice was not quite steady, 'you'll have to join the end of the queue. What was it the poet said?' He couldn't remember. He gave a sort of wave at Oswald, and then turned. He heard the front door close. He cried out, 'Oh God,' and was immediately ashamed for doing so. He was about to tell himself that it was of course the wind that had blown the door shut when a familiar voice said:

'It's all right. Only me.'

Tom emerged from the alcove. 'I hope I didn't frighten you,' said Mr Timmins, who stood near the door. His dressing gown sleeve was still rolled up.

'Frighten me? Frighten me? Heavens no. I'm – I'm surprised, though – I'll give you that. Mr Timmins, would you mind very much if I asked how the hell you managed to escape?'

'Not at all,' said Mr Timmins. 'You can ask.' There was silence.

'Night nurse didn't find you, did she?'

'No, no.'

'And you've not spoken to her on your way down?'

'No.'

'You promise?'

'I promise.'

Tom gave a low whistle of relief. 'But you didn't get free on your own, I bet. Who helped you? Tell me.'

Mr Timmins said nothing. He smiled.

'Tell me,' repeated Tom. He was already planning a cover-up.

'Tom, listen,' said Mr Timmins. 'I have a proposal to make. Don't know how you'll feel about this, but, well, I've thought it through, and I've made up my mind. I'd still like to do the experiment. Tonight. Straight away. If it's all the same to you.'

'What?'

'The thing is, Tom – it seems to me that we can't possibly pull back now – not when we have the chance of making such an important breakthrough in the field of human knowledge. So what do you think? How about it?'

Tom looked at Mr Timmins. 'Fine,' he said at last, without total conviction. 'Great.' He was trying to accommodate himself to the idea of Mr Timmins making the ultimate sacrifice in pursuit of the advancement of learning.

'Mr Timmins,' he said, 'I very much appreciate this.' He made a vague gesture with his hands. 'Words fail me. What can I say? But if you're absolutely sure – let's proceed back to the bathroom, shall we?'

Mr Timmins shook his head. 'No, Tom. Actually, Tom, I'd like us to carry out the experiment here.'

'Here?' queried Tom. 'But that's not possible, Mr Timmins. No scales.'

Mr Timmins was adamant. 'Here. Has to be. I'm not taking part otherwise.'

'I don't understand.' Tom felt he was being cheated. 'How are we to manage?'

'You'll see,' replied Mr Timmins. 'Oh, by the way – I've brought these with me.' He drew the piece of rope and the packet of sticking plaster out of his dressing gown pocket. 'Thought they might come in handy.' He glanced up at Tom. 'You cold, Tom? Sorry about that. Don't feel it so much myself.' He took a step or two towards Tom. The porter's eyes widened. 'I gather it was Oswald you ferried down here,' continued Mr Timmins. 'Ah well – comes to us all eventually. Though in my case,' – he was now within a yard of Tom – 'I'd much rather it had been later than sooner.'

Mr Timmins leant forward. Tom, uttering something that

started as a remark and ended as an unintelligible stammer, put out a pathetic hand to try and ward Mr Timmins off, but found that there was nothing of him to touch. He gasped.

'No need to be alarmed, Tom. Just another spiritual manifestation to add to the number you claim to have witnessed. Yes, Tom – I've escaped my earthly bonds. I had a heart attack. I'm afraid your attempted experiment induced a massive seizure. I was dead within minutes.' Mr Timmins sighed. 'What a stupid waste. I had so much to look forward to, especially without the wife and kids.' He paused. 'Anyway. To work. The experiment.'

'Not possible,' jabbered Tom. 'No scales. No scales.'

'Tom,' murmured Mr Timmins. 'Calm yourself. Please.' He grinned. 'Tom! My dear Tom! You weren't beginning to think, were you, that I wanted to perform the weighing experiment on your own person?'

Tom replied, in a faint voice, that the idea had crossed his mind. 'I mean,' he added, 'you do hear, don't you, of vengeful ghosts and suchlike?'

Mr Timmins agreed. 'Indeed you do. But the thing is, Tom: it's not *that* experiment that interests me. It's the other one.'

'The other one?'

'You remember. The one you tried on the rat. The one you thought might be a little, you know – messy.'

Tom tried to scream. Mr Timmins leapt upon him and with a strength that easily overcame Tom's feeble resistance quickly gagged the porter and began to bind him. 'What an achievement it would be,' said Mr Timmins, 'to find where the soul is located; to prise it from the body.' He hoisted Tom onto a large stone slab. 'And just think, Tom, what a splendid contribution you will have made to this discovery.'

On the wall by the *post mortem* slab was an array of instruments: scalpels, saws, drills. Mr Timmins looked at them with interest, and glanced back at Tom. The porter jerked his head from side to side in disbelief. 'Keep calm, Tom,' said Mr Timmins softly. 'I'm not going to kill you. Not until I've found your soul, I mean. I'm assuming, of course, that you do have a soul.'

He removed the largest saw from the selection, and gripped it tightly. 'Right then. Are you ready?'

MUSIC LOVERS

Nick Warburton

*Nick Warburton was born in 1947 and is married with one son.
He gave up teaching in primary schools after ten years to try
writing (also doing part-time work in libraries and selling on craft
stalls). He writes children's books, radio, stage and television
scripts and in 1985 was joint winner of the BBC/Radio Times
Drama Award for CONVERSATION FROM THE ENGINE ROOM.*

Miss Eames hurried into the shadow of the churchyard. It wasn't like her to be late and she was
annoyed with herself for allowing Mother to cling so.
Tonight of all nights. By the time she reached the hall on the
far side of the church she was nearly ten minutes late. Perhaps that was why she made such a clatter going in. Usually
she was so careful about such things.

Mr Pauley was standing by the tape machine with his eyes
closed. Whispers of lute music hung in the empty hall. That
piece, was it? Miss Eames stood still and bit her lip. But the
door banged against the wall and a scatter of dried leaves
blew across the floor.

'Oh, Mr Pauley . . .' she said. 'I'm so sorry. Barging in like
this . . .'

Mr Pauley fumbled with the machine and the music
stopped. He told Miss Eames not to worry. It didn't matter.

'But Bach, Mr Pauley. In the middle of Bach. What must
you think?'

'Please don't concern yourself,' said Mr Pauley, looking
intently at the floor. 'And it wasn't Bach. Just a piece by
some Frenchman, I think. So no great sacrilege there.'

Miss Eames relaxed a little. She wasn't the last to arrive,
she noticed. In fact she was the first. Mr Pauley made light of

it but she guessed that he was a little hurt by the lack of support from the group.

'I'm glad you came,' he told her. 'I would've felt foolish playing my little selection to myself. I could've done that at home. On superior equipment.'

Really, it was too bad of the others to be so lax. Surely they knew how nervous Mr Pauley was about addressing them? And, even if guitars and lutes weren't quite their thing, they could at least have made an effort. Miss Eames cleared her throat and said:

'I do love guitars and lutes, Mr Pauley. I feel they're my particular thing.'

She hesitated and risked a look at him. She really needed to see his face but his back was turned. He stood with his hands bunched in his coat pocket.

'And I *was* pleased to see that you had the Sarabande and Bourrée,' she went on. 'You know, the Bach. Such a lovely piece. Almost perfect. In the right hands, of course.'

'Ah yes,' he said turning. 'As always. The interpretation must be right, mustn't it?'

'May I ask who you've got on your recording?'

He moved quickly to a small pile of cassettes by the tape machine. He shuffled through them but came to a stop after looking at two or three.

'I do hate it when people sing along, don't you?' he said suddenly.

'Sing along?'

He seemed to have forgotten Miss Eames's request about the lute piece. Sometimes people were so bad at answering questions, she felt.

'They sing along with the music,' said Mr Pauley. 'Hadn't you noticed?'

'Oh yes.'

'Like Maurice. Pom-pom-pomming all the time. I sometimes wonder why he buys records. I mean, he can't possibly hear them properly.'

'He probably doesn't know he's doing it,' said Miss Eames.

'Then perhaps he should be told. After all, it is annoying.'

The chairs had been arranged in a circle and they sat down, neither close to nor facing each other. After a while they both looked towards the door, at the same moment, as if willing someone else to join them. Miss Eames coughed a little and Mr Pauley looked at her with raised eyebrows, expecting her to say something perhaps. She smiled and looked away.

'I try to hold my breath,' he said.

'Sorry?'

'In the quieter passages. I hold my breath, so that I can hear nothing but the music.'

'Really?'

'Yes,' he said, leaning forward and edging his chair round slightly. 'It's possible to improve with practice so that you hardly know you're doing it. I can, for example, do the slow movement of the Emperor Concerto with very few breaths indeed. Hibernation rate, almost. Not that I count, of course. Have you ever tried?'

'Holding my breath?'

'Yes.'

'No.'

'You should.'

By this time it looked as if the others weren't going to turn up at all and Miss Eames was feeling responsible for them. She would have phoned round to jog their memories, she explained, but she wasn't on the phone. Mother didn't like phones.

Mr Pauley shrugged and gave her a little smile. Oh, it was such a pity. The poor man had obviously put so much work into a selection nobody was going to hear. And he looked so vulnerable, bunched up inside his coat, as if he was afraid to take it off. This is the penalty of sensitivity, thought Miss

Eames. And, certainly, Mr Pauley was a sensitive man.

As if to demonstrate this aspect of his character, Mr Pauley sat stiffly back in his chair, a sudden alertness in his eyes. He hurried to the door, flung it open and looked out.

'What is it?' asked Miss Eames.

'A sound,' he said. 'Didn't you hear it?'

She strained to hear but all she could make out was the darkness moving through bare branches, and dead leaves on gravel. Unless . . . For some unaccountable reason, that lute piece, the Sarabande and Bourrée, came back to her. It was in her head, faint but clear. Surely Mr Pauley couldn't have heard it too?

'Nothing,' said Mr Pauley pulling the door to. 'But I think I'll lock it, just to make sure. Listening to music makes one sensitive to all kinds of sounds, Miss Eames, don't you think?'

'Oh yes,' she said. 'I sometimes wonder . . .'

'What?'

'You'll think I'm silly.'

'I'm sure I won't.'

'Well,' she went on, lowering her voice. 'I sometimes wonder whether one is actually *in touch* with a performer, in a kind of way. As if one can hear something beyond the music . . .'

'That's not silly,' he said unexpectedly. 'I know exactly what you mean.'

She saw in his eyes that he was telling the truth and she decided to ask the question that had been in the back of her mind all evening.

'Mr Pauley, do you know James Wilson? He was killed in that plane crash last year . . .'

'Yes,' said Mr Pauley, almost whispering. 'Yes, of course.'

'Well, I used to feel that kind of thing – being in touch with a person – while I was listening to his music. It was almost like a conversation. Except that actual conversation is, well, flat.'

'Yes, indeed, Miss Eames. It falls short, doesn't it?'

'Mr Pauley,' she said, clearing her throat, 'James Wilson isn't, by any chance, playing the Sarabande and Bourrée on your tape, is he? I've been rather afraid that he might be.'

'Afraid, Miss Eames?'

'Yes.' She allowed only the smallest hesitation before continuing. 'I have a little confession to make. I almost didn't come this evening. When I saw from your programme that you were intending to play the Sarabande and Bourrée, my heart missed a beat. I wasn't sure that I could face it.'

'But why not?'

'James Wilson played that piece in his last concert, a week before he died. I was there and it was . . . perfect. Perfection is not a thing you meet very often in life. I don't, anyway.'

'And you fear the recording may not have captured that?'

'Yes.'

'Then, of course, I shall check, Miss Eames,' he said and he took up the cassettes again.

She watched his face and could tell, without the slightest doubt, when he came to the Bach. It was as she feared. James Wilson at the Thornton Rooms.

He mumbled an apology, as if it was his fault, and said he would put the tape aside. They wouldn't listen to it. Of course. He didn't want to upset her . . .

'Unless . . .'

'What?' she asked.

'Well, you don't think the recording might *renew* that conversation you were talking about?'

'Renew it? How?'

'Beyond James Wilson's death, as it were . . .'

Miss Eames blinked at him and sat back in her chair.

'Oh no,' she said. 'I wouldn't want that at all.'

So Mr Pauley, briskly changing the mood, suggested that they should stop talking and listen to a quite different piece instead; a little Jacques Bittner, perhaps. He fumbled through his tapes and slotted one into the machine. Then he addressed Miss Eames coolly on the subject of Bittner for two or three minutes, as if she were twenty complete strangers taking notes. It seemed to be a relief to both of them when they were able to sit down with their eyes closed and simply listen to the music.

Then time became an endless plain of sound for Miss Eames. The fussy world faded and she became completely unaware of the bleak and empty church hall.

Until Mr Pauley put his hand on her arm.

'I'm sorry,' he said, seeing how she jumped. 'I thought you were unwell.'

'I'm not unwell, Mr Pauley. I was listening, that's all.'

'It's just that . . . I thought you were choking. You coughed.'

'Did I? I wasn't aware . . .'

'You did. It was a little disconcerting.'

'I . . . I was involved,' she said. 'I didn't hear myself cough.'

'No. Possibly it's something you're used to.'

'Used to? You mean it happened more than once?'

'Yes. It's a sort of nervous tickle. Rather like Maurice's pom-pomming. I believe that's nervous too. You say you haven't tried holding your breath?'

'No.'

'You could try that.'

'Except that I don't know I'm doing it.'

'Well, you do now.'

'Oh dear.'

His face was more intent and open than it had been before. And he wasn't looking at the floor quite so much.

'Perhaps I can help you with that cough, Miss Eames,' he said suddenly.

'How could you do that?'

'You seem such a nervous person. So quiet . . .'

'I'm quiet, Mr Pauley? I must say that's rather good, coming from you. You never say a word in some meetings . . .'

'I know,' he cut in. 'And I'm beginning to think I'm wrong. In fact, it's my turn to confess now, Miss Eames.'

'To confess? To confess what?'

'This meeting. None of the others knows about it.'

'What?'

'They have invitations, of course. Similar to yours except that they give tomorrow as the date.'

'Tomorrow? But why?'

'I wanted to talk to you. Alone.'

'Surely, Mr Pauley, you could have asked me. Why go through all this . . . scheming?'

'Would you have come if I'd asked you?'

'I might.'

'Would you?'

She looked up at him. His pale eyes were searching her face.

'No,' she smiled. 'I suppose not.'

All this was less of a surprise to her than it might have been. She recalled moments in previous meetings, when they had been listening to some piece of music and she had chanced to look across the hall at him. How often his attention seemed to be on her rather than the music. And yet, with Maurice and the others chattering away during the coffee breaks, they had never managed to exchange more than a dozen words over the weeks.

'Miss Eames,' he said, 'there's something I want you to hear. Without the others.'

'Please, Mr Pauley. Go ahead.'

She was expecting him to speak, to say something that had been stuck somewhere inside him until this moment of being alone. She prepared herself, but he didn't speak. He jumped up and darted over to the tape machine.

'It's a piece of music,' he said. 'Rather special. As a matter of fact, I was playing it as you came in.'

'The French piece?'

'No,' he laughed. 'It wasn't French. Of course it wasn't. It was the Sarabande and Bourrée. I just didn't think you were quite ready for it at that moment.'

'But you didn't know I knew it.'

'Didn't I?'

'Well, how could you?'

He didn't answer, holding up his hand for silence instead. Then he started the tape. The Sarabande began to fill the hall. Unmistakeably James Wilson. Miss Eames listened, puzzled.

'There,' said Mr Pauley switching the machine off. 'Did you hear that?'

'I'm sorry,' she said. 'Hear what?'

'It was perfectly clear, Miss Eames. As clear as the day it was recorded.'

'In the Thornton Rooms?'

'Well of course.'

'But you weren't there.'

'Yes I was,' said Mr Pauley quickly. 'I sat behind you. You wore a blue straw hat.'

'I'm afraid I don't quite understand . . .'

'Then listen carefully and you will.'

He changed the tape and again held up his hand for silence. Miss Eames, however, didn't need a warning. She had no intention of interrupting. She wanted to know what Mr Pauley meant by all this. Why all these plans? Why the deception? Could he not simply say what was in his thoughts?

Again the Sarabande and Bourrée filled the hall. But this time there was something different about it. The same section was playing over and over again. And at the end of each repeated phrase there was another sound. Something Miss

Eames hadn't noticed before.

A cough. A tiny cough. Over and over again.

She looked up at Mr Pauley and the sight of his face, tight and strange, turned her heart cold.

'Please,' she said. 'Turn it off.'

Mr Pauley did so. He took a long breath and looked at her. And spoke softly, with great control.

'Yes. It does . . . grate, doesn't it?'

'Was . . . was that me?'

'Yes. Well the cough was you. The lute was James Wilson.'

Miss Eames felt as if she were teetering on some high wire. She didn't understand what was happening in the room. She didn't know whether Mr Pauley was being amusing, or intimate . . . or what? She stood up uncertainly and muttered something about going to see the vicar.

And Mr Pauley grabbed her arm, twisting it till she had to sit down.

'Don't touch me! Don't touch me!' she cried.

'Calm down, Miss Eames. You're becoming irrational. It's most unlike you.'

'I'm sorry. I've just remembered I have to phone Mother. I always phone her about this time because she worries so and . . .'

'But Mother isn't on the phone, Miss Eames. Remember?'

'You're getting me all confused, Mr Pauley,' she said and she could hear the tremble in her voice.

'Then I'll be happy to explain,' he said with a polite little nod. 'I was most anxious to get the James Wilson recording. To see if they had managed to get rid of that ugly little cough. As you've heard, they didn't. The recording captured everything. Everything, Miss Eames.'

'But I couldn't help that . . .'

'Yes you could. Of course you could.'

He paused and moved away from her. Confident. At ease now.

'It's strange but I *have* to listen to that recording now,' he continued. 'I have no will in the matter. To begin with I had to listen to see if the blemish was there. Then I had to listen to see if I could manage to ignore it. Then again, and again. And again. Each time waiting for the cough and hearing less and less of the music!'

There was an implacable anger in his voice now. He allowed it to swell and watched Miss Eames cower beneath it. Very deliberately he pulled something from his coat pocket. A pair of yellow gloves.

'I can never listen to that music again without thinking of your cough,' he said. 'Even if James Wilson were to rise from the grave and play the piece through to perfection, the ghost of that unnecessary blemish would still be there. I know exactly where it comes and if I don't hear it I won't be able to prevent myself recreating it, deep inside my head!'

'Please, Mr Pauley,' she begged, 'what can I do?'

She felt her throat tickle and put her fingers to it to stifle a cough. No, she thought. Not now. I mustn't cough now . . .

'You've destroyed something beautiful, Miss Eames,' he said. 'You must be made to pay for that.'

He took two quick steps towards her, flourishing the gloves. They flashed in the air, like the hands of a magician. Then he pressed his thumbs into her neck and his lips split in a smile of exertion.

'Oh dear,' he breathed. 'Poor you. But I did say I'd get rid of that cough for you, didn't I?'

MIND WELL THE TREE

William Ingram

Writer/actor, William Ingram lives in South Wales. He is probably one of the most prolific and successful writers of radio drama, with some 400 plays to his credit. He is no stranger to writing in the horror genre. For three years he was the major contributor to the highly popular BBC series, THE PRICE OF FEAR, starring Vincent Price.

Although, as head of his own business consultancy firm, David Hollis was extremely well-off, the news that he'd been made sole heir of his Aunt Hestor's estate came as a very pleasant surprise. True, he was her only surviving relative but, not to put too fine a point on it, their relationship had always been cool. A bequest to the local Cats' and Dogs' Home would have seemed much more on the cards.

The will had been drawn up some years before, but the codicil had been added literally minutes before the old lady's death. It was written in her own hand and heavily underlined.

Mind well the tree.

The tree in question was an ancient elm. It stood at the bottom of the garden and had given the house its name: Elm Cottage. David and his wife Helen stood looking up at it, trying to give the odd instruction some significance.

'It doesn't mean anything,' he pronounced. 'The old girl was obviously dotty when I first met her, some thirty years back. She simply got dottier. In any event, from the look of the thing, it won't need minding much longer. It's rotten. Dangerous too, if you ask me. If we had any sense we'd get that gardener fellow . . . what's his daft name? Taff?'

'Shwn,' Helen prompted.

'Shwn! I ask you! Anyway, we'll get him to chop the ruddy thing down.'

'Darling, we can't do that. It's a condition of our inheriting the house in the first place.'

'So, we'll give it a very brief stay of execution. Then it's the chain-saw for you, my old beauty.'

He gave it a hefty kick. Helen was aware of it reverberating through the gnarled, half-hollow trunk. It seemed to shudder in an almost human sense: a feeling of victimisation which it reacted to, resented. Helen turned to comment on the fact, but David was already half-way across the sunlit lawn. He called back to her.

'Come on. We'll get that Gwen woman to make us some tea.'

David did not stay overnight. At the last minute, he'd invented an urgent business appointment. He insisted that Helen should 'suit herself'.

'If you really don't mind, I'll stay on then,' she had said. 'It'll give me a chance to explore the place and get some work done. That damned publisher keeps after me for my proofs. This will give me the chance to take the phone off the hook and get on with it. You're quite sure you don't mind? Because, if you do . . .'

'I said suit yourself, didn't I?'

'We can expect you down for the weekend, though? David?'

'We'll see how things work out.'

He had slammed the car door and was already heading off down the drive.

The description of the place as a 'cottage' could not have been further off the mark. The rooms were large and airy, but furnished in a chintz and horse-brass fashion. They still retained the cottage atmosphere though – a feeling of warmth and welcoming friendliness. But there was one room that Gwen, the housekeeper, omitted from her guided tour. Helen only became aware of the fact some days later when she was writing in the garden and happened to glance up at the eaves. She noticed a single, small window, an attic window, almost hidden by the thatch. When questioned, Gwen dismissed it.

'Just a bit of a box-room, Mum. Not worth the mentioning.' But Helen sensed a certain wariness, almost a feeling of foreboding, in her tone.

'I'd still like to see it, Gwen.' She was already on her way. 'No, don't bother coming. I'm sure I can find the way.'

'But it's not worth climbing the stairs for, Mum.'

Helen sensed something approaching fear in her voice.

Just a box-room. It was almost cell-like in its cramped austerity. A bed, a small washstand with china bowl and jug, a chair with a rough, rush seat, and . . . a trunk. A large, old-fashioned trunk. Wooden, with brass fittings and bound round with a length of ancient-looking hemp. It stood apart, crowding the darkest corner of the room. As Helen knelt to open it, she could not explain her feeling of guilty intrusion. It was as though she were about to enter forbidden territory, explore where she had no right. She brushed away the dust. Across the lid of the chest, in uneven, childlike characters, she made out a name.

'C . . . A . . . E . . . N.'

'Caenwyn Davies was her name, Mum.' Gwen stood in the door, completing it for her.

'Did she live in, then?'

'Oh yes.'

'A servant?'

Gwen paused. 'Very close to Miss Hestor. Very close.'

Helen's attention returned to the trunk. 'Tied with . . . hemp? As though she were all packed to leave but . . . Did she leave, Gwen?'

Gwen's hesitation was unmistakable. 'Oh yes. She left.'

Shwn was calling up from the hall. He spoke in Welsh, but his concern would have been obvious in any language. Gwen looked sheepish.

'He wants me down there now, Mum. Important, he says. Will I leave you, then?'

'Of course. I'll be all right, Gwen. Down in a minute.'

As she left the room, Gwen called back to her. 'Mind well the stairs, Mum. They narrow on the turning.'

Alone, her attention returned to the trunk. She untied the hemp. It wasn't locked. A layer of tissue paper protected the contents. She folded it carefully, laid it to one side. And it was then she felt a 'presence' in the room. She stayed quite still. Quite, quite still. And then, a sound of gentle humming. As though of a young girl at her needlework. The voice, when it came, had a soft, Welsh lilt.

'Poor things, Mum. But all my own. The dress I made myself. A wedding dress . . . or so t'was meant to be.'

Helen held it up.

'Blue, like the sky. "The colour of your eyes, Caenwyn my own true love," was what he said. And, about the bodice, fine-worked forget-me-nots.' A gentle sob in the voice now. 'Oh, poor, poor Caenwyn. Forget me not. Forget me not.'

And then silence. Only the empty silence.

Several days later, David rang to say he wouldn't be down for the weekend after all. His excuse sounded lame, but Helen had learned, from long experience, not to press the matter. She concentrated on her work.

She sat in the garden: but the heat was oppressive and the words refused to come. She was about to call for Shwn and ask him to move her table to somewhere more shady when she remembered the small bench beneath the elm.

It was cool there. Still and cool.

She'd barely opened her notebook, when she heard the voice. The same voice she'd heard in that attic bedroom. A gentle humming at first, then becoming a plaintive song.

> *Idle days in summer time,*
> *In pleasant summer weather,*
> *Two lovers passed together.*

Helen stayed quite still. 'Caenwyn? Is that you, Caenwyn?'

'Caenwyn. Is me, Caenwyn. See, in the bark, by your head where you sit? True loves' hearts, intertwined.' Then a sadder note. 'But see where he gouged his name out? Oh, see where he done it then.'

Helen explored the rough-cut heart and initials with her fingers. And, something else, even as she felt it . . . sap. From a dead tree? Sap? It was as though the ancient elm were . . . bleeding. For no reason she could possibly explain, Helen put her fingers to her lips. But the taste was not of sap at all. Salt. The unmistakable taste of salt. The salt of tears.

Helen stood transfixed. Until the sudden cracking of the bough overhead. Then, the briefest moment of terror as it came crashing towards her.

Helen recovered consciousness in her bedroom. Gwen and Shwn, all anxious concern, were leaning over her.

'You'll be all right now, Mum. You'll be all right.'

Helen attempted to sit up, but Gwen pressed her gently but firmly back on to the pillows.

'It was the tree. Wasn't it, Shwn?'

'And all my stupid fault, Mum. When I spotted you crossing the lawn, I should have thought to . . .' He stopped in mid-sentence.

'Warn me, Shwn?'

He looked away. 'Tried to persuade you anyway.'

369

'To stay away from the place? It would have made no difference, Shwn. I'd have gone anyway. To see for myself. It would have made no difference. It was what you tried to do when I demanded to be shown the attic bedroom, wasn't it, Gwen? Caenwyn's room? Her trunk already packed and tied for leaving. Why should Miss Hestor insist on it all remaining just as she left it, untouched for all the long years? Why, Gwen? You owe me that.'

Gwen looked at her husband. Her voice was barely audible.

'Shwn knew Caenwyn Davies, Mum.'

He nodded. 'Only distant, like. Don't know the whole story. Nobody knows it all. But Caenwyn wasn't just a live-in servant. More "family", far as Miss Hestor was concerned. Happy to stay here. Happy as the day, Caenwyn. And always that old song on her lips. Until . . . until . . .' He could not go on, shook his head.

Helen pressed him. 'Tell me, Shwn. Please.'

'All her happiness stopped. Talk and rumour is all to go by. That's all.'

Gwen continued for him. 'Young love, Mum. But secret love. And Caenwyn all set to leave with him, and happy ever after? Yes, and her trunk all packed and final proof of that.'

'Final? Why final, Gwen?'

'No note to say goodbye. No reason given.' She paused. 'It was the best part of day and night before Miss Hestor found her. Hanging from that old elm. And Miss Hestor gave orders, "Tree never to be felled in her lifetime, or even after." Sacred to her memory, in a manner of speaking. Poor Caenwyn. Always so happy. Always that old song on her lips.'

But Helen was barely listening. Her thoughts returned to the old lady's will. *Mind well the tree*. In a flash of revelation, its meaning was all too clear.

* * *

'*Mind well the tree*, David. Your Aunt's last words, David. Her exact last words.'

As he undressed for bed, David was in no mood to be attentive. He'd resented coming down in the first place, and now this nonsense. It was all too much.

'I'm warning you, Helen. Weekend or not, keep this rubbish up and I'm on the next train out of here.'

Helen persisted. 'Her exact last words. I rang her solicitor and checked.'

'Then he must have thought you several kinds of idiot.'

There was a new urgency in her voice. 'Not *tend* the tree, not *care for* the tree. MIND. It wasn't meant as an appeal, it was a warning. The girl did hang herself from it, David. Just the way they said she did.'

'Which is the only sad part of the whole ridiculous business. The rest is pure fantasy.'

He was in his pyjamas now, climbing into bed beside her. He switched off the bedside lamp. Helen sensed the hostile silence. It was a while before she found the courage to ask it.

'Do you remember her, David?'

'What now?'

'David, please tell me.'

'How the hell would I?'

'It's thirty odd years ago since she died. But it must have been about the time you were visiting.'

He turned impatiently from her. 'Is this just morbid interest, or something more searching?'

'I want to know.'

'For God's sake, Helen! If the girl was working here then, she was just a servant. I probably never set eyes on her.' He sensed her disbelief. 'All right, if you don't believe me, at least give me credit for being a bit selective. Besides, under Aunt Hestor's eagle eye, there wouldn't have been a cat in hell's chance of anything untoward. Satisfied?'

'She was expecting a child, David.' Helen pronounced the

fact without realising it, certainly without knowing why. It was almost as though . . . as though someone else were saying it, through her.

'How the hell do you know that?' His voice had a note of inner intensity that gave him away.

'I . . . I don't know.'

'Fanciful nonsense! She was a domestic, not one of your idiotic heroines.' He turned away from her.

There was no mistaking the hostile silence between them. It frightened Helen. She was the first to breach it.

'You think I'm some kind of absolute fool, don't you?'

His answer was to hold her close. His voice immediately reassuring. 'I don't think anything of the sort. I think you're a brilliant novelist and that imagination is part of the craft, but . . . well, to put it bluntly, you've probably been grafting a bit too hard. You've simply allowed that wonderful imagination of yours to spill over into real life. Perhaps this Caenwyn of yours did exist . . .'

'I know she did.'

'All right. But for the rest of it? You've taken a few simple facts and, thanks to our two fanciful Welsh yokels, turned them into some turgid, human drama which has no foundation in reality.'

'Have I, David? Is that what I've done?'

'Take my word for it. It's all pure fantasy, my love.' He held her even closer. 'There's no harm in it. I wouldn't mind, except that now you're trying to involve me in your fanciful machinations, and . . . well, it simply isn't good enough. Is it now? Without trust, where the hell are we? It's simply not good enough.' He kissed her lightly and turned away again.

Sometime later, Helen called his name. She wanted to, needed to, apologise. He was either asleep or pretending to be.

The tapping at the window was gentle at first. Then it

became more insistent. To begin with, Helen tried to ignore it. Eventually, she felt forced to investigate. She opened the casement window. The tapping had stopped. A tapping like the branch of a tree against the pane. Except that there was no tree. Not near the house. There was only one tree. It stood at the bottom of the garden, slate grey in the fitful moonlight.

It was still night. But blackest night.

It was Caenwyn that did the deed but Helen's hand that held the carving knife. She wore the wedding dress from the old, brass-bound trunk. Caenwyn's trunk. Her voice was different, modulated to a gentle, Welsh lilt. Because of the sleeping pills he'd taken, it did not reach David in his half-drugged sleep.

'Caenwyn, come back. Come back to visit her one, her own, David. See? Wedding dress and ring of troth. When her David promised always to be true? Remember when her David carved their names on the tree and promised always to be true?' David stirred but did not wake. 'Wedding dress, my David. Or so 'twas meant to be. Colour of blue, like sky. "The colour of your eyes, Caenwyn my one, my only love," was what you said. And, about the bodice, fine-worked forget-me-nots. Forget . . . me . . . not.'

For a barely perceptible instant, he opened his eyes and looked up at her. The knife plunged home. He was probably dead from that very first thrust. It did not stop her.

We shall never know the reason for his aunt's deathbed warning. Last minute forgiveness? Or, perhaps, a premonition of a fate even more terrible than her beloved Caenwyn's desertion and betrayal? It went unheeded.

They found him hanging from the elm, the length of hemp about his neck. His heart, gouged out, lay at her feet. She. Helen? Or was it Caenwyn? She sat there, oblivious to the smirch of his blood, the thick of the flies.

Where she has gone, she speaks no word. Only the song. It echoes from her cell, down the tight-locked corridors.

> *Idle days in summer time,*
> *In pleasant summer weather,*
> *Two lovers passed together.*

She sings it in Welsh. It fills the night.

SURVIVAL

John Wyndham

One of Britain's best-known science fiction writers, John Wyndham drew his inspiration partly from H. G. Wells, and liked to describe his work as 'logical fantasy'. Probably the most popular of his stories are THE DAY OF THE TRIFFIDS and THE CHRYSALIDS where catastrophic, usually fantastical events occur against the background of comfortable English life. Several of his works have been filmed and televised.

———————

As the spaceport bus trundled unhurriedly over the mile or more of open field that separated the terminal buildings from the embarkation hoist, Mrs Feltham stared intently forward across the receding row of shoulders in front of her. The ship stood up on the plain like an isolated silver spire. Near its bow she could see the intense blue light which proclaimed it all but ready to take off. Among and around the great tailfins, dwarf vehicles and little dots of men moved in a fuss of final preparations. Mrs Feltham glared at the scene, at this moment loathing it and all the inventions of men, with a hard, hopeless hatred.

Presently she withdrew her gaze from the distance and focused it on the back of her son-in-law's head, a yard in front of her. She hated him, too.

She turned, darting a swift glance at the face of her daughter in the seat beside her. Alice looked pale; her lips were firmly set, her eyes fixed straight ahead.

Mrs Feltham hesitated. Her glance returned to the spaceship. She decided on one last effort. Under cover of the bus noise she said:

'Alice, darling, it's not too late, even now, you know.'

The girl did not look at her. There was no sign that she had heard, save that her lips compressed a little more firmly. Then they parted.

'Mother, please!' she said.

But Mrs Feltham, once started, had to go on.

'It's for your own sake, darling. All you have to do is to say you've changed your mind.'

The girl held a protesting silence.

'Nobody would blame you,' Mrs Feltham persisted. 'They'd not think a bit worse of you. After all, everybody knows that Mars is no place for –'

'Mother, please stop it,' interrupted the girl. The sharpness of her tone took Mrs Feltham aback for a moment. She hesitated. But time was growing too short to allow herself the luxury of offended dignity. She went on:

'You're not used to the sort of life you'll have to live there, darling. Absolutely primitive. No kind of life for any woman. After all, dear, it is only a five-year appointment for David. I'm sure if he really loves you he'd rather know that you *are* safe here and waiting –'

The girl said, harshly:

'We've been over all this before, Mother. I tell you it's no good. I'm not a child. I've thought it out, and I've made up my mind.'

Mrs Feltham sat silent for some moments. The bus swayed on across the field, and the rocketship seemed to tower further into the sky.

'If you had a child of your own –' she said half to herself '– well, I expect some day you will. Then you will begin to understand. . .'

'I think it's you who don't understand,' Alice said. 'This is hard enough, anyway. You're only making it harder for me.'

'My darling, I love you. I gave birth to you. I've watched over you always and I *know* you. I *know* this can't be the kind of life for you. If you were a hard, hoydenish kind of girl, well, perhaps – but you aren't, darling. You know quite well you aren't.'

'Perhaps you don't know me quite as well as you imagine you do, Mother.'

Mrs Feltham shook her head. She kept her eyes averted, boring jealousy into the back of her son-in-law's head.

'He's taken you right away from me,' she said dully.

'That's not true, Mother. It's – well, I'm no longer a child. I'm a woman with a life of my own to live.'

'"Whither thou goest, I will go . . ."' said Mrs Feltham reflectively. 'But that doesn't really hold now, you know. It was all right for a tribe of nomads, but nowadays the wives of soldiers, sailors, pilots, spacemen –'

'It's more than that, Mother. You don't understand. I must become adult and real to myself . . .'

The bus rolled to a stop, puny and toylike beside the ship that seemed too large ever to lift. The passengers got out and stood staring upwards along the shining side. Mr Feltham put his arms round his daughter. Alice clung to him, tears in her eyes. In an unsteady voice he murmured:

'Good-bye, my dear. And all the luck there is.'

He released her, and shook hands with his son-in-law.

'Keep her safe, David. She's everything –'

'I know. I will. Don't you worry.'

Mrs Feltham kissed her daughter farewell, and forced herself to shake hands with her son-in-law.

A voice from the hoist called: 'All passengers aboard, please!'

The doors of the hoist closed. Mr Feltham avoided his wife's eyes. He put his arm round her waist, and led her back to the bus in silence.

As they made their way, in company with a dozen other vehicles, back to the shelter of the terminal, Mrs Feltham alternately dabbed her eyes with a wisp of white handkerchief and cast glances back at the spaceship standing tall, inert, and apparently deserted now. Her hand slid into her husband's.

'I can't believe it even now,' she said. 'It's so utterly unlike her. Would you ever have thought that our little Alice . . ? Oh, why did she have to marry him . . ?' Her voice trailed to a whimper.

Her husband pressed her fingers, without speaking.

'It wouldn't be so surprising with some girls,' she went on. 'But Alice was always so quiet. I used to worry because she was so quiet – I mean in case she might become one of those timid bores. Do you remember how the other children used to call her Mouse?

'And now this! Five years in that dreadful place! Oh, she'll never stand it, Henry. I know she won't, she's not the type. Why didn't you put your foot down, Henry? They'd have listened to you. You could have stopped it.'

Her husband sighed. 'There are times when one can give advice, Miriam, though it's scarcely ever popular, but what one must not do is to try to live other people's lives for them. Alice is a woman now, with her own rights. Who am I to say what's best for her?'

'But you could have stopped her going.'

'Perhaps – but I didn't care for the price.'

She was silent for some seconds, then her fingers tightened on his hand.

'Henry – Henry, I don't think we shall ever see them again. I feel it.'

'Come, come, dear. They'll be back safe and sound, you'll see.'

'You don't really believe that, Henry. You're just trying to cheer me up. Oh, why, why must she go to that horrible place? She's so young. She could have waited five years. Why is she so stubborn, so hard – not like my little Mouse at all?'

Her husband patted her hand reassuringly.

'You must try to stop thinking of her as a child, Miriam. She's not; she's a woman now and if all our women were mice, it would be a poor outlook for our survival . . .'

The Navigating Officer of the s/r *Falcon* approached his captain.

'The deviation, sir.'

Captain Winters took the piece of paper held out to him.

'One point three six five degrees,' he read out. 'H'm. Not bad. Not at all bad, considering. South-east sector again. Why are nearly all deviations in the S.E. sector, I wonder, Mr Carter?'

'Maybe they'll find out when we've been at the game a bit longer, sir. Right now it's just one of those things.'

'Odd, all the same. Well, we'd better correct it before it gets any bigger.'

The Captain loosened the expanding book-rack in front of him and pulled out a set of tables. He consulted them and scribbled down the result.

'Check, Mr Carter.'

The navigator compared the figures with the table, and approved.

'Good. How's she lying?' asked the Captain.

'Almost broadside, with a very slow roll, sir.'

'You can handle it. I'll observe visually. Align her and stabilise. Ten seconds on starboard laterals at force two. She should take about thirty minutes, twenty seconds to swing over, but we'll watch that. Then neutralise with the port laterals at force two. Okay?'

'Very good, sir.' The Navigating Officer sat down in the control chair, and fastened the belt. He looked over the keys and switches carefully.

'I'd better warn 'em. May be a bit of a jolt,' said the Captain. He switched on the address system, and pulled the microphone bracket to him.

'Attention all! Attention all! We are about to correct course. There will be several impulses. None of them will be violent, but all fragile objects should be secured, and you are advised to seat yourselves and use the safety belts. The operation will take approximately half an hour and will start in five minutes from now. I shall inform you when it has been completed. That is all.' He switched off.

'Some fool always thinks the ship's been holed by a meteor if you don't spoon it out,' he added. 'Have that woman in hysterics, most likely. Doesn't do any good.' He pondered idly. 'I wonder what the devil she thinks she's doing out here, anyway. A quiet little thing like that; what she ought to be doing is sitting in some village back home, knitting.'

'She knits here,' observed the Navigating Officer.

'I know – and think what it implies! What's the idea of that kind going to Mars? She'll be as homesick as hell, and hate every foot of the place on sight. That husband of hers ought to have had more sense. Comes damn near cruelty to children.'

'It mightn't be his fault, sir. I mean, some of those quiet ones can be amazingly stubborn.'

The captain eyed his officer speculatively.

'Well, I'm not a man of wide experience, but I know what I'd say to my wife if she thought of coming along.'

'But you can't have a proper ding-dong with those quiet ones, sir. They kind of featherbed the whole thing, and then get their own way in the end.'

'I'll overlook the implication of the first part of that remark, Mr Carter, but out of this extensive knowledge of women can you suggest to me why the devil she is here if he didn't drag her along? It isn't as if Mars were domestically hazardous, like a convention.'

'Well, sir – she strikes me as the devoted type. Scared of her

own shadow ordinarily, but with an awful amount of deter-
mination when the right string's pulled. It's sort of – well,
you've heard of ewes facing lions in defence of their cubs,
haven't you?'

'Assuming that you mean lambs,' said the Captain, 'the
answers would be, A: I've always doubted it; and, B: she
doesn't have any.'

'I was just trying to indicate the type, sir.'

The Captain scratched his cheek with his forefinger.

'You may be right, but I know if I were going to take a wife
to Mars, which heaven forbid, I'd feel a tough, gun-toting
Momma was less of a liability. What's his job there?'

'Taking charge of a mining company office, I think.'

'Office hours, huh? Well, maybe it'll work out some way,
but I still say the poor little thing ought to be in her own
kitchen. She'll spend half the time scared to death, and the
rest of it pining for home comforts.' He glanced at the clock.
'They've had enough time to batten down the chamber-pots
now. Let's get busy.'

He fastened his own safety-belt, swung the screen in front
of him on its pivot, switching it on as he did so, and leaned
back, watching the panorama of stars move slowly across it.

'All set, Mr Carter?'

The Navigating Officer switched on a fuel line, and poised
his right hand above a key.

'All set, sir.'

'Okay. Straighten her up.'

The Navigating Officer glued his attention to the pointers
before him. He tapped the key beneath his fingers experi-
mentally. Nothing happened. A slight double furrow
appeared between his brows. He tapped again. Still there
was no response.

'Get on with it, man,' said the Captain irritably.

The Navigating Officer decided to try twisting her the
other way. He tapped one of the keys under his left hand.

This time there was response without delay. The whole ship jumped violently sideways and trembled. A crash jangled back and forth through the metal members around them like a diminishing echo.

Only the safety belt kept the Navigating Officer in his seat. He stared stupidly at the gyrating pointers before him. On the screen the stars were streaking across like a shower of fireworks. The Captain watched the display in ominous silence for a moment, then he said coldly:

'Perhaps when you have had your fun, Mr Carter, you will kindly straighen her up.'

The navigator pulled himself together. He chose a key, and pressed it. Nothing happened. He tried another. Still the needles on the dials revolved smoothly. A slight sweat broke out on his forehead. He switched to another fuel line, and tried again.

The Captain lay back in his chair, watching the heavens stream across his screen.

'Well?' he demanded curtly.

'There's – no response, sir.'

Captain Winters unfastened his safety belt and clacked across the floor on his magnetic soles. He jerked his head for the other to get out of his seat, and took his place. He checked the fuel line switches. He pressed a key. There was no impulse: the pointers continued to turn without a check. He tried other keys, fruitlessly. He looked up and met the navigator's eyes. After a long moment he moved back to his own desk, and flipped a switch. A voice broke into the room:

'– would I know? All I know is that the old can's just bowling along head over elbow, and that ain't no kind of way to run a bloody spaceship. If you ask me –'

'Jevons,' snapped the Captain.

The voice broke off abruptly.

'Yes, sir?' it said, in a differeent tone.

'The laterals aren't firing.'

'No, sir,' the voice agreed.

'Wake up, man. I mean they *won't* fire. They packed up.'

'What – all of 'em, sir?'

'The only ones that have responded are the port laterals – and they shouldn't have kicked the way they did. Better send someone outside to look at 'em. I didn't like that kick.'

'Very good, sir.'

The Captain flipped the communicator switch back, and pulled over the announcement mike.

'Attention, please. You may release all safety belts and proceed as normal. Correction of course has been postponed. You will be warned before it is resumed. That is all.'

Captain and navigator looked at one another again. Their faces were grave, and their eyes troubled . . .

Captain Winters studied his audience. It comprised everyone aboard the *Falcon*. Fourteen men and one woman. Six of the men were his crew; the rest passengers. He watched them as they found theselves places in the ship's small living-room. He would have been happier if his cargo had consisted of more freight and fewer passengers. Passengers, having nothing to occupy them, were always making mischief one way and another. Moreover, it was not a quiet subservient type of man who recommended himself for a job as a miner, prospector, or general adventurer on Mars.

The woman could have caused a great deal of trouble aboard had she been so minded. Luckily she was diffident, self-effacing. But even though at times she was irritatingly without spirit, he thanked his luck that she had not turned out to be some incendiary blonde who would only add to his troubles.

All the same, he reminded himself, regarding her as she sat beside her husband, she could not be quite as meek as she looked. Carter must have been right when he spoke of a stiffening motive somewhere – without that she could never have started on the journey at all, and she would certainly not be coming through steadfast and uncomplaining so far. He glanced at the woman's husband. Queer creatures, women. Morgan was all right, but there was nothing about him, one would have said, to lead a woman on a trip like this . . .

He waited until they had finished shuffling around and fitting themselves in. Silence fell. He let his gaze dwell on each face in turn. His own expression was serious.

'Mrs Morgan and gentlemen,' he began. 'I have called you here together because it seemed best to me that each of you should have a clear understanding of our present position.

'It is this. Our lateral tubes have failed. They are, for reasons which we have not yet been able to ascertain, useless. In the case of the port laterals they are burnt out, and irreplaceable.

'In case some of you do not know what that implies, I should tell you that it is upon the laterals that the navigation of the ship depends. The main drive tubes give us the initial impetus for take-off. After that they are shut off, leaving us in free fall. Any deviations from the course plotted are corrected by suitable bursts from the laterals.

'But it is not only for steering that we use them. In landing, which is an infinitely more complex job than take-off, they are essential. We brake by reversing the ship and using the main drive to check our speed. But I think you can scarcely fail to realise that it is an operation of the greatest delicacy to keep the huge mass of such a ship as this perfectly balanced upon the thrust of her drive as she descends. It is the laterals which make such balance possible. Without them it cannot be done.'

A dead silence held the room for some seconds. Then a voice asked, drawling:

'What you're saying, Captain, is, the way things are, we can neither steer nor land – is that it?'

Captain Winters looked at the speaker. He was a big man. Without exerting himself, and, apparently, without intention, he seemed to possess a natural domination over the rest.

'That is exactly what I mean,' he replied.

A tenseness came over the room. There was the sound of a quickly drawn breath here and there.

The man with the slow voice nodded, fatalistically. Someone else asked:

'Does that mean that we might crash on Mars?'

'No,' said the Captain. 'If we go on travelling as we are now, slightly off course, we shall miss Mars altogether.'

'And so go on out to play tag with the asteroids,' another voice suggested.

'That is what would happen if we did nothing about it. But there is a way we can stop that, if we can manage it.' The Captain paused, aware that he had their absorbed attention. He continued:

'You must all be well aware from the peculiar behaviour of space as seen from our ports that we are now tumbling along all as – er – head over heels. This is due to the explosion of the port laterals. It is a highly unorthodox method of travelling, but it does mean that by an impulse from our main tubes given at exactly the critical moment we should be able to alter our course approximately as we require.'

'And how much good is that going to do us if we can't land?' somebody wanted to know. The Captain ignored the interruption. He continued:

'I have been in touch by radio with both home and Mars, and have reported our state. I have also informed them that I intend to attempt the one possible course open to me. That is of using the main drive in an attempt to throw the ship into an orbit about Mars.

'If that is successful we shall avoid two dangers – that of shooting on towards the outer parts of the system, and of crashing on Mars. I think we have a good chance of bringing it off.'

When he stopped speaking he saw alarm in several faces, thoughtful concentration in others. He noticed Mrs Morgan holding tightly to her husband's hand, her face a little paler than usual. It was the man with the drawl who broke the silence.

'You *think* there is a good chance?' he repeated questioningly.

'I do. I also think it is the only chance. But I'm not going to try to fool you by pretending complete confidence. It's too serious for that.'

'And if we do get into this orbit?'

'They will try to keep a radar fix on us, and send help as soon as possible.'

'H'm,' said the questioner. 'And what do you personally think about that, Captain?'

'I – well, it isn't going to be easy. But we're all in this together, so I'll tell you just what they told me. At the very best we can't expect them to reach us for some months. The ship will have to come from Earth. The two planets are well past conjunction now. I'm afraid it's going to mean quite a wait.'

'Can we – hold out long enough, Captain?'

'According to my calculations we should be able to hold out for about seventeen or eighteen weeks.'

'And that will be long enough?'

'It'll have to be.'

He broke the thoughtful pause that followed by continuing in a brisker manner.

'This is not going to be comfortable, or pleasant. But, if we all play our parts, and keep strictly to the necessary measures, it can be done. Now, there are three essentials: air to breathe – well, luckily we shan't have to worry about that. The regeneration plant and stock of spare cylinders, and cylinders in cargo will look after that for a long time. Water will be rationed. Two pints each every twenty-four hours, for *everything*. Luckily we shall be able to draw water from the fuel tanks, or it would be a great deal less than that. The thing that is going to be our most serious worry is food.'

He explained his proposals further, with patient clarity. At the end he added: 'And now I expect you have some questions?'

A small, wiry man with a weather-beaten face asked:

'Is there no hope at all of getting the lateral tubes to work again?'

Captain Winters shook his head.

'Negligible. The impellent section of a ship is not constructed to be accessible in space. We shall keep on trying, of course, but even if the others could be made to fire, we should still be unable to repair the port laterals.'

He did his best to answer the few more questions that followed in ways that held a balance between easy confidence and despondency. The prospect was by no means good. Before help could possibly reach them they were all going to need all the nerve and resolution they had – and out of sixteen persons some must be weaker than others.

His gaze rested again on Alice Morgan and her husband beside her. Her presence was certainly a possible source of trouble. When it came to the pinch the man would have more strain on account of her – and, most likely, fewer scruples.

Since the woman was here, she must share the consequences equally with the rest. There could be no privilege. In a sharp emergency one could afford a heroic gesture, but preferential treatment of any one person in the long ordeal which they must face would create an impossible situation. Make any allowances for her, and you would be called on to make allowances for others on health or other grounds – with heaven knew what complications to follow.

A fair chance with the rest was the best he could do for her – not, he felt, looking at her as she clutched her husband's hand and looked at him from wide eyes in a pale face, not a very good best.

He hoped she would not be the first to go under. It would be better for morale if she were not the very first . . .

She was not the first to go. For nearly three months nobody went.

The *Falcon*, by means of skilfully timed bursts on the main tubes, had succeeded in nudging herself into an orbital relationship with Mars. After that, there was little that the crew could do for her. At the distance of equilibrium she had become a very minor satellite, rolling and tumbling on her circular course, destined, so far as anyone could see, to continue this untidy progress until help reached them, or perhaps for ever . . .

Inboard, the complexity of her twisting somersaults was not perceptible unless one deliberately uncovered a port. If one did, the crazy cavortings of the universe outside produced such a sense of bewilderment that one gladly shut the cover again to preserve the illusion of stability within. Even Captain Winters and the Navigating Officer took their observations as swiftly as possible and were relieved when they had shut the whizzing constellations off the screen, and could take refuge in relativity.

For all her occupants the *Falcon* had become a small, independent world, very sharply finite in space, and scarcely less so in time.

It was, moreover, a world with a very low standard of living; a community with short tempers, weakening distempers, aching bellies, and ragged nerves. It was a group in which each man watched on a trigger of suspicion for a hairsbreadth difference in the next man's ration, and where the little he ate so avidly was not enough to quiet the rumblings of his stomach. He was ravenous when he went to sleep; more ravenous when he woke from dreams of food.

Men who had started from Earth full-bodied were now gaunt and lean, their faces had hardened from curved contours into angled planes and changed their healthy colours for a grey pallor in which their eyes glittered unnaturally. They had all grown weaker. The weakest lay on their couches torpidly. The more fortunate looked at them from time to time with a question in their eyes. It was not difficult to read the question: 'Why do we go on wasting good food on this guy? Looks like he's booked, anyway.' But as yet no one had taken up that booking.

The situation was worse than Captain Winters had foreseen. There had been bad stowage. The cans in several cases of meat had collapsed under the terrific pressure of other cans above them during take-off. The resulting mess was now describing an orbit of its own around the ship. He had had to throw it out secretly. If the men had known of it, they would have eaten it gladly, maggots and all. Another case shown on his inventory had disappeared. He still did not know how. The ship had been searched for it without trace. Much of the emergency stores consisted of dehydrated foods for which he dared not spare sufficient water, so that though edible they were painfully unattractive. They had been intended simply as a supplement in case the estimated time was overrun, and were not extensive. Little in the cargo was edible, and that mostly small cans of luxuries. As a result, he had had to reduce the rations expected to stretch meagrely over seventeeen weeks. And even so, they would not last that long.

The first who did go owed it neither to sickness nor malnutrition, but to accident.

Jevons, the chief engineer, maintained that the only way to locate and correct the trouble with the laterals was to effect an entry into the propellent section of the ship. Owing to the tanks which backed up against the bulkhead separating the sections this could not be achieved from within the ship herself.

It had proved impossible with the tools available to cut a slice out of the hull; the temperature of space and the conductivity of the hull caused all their heat to run away and dissipate itself without making the least impression on the tough skin. The one way he could see of getting in was to cut away round the burnt-out tubes of the port laterals. It was debatable whether this was worthwhile since the other laterals would be still unbalanced on the port side, but where he found opposition solidly against him was in the matter of using precious oxygen to operate his cutters. He had to accept that ban, but he refused to relinquish his plan altogether.

'Very well,' he said, grimly. 'We're like rats in a trap, but Bowman and I aim to do more than just keep the trap going, and we're going to try, even if we have to cut our way into the damned ship by hand.'

Captain Winters had OK'd that; not that he believed that anything useful would come of it, but it would keep Jevons quiet, and do no one else any harm. So for weeks Jevons and Bowman had got into their spacesuits and worked their shifts. Oblivious after a time of the wheeling heavens about them, they kept doggedly on with their sawing and filing. Their progress, pitifully slow at best, had grown even slower as they became weaker.

Just what Bowman was attempting when he met his end still remained a mystery. He had not confided in Jevons. All that anyone knew about it was the sudden lurch of the ship and the clang of reverberations running up and down the hull. Possibly it was an accident. More likely he had become impatient and laid a small charge to blast an opening.

For the first time for weeks ports were uncovered and

faces looked out giddily at the wheeling stars. Bowman came into sight. He was drifting inertly, a dozen yards or more outboard. His suit was deflated, and a large gash showed in the material of the left sleeve.

The consciousness of a corpse floating round and round you like a minor moon is no improver of already lowered morale. Push it away, and it still circles, though at a greater distance. Some day a proper ceremony for the situation would be invented – perhaps a small rocket would launch the poor remains upon their last, infinite voyage. Meanwhile, lacking a precedent, Captain Winters decided to pay the body the decent respect of having it brought inboard. The refrigeration plant had to be kept going to preserve the small remaining stocks of food, but several sections of it were empty . . .

A day and a night by the clock had passed since the provisional interment of Bowman when a modest knock came on the control-room door. The Captain laid blotting paper carefully over his latest entry in the log, and closed the book.

'Come in,' he said.

The door opened just widely enough to admit Alice Morgan. She slipped in, and shut it behind her. He was somewhat surprised to see her. She had kept sedulously in the background, putting the few requests she had made through the intermediation of her husband. He noticed the changes in her. She was haggard now as they all were and her eyes anxious. She was also nervous. The fingers of her thin hands sought one another and interlocked themselves for confidence. Clearly she was having to push herself to raise whatever was in her mind. He smiled in order to encourage her.

'Come and sit down, Mrs Morgan,' he invited, amiably.

She crossed the room with a slight clicking from her magnetic soles, and took the chair he indicated. She seated herself uneasily, and on the forward edge.

It had been sheer cruelty to bring her on this voyage, he

reflected again. She had been at least a pretty little thing, now she was no longer that. Why couldn't that fool husband of hers have left her in a proper setting – a nice quiet suburb, a gentle routine, a life where she would be protected from exaction and alarm alike. It surprised him again that she had had the resolution and the stamina to survive conditions on the *Falcon* as long as this. Fate would probably have been kinder to her if it had disallowed that. He spoke to her quietly, for she perched rather than sat, making him think of a bird ready to take off at any sudden movement.

'And what can I do for you, Mrs Morgan?'

Alice's fingers twined and intertwined. She watched them doing it. She looked up, opened her mouth to speak, closed it again.

'It isn't very easy,' she murmured apologetically.

Trying to help her, he said:

'No need to be nervous, Mrs Morgan. Just tell me what's on your mind. Has one of them been – bothering you?'

She shook her head.

'Oh, no, Captain Winters. It's nothing like that at all.'

'What is it, then?'

'It's – it's the rations, Captain. I'm not getting enough food.'

The kindly concern froze out of his face.

'None of us is,' he told her, shortly.

'I know,' she said, hurriedly. 'I know, but –'

'But what?' he inquired in a chill tone.

She drew a breath.

'There's the man who died yesterday. Bowman. I thought if I could have his rations –'

The sentence trailed away as she saw the expression on the Captain's face.

He was not acting. He was feeling just as shocked as he looked. Of all the impudent suggestions that ever had come his way, none had astounded him more. He gazed dumbfounded at the source of the outrageous proposition. Her eyes met his, but, oddly, with less timidity than before. There was no sign of shame in them.

'I've *got* to have more food,' she said, intensely.

Captain Winters' anger mounted.

'So you thought you'd just snatch a dead man's share as well as your own! I'd better not tell you in words just where I class that suggestion, young woman. But you can understand this: we share, and we share equally. What Bowman's death means to us is that we can keep on having the same ration for a little longer – that, and only that. And now I think you had better go.'

But Alice Morgan made no move to go. She sat there with her lips pressed together, her eyes a little narrowed, quite still save that her hands trembled. Even through his indignation the Captain felt surprise, as though he had watched a hearth cat suddenly become a hunter. She said stubbornly:

'I haven't asked for any privilege until now, Captain. I wouldn't ask you now if it weren't absolutely necessary. But that man's death gives us a margin now. And I *must* have more food.'

The Captain controlled himself with an effort.

'Bowman's death has *not* given us a margin, or a windfall – all it has done is to extend by a day or two the chance of our survival. Do you think that every one of us doesn't ache just as much as you do for more food? In all my considerable experience of effrontery –'

She raised her thin hand to stop him. The hardness of her eyes made him wonder why he had ever thought her timid.

'Captain. Look at me!' she said, in a harsh tone.

He looked. Presently his expression of anger faded into shocked astonishment. A faint tinge of pink stole into her pale cheeks.

'Yes,' she said. 'You see, you've *got* to give me more food. My baby *must* have the chance to live.'

The Captain continued to stare at her as if mesmerised. Presently he shut his eyes, and passed his hand over his brow.

'God in heaven. This is terrible,' he murmured.

Alice Morgan said seriously, as if she had already considered that very point:

'No. It isn't terrible – not if my baby lives.' He looked at her helplessly, without speaking. She went on:

'It wouldn't be robbing anyone, you see. Bowman doesn't need his rations any more – but my baby does. It's quite simple, really.' She looked questioningly at the Captain. He had no comment ready. She continued: 'So you couldn't call it unfair. After all, I'm two people now, really, aren't I? I *need* more food. If you don't let me have it you will be murdering my baby. So you *must . . . must . . .* My baby has *got* to live – he's got to . . .'

When she had gone Captain Winters mopped his forehead, unlocked his private drawer, and took out one of his carefully hoarded bottles of whisky. He had the self-restraint to take only a small pull on the drinking-tube and then put it back. It revived him a little, but his eyes were still shocked and worried.

Would it not have been kinder in the end to tell the woman that her baby had no chance at all of being born? That would have been honest; but he doubted whether the coiner of the phrase about honesty being the best policy had known a great deal about group-morale. Had he told her that, it would have been impossible to avoid telling her why, and once she knew why it would have been impossible for her not to confide it, if only to her husband. And then it would be too late.

The Captain opened the top drawer, and regarded the pistol within. There was always that. He was tempted to take hold of it now and use it. There wasn't much use in playing the silly game out. Sooner or later it would have to come to that, anyway.

He frowned at it, hesitating. Then he put out his right hand and gave the thing a flip with his finger, sending it floating to the back of the drawer, out of sight. He closed the drawer. Not yet . . .

But perhaps he had better begin to carry it soon. So far, his authority had held. There had been nothing worse than safety-valve grumbling. But a time would come when he was going to need the pistol either for them or himself.

If they should begin to suspect that the encouraging bulletins that he pinned up on the board from time to time were fakes: if they should somehow find out that the rescue ship which they believed to be hurtling through space towards them had not, in fact, even been able to take off from Earth – that was when hell would start breaking loose.

It might be safer if there were to be an accident with the radio equipment before long . . .

'Taken your time, haven't you?' Captain Winters asked. He spoke shortly because he was irritable, not because it mattered in the least how long anyone took over anything now.

The Navigating Officer made no reply. His boots clicked across the floor. A key and an identity bracelet drifted towards the Captain, an inch or so above the surface of his desk. He put out a hand to check them.

'I –' he began. Then he caught sight of the other's face. 'Good God, man, what's the matter with you?'

He felt some compunction. He wanted Bowman's identity bracelet for the record, but there had been no real need to send Carter for it. A man who had died Bowman's death would be a piteous sight. That was why they had left him still in his spacesuit instead of undressing him. All the same, he had thought that Carter was tougher stuff. He brought out a bottle. The last bottle.

'Better have a shot of this,' he said.

The navigator did, and put his head in his hands. The Captain carefully rescued the bottle from its mid-air drift, and put it away. Presently the Navigating Officer said, without looking up:

'I'm sorry, sir.'

'That's okay, Carter. Nasty job. Should have done it myself.'

The other shuddered slightly. A minute passed in silence while he got a grip on himself. Then he looked up and met the Captain's eyes.

'It – it wasn't just that, sir.'

The Captain looked puzzled.

'How do you mean?' he asked.

The officer's lips trembled. He did not form his words properly, and he stammered.

'Pull yourself together. What are you trying to say?' The Captain spoke sharply to stiffen him.

Carter jerked his head slightly. His lips stopped trembling.

'He – he –' he floundered; then he tried again, in a rush. 'He – hasn't any legs, sir.'

'Who? What *is* this? You mean Bowman hasn't any legs?'

'Y – yes, sir.'

'Nonsense, man. I was there when he was brought in. So were you. He had legs all right.'

'Yes, sir. He did have legs then – but he hasn't now!'

The Captain sat very still. For some seconds there was no sound in the control-room but the clicking of the chronometer. Then he spoke with difficulty, getting no further than two words:

'You mean – ?'

'What else could it be, sir?'

'*God in heaven!*' gasped the Captain.

He sat staring with eyes that had taken on the horror that lay in the other man's . . .

*   *   *

Two men moved silently, with socks over their magnetic soles. They stopped opposite the door of one of the refrigeration compartments. One of them produced a slender key. He slipped it into the lock, felt delicately with it among the wards for a moment, and then turned it with a click. As the door swung open a pistol fired twice from within the refrigerator. The man who was pulling the door sagged at the knees, and hung in mid-air.

The other man was still behind the half-opened door. He snatched a pistol from his pocket and slid it swiftly round the corner of the door, pointing into the refrigerator. He pulled the trigger twice.

A figure in a spacesuit launched itself out of the refrigerator, sailing uncannily across the room. The other man shot at it as it swept past him. The spacesuited figure collided with the opposite wall, recoiled slightly, and hung there. Before it could turn and use the pistol in its hand, the other man fired again. The figure jerked, and floated back against the wall. The man kept his pistol trained, but the spacesuit swayed there, flaccid and inert.

The door by which the men had entered opened with a sudden clang. The Navigating Officer on the threshold did not hesitate. He fired slightly after the other, but he kept on firing . . .

When his pistol was empty the man in front of him swayed queerly, anchored by his boots; there was no other movement in him. The Navigating Officer put out a hand and steadied himself by the doorframe. Then, slowly and painfully, he made his way across to the figure in the spacesuit. There were gashes in the suit. He managed to unlock the helmet and pull it away.

The Captain's face looked somewhat greyer than undernourishment had made it. His eyes opened slowly. He said in a whisper:

'Your job now, Carter. Good luck!'

The Navigating Officer tried to answer, but there were no words, only a bubbling of blood in his throat. His hands relaxed. There was a dark stain still spreading on his uniform. Presently his body hung listlessly swaying beside his Captain's.

'I figured they were going to last a lot longer than this,' said the small man with the sandy moustache.

The man with the drawl looked at him steadily.

'Oh, you did, did you? And do you reckon your figuring's reliable?'

The smaller man shifted awkwardly. He ran the tip of his tongue along his lips.

'Well, there was Bowman. Then those four. Then the two that died. That's seven.'

'Sure. That's seven. Well?' inquired the big man softly. He was not as big as he had been, but he still had a large frame. Under his intent regard the emaciated small man seemed to shrivel a little more.

'Er – nothing. Maybe my figuring was kind of hopeful,' he said.

'Maybe. My advice to you is to quit figuring and keep on hoping. Huh?'

'The small man wilted. 'Er – yes. I guess so.'

The big man looked round the living-room, counting heads.

'Okay. Let's start,' he said.

A silence fell on the rest. They gazed at him with uneasy fascination. They fidgeted. One or two nibbled at their finger nails. The big man leaned forward. He put a spacehelmet, inverted, on the table. In his customary leisurely fashion he said:

'We shall draw for it. Each of us will take a paper and hold it up unopened until I give the word. *Un*opened. Got that?'

They nodded. Every eye was fixed intently upon his face.

'Good. Now one of those pieces of paper in the helmet is marked with a cross. Ray, I want you to count the pieces there and make sure that there are nine –'

'Eight!' said Alice Morgan's voice sharply.

All the heads turned towards her as if pulled by strings. The faces looked startled, as though the owners might have heard a turtle-dove roar. Alice sat embarrassed under the combined gaze, but she held herself steady and her mouth was set in a straight line. The man in charge of the proceedings studied her.

'Well, well,' he drawled. 'So you don't want to take a hand in our little game!'

'No,' said Alice.

'You've shared equally with us so far – but now we have reached this regrettable stage you don't want to?'

'No,' agreed Alice again.

He raised his eyebrows.

'You are appealing to our chivalry, perhaps?'

'No,' said Alice once more. 'I'm denying the equity of what you call your game. The one who draws the cross dies – isn't that the plan?'

'*Pro bono publico*,' said the big man. 'Deplorable, of course, but unfortunately necessary.'

'But if *I* draw it, two must die. Do you call that equitable?' Alice asked.

The group looked taken aback. Alice waited.

The big man fumbled it. For once he was at a loss.

'Well,' said Alice, 'isn't that so?'

One of the others broke the silence to observe: 'The question of the exact stage when the personality, the soul of the individual, takes form is still highly debatable. Some have held that until there is separate existence –'

The drawling voice of the big man cut him short. 'I think we can leave that point to the theologians, Sam. This is more in the Wisdom of Solomon class. The point would seem to be that Mrs Morgan claims exemption on account of her condition.'

'My baby has a right to live,' Alice said doggedly.

'We all have a right to live. We all want to live,' someone put in.

'Why should you – ?' another began; but the drawling voice dominated again:

'Very well, gentlemen. Let us be formal. Let us be democratic. We will vote on it. The question is put: do you consider Mrs Morgan's claim to be valid – or should she take her chance with the rest of us? Those in –'

'Just a minute,' said Alice, in a firmer voice than any of them had heard her use. 'Before you start voting on that you'd better listen to me a bit.' She looked round, making sure she had the attention of all of them. She had; and their astonishment as well.

'Now the first thing is that I am a lot more important than any of you,' she told them simply. 'No, you needn't smile. I am – and I'll tell you why.

'Before the radio broke down –'

'Before the Captain wrecked it, you mean,' someone corrected her.

'Well, before it became useless,' she compromised. 'Captain Winters was in regular touch with home. He gave them news of us. The news that the Press wanted most was about me. Women, particularly women in unusual situations, are always news. He told me I was in the headlines: GIRL-WIFE IN DOOM ROCKET, WOMAN'S SPACEWRECK ORDEAL, that sort of thing. And if you haven't forgotten how newspapers look, you can imagine the leads, too: "Trapped in their living space tomb, a girl and fifteen men now wheel helplessly around the planet Mars . . ."

'All of you are just men – hulks, like the ship, I am a woman, therefore my position is romantic, so I am young, glamorous, beautiful . . .' Her thin face showed for a

400

moment the trace of a wry smile. 'I am a heroine . . .'

She paused, letting the idea sink in. Then she went on:

'I was a heroine even before Captain Winters told them that I was pregnant. But after that I became a phenomenon. There were demands for interviews, I wrote one, and Captain Winters transmitted it for me. There have been interviews with my parents and my friends, anyone who knew me. And now an enormous number of people know a great deal about me. They are intensely interested in me. They are even more interested in my baby – which is likely to be the first baby ever born in a spaceship . . .

'Now do you begin to see? You have a fine tale ready. Bowman, my husband, Captain Winters, and the rest were heroically struggling to repair the port laterals. There was an explosion. It blew them all away out into space.

'You may get away with that. But if there is no trace of me and my baby – or of our bodies – *then* what are you going to say? How will you explain that?'

She looked round the faces again.

'Well, what *are* you going to say? That I, too, was outside repairing the port laterals? That I committed suicide by shooting myself out to space with a rocket?

'Just think it over. The whole world's press is wanting to know about me – with all the details. It'll have to be a mighty good story to stand up to that. And if it doesn't stand up – well, the rescue won't have done you much good.

'You'll not have a chance in hell. You'll hang, or you'll fry, every one of you – unless it happens they lynch you first . . .'

There was silence in the room as she finished speaking. Most of the faces showed the astonishment of men ferociously attacked by a Pekinese, and at a loss for suitable comment.

The big man sat sunk in reflection for a minute or more. Then he looked up, rubbing the stubble on his sharp-boned chin thoughtfully. He glanced round the others and then let his eyes rest on Alice. For a moment there was a twitch at the corner of his mouth.

'Madam,' he drawled, 'you are probably a great loss to the legal profession.' He turned away. 'We shall have to reconsider this matter before our next meeting. But, for the present, Ray, *eight* pieces of paper as the lady said . . .'

'It's her!' said the Second, over the Skipper's shoulder.

The Skipper moved irritably. 'Of course it's her. What else'd you expect to find whirling through space like a sozzled owl?' He studied the screen for a moment. 'Not a sign. Every port covered.'

'Do you think there's a chance, Skipper?'

'What, after all this time? No, Tommy, not a ghost of it. We're – just the morticians, I guess.'

'How'll we get aboard her, Skip?'

The Skipper watched the gyrations of the *Falcon* with a calculating eye.

'Well, there aren't any rules, but I reckon if we can get a cable on her we *might* be able to play her gently, like a big fish. It'll be tricky, though.'

Tricky, it was. Five times the magnet projected from the rescue ship failed to make contact. The sixth attempt was better judged. When the magnet drifted close to the *Falcon* the current was switched on for a moment. It changed course, and floated nearer to the ship. When it was almost in contact the switch went over again. It darted forward, and glued itself limpet-like to the hull.

Then followed the long game of playing the *Falcon*; of keeping tension on the cable between the two ships, but not too much tension, and of holding the rescue ship from being herself thrown into a roll by the pull. Three times the cable parted, but at last, after weary hours of adroit manoeuvre by the rescue ship the derelict's motion had been reduced to a slow twist. There was still no trace of life aboard. The rescue ship closed a little.

The Captain, the Third Officer, and the doctor fastened on their spacesuits and went outboard. They made their way forward to the winch. The Captain looped a short length of line over the cable, and fastened both ends of it to his belt. He laid hold of the cable with both hands, and with a heave sent himself skimming into space. The others followed him along the guiding cable.

They gathered beside the *Falcon*'s entrance port. The Third Officer took a crank from his satchel. He inserted it in an opening, and began to turn until he was satisfied that the inner door of the airlock was closed. When it would turn no more, he withdrew it, and fitted it into the next opening; that should set the motors pumping air out of the lock – if there were air, and if there were still current to work the motors. The Captain held a microphone against the hull, and listened. He caught a humming.

'Okay. They're running,' he said.

He waited until the humming stopped.

'Right. Open her up,' he directed.

The Third Officer inserted his crank again and wound it. The main port opened inwards, leaving a dark gap in the shining hull. The three looked at the opening sombrely for some seconds. With a grim quietness the Captain's voice said: 'Well. Here we go!'

They moved carefully and slowly into the blackness, listening.

The Third Officer's voice murmured:

> *The silence that is in the starry sky,*
> *The sleep that is among the lonely hills . . .*

Presently the Captain's voice asked:

'How's the air, Doc?'

The doctor looked at his gauges.

'It's okay,' he said, in some surprise. 'Pressure's about six

403

ounces down, that's all.' He began to unfasten his helmet. The others copied him. The Captain made a face as he took his off.

'The place stinks,' he said, uneasily. 'Let's – get on with it.'

He led the way towards the lounge. They entered it apprehensively.

The scene was uncanny and bewildering. Though the gyrations of the *Falcon* had been reduced, every loose object in her continued to circle until it met a solid obstruction and bounced off it upon a new course. The result was a medley of wayward items churning slowly hither and thither.

'Nobody here, anyway,' said the Captain, practically. 'Doc, do you think –?'

He broke off at the sight of the doctor's strange expression. He followed the line of the other's gaze. The doctor was looking at the drifting flotsam of the place. Among the flow of books, cans, playing-cards, boots, and miscellaneous rubbish, his attention was riveted upon a bone. It was large and clean and had been cracked open.

The Captain nudged him. 'What's the matter, Doc?'

The doctor turned unseeing eyes upon him for a moment, and then looked back at the drifting bone.

'That' – he said in an unsteady voice – 'that, Skipper is a human femur.'

In the long moment that followed while they stared at the grisly relic the silence which had lain over the *Falcon* was broken. The sound of a voice rose, thin, uncertain, but perfectly clear. The three looked incredulously at one another as they listened:

> *Rock-a-bye baby*
> *On the tree top*
> *When the wind blows*
> *The cradle will rock . . .*

Alice sat on the side of her bunk swaying a little, and holding her baby to her. It smiled, and reached up one miniature hand to pat her cheek as she sang:

> . . .*When the bough breaks*
> *The cradle will fall.*
> *Down will –*

Her song cut off suddenly at the click of the opening door. For a moment she stared as blankly at the three figures in the opening as they at her. Her face was a mask with harsh lines drawn from the points where the skin was stretched tightly over the bones. Then a trace of expression came over it. Her eyes brightened. Her lips curved in a travesty of a smile.

She loosed her arms from about the baby, and it hung there in mid air, chuckling a little to itself. She slid her right hand under the pillow of the bunk, and drew it out again, holding a pistol.

The black shape of the pistol looked enormous in her transparently thin hand as she pointed it at the men who stood transfixed in the doorway.

'Look, baby,' she said. 'Look there! Food! Lovely food . . .'

'Survival' was dramatised for BBC Radio 4 by Pat Hooker.

A DAY AT
THE DENTIST'S

James Saunders

*James Saunders has been writing radio plays since the early
1950s. One of them, MENOCCHIO, won a Giles Cooper Award.
Another, THE MAGIC BATHROOM, was a BBC Radio Drama
entry for the Prix Italia. He has also written extensively for
television and for theatre. His stage plays include
NEXT TIME I'LL SING TO YOU and BODIES.*

It's not a matter of money,' said Mr Charles's receptionist-
cum-assistant, Betty, feeling her face redden with exasperation. (Who does he think he is? she thought.) 'He's on
his last patient now, and he's got to get away early.'

'Tomorrow then. Tomorrow morning.'

'Mr Charles is retiring. This is his last day.'

Just then Mr Charles called her in on the intercom to
make up some amalgam. As she left the waiting-room the
brash man with the flash tie called after her:

'Tell him I'll pay anything! I'll wait!'

'Who was that?' asked Mr Charles as he attended to Mrs
Phelps's cavity – to Mozart, her favourite composer.

'His filling's come out. I told him you couldn't possibly see
him.'

'No, no, I must get away to help with the packing.' (The
Charles's were going on a cruise to celebrate his early but
well-earned retirement.) 'Is he on our books? It can't be one
of my fillings, mine don't drop out. Do they, Mrs Phelps?'

'Aangh,'said Mrs Phelps.

'He says it is,' said Betty. (But that sort say anything to get
what they want, she thought.)

'Impossible. What's his name?'

'Houseman. Fred Houseman.'

'Aangh!' cried Mrs Phelps as the probe dug into her gum.

As Betty tidied the waiting-room for the last time, putting the *Spectator*s and *Lady*s into neat piles, she decided she'd never fathom men, not even nice simple Mr Charles. To seem so upset over hurting Mrs Phelps, even if he did pride himself on *never* hurting *anyone*; and then to change his mind about seeing that *awful* man, who winked at her as she showed him in, the nerve. And then to tell her he wouldn't need her any more and she could call to say her good-byes in the morning. Was he going to treat the man or not?

In the surgery Fred Houseman was being belligerent – it was his fear speaking.

'I'll put my cards on the table. I can't stand dentists, must have had a bad time as a kid, so –'

'You don't have to explain,' said Mr Charles. 'I remember you.'

'After ten years? Did I make that much fuss?'

'You did indeed.'

'Luckily I've got perfect teeth, except for this one.'

'What I don't understand,' said Mr Charles, 'is how you managed to dislodge one of my fillings.'

'Bit of chicken bone. In a health-food restaurant, would you believe?'

Mr Charles laughed.

'You never know where you're safe,' he said.

'Anyway, you managed to get me to relax last time, that's why I've come to you now. I don't know how you did it and I don't care, just do the same again, put the damn filling in and let me get the hell out of here.'

'All in good time,' said Mr Charles. 'First we have to cope with your phobia. After that the filling is nothing. Sit down and tell me about yourself. Don't look so terrified, I mean the easy chair.'

Then Mr Charles got him to talk, though his fingers were still clenched hard on the arms of the easy chair. He'd moved out of the area nine years ago, to a super detached house where he lived with his lovely wife and smashing kiddie. He was a self-made man, he'd always got what he wanted; done well for himself. That very morning he'd done a particularly clever bit of business in town, he was planning to spend the evening there to celebrate.

'You don't want to get back to your nice house, give your wife a surprise, take her some flowers perhaps?'

'What do you mean?'

'But it's nice to feel fancy-free sometimes, I quite understand; wander the town, take what turns up; forbidden fruit tastes sweeter, eh?'

'Look, what are you getting at?' said Houseman.

'Have I annoyed you?'

'You're damned right. You're digging at me. Why don't I go home to my wife, what am I going to do in town, what business is that of yours? I came here to get my filling put back, not for an inquisition. Why don't you damned well get on with it?'

'Splendid,' said Mr Charles. 'Just testing.'

'You mean you were putting my back up on purpose?'

'Oh yes.' And Mr Charles explained his method. 'You're a bad case, you know, the worst I've come across. I'll tell you something: you've no intention of sitting in that chair, let alone letting me anywhere near your teeth. You're terrified. And being the man you are, you're just waiting for the moment when you can feel justified in turning your terror into anger, and storming out. And what can I do then? I can't put you in a strait-jacket, can I? Your phobia, you know, is like a little devil inside you. And do you know how they used to drive the devil out of people they thought were possessed? They'd taunt that devil to loosen him up, twist him this way and that to dislodge him, and when he felt his roots beginning to slip that devil would get really angry. Then the exorcist knew he was winning. We don't call them devils anymore, of course, we use psychiatric terms for them, but the principle is the same. Getting you angry, turning your fear into anger, is all part of the process. Trust me. Now, do you want to leave?'

'No, of course not!'

'You do really. Never mind, after today you'll never worry about going to the dentist again. I guarantee it. Now let's have a little music. What music do you play when you want to forget the unpleasant things of life?'

'I don't have much time for music.'

'Oh come now. Put it this way: you've taken a young lady out to a restaurant, nice meal, rather pricey but you hope it's going to pay off. A taxi back to your place to show her your collection of Toby jugs –'

'How the hell did you know about my Toby jugs?'

'Have I hit the button? Well, I never! I'm on your wavelength, Mr Houseman, that's a good sign. So you've got the lady into your bachelor flat, this is before you married, of course, let's say ten years ago. There you both are, sitting on the sofa with a brandy or a scotch, wondering if the time has come to make the next move. You put on a little music to smooth things along –'

'Look, I don't think this is necessary – '

'Mr Houseman, I have to ask that you trust me. Well, I'll choose something for you, I have quite a selection of tapes here, all part of the process. Now, let's see . . .'

Mr Charles inserted a tape; 'mood music' wafted through the air like scented honey.

'I used to have that album,' said Fred Houseman.

'So I've hit the nail on the head again? That is good. Because you see, Mr Houseman, there's an interesting parallel between *you* trying to coax a young lady into your bed – before you were married, of course, with your lovely wife and smashing kiddie – and *me* trying to coax you into my dentist's chair. You hate the very idea: the indignity of having the prying fingers of a stranger in your mouth, and worse still, the dreadful machinery violating you, the drill –'

'Do you have to talk about it?'

'Yes, I do. Trust me. Some fool of a dentist mistreated you as a child, forced your mouth open perhaps regardless of your cries, inserted his instruments –'

Houseman groaned.

'What am I to you then but a potential rapist, intent on assaulting your most secret, most vulnerable places? Rape is a terrible thing, don't you agree? So you see, I have to convince you that it doesn't have to be like that, that it can be a painless experience, even pleasant.'

'You've got a job on,' said Houseman.

'Ah, but think back to the young lady in your flat. She hasn't left yet, she must know what you're after by now but she's still there. And look, when you make a joke, she laughs. When they laugh with you, the battle's as good as won. Isn't that so?'

Fred Houseman laughed. 'Too right.'

'And you challenged me, "You've got a job on." In other words, "Go ahead and try." Isn't it the same with women? When you sense that they're challenging you, don't you know you're on the last lap?'

'Absolutely!' said Houseman, laughing.

Mr Charles laughed too, they laughed together as the music played softly. And before long, reassured that Mr Charles would not touch him, would not even look in his mouth, Fred Houseman agreed to try out the chair.

'Don't worry, you can get down any time you like.'

Then Houseman even agreed, laughing, to try on the apron thing with long sleeves.

'Splendid,' said Mr Charles. 'Now I'll just tie these tapes at the back . . .'

Fred Houseman stared down as his arms were pulled round him.

'This is a – this is a strait-jacket!'

'That's right.'

'What are you doing now?'

Just tying your ankles, so you don't kick. Don't bother to struggle, it's very strong. I had it all specially made, and we tested it together, my wife and I.'

'If this is part of your so-called therapy I've had enough of it,' said Houseman. 'Let me out!'

But Mr Charles took no notice. He was calling his wife on the intercom, asking her to come down because he had a special treat for her.

'God, this is a nightmare,' said Houseman. 'Let me out. Please – you promised!'

'Promises, promises,' said Mr Charles. And when Houseman began to shout he explained that Betty had gone home and the windows were double-glazed and that if Houseman made any more noise he would have a piece of machinery wedged in his mouth. And Houseman was quiet for a while, his eyes staring and beads of sweat on his forehead.

'About ten years ago, it was. You may not remember the woman, Mr Houseman, I daresay she was one of many, but you must remember the case. Yes, I see that you do. I was very distressed to read about it in the paper, I've always had a hatred of physical violence. And that you actually got away with it. I knew you were guilty. I knew *her*, you see, as a patient, a sweet child, I knew she was not capable of such things as came out at the trial. And I saw the change that came over her afterwards. Her teeth were always good, but she took to seeing me regularly after it was all over, after she'd lost the case and thus been branded as a – perverted woman. She knew I was gentle, you see, and she needed to remind herself that there was in the world at least one *gentle* man. And I was a good deal older, that helped. She could treat me as a father. She'd sit in that chair and while I pretended to examine her teeth I'd talk to her, try to comfort her. Anyway, the long and short of it was that we married. It wasn't only pity, though; she attracted me too. You'll understand that.'

'Please . . .' said Houseman.

'Only, after her beastly experience with you there were difficulties. She couldn't bear to be touched, not even by me. She told me about it eventually: the good-looking man who took her out for a meal, how he persuaded her to drop into his place for a brandy and to see his collection of Toby jugs, she was so innocent. And soft music, this music . . . And the rest . . . And the court case, her humiliation, his crowing to his friends after it was over, spreading stories, yes, I heard. And then having to get rid of the child, did you know that?'

'Oh my God . . .'

'To her it was a sin, but she had to commit it, or she'd have gone mad; a sin she paid for, because afterwards she was told she could bear no more children. That's one of the debts you owe us.'

'I didn't know. Please . . .'

'Then one day in you came for a filling. I recognised you, she'd once pointed you out in the street, with terror. You sat in my chair, and I could do nothing. I asked you to come back, but you didn't. So I waited, and prepared, just in case. And here we are. Better late than never, eh?'

'Look, I'm not short of money. If there's anything I –'

'Wait, you haven't heard the best bit. A very strange thing happened when I told her I'd had you in this very chair. She said: "What would you have liked to do?" And I told her. And her eyes – lit up.'

He looked down at Houseman, and smiled.

'That night, for the first time . . . I'd made a mistake, you see, with my gentleness. My innocent child . . . Your fault,

Mr Houseman, another debt. We talked fantasies that night; nasty fantasies; about you. And for the first time, as we talked, she allowed me to touch her. And that's how it's had to be ever since. You've been with us every time we made love, Fred. Isn't that nice? They were her idea, the strait-jacket and the ankle-straps. She wanted to feel that somehow, some day, her fantasies would take on flesh. And here you are, at the eleventh hour. She won't be long now. She'll be preparing.'

'You can't do this!' said Houseman. 'I won't have it! Help! Help! Aangh!'

'That's it, open wide,' said Mr Charles as he inserted the clamp.

When Mrs Charles came in she gave a long look at the dentist's chair; then she smiled tenderly at her husband. He smiled back. Then she gazed down at Houseman, touched him with the tip of one finger, and gave a long sigh.

'Isn't she beautiful, Fred? Isn't she?' said Mr Charles.

'Aangh,' said Fred Houseman.

'Why don't you loosen his clothing here a little, my dear?' said Mr Charles.

'Aangh.'

'Now, where shall we start? You first, my darling, it's your treat.'

Mrs Charles sighed again. Her eyes lit up. Then the sweet sound of the music was covered by the shrill whine of the drill.